DEBT

NINA G. JONES

DEBT

Copyright © 2014 Nina G. Jones
All rights reserved.

Interior Design and Formatting by:
Christine Borgford, Perfectly Publishable

All rights reserved.
Without limiting the rights under copyright reserved above, no part of this publication may be reproduced, stored in or introduced into a retrieval system, or transmitted, in any form, or by any means (electronic, mechanical, photocopying, recording, or otherwise) without the prior written permission of both the copyright owner and the above publisher of this book.

This is a work of fiction. Names, characters, places, brands, media, and incidents are either the product of the author's imagination or are used fictitiously. The author acknowledges the trademarked status and trademark owners of various products, bands, and/or restaurants referenced in this work of fiction, which have been used without permission. The publication/use of these trademarks is not authorized, associated with, or sponsored by the trademark owners.

To those who have ever stood up to a lion in a lions' pit.

A NOTE FROM NINA

Dear reader,

As I wrote this novel, so many of the scenes in my head had specific songs as a backtrack. I wanted to give the reader the opportunity to experience the novel in this way, if they so choose.

You will notice a song title at the top of certain chapters or sections. These were songs I associated with certain scenes.

If you are on Spotify, you can search for "Nina G. Jones" and find the DEBT playlist there. The playlist has a few extra songs included that did not make it into the book.

Please also note that this book deals with some difficult themes of abuse, including graphic descriptions. If you are sensitive to these issues or if they are a trigger, this may not be the book for you.

Kindest regards,

Nina G. Jones

PROLOGUE

14 Years Earlier

<u>The Smashing Pumpkins – To Forgive</u>

Pressure. Unrelenting pressure. That is the first sensation I am aware of as I regain consciousness. My head feels like it might explode. As I try to open my eyes the fluorescent light sears my pupils. I pinch them shut again so they can adjust.

I try and lift my arm to shield my eyes from the glare, and that's when I feel the throbbing. Like some sort of domino effect, everything else begins to hurt. My entire body aches.

"Sil? Sil? You up?" It's my father's voice. *Shit.*

I open my mouth to respond, but choke on the dryness in my throat.

"Hold on. Have some water," he says kindly. Shit must be really bad if he's being nice.

I feel a straw poke at my lips and I suck. The lukewarm water coating my mouth might be the best thing I have ever tasted.

Through blurry eyes, I look at him, trying to recall what got me here, and then I remember: the letter, the forest, and Jude...Jude!

"Where's Jude?" I ask, panicked. I try to sit up but collapse, wincing.

"Calm down, Silvio," he says sternly. My eyes focus on his swollen cheek and the stitches under his left eye. "She's fine. Now just keep your mouth shut for a second and listen." I knew he couldn't keep up the sympathetic act for long.

I fall back onto the pillow, exhausted and woozy from the sedation.

"Do you remember what happened?"

I hesitate. I have never felt like he has had my best interests in mind, and even here, lying in a hospital bed, I still don't.

"Yeah. Well, most of it."

"Well, now you don't."

"What?" I ask, trying to focus my cloudy thoughts. "What are you talking about?"

"Don't fucking question me."

This doesn't make any sense. Yeah, he's a piece of shit, but why wouldn't he care? We're still his kids.

"I don't understand—"

He grips my throat and squeezes forcefully. "You don't remember a fucking thing, you little shit," he hisses. "Neither does Jude. Case closed. After what you pulled the other night, you're lucky I don't kill you myself. Some things just need to be forgotten."

When he lets go, I cough and gasp for air. With every inhale and exhale it feels like a bat is being taken to my ribcage. I must have some broken ribs. And then I realize it: Tripp's father must have paid mine off to cover up what happened.

"Did they pay you?"

"That's none of your goddamn business. It's about time I got paid. Having to raise you and your sister ain't cheap."

This fucking town. This piece of shit town and everyone in it. I swear I'll burn it to the ground one day.

"Now, I'm going to tell Sheriff Tibbett you're up. And he's gonna to ask you what happened. You're going to say you don't remember. And we are all gonna move on. And if you don't, you are gonna have more broken bones than you do already. And your sister, everyone will know what happened to her. She'll be damaged goods. Understand?"

CHAPTER ONE

Mia

"Any plans this weekend?" Laney asks from the adjacent cubicle.

"Uhhh, not really. I might catch up with a friend. Other than that, I think I'll loaf. How about you?"

"Well...Luke is taking me out to a fancy restaurant on Saturday," she says, popping her head over the wall. "I don't know, I have a feeling...this is it!"

I pull off my headphones, which are supposed to be a universal signal that I don't want to chat, but she's got my attention. "You mean, you think he's going to propose?"

"Yup!" She says gleefully.

"Well that's great!" I say. I really mean that, but there's a little knot that forms in my stomach. Laney is sweet, don't get me wrong, but she's one of those girls whose life revolves around the end game of marriage. It's always, Luke this and Luke that. A year and a half ago, it was Matt this and Matt that until they broke up. And if I get too deep into this chat with her, it'll turn around to me, and she'll start asking if I am seeing anyone, and then she'll try to set me up. Laney seems to be absolutely terrified that I will be alone. Me, I am okay with that. Well, maybe not okay, but I am tired of defending my quiet love life to her. "Good luck!" I say, telegraphing my hands to my earphones so that she sees I am ending the conversation.

"Tonight though..." *damn, she's pulling me in,* "me and Luke are going to hang out with some of his old college friends. And guess what? A few of them are siiiiiingle!"

There's that knot in my stomach, getting tighter. I just told her I have no set plans. She fucking trapped me.

Just then, Dewey stops at our desks. Dewey is our boss and the owner of Alea Intimate Toys for Women. Basically, we make sex toys; beautiful, high-end, designer sex toys for women. That might be why I find myself alone. I have access to the best toys on the market. Most guys can't keep my interest when I have the Aphrodite with "rotating feature" in my nightstand drawer. Okay, that's not true. I am really alone because most men bore me. Not just in the bedroom, but outside of it. Now, I'm putting my energy into building my career. I am independent, perhaps to a fault. From what I've seen — and dated — I just don't feel like most men have anything to offer that I can't do for myself. Trudging through the endless droves of bros and bankers got old fast, so I declared a hiatus. A nine-month hiatus so far.

"Dewey!" I call out, happy to see him, especially since he just saved me from one of Laney's hookups.

He glances at his watch. "I'm feeling generous today. I'm thinking you all can go home an hour early."

"That's why we love you," I smile.

Just as I say that, my phone pings.

Want to hang out tonight?

Oh thank god! The friend I might have plans with just came through, bless her soul!

Sure! Want to come over around 6?

It's on, I'll bring the booze!

I lounge on my sofa, comfy in a tank and sweats, already sipping on some wine when my doorbell rings.

I have known Tiff long enough to recognize the look on her face as soon as I open the door. She's trying to play it cool, but she's about to burst. She really wants to tell me something. It also explains why she is uncharacteristically prompt this evening.

"I brought snacks!" she says, making a beeline to my kitchen and dumping the grocery bags on the counter.

"Thank you. How's it going?" I ask, giving her a tight hug. "You saved me from Laney, by the way."

"Oh god, that girl..." Tiff replies. I would say Tiffany is the antithesis of Laney. Laney probably looks out of her window every night and wishes on a star that some Prince Charming would come and sweep her off of her feet. Tiff is a blue, or purple, or green-haired, tatted, combat-boot wearing owner of a popular bar. She inherited it from her dad, along with her no-nonsense personality. I met her when I graduated from Marquette University eight years ago. I rented one of the two shitty apartments above her bar, and she lived in the other one. We quickly became fast friends. "Why don't you tell her to fuck off?"

"Because she's nice, and I work with her. It's not a bar, I can't tell my co-workers to go fuck themselves."

"You sell dildos, not stocks and bonds."

"All the more reason to be professional, Tiff. We surround ourselves with sex all day, so we have to make sure we exude professionalism. And again, I know I bitch about her, but she's trying to help, she just doesn't understand I don't want or need it."

"Don't you just love unsolicited advice from people who don't have their own shit together? She's trying to get you hitched and she can't keep a guy to save her life."

We bring a large bottle of Moscato, a couple of glasses, and plates of food over to the sofa, cozying up under some blankets as we catch up on our lives. An hour goes by and we kill the Moscato, but I can tell there is something Tiff's still not telling me.

"So...what's on your mind?" I ask.

"Hmmm?" she innocently asks, reaching for a piece of cheese and a cracker.

"I could tell as soon as you walked in the door, there was something you wanted to tell me. So tell me."

"I hate you sometimes. You know me too well."

"Tell me!" I insist, pulling a blanket away from her as she fights to keep it on her side of the couch.

"Okay..." she lingers, half because she's thinking about how to phrase it and half because she's tipsy. She takes a big sigh, slapping a hand on her thigh. "Okay. Remember we talked a long time ago about like our biggest fantasies?"

"Yeeeeesss..." I reply hesitantly, wondering where she could possibly be going with this.

"Okay, we both agreed that it would like be hot to have a guy like role play that he was a stranger that like, broke into our house or something and then like fucks the shit out of us."

The number of likes in her sentence is directly proportional to the level of discomfort I am beginning to feel.

"Yeah, I remember that."

"And you know I'm a kinky bitch, and you're a closet kinky bitch."

"Maybe not the exact words I would use, but yes, I enjoy a variety of bedroom activities."

"Okay, so hear me out: I did it!" she blurts.

"Wait. Wait. Wait," I reply, shaking my head as I try to digest her words. "What do you mean, you did it? You broke into someone's house and fucked them?"

"No!" she says, as if *I* am the crazy one. "I hired someone to attack me."

CHAPTER TWO

Mia

"What?" I ask, still not comprehending what she's saying. "Tiff, just spell this out for me because either I am just too stupid to understand this or too drunk."

She laughs. Clearly, whatever nervousness she felt about telling me has dissolved. "Okay, so I have a regular that comes into the bar. Over time I got to know her — turns out she's a high-priced call girl. Well, one night she starts telling me about this service and she gives me this card."

Tiff pulls out a black card that simply says: www.happykitty.onion

"What the hell...?" I ask, picking it up and looking it over.

"She told me they specialize in rape and attack fantasies. You go online and fill out a survey, and they send someone. All the guys are supposed to be fucking hot, clean, and have gorgeous dicks."

I listen to her with my mouth agape.

"I know what you're thinking, but it's a totally professional operation. The website is probably like proxied a bajillion times and it's in the deep web. It's a lot like the card, black background, no info, just a survey, and then you pay. And then you wait."

"Woah, woah…you are making this sound way too simple. So how do you know when to expect him? How do you know you are not actually being attacked? And are you saying you actually went through with this?"

"You don't know exactly when to expect him. You fill out a survey about times and locations you would like to be 'accosted.' So there is a window of time, but you don't know exactly when. And they always wear suits. It's like an invisible uniform. 'Cause they're well-dressed, so the odds of an actual rapist wearing Hugo Boss is slim. You need to be alone; otherwise they'll bail and try one more time. But there are fail-safes. There is a question you can ask that only he would know the answer to, and a safeword to make him stop."

"How do you know all this?"

"It's all referral based, the site doesn't hold any info. So the chick that gave me the card answered all my questions. She does some kinky shit herself. She gets paid a fuck-ton to tie up and spank old CEOs and shit."

"Tell me you didn't do this!" I ask with a mixture of disappointment and curiosity.

"I did," she says, like someone who was busted stealing leftovers from the fridge.

"I cannot believe you!" I scold, trying to muster up disapproval, but somehow her crazy is rubbing off on me, because I want to know more.

"Mia, it was fucking incredible. I mean, wild, animalistic, brutal!" She raises her palms up and then clenches them into fists as she closes her eyes. "I came like three times! Hard! The guy was gorgeous. His cock, oh god!" she says, as if she is reliving the entire thing again.

"How? Where?"

"As I was closing up the bar," she says slyly. "I made plans to close it alone one night and put it as an available time slot. Bingo," she says, pointing to an invisible button in the air.

Again, I am speechless, and now, oddly envious.

"He came up behind me and covered my mouth. My first reaction was to scream, panic. I flailed. But he was so big and strong, there was no way I could fight back. It's like even though I knew it was set up by me, my nervous system freaked the fuck out. He pushed me into the bar and locked the door behind me. Then he dragged me to the office in the back. That's when I got a look at him. Fucking gorgeous. Tanned, his face, his eyes. Everything," she swoons.

"I cannot believe what I am hearing." My heart races as I wait for her to continue. "This is insane!"

"He pushes me to my knees and I can't even—he's pulling my hair, biting, just roughing me around. Talking dirty. I was still scared, but so aroused. I kept thinking I should stop it, but I didn't want to."

"You're nuts!" I yell, but a smile is plastered across my face.

"His dick. Oh my god. You need to plaster mold that shit and use it for your next dildo at Alea. He fucked me every which way. I came so hard, the hardest I have ever come in my life. I was seeing stars!"

By this time, I am pacing around the couch. This is just too much.

Then she pauses, takes a breath, and looks me in the eyes. "Mia, you *have* to do this."

"Me? What? You've lost your fuckin' mind!"

"As your best friend, and someone you confessed having this fantasy to, I am telling you, you will never have sex like this. It's like fight or flight sex, the adrenaline is so strong. I am telling you, you have got to try it."

"Listen, I'm not judging, but you're crazy. I am not nearly as ballsy as you. I mean what if the police bust them or something and our names come out?" The fact that my first concern is getting caught, and not the morality of the arrangement itself, makes me distrustful of myself.

"Like I said, it's on the deep web. You use a special browser, a VPN, and you pay with bitcoins. It's all encrypted. It's nearly impossible for them to be caught. Discretion is the whole point. It's a way to safely and shamelessly fulfill your fantasy."

"I—I don't know..." I say, picking up the card and looking at it. "Sex with a total stranger?"

"How is it any different than a one night stand?"

"And what if I want him to stop and he doesn't?"

"They only exist through word of mouth, their reputation would be destroyed if they didn't respect the boundaries they put forth. The guy did his thing and then left. We didn't exchange words. It was anonymous and beautiful."

My belly tingles at those last words.

"You really want me to try this? Huh?"

"Yes, it's not cheap, but at least do it once. Before you die, you need to feel what this is like. Also, I get the next fuck at 50% off."

"Are you kidding me?" I laugh in disbelief as I flick the card at her. "You're trying to get me to do this for a discount?"

"No! I am doing it again no matter what. Just trying to do the full disclosure thing."

"Sorry my friend, but I don't think I am as adventurous as you."

"Just keep the card, no pressure. If you do, use the number I wrote on the back. It's my referral code," she winks.

CHAPTER THREE

Mia

This is ridiculous. It's been a week since Tiff told me about this rape-for-hire service and I STILL can't sleep.

I am disgusted with myself because each day I think about it, I reason with myself more and more. I justify going through with it.

I mean, it's my body, right? It's my sexuality. All we talk about at Alea is empowering women to explore their sexuality, to not be ashamed. But this—this feels so dirty and wrong. And I think that's why every time I think about it, heat rises from my belly and gives me goosebumps all over my arms.

I have never seen Tiff so excited about anything before. Not even close. Ever since she told me about it, I have thought about that look of jubilation on her face with such envy.

That's what *I* want to feel. I don't want a picket fence or some guy to take me to the movies on a date. I want the look that was in Tiff's eyes. That high, that hysterical lust, that frenzy.

At least I want that before I might have to settle for something else one day.

I've had rough sex before, but it was always guarded. I've been close to that magic Tiff described, but didn't get to that deep animalistic part of me. And I craved that. The guy I was with seemed unsure, playing a role that he was afraid might cross some line. I didn't just want rough, I wanted painful, I wanted degradation. I wanted someone to take me out of my head. No—force me out of my head. To violently thrust me away from convention. I am so "together" and I have always wanted to find someone who would make me a chaotic mess. But the level of aggression I wanted was not something anyone I had dated could provide. They just couldn't–or wouldn't--go to that place. Maybe you can't get that with someone who is familiar. Because after all is said and done, you have to face that person in the real world. It's hard to be both uncivilized and normal with the same person. Maybe that's why this service exists in the first place.

I enjoy the kind of porn that would be humiliating to me should anyone find out: spanking, tying, pulling, pinching. Actors pretending to capture women and have their way with them. But that was just pretend. This skirted the line between pretend and reality.

I toss and turn on my pillow. *No. No. No. No.*

What the hell is wrong with you? Are you seriously considering letting a stranger rough you up and fuck you? You have officially lost your mind!

This time, I sit up in bed, wide awake. I'm just going to look, just browse the site. Just dip a toe into this filthy water.

DEBT

I make my way out to my living room, sit on the floor in front of my coffee table and pull open my laptop.

I type in the url, but it brings me to a parked page.

Wait, Tiff said something about the deep web. I have heard of this. I need a VPN and some special browser.

A few Google searches and a glass of wine later, I am up and running on the deep, dark, web. This is the dark alleyway of the internet, where you can order drugs, prostitutes, and find illegal porn.

It's 2am and I am lurking on the deep web for a male prostitute to mock-rape me. This calls for more wine.

I walk to the kitchen, shaking my head at myself as I refill my glass. I settle back down at the coffee table.

Here I am, staring at this black page in front of me. It's a survey.

At the very top it says:

ABSOLUTELY NO REFUNDS. THIS TRANSACTION CANNOT BE CANCELLED ONCE SUBMITTED. YOU WILL NEED TO USE YOUR DESIGNATED SAFE WORD TO CANCEL THE APPOINTMENT AT TIME OF DELIVERY.

This is some heavy shit.

How did you hear about us?

Enter referral code here.

Okay, I am just going to fiddle around, fill it out for fun. I grab Tiff's card and enter her referral code.

Please select your preferences in a sexual partner. Select all that apply.

There are a gazillion checkboxes to choose from and I select with abandon:

Tall
Athletic/Muscular
Dark hair
Tattoos
Skin tone: Fair skin or Olive skin
Eye color: No preference
Body hair- Trimmed (not fully shaven) or shaven
Facial hair- Stubble or clean shaven

This is like building my perfect man!

Next is the schedule. I select dates from a calendar and then schedule in time slots and locations for the availability of my fake rape. I laugh to myself as I fill out this part. *Yes, I'd like to schedule my assault for Thursday at 6pm. Yes, my place is fine.*

Then there is a list of sexual preferences. Again I must select all that apply. This one baffles me. I mean, I know all the normal stuff I like, and things I have fantasized about, but the options are some I had never considered.

Do I like to be choked/spanked/cut?

I leave that part blank, select other. In the comment box, I type: *I am open, but nothing too painful. And NO KNIVES.*

Unexpectedly, I come across a health questionnaire. It reminds me a lot of the questions one is asked when donating blood.

In the past 12 months have you:

Had sexual contact with anyone who has HIV/AIDS or has had a ‰positive test for the HIV/AIDS virus?

Had or been treated for syphilis or gonorrhea?

Had sexual contact with a prostitute or anyone else who takes money or drugs or other payment for sex?

Ha! That last question makes me laugh to myself. Presumably, I might be precluded from this service if I actually used another service. Happy Kitty: *Prostitutional* Services for People Who Don't Use Prostitutes.

Is "prostitutional" a word? Well, it should be.

The health questionnaire only provides a thin veil of assurance. Clearly Happy Kitty is no street pimp with a cane and feathered hat, but the idea of being that intimate with a stranger, no matter how sexy he is, is panic-inducing.

I wonder who these men are that perform this service. Do they have day jobs? Are they pillars of their community? How does Happy Kitty even recruit this handsome, supposedly healthy stable of men?

As I fill out each subsequent part of the form, the idea of me actually doing this becomes easier and easier. It's no different than applying for a job or donating blood, it's so...clinical. I'm just putting words onto a web page. I can't connect that this will actually lead to something real, something potentially life-changing.

Three wine glasses in, I reach the bottom of the form.

The button stares back at me: SUBMIT.

Just below is that same warning that was on the top of the form. This is it, if I press this button, the only way I can stop it is by saying my safeword to my attacker, face to face. I selected the word "rainbow," certain that is something I would never shout during sex unless I wanted it to end.

And oh, I will also be losing $900 dollars.

I dangle my finger above my trackpad. Inching it closer and then pulling it away, testing and tempting myself. Daring myself.

All it takes is a second. No, less than a second. I just press that button. I take a chance on something crazy. I can just press it, and then it's over. Once submitted, I leave myself with no choice but to go through with at least coming face to face with this guy.

This time, my finger lays on the trackpad. I could literally sneeze and accidentally do this, but something keeps holding me back. Maybe it's the smidgen of sanity I have left.

"Woah!" I say to myself, slamming down the screen of my laptop, getting up to my feet, and circling away.

What in the hell am I thinking?

I run my hands through my hair and my eyes drift back to the computer. It's almost magnetic. It's taunting me.

I've done the whole normal thing. I've tried it, and I'm not cut out for it. I came from a small town where all anyone ever wanted to do was to fit into a box and I left that shit for a reason.

I need more. And this is the only thing in my life that might be that: More.

Besides, Tiff did it, and she would never steer me wrong.

I run over to my laptop, flip it open and the screen reappears.

I shut my eyes and wince, as if I am about to rip off duct tape, and slam my finger down on the trackpad, feeling the faint click under my index finger.

I open my eyes and in front of me the screen says:

Transaction successful.
Safeword: Rainbow
Your secret question: Have you ever danced with the devil in the pale moonlight?
Correct Answer: Pineapples.

Watch your back.

Sincerely,
Happy Kitty

A wave of relief rushes over me, it's done. It's out of my hands now. But then, just as quickly, a surge hits my stomach, my head feels spacey.

I'm not crazy like Tiff, I don't get into fist fights with men at bars. I design pretty dildos!

Dear lord, what have I done?

The surge in my gut rises to my throat and I run to the bathroom to purge the contents of my stomach.

CHAPTER FOUR

Mia

Today is Dewey's birthday and we are celebrating after work at the rooftop deck of Cafe Benelux.

It's been a week since in a terrible moment of weakness and poor judgment, I clicked on the word: SUBMIT.

I didn't realize when I filled out the schedule, that Dewey's birthday party would also fall on the first day I made available for my mystery rapist-for-hire man to pay a visit.

My stomach has been swimming all day. The only things that keep me from completely losing my shit is the fact that: 1) I will be surrounded by people pretty much until I go to bed and 2) I doubt that anyone would come after me on day one, that's just too easy. Tiff told me she waited a week and a half for her attacker.

So I recite my safe word over and over again. I elect to use it as soon as he lays his hands on me. This whole thing was a terrible idea. I am not Tiff, or that call girl. I am Mia, and while I like to think of myself as sexual and kinky, I am not fucking nuts.

Oh and Tiff, I haven't told her anything. I just want to forget this ever happened.

Laney is crying on my shoulder. She's hammered. Luke didn't propose. He took her to this nice restaurant to tell her he got a new job offer in San Francisco. She won't move unless he commits fully, and well...there was no ring.

"I don't know what I'm gonna doooooo," she says, her face a mess of smudged lipstick and mascara.

"There, there," I say, as my eyes scan the bar for any impeccably-dressed, tall, sexy lurkers. I feel like I am being watched, like I am a gazelle being spied on from a distance by a low-lying tiger. *It's just nerves Mia. You can tell him to stop. Then you will be $900 poorer, but still have your dignity intact.*

Alea parties can get a little reckless, as this group likes to have a good time. But it's getting late, and like Laney, I have had far too many drinks. I am ready to go home and pass out in my comfy bed.

I have a plan: grab a taxi, slip the driver an extra ten and ask him to wait until I am safely in my home before leaving. Fool proof!

I idle in the back seat of the cab, relieved that I have made it one day without a freakish erotic encounter. As rehearsed, despite my mild drunkenness, I am able to communicate with the driver that I would like him to make sure I have entered my home and closed the door behind me. He even suggested I switch the lights on and off to signal he could go.

And so, I followed the exact protocol. I pulled my keys out of my purse and let myself in. I turned the lights on off a few times, watched the driver leave through my front window, and then proceeded to let out a sigh of relief.

I made it.

I kick off my shoes and turn on my cd player, suddenly in a gleeful mood. Things are pretty good: I love my job, I have a great buzz, and some time to myself after socializing and partying for hours and hours.

I dance alone in my living room and have a sudden pang of hunger. I shimmy my way to the fridge, mouthing the words to some classic Backstreet Boys.

Just as I open the fridge and poke my head in, the music stops. I stand tall, hoping it'll play again. "Dammit!" I say to myself. The song was just about to get to my favorite part. The cd and player are old and occasionally the music skips. But this time, the song doesn't start up again. This time, what should be a minor inconvenience send chills up my arms; the fine hairs stand at attention as if I touched static.

Then the living room light turns off.

I don't even have time to get scared, or analyze what is happening. I turn my head to investigate and I see a dark shadow hanging over me.

He is tall and his shoulders are broad. He might be, I don't know 6'3" or 6'4"?

I open my mouth to say something. What? I don't even know, and he puts a gloved hand over my mouth.

"Don't say a fucking word, bitch."

CHAPTER FIVE

Tax

It's already 11pm and my patience is growing very fucking thin. I know she's at a party, but I don't give a shit. I want her here now.

Finally, I hear a car pull up front. A taxi. Perfect. She's alone just as I expected.

I watch Mia from a closet as she enters the house and locks the door behind her. She even does this thing where she switches the light on and off. Stupid little bitch.

It's tempting to jump out now, but I need to be patient. I have to catch her completely off guard and without warning.

She's wobbling all over the place, she must be hammered. I couldn't have asked for a better setup: drunk people are easy to overpower. Not that I am worried about her tiny ass putting up a good fight.

She kicks off her shoes and pulls off her sweater, and I admire the curves of her body in her white tank top and tight jeans. Her tits are perfect, full but still perky, and right now her nipples are hard, poking right through the thin material of her tank. Her ass is round and tight. Her body has changed over the years, filling out in all the right places. My dick throbs thinking about the things I would do to her.

Now if this bitch would just go to the bedroom, I could get started. Her living room window faces the main street and she *will* scream. Her bedroom, on the other hand, is towards the back of the house and faces the backyard. Wrestling on a bed is much quieter than in a living room full of lamps and bookshelves filled with random bullshit. How many fucking knickknacks does one human being require? Is that a porcelain cat? Honestly, I'm putting her out of her misery. She should thank me.

Anyway, I want to take my time with her, so I need to wait just a little bit longer. Shit, I've already waited fourteen years.

I cannot believe this shit, she's turning on her stereo.

What is this godforsaken tripe she's listening to? Of course, fucking Backstreet Boys.

I can't help but smile a little when she dances. She's so carefree right now. She thinks she's safe.

But she doesn't understand that tonight is the night she dies.

Mia

Nine Inch Nails – Closer

I cry out, but the sound is muffled by his hand. He holds me, firmly against him, waiting out my thrashing. My legs flail into the fridge, knocking over a tub of cottage cheese that explodes on the kitchen floor. Another kick dislodges a shelf and Tupperware containers slide to the floor.

I knew this was coming, but it doesn't make me any less frightened as adrenaline floods my body. My heart revs up. I feel stronger, like my muscles are supercharged, but even still, his grip on me is immoveable. And while I am more alert, there is a strange fog surrounding my thoughts. I have all this fresh mental energy from the terror, but I am unable to focus on anything other than his hand on my mouth. I just need to get his hand off my fucking mouth. But this guy is made of stone: heavy, massive, dense. I can tell he is only using a fraction of his strength against me, while I am using everything I have, and losing energy with each kick.

Then my mind jumps to something Tiff mentioned, how she was scared, how she flailed, but eventually she went with it. Suddenly, I realize my only way to freedom is passivity. I can't say a safeword unless I calm down. Then he'll move his hand so I can speak. It makes sense, this whole thing relies on anonymity, if a neighbor hears me scream and calls the cops, then our cover is blown.

I breathe heavily into the stranger's gloved hand as I try and relax my body. In that moment, my senses become acute. I can feel the bulges of his muscles pressing against my body. I can smell him: slight hints of musk, pine and vanilla mixed with his body chemistry. He is warm, and his warmth spreads to my exposed shoulders and through the fabric of my clothing.

As I relax, the tension of his grip subsides and I notice we pant in unison, his chest expanding into the curve of my upper back with each breath we take.

Eventually, aside from my heavy panting, I become still.

"I am going to move my hand from your face, but don't fucking scream. You scream and I will fuck you up. Do you understand?" he asks. His voice is deep and rich; it sends chills through my core. Not of terror, but arousal. I haven't gotten a good look at him, but just his stature, strength, smell, and voice scream masculinity. Dominance. Ferocity. The things I tried to find but never could. I already feel in this moment a blazing in my core that I have never felt before and he's barely done anything. Goosebumps raise on my arms and neck, my nipples tingle against the fabric of my tank.

I nod my head frantically. He slowly slides away his hand.

He's here. I can say the word. I can scream it, but I don't have to do it yet. I can do it at any point.

And right now, for some inexplicable reason, I don't want to.

And that's when I feel the thick rock-hardness pressing on my backside. I haven't been with a man in so long, and there is something primal about this encounter. The way this massive man stands above me, his scent, the baritone of his voice, the feeling of his desire for me pressing into my back. There are no pleasantries, no small talk, it's a man who wants to fuck a woman. Not just fuck her, but take her.

I hold onto the safeword, it makes me feel safe. It reminds me that I still have ultimate control. But right now, at this moment, I want more.

I press my ass against him, and crane my neck back. His firm grip on me loosens as I spin to face him.

The glow of the fridge light casts on him and gives me a shadowy view of the mysterious stranger: he is as tall as I estimated, and he is well-dressed, in a black tailored suit with a white shirt, no tie. Through the unbuttoned top of the shirt, I can tell he is muscled. But I can't see his face, because it's covered in a ski mask. All I can see are two dark eyes staring back at me and two full lips peeking through the mouth hole.

There is a moment of stillness. It may have only been a second, but the adrenaline makes everything feel fast and slow at the same time. Tentatively, I reach out to touch the mask and his large hand snaps up and snatches my wrist painfully, twisting it.

"Ahhh," I call out in pain. But the pain is fleeting, it's more of a reminder than it is meant to hurt.

"Shut the fuck up," he says coarsely.

And I do. I don't say a word, but our heavy breathing fills the quiet air of my house.

The fridge closes with a thud and the entire house goes dark.

The leather glove slides up my stomach, over my hardened nipple, up my neck and roughly yanks my ponytail.

Again I call out.

His other hand covers my mouth. "Shhhhh."

The length of his erection presses against my stomach and again, almost involuntarily, I snake against it.

"Is this what you want? You little fucking whore?"

I bite my lip. I can stop this, I can make him go away. I can say the word I have rehearsed all week, convinced this was something I absolutely did not want.

I nod.

He pushes me against the fridge, the cold stainless steel contrasting with the warmness of his body electrifies me. I mewl, a combination of arousal and passivity to his overwhelming will.

Then he bites my neck. At first it feels nice, like a love bite, and then he digs in hard, so hard, an alarming pain jolts through my flesh and instinctively, I flail my fists at him. He catches them, and twists them behind my back.

The spot where he bit radiates with pain, so that I feel his mark on a spot where he isn't even touching me any longer. The way he branded me with his mouth like that makes me hot. The dark figure drags me to the living room, bumping into a lounge chair as I fight to free my arms, and throws me down on the rug, face first.

His hand presses on the small of my back to still me as I feel the cold blade touch my flesh. My almost passive acceptance up until this point makes way for defiance as I buck my ass against his crotch. I am surprised that I am able to move his solid mass, a side effect of the adrenaline coursing through my muscles. But he reacts by bearing his weight down on me, rendering me unable to budge. Frustration and anger boil through me. I wonder if I should say the word and end this. They fucked up, betraying my trust by bringing the implement I banned. Images of slits on my skin and blood pervade my thoughts and I gasp for oxygen, choking on panic, unable to push out air to form a word. Finally, a sound emerges from my throat.

Just as I am about to scream something about knives, I hear the threads of my tank tearing as the stretchy material snaps away from my body, the knife cutting through it like warm butter.

The drafty air runs over my exposed skin and in that moment I realize this is really happening. I am drunk, face down, and topless with a stranger I paid to fuck me. This is arriving at a point that I cannot simply write off as poor judgment, curiosity, or even a few glasses of wine. I am making a clear decision if I don't put this to an end.

But I still don't want him to stop.

He rolls me over on my back, my eyes have adjusted to the darkness and the street light sifting through the windows gives me another view of him. His suit jacket is now gone, and I have a better view of his body: the strong v-taper of his wide shoulders and narrow waist. His collarbone is chiseled and prominent. It's not a feature I ever noticed on a man, let alone found sexy, until I notice his.

He straddles me, heaving like a beast in heat, and it awakens a surge of tingling warmth that emanates from between my legs. The pressure builds. I need to be touched, to be relieved of the tension that is blooming from this area to the rest of my body.

I reach out for his belt, accepting my role in this whole thing, and again he grabs my wrists. There is another moment of stillness, as I wait for what he will do to me, and then he slams my hands on the floor above me. He collects my wrists into one hand, while reaching down to my breasts, firmed with arousal, and pinches my nipple.

I moan and gyrate my hips in response. I want his mouth on me. And I want him to remove the fucking mask.

"Stay still," he commands, squeezing hard on my wrists. I wince in pain, but it only makes me more sensitive to the brewing erotic warmth below my bellybutton.

"Please, suck them," I beg submissively. And instantly, I realize the other component that makes this so fucking hot: Yes it's the primal, animalistic abandon of it all, but it's also the anonymity: I can say whatever I want, because I don't care what he thinks of me.

He makes a throaty sound. One of hesitation. Tiff saw the face of her attacker, and I want to see mine. "I want your mouth on me. Without the mask," I beg. "You can do whatever," I say, my voice quivering from a vague sense of fear and an intense arousal. It's me surrendering to his will.

He leans over me, his hand still pinning my arms to the floor, his bodyweight straddled over mine, and there is just a hollow silence in the dark house. But after a few tense seconds, my ears train on the sound of our breathing, my eyes scan the outline of our chests, nearing and distancing with each inhale and exhale. It's an a cappella song of sexual intensity and fear.

Then without warning, he thrusts the mask up, wearing it like a hat, so that I can make out some of his face. It's shadowy and hard for me to get a clear view, but I can tell he's striking: an angled jawline, full lips, a Roman nose. My eyes wander down to his neck and the large, colorful neck tattoo that seems to pierce through the darkness of the room. A jumble of snakes, they come to life as the cords of his neck muscles tense and relax. Before my eyes can focus any further, he dives down, mouthing my breasts, his stubble scratching against my soft skin. He bites me again so that I writhe against him, both fighting and receiving him.

"Fuck!" I call out. His mouth is all over my torso, savagely kissing, biting, consuming. I can't tell what stings and what pleases me as he mixes softness with savagery.

I want it so much that my body fights him, again trying to buck him off of me. I know it's pointless, but I want him closer, I want his body on my body. Every action of mine receives an equal but opposite reaction. The more I fight, the closer he gets.

His body presses against mine, rendering me helpless, but I don't feel helpless because I chose this. Despite what I told myself this week, a part of me that had been hiding, tucked away by civility and propriety, had the guts to break out. I tried to put her back in hiding, but this man on top of me is dragging her out, kicking and screaming. I *want* this big, rough man, taking my body for his pleasure.

He pulls both of his hands away from me to unbutton my jeans and then he reaches for the knife. My eyes grow with fear. *Do I say the safeword? Do I remind him that I requested no knives in the survey?*

I choose to wait it out a few more seconds and see what he will do. Now that the knife has already been used, it isn't as threatening as it was in the mental images I had created. In fact, in this darkness, it glints, reflecting the amber light of the street lamps. Ironically, the most sinister tool is the only source of light between us. He slides the flat side of the knife under the open crotch of my jeans and then turns the blade up and out, cutting through the denim. Once there is a slash, he takes his two strong hands and rips the jeans effortlessly, tearing the fabric away from my body and exposing me to him.

A flimsy piece of lace is now the only barrier between me and this intoxicating stranger. He uses the knife to pluck at the two strings securing the thong to my hips. They snap away effortlessly and he balls up the panties in his hand and squeezes my cheeks roughly.

"Open your mouth."

I relax my jaw, as he uses his leather-covered hand to shove my panties into my mouth. It's almost too much: the filth, the excitement, the trepidation. It's like I am teetering on the edge of a building and losing my balance. It's that heightened feeling of terror and excitement you feel as you fight to keep your footing, except, while that feeling usually lasts just a second or two, this is persistent and unrelenting.

My eyes are again drawn to his tattoo as the pit of snakes wriggle on his neck. I want to bite him, I want to kiss him, but he won't let me touch him.

"Don't move your fucking hands," he says. I haven't moved them since he pinned them overhead. His message was loud and clear long before he had to utter the words.

I watch in heady, adrenaline-fueled lust as he pulls open his belt, and the leather-clad hand reaches in to pull out his cock. I catch myself gasping at its outline in the shadowy living room: it's thick and long. This much I expected from rubbing up against him, but the shaft is smooth and symmetrical, the head is thick and pretty. It's...beautiful. And it curves up. *My god, it curves.*

I am an expert in creating toys to please females, and if there was ever a cock created by the hands of god to maximize a woman's pleasure, it's the one being held by the leather glove in front of me.

He reaches down and grabs me by my ponytail, pulling me to a seated position. He glides the panties out of my mouth, like a magician would.

"Lick it."

I hesitate, my head spinning from the constant level change, reminding me that I am still very drunk. He still holds his hard dick in his hand, just in front of my lips. With each deep breath I take, they graze his head before my mouth shrinks away from it. He tightens his grip on my hair, jerking my head ever so slightly in silent insistence.

Until this point, this was a violent dance, with the stranger taking the lead. But that's all it was. If I do what he asks—tells—me to do, I will forever be a different Mia. As open as I consider myself to be about my sexuality, I have also always been very responsible. This was more than irresponsible, this was reckless, this was careless…I would never see myself the same way again.

I had moved inch by inch, starting with even keeping the card that Tiff handed me the night she told me about the service. And now, I look back to that day and I realize I am already miles away from the person who scoffed at the idea. Like bobbing in an ocean current, I had drifted into this man's ferocious grip, and I didn't even really feel myself moving. I am already here, so far away from someone who wouldn't consider taking this man in my mouth. There is no going back.

And then hesitantly, but obediently, I faintly stick my tongue out right at the very tip of his cock, and I taste the fluid of his arousal lingering on its tip.

With each lick I am a little more generous. And he becomes greedier.

"Suck it, bitch."

I snarl at that word. I hate that fucking word and he keeps using it against me. But the anger, it makes me more heated, more wanton, and I find myself pursing my lips around him. *I'll show him a bitch, he'll be moaning my name.* His hands reach back and his fingers comb through my hair, leading my head at the pace he wants.

He wants. But I want too, so I suck vigorously, passionately, because I want to tempt him to give me more.

The scent of his groin, a faint mix of soap and his natural pheromones make my pussy swell with need.

I am all in.

He guides my hands up, giving me permission to use them on his cock and balls. I cup and massage his balls with one hand as I use the other on his shaft.

His mouth is closed, but raspy groans escape the back of his throat and I fear he might release before I have had any satisfaction.

I pull away. I know he will anger, but I don't care.

I look straight into his dark eyes, soulless caverns, and I beg without saying a word.

"You want me to fuck you," he replies. It's not really a question, it's more of a confirmation.

I don't say anything, but I continue to plead with my eyes.

He smirks, a smug, cocky smirk. Then he shoves my mouth back onto him and I continue licking, sucking, rubbing. He fucks my face with no concern for my comfort, shoving himself to the back of my throat. The ferocity only makes me desire his cock in my pussy even more. Then he pulls out of my mouth. He's going to fuck me, but on his terms.

He places his cool leather hands on my inner thighs and angrily pushes them apart. My initial reaction is to resist, a sheer reflex to the force of his movement, but my inner thigh muscles relent to his strength almost instantly. His face disappears below as I feel his tongue slide inside of me. I moan loudly, my legs react by trying to wrap around him, but he clamps down on my inner thighs with his fingers and the sensitive nerves in that area scream in pain.

I mew like a cat in heat, as the alarming pain dulls into warm waves of wetness from my pussy. I can feel myself readying, but it's more than readying, it's as though my pussy is willing him, inviting him with slick warmth.

The dark stranger runs a flat tongue up my entire opening, lapping up the juice he has summoned from my body. I shudder from the overwhelming eroticism of the act, the way he is tasting the fruits of his complete tyranny over my body.

Then he eats me, with abandon, like someone who has thirsted for me for so long and is finally able to quench himself.

It's been so long since I have had the warmth of someone's mouth on my pussy, and this feeling, this level of arousal and passion and heat is something I have never experienced. I bellow like an animal, with no name to call out, no true identity to ascribe to the person whose mouth engulfs my pussy. We aren't even people, we are just sex. That is all we are to each other.

He sucks on my clit, and though I am not supposed to, my hands reach down to him, squeezing the fabric of the ski mask that rests on his head as an explosion of relief and energy erupts from my clit. Pulses of electric warmth roll away from my core like a shattering earthquake.

I call out horrible, filthy words as my hips thrust against his face. His tongue and lips continue to dance along my pussy as each wave becomes fainter.

"We're not fucking done." His words vibrate into my sensitive flesh.

Thank god. I need to feel that beautiful cock inside of me.

He pulls me up to my knees, and I fall forward into his chest. It's like a wall, and it reminds me how vulnerable I am. He handles me like I am a doll, like I have no substance, just useless filling.

Maybe that is what I am to him: a living, breathing sex toy.

My eyes trail up to the tattoo and for some stupid reason, I try to kiss it.

My neck is whipped back by a firm tug on my ponytail. "This is my last warning. Do not kiss me and keep your hands to yourself."

He stands and brings me to my feet by my ponytail, dragging me to my couch. The couch where just two weeks ago, Tiff told me about her experience. The stranger throws me face-first onto it, so that I am on my knees, my chest resting against the backrest.

His hands roughly pull on my hips to prop my ass out. His swollen head rubs up and down my slippery slit. I bite my lips and scrunch my face from the agony of his teasing. I stopped thinking about the fact that this is a rape-for-hire as soon as my tongue lapped up his precum. I stopped considering using the safe word as soon as he put his mouth on my mound. All logic, common sense, and morality has escaped my thoughts.

My house is a pit of snakes right now, like the tattoo on his neck.

His fingers rake through the base of my ponytail. "Beg for it, you little slut."

My chest quivers. How did this happen? How am I here, begging my fake rapist to fuck me? But he's got me in a corner: I can feel the warmth of his head resting against the hypersensitive lips of my pussy; the muscles of my inner walls clench around emptiness begging to be filled. My body won't let me stop.

But, I hesitate. How much more can he taunt me and degrade me? I have been thrown around, called a bitch, a slut, my clothes have been torn, bite marks linger on my skin.

He slides it up and down again, slowly, teasing and enticing me.

All of my muscles melt, almost dissolving me into a puddle on the couch as I purr. He pulls my hair again, awakening all of my muscles, making me taut and ready to receive his violence.

His stubble flares the nerve endings on my cheek and his lips caress the curve of my ear, "I said beg." His fist grips at the roots of my hair painfully.

A throbbing deep inside of me stubbornly insists on release. It's no longer a desire. It has become a need, absolving me of the burden of free will.

"Please..." I whimper in a shaky voice.

"Louder." His low, gritty tone is a thin veil for the note of pleasure in his voice.

"Please," I say more firmly.

"Louder," he says cruelly.

"Please," I project.

He slips his head inside of me as I gasp and then he stops.

"Louder, bitch." He won't be satisfied until I am completely stripped of dignity.

"Please!" It's just below a yell, but my voice is jagged with shame.

He pushes his entire length into me, wrathfully.

I cry out, throwing my head back and gripping the top of the couch. His cock curves into me deeply, painfully.

"Don't stop begging, and loud so I can hear you cry."

He pulls out almost all the way and impales me again. "Please!" I cry, arching my back to brace for the impact of his cock.

He hits a rhythm, each thrust complete with my vocal begging. The more I beg, the louder I beg, the more he fucks me.

The otherwise silent house is filled with the sounds of his hips slapping the soft flesh of my ass, the sounds of my juices sloshing around his cock, and my loud, crying plead: "Please! Please! Please! Please!" My voice vibrates from the stranger's violent thrusting against my body.

"That's right, fucking whore," he grumbles.

If I stop begging, he stops. It's humiliating, it's dirty, and yet it somehow turns on every erogenous zone in my body.

His balls violently slap against me, reminding me of his conquering with each tap and awakening even more nerve endings just behind my pussy.

This stranger violently thrusting into me as I shamelessly beg for his dick makes me feel like a star bursting bright. Like sex is pouring out of my every orifice, every pore. My mind is honed in on him and only him. This is the abandon I have been looking for. Shame and decency have long gone out the window. I can be freely sexual. I can admit I want cock, I want cum, I want my hair to be pulled, I want my nipples to be pinched. I can howl as loud as I want. Nothing else fucking matters but the feeling of this man's cock pressing against the walls of my pussy.

Eventually, he stays inside of me instead of pulling in and out. He maintains a steady contact and friction with my walls as his cock rubs deep inside of me. The tension builds and builds.

Everything tightens: every pore on my body shrinks, my nipples minimize to their smallest, most sensitive point, his stubble burns against my neck, the muscles inside of my thighs clench, his warm breath blows against my cheek.

"Please!" I beg at my loudest, the scratchy husk of certainty cloaking my voice. He cannot stop now, he has to take me all the way. His hand reaches around and he rubs my mound, giving the perfect amount of attention to my overstimulated clit.

I tighten, and tighten, everything shrinking to its most compact point around his hard cock, and then BOOM. Everything releases. Everything bursts, erupts, shatters.

I hear my own voice fill the room: a shaky, quavering cry. He covers my mouth with his gloved hand, because it's so loud, it might grab a neighbor's attention.

As my walls contract around him and my body erupts, his cocks swells in me, his grip around me tightens. The stranger keeps his pace, covering my mouth with one hand and clenching a breast with the other, rolling a nipple between his fingers. And before I am even done coming down, I start to build again with him.

I can't believe I am about to have another orgasm before the first one has even finished. This time his groans almost become growls, he bites my neck, stopping right at the pressure before I would scream in pain.

He squeezes my breast so hard I yelp and then his cock pulsates inside of me as he grunts into my neck, his warm groans envelop me. His warmth shoots inside of me, and I come again around his throbbing cock.

Reckless. Irresponsible. Dirty. Dangerous.
Exhilarating. Erotic. Wild. Euphoric.
How can one thing be all of those?

How can peering into the gutter of my soul feel like I just touched heaven?

CHAPTER SIX

Mia

"Get up," he says between breaths as he pulls down his mask to cover his face again.

My ears ring from the intensity of the multiple orgasms. My hearing is dampened, smothered. The stranger's voice sounds distant, like I am underwater. It's like a nearby bomb went off. I swallow hard, desperately trying to regain my bearings and clear my hearing.

"Huh?" I ask, exhausted and mentally shattered. I guess his act isn't over. I try desperately to cope with the physical aftermath of what just happened, while still trying to be present with the man who just lit my word ablaze. I glance over to the floor and my clothes are shredded and strewn about. A lamp is turned over along with some knick-knacks, and the rug is warped. *Maybe a bomb did go off?*

He yanks me by my elbow and up to my feet. "Come on." His voice is deep, gravely, and devoid of patience.

He drags me to the bathroom, whips open the shower curtain, and turns on the shower. "Get in."

I look at him hesitantly as he grips my upper arm and I step in. Stranger yanks the curtain closed except for a small gap so he can watch. "Clean your pussy." He peeks through the opening and watches me as I soap myself up. When he appears to be satisfied, he closes all the way.

Finally alone, I look down at my hands and they are still trembling from our encounter.

I think about what I should say. *Should I thank him for his services? What the hell just happened? What is happening? Who the fuck am I and what did I just do?*

I just let a complete stranger fuck me raw! Oh my god. Holy fuck. Holy fucking fuck.

The shower is sobering and panic hits me hard. My chest tightens as I lean against the cold tile and aggressively scrub my skin with a bar of soap. My legs are still jello and I can barely keep myself up. Shivers run up and down my body like aftershocks, reminding me of the intense pleasure at the hands of a man whose name I don't even know.

My sympathetic nervous system fires on all cylinders, rendering me unable to relax or complete a coherent thought and reducing me to a ball of nervous physical energy.

I don't know how I feel about anything right now. What I did was stupid, thoughtless, and fucking crazy. And yet, it was the most insane, erotic, exhilarating and sensual experience of my life. I have never come that hard that many times. I have never just let go the way I did in that living room.

I have never had a man just fuck me like that, with pure lust and physical desire, without either one of us giving a single shit about convention or feelings or propriety. It was rude, vulgar, wrong...immoral. There was no discomfort or awkwardness. Shame did not exist when he took me. But now, alone behind the shower curtain, I couldn't wash off the fresh coat of shame no matter how much I scrubbed.

My logical mind pulls me back into the present. There is a sexy, but strange man still in my house. I thrust the curtain open and the bathroom is empty. I turn off the shower, wrap myself in a towel, and cautiously step out of the bathroom, dripping wet. The house is still completely dark.

"Hello?" I call out. "Are you still here?"

I tip toe through every room, leaving a trail of water in my wake, remains of a pointless attempt at washing the filth off of my flesh. But it's too late, he's already inside of me and under my skin. Despite all the meticulous planning, I sense the irrational threat of danger. I shouldn't, this guy is a professional. But still, I don't know him.

I don't know a single thing about him.

I pace silently from one empty room to the next, ending up in the living room. A chair is on its side, a lamp turned over, the rug is crumpled, my tattered clothes are in a heap, the adjoining kitchen floor is a mess of food and Tupperware.

Then I realize that just as quickly as Stranger swooped into my life...

He is gone.

Tax

I slam my car door shut and tomahawk my fist against the steering wheel.

What the fuck just happened?

That did NOT go according to plan.

I throw my head back and run my hands over my face, taking in a deep breath. Her scent lingers on my clothes, a sweet, soapy smell. I can still taste her on my lips, and it reminds me of the way her pussy bloomed for me, the way she begged me to fuck her, the way she tremored around my cock.

I rip my jacket off, trying to rid myself of her. Of that bitch's essence.

Still breathless, I fiddle with the hunting knife that I had planned on using tonight. And I did use it, but not the way I had planned.

This shit was not supposed to go down like this. This was supposed to be the end. The grand finale. Everything was supposed to come full circle.

But I lost my focus and blew it.

When it comes to the mission, I have always succeeded the first time around, so this territory is foreign to me. But I'll take it as a sign that her end should be far more ceremonious.

I never thought I would say this, but...*on to plan B.*

CHAPTER SEVEN

Mia

"Mia!"

I nearly hit the ceiling as Dewey calls my name, tapping my shoulder.

"Uh...oh, hi...what's up?"

"Didn't mean to startle you, but I called your name about five times already. Maybe you should turn your headphones down? I'd hate for you to lose your hearing, my friend."

I push out a fake smile. "You know me, I get so focused in on things." *I am so lying right now.* There is only one reason why my mind is elsewhere.

"Anyway, I just wanted to catch you. Before you go home today, I'd like you to stop by my office. There are some things I would like to talk to you about."

"Uh...sure. Of course. Is everything alright?"

"Yeah," he says brushing off my concern by waving his hand in the air. "*We'll talk...*" he mouths as he walks away.

A private meeting when everyone has left the office is not like Dewey and it makes me nervous. Well, during these past five days, everything has made me nervous. Honestly, I wasn't even listening to music, I just wore my earphones so people would generally leave me alone. But my thoughts have not stopped drifting back to that night.

I still don't know how I feel about it. It's a mixture of things. Like I am walking around with a dirty little secret. I have these intense introspective moments of disgust with myself. And then there's fear because of the unprotected sex (the promise of an STD-free experience from this mysterious service isn't quite as assuring as I thought it would be now that it's all said and done). But a larger portion of the time, my mind drifts back to specific moments or memories.

I think about the pinch of his bites on my skin, the way his stubble pricked against my stomach as he licked his way down between my legs. I remember *his smell*...an intoxicating mixture of man and cologne. I think about his thick, curved cock and how it rubbed me in all the right places, and the way he forced me to beg until I had no inhibitions left. It fills my stomach with butterflies. I can't eat. I can't sleep. I can't even focus at the job I love.

And I think that's why Dewey wants to see me. He keeps asking me if something is different, if everything is okay. I have worked here for eight years now, and we know each other pretty well. He's that kind of guy, he cares. And he probably wants to ask me when the office is quiet.

I barely remember anything from this work week because all I have done is relive pieces of Friday night.

Yet, I can't bring myself to press that "SUBMIT" button again. There is a filthiness that makes it the type of experience that knocks you on your ass for a week after it happened, but also it sickens you. It makes you feel wrong. Because it is wrong, *right*? What I did? I hired a strange man to come into my house and violate me.

I don't care how many people have done it. I don't care if the guy would stop when I say *rainbow*, there is something seriously wrong with this scenario.

And yet, why is that I find myself smiling at random moments? Why have I held on to the torn tank top that still has his smell on it?

I think I made a huge mistake. A terrible, amazing, unforgettable mistake.

———※———

"Have a seat," Dewey says to me as I enter his office, while still looking at his computer screen. He's trying to act casual, but I sense he's covering up something heavy.

I sit across from him as he looks up as me and purses his lips.

"Dewey...what's going on? You seem reaaaaally serious," I say nervously.

"You're the first person I am telling this to, so it's hard to utter the words..." He takes a deep breath before pushing out: "I've sold Alea."

"You sold the company?" I ask in disbelief. Alea is his baby, a company he built from the ground up with his wife, Barb. I have been with him since nearly the beginning, being the second person he hired. Together, we grew Alea from a company making fifty thousand a year to nearly ten million. I know Alea is his, but I have to say, it hurts to be blindsided like this.

"Hear me out. You know Barb has had her health problems, and I want to spend more time with her. We want to do some traveling. A buyer came with an offer I could not refuse. But you know I love you guys and I would never leave you all hanging. The buyer wants to be a silent owner, while the company runs as-is. They understand that the people here make it so great, and trying to come in and change what we have would hinder Alea's success. So Alea's new parent company, Draconi Corp, will simply check in with the head of Alea to analyze numbers, maybe work on some strategy, but everything stays the same. It'll be like it has always been."

While I am relieved, I wonder if it will ever be like it's always been. Dewey is the heart of this company, and being bought out by some bigger entity always means there will be changes, no matter what promises were made.

"But, if you're gone, how can it be the same? Who will be our boss?" I ask.

Dewey smiles. "Why do you think you're the first person I'm telling?"

"Wuh?" I ask skeptically. I think I know what he's getting at, but I don't want to jump to conclusions. Because it would be a really big friggin' deal.

"Because it's you, Mia. I want you to take my place."

I gasp, trying to hold down the knot that forms in my throat.

"Mia, you are Alea's longest standing employee, and no one understands the culture and the business side of Alea like you. You have helped me grow this company to what it is today. I would have no other person take my place. I told Draconi that putting you at the helm would be the only way to guarantee a seamless transition. They agree and see your move to my spot as an investment and are prepared to pay you really well. I mean, life-changingly well."

"I don't know what to say," I reply, shaking my head in disbelief. I love working here, and I worked my ass off, but it never really felt that way because it was always a joy.

"Say you'll take my spot, so I know Alea is in good hands."

"You know Alea is my baby too. God, I am going to miss you and Barb, but I would be happy and honored to make sure Alea keeps being awesome."

I hug Dewey as tears trickle down my cheeks. I am touched by his trust in me and thrilled to be promoted, but I am going to really miss him.

And for a moment, I forget about the completely stupid and irresponsible decision I made just days before.

CHAPTER EIGHT

Mia

I walk through the empty garage of the office building with a huge smile on my face. I have worked so hard to help grow Alea, and I have always felt so fortunate to work here. Not many people can say they love their job and their boss.

But my happiness is bittersweet, because I do love my bosses. Barb used to be a regular fixture at Alea until she was diagnosed with lupus and had to take leave about a year ago. It was hard enough losing her motherly presence in the office, and now I would be losing Dewey too. It would become my job to maintain the culture of strong work ethic, openness and fun they had established at Alea.

I won't lie, the responsibility makes me nervous, but I know Dewey is right. If there is anyone who is qualified for this job, it's me. I built Alea alongside Barb and Dewey; I know everything about the manufacturing side and I helped build our current distribution channels. I just hope that this new group that has acquired Alea respects our wishes to keep the company running the way it has until now.

My footsteps echo through the cavernous empty parking lot as I walk towards my car from the stairwell. I have always felt safe in this garage. We have a small office building and the parking lot is secure. Only someone with an access code can enter. Since Alea has a mostly female staff, safety was important when we hunted for office buildings.

Tonight though, I feel a strange sensation as I walk through the empty lot, like I am being watched. I stop and scan the open space, my car being the only one still there. I don't see anyone, and I chalk it up to my residual nerves from Friday.

I pick up my pace as I fumble with my keys, hitting the button on my keyless entry to hear the comforting click of my car doors unlocking. I slide into my car as quickly as I can, letting out a huge sigh of relief as I lock the doors to my car and almost recklessly back out of my spot and drive away.

Just then, my phone rings, startling me. I'm still jittery from the uneasy feeling I had in the parking lot. It's Tiff. I debate answering the phone. I still haven't told her about that night. At first I was convinced it would be moot since I was not going to go through with it, and I didn't want her trying to change my mind. Then when it happened, I was so conflicted that I wasn't ready to share the news with her. I figured eventually she'd get a discount and realize it was me, but Tiff has hundreds of friends. *Lots* of freaky friends. I am certain I am not the only referral she put out there.

This whole Happy Kitty thing was supposed to go away. Unlike Tiff, who seemed to feel conflict-free elation about the whole thing, I am battling with what I did. But I have avoided her since the night she came to my place, and that's not like me. So, I take a breath and answer her call through the Bluetooth system in my car.

"Hey," I say, trying to act like everything is all hunky dory.

"Hey," Tiff says, somewhat caught off-guard, as if she didn't expect me to answer.

"What's up?"

"Oh not much, just wanted to check in. I haven't spoken to you since I think I freaked you out about that whole experience I had."

I shake my head even though she can't see me. "Oh, no...I've just been busy with work."

"Did I come on too strong? I know I have a tendency to do that when I'm passionate about stuff."

"You do, but no. I love that you stand behind things that you love and you become like a street-corner preacher about it. I mean, if I am being honest, it was a shock. But I think you know by now that nothing, short of mass-murder or something, is too shocking for me. So just don't go on a killing spree and we're good."

I hear Tiff let out a sigh of relief. "I meant what I said, about how I think you should do it..." My fingers choke the steering wheel. "But, I know you're not comfortable with it. So, let's just forget I mentioned it. Unless you do want to do it, then you can talk to me about it, if you want, of course. Lord knows I'll be doing it again when I can spare the money, and I sure as hell will be giving you the play by play."

"Thanks," I say, wondering if I am currently lying by omission. "I appreciate you thinking of me, even if it is in regards to really freaky sexcapades."

She laughs. "Just sayin', you are missing on the really good D." *Oh no, my friend, I got the good D. I got the BEST D. I got the D that's ruined me for other guys.* My brain, working on overdrive, to think of the most natural response, leaves a few seconds of silence between us. "So, what else is new?" she asks.

"Well...big news actually. Dewey sold Alea and I am taking over as President."

"Are you serious?"

"Yes! I think I've been too shocked to be excited. And I am sad that Dewey is leaving."

"Oh you'll get over it, boss lady. This calls for a celebration!"

Normally, I would be down, but I don't want to see Tiff quite yet. This phone conversation has me tense enough. I need to get back to a somewhat normal state of mind before she and I get together again.

"Can I take a rain check? I am so effin' tired."

"Fine, you stick in the mud."

"Okay, I promise, we'll celebrate soon. Love ya."

"Love ya too."

During the rest of the drive home, the feeling of disgust that has visited intermittently since Friday makes a reappearance. My dubious conversation with Tiff only helped it resurface. Here I am, with everything I have ever wanted, and yet, I had to find a way to fuck things up just a little bit. I try to focus on the positive: we all make bad judgment calls. In a few weeks, this will be a distant memory, a secret I will carry with me. But hopefully the shame will dull, and the feeling of filth will subside. Like Tiff said, it's a lot like a rough one-night stand. That's all it was, a really intense, multiple-orgasmic, mind-fucking one night stand.

I pull into my driveway, turn off my car, and grab my purse and jacket before slipping out. Just when I slam the car door shut, I see the bushes in front of my patio rustle, followed by a shuffling sound.

Before my eyes can focus on the commotion, there is a shadowy figure thrusting upon me. My keys and bag fall to the floor as I slam onto my car.

I gasp loudly.

"Shut up," he says.

My flood lights glare on the driveway so I can see him clearly.

He is wearing a grey suit and he's tall, with a chiseled jawline. He's very handsome and well-groomed. This guy doesn't look like a mugger. Do I know him? Could it be *him*? Did he come back for more?

Impossible. I only paid for one encounter and I got more than my money's worth.

Panic sets in. Just because it happened once before does not make this instance any less terrifying.

"Get in the car," he says, squeezing my arm and opening the back seat. "Now."

This doesn't make sense. None of this makes sense. This already happened. Why—how—is this happening again?

I hesitate, trying to make sense of my double attack. Is this some sort of extra level of mindfuck? I'm so confused. Is this guy really attacking me? Is he even part of Happy Kitty?

I look into his cold eyes and immediately realize they are blue. The house was dark the first time, but I am certain the other guy's eyes were brown.

"I...who are you?" I ask.

"Shut up and get in the car," he whispers furiously. He drags me by my arm closer to the rear door. And while he's being rough, there is still a level of self-restraint, like he isn't really intending to punish me. It feels like he's *acting*.

In a flash, I remember the clue that will reveal for certain if this is the guy who attacked me in my house: the neck tat.

I look over to his right side, and there is no sign of the snakes peeking up from his collar. The other guy's tat ran up the entire length of his neck, threatening to slither up his jawline.

It's not him. It's not him.

It's not him?

Then who his this? And who the FUCK was the other guy?

"RAINBOW!" I call out. "RAINBOW!"

The guys eyes softly squint and he releases his grip on my arm.

"It's okay," he says. "I'm stopping. It's okay."

It's like I flicked an off switch on his persona.

"Are you with...the website?" I ask in a shaky voice.

"We are terminating the encounter. Just go into your house. You are safe. This is over. You won't see me again."

"But...but...someone already came..."

The handsome face looks back at me in disbelief, like I am completely unhinged.

"That's not possible."

My voice is trembling. "No...yes, yes it is possible. Someone came last Friday. He had on a suit. He..."

And that's when I realize that something is terribly wrong.

I never verified the mystery man by asking him the optional secret question, he was wearing a mask, he didn't approach me on my driveway as specified, he was in my house.

He had a knife. Holy shit, he had a KNIFE.

"I have to go. You are safe, the encounter is terminated," he says as if rehearsing some line he's been fed. And then he jogs back into the dark where he came from, leaving me speechless and confused on my driveway.

If the dark stranger wasn't someone I hired to attack me, then where did he come from? Who is he?

Did I have sex with someone who genuinely broke into my house?

Did I actually have sex with my rapist?

CHAPTER NINE

Tax

I watch the whole thing go down. I've been following her since Friday, knowing she would be approached by some asshole within the next couple of weeks. And the thought she might let him do what I did to her enraged me.

I was prepared to fuck up the cocksucker if he got anywhere past the confrontation stage, and then I would drag her into the house and fuck her again. I would make her remember me.

But she stopped him. Within seconds, the guy just ran back into the bushes. I can't help but laugh here in my car. Her mind must be spinning. She must be so fucking confused. She's probably wondering who I am and where I came from.

She's just standing there in shock, her purse and keys still splayed on the driveway at her feet. Part of me wants to get out of the car just to see her again, to monopolize on her confusion and then drag her into the house and make her scream as I shove my cock into her creamy pussy.

When I pressed up against her that night I broke into her house, I smelled her shampoo, felt her soft skin, and my cock rebelled, morphing my intentions from rage to lust. And since that night the lust hasn't waned.

But I have to keep my distance, because she won't be around for long.

I must admit though, there is something immensely satisfying about the fact she rejected that fucker.

Because I know it's me she wants.

Mia

I pace my living room frantically, in tears.

I don't know what to do. I don't know what happened. It's like I am being punished for being a dirty slut. I wanted a stranger to sneak up on me and fuck me? Well, I got it.

I can't call the police. How could I even begin to explain myself? I never even said no to the guy. I begged him. I pleaded with him over and over to fuck me.

Fuuuuuuuuck.

I grab my cell phone and stare at it for a while. I could call Tiff, but now I am even less prepared to tell her about that night. This whole fucking thing has turned into a nightmare. I know Tiff would help me, but even in front of her, I would feel so stupid. Because I am an idiot. I got carried away. I felt him, I smelled him, I saw him, and I lost all sense. In my eyes, he was physical perfection, he checked off all the boxes I selected in my little "perfect man survey" for Happy Kitty. In his arms, all the so called foolproof fail-safes were worthless. Foolproof my ass. They weren't prepared for a fool as big as me.

There is no recourse. I may have to come to terms with the fact that I will never have answers about what happened to me that night. Some guy broke in my house with the purpose of...I don't know...raping or robbing me, and I fucked his brains out! He might attack some other innocent woman because I didn't stop him or report him.

Oh god, I need to see a doctor right away. Sure he wore an expensive suit and was impeccably groomed, but that doesn't mean shit.

This isn't right. How can someone who prides herself on being smart, hardworking and intelligent do something so impetuous? I always had these desires, these fantasies of a man having his way with me, but that was all they were meant to be: fantasies. And now I have pulled that world into the life I have so carefully crafted for myself and it's already more than I bargained for.

Then fear strikes. He was in my house. He gained entry into my house without breaking the door. Maybe he has a key, maybe he opened a window. I don't know. But I know I have to get out. I don't think I am safe in my own home.

I run into my bedroom and grab an overnight bag, yanking clothes from my closet and dresser and haphazardly throwing them in. Within minutes, I am out the door and back in my car, driving to the nearest motel and looking at my rear view mirror like some paranoid freak.

Never have I felt so alone. Never have I missed my dad like I do right now. I couldn't have told him about the bind I am in, but just talking to him would have made me feel safe. He always made me feel safe.

CHAPTER TEN

Mia

It's been two and half weeks. Two and a half weeks since that man came into my house and shattered everything I knew about myself. I still think about him all the time. I still battle with mixed feelings of disgust and lust.

I am terrified because I have no answers. If I knew who he was, what he was doing in my house, I would have something to hide from. But he might as well be a ghost. He could be anywhere.

Above all, there is one thing that frightens me more than anything: I think I might never feel the way I felt that night with anyone ever again. And I hate myself for thinking that.

I went to see my gynecologist last week. Since I had my annual recently, I had to request a new full STD screening. She's a professional, and never batted an eyelash as to why I would want such a thing, but I couldn't help and project my feelings of shame onto her. I felt like she could smell the stench of my sluttiness in her presence. I am so glad that despite my self-imposed slower than normal sex-life, I stayed on my birth control pills instead of taking a break like I had considered. Because THAT would have been epically disastrous. The STD tests came back negative, but I'd have to come back in six long months for another HIV screening. Because I am an imbecile who has unprotected sex with a stranger.

Today should be the happiest day of my life. I am officially the President of Alea Intimate Toys for Women. I have a job that makes me so happy, I have jumped up to a new income bracket, I have a nice house, I am healthy. But this week has been filled with inner turmoil so strong that it shakes me to my core every day.

I still can't sleep or eat. I hope this will pass, but the stress of acclimating to the new role has only compounded the distress I already feel about my personal life.

To top it off, I am on my way to my first meeting with the new owners of Alea. It's my first face to face with them, and Dewey will be there too, to symbolically pass the torch, I assume. One thing has been confirmed for me already: when they say they are silent, they mean SILENT. The meeting has been scheduled for 5am, three hours before our earliest employee is scheduled to appear in the office. It appears they have no interest in mingling with their new minions. They want to make sure I am steering the ship correctly, that their investment is being well taken care of, and that's the extent of their involvement in Alea.

I hope that's a sign that they are keeping their promise to Dewey, that they will keep out of the day to day management of the company and not that they will be some faceless entity, giving me orders that I must singlehandedly pass down to my co-workers. Because the latter could really alienate me from the people I have worked with for so many years.

I pull into the garage at the office building and my stomach tightens as I recall the last time I was alone in this empty lot. It was the night I learned that I had screwed up majorly and allowed a home invader to have me.

I had a gut feeling something was wrong that night before the actual-fake attacker approached me in my driveway. My instincts were right, something was about to go terribly wrong, but then why did my instincts fail me so miserably the first time?

As I exit the car, I smooth out my pencil skirt and blouse. Usually, we dress casually in the office. We are an eclectic bunch and almost anything goes. But today I am trying to look more civilized for my new role and out of respect to our guests. I quickly touch up my lipstick on the side view mirror and smooth my hair back.

I take a deep breath, trying to relieve the tension that seems to have made a permanent home in my muscles these days. Then I make my way to the door leading to the building. My heels clamor loudly in the empty lot, reminding me how alone I am, how alone I feel.

Relax, get your game face on. You are a professional. Keep your personal shit out of the office.

The door to Alea is unlocked, and I figured it would be, as I assume Dewey made his way into the office before me. All the lights are off, except the one inside of the conference room. I glance at my phone. 4:55am. I'm not late, so that's good. I assume all parties are inside, but I can't tell since the blinds are drawn over the glass enclosure.

I head to the conference room door, forcing a huge smile on my face as I pass the threshold.

On the far end stands a towering man in an expensive-looking navy blue suit. He's facing away from the door, studying our product line proudly displayed along some open glass shelves. My eyes dart around the room for Dewey, but he's nowhere in sight.

I clear my throat to make my presence known to the looming figure across the room.

He turns smoothly, as if he is unsurprised by my presence. Before he even faces me, my nose picks up on something familiar...it's the faintest hint of cologne, I believe. But before I can place its origin, my eyes land on a visual target, like two heat seeking missiles.

And I don't even think. My reaction is pure instinct: my throat goes dry, my heart pumps rapidly, my thoughts shrivel into a collage.

Because what my eyes narrow in on is a vibrantly colored neck tattoo, a pit of snakes, that curl and crawl up his neck.

Tax

Joy.

Not many things in life bring me joy. But the look on that bitch's face when she recognizes me makes me downright gleeful.

She has no idea what hit her.

"Nice to meet you, Ms. Mia Tibbett," I say. I keep a disinterested tone, but I am enjoying the fuck out of this moment.

"I uh...I..."

It's hard not to laugh. Her complete confusion, her discomfort: I live for this shit.

"Is the feeling not mutual?" I ask.

"No! Of course," she says, clearly lying. She might be afraid for her safety. Doesn't the bitch realize if I fucking wanted to kill her she'd have been dead weeks ago?

Mia goes pale. She might pass out. I study her as her thoughts race, she is pathetically transparent. I can tell she's trying to figure out if I know that she knows.

Bitch, I'm not hiding.

"But this isn't our first time meeting, is it?" I ask with a smug grin.

Her face almost melts off. I'm done playing games. Well, not really, but I am done playing whodunnit with her.

She starts to breathe heavy, almost hyperventilating. I love it. "Who...are you?" She slowly backs away as if she thinks she has the option of leaving.

"I'm the owner of Draconi Corp. I purchased Alea. I was told you are essential to this company's success, that you know everything there is to know."

"Where's Dewey?"

"Oh, I told him we didn't need him this morning. No crutches for you Mia. You run Alea now, under my ownership, of course. He no longer has any affiliation to Alea and was solely coming to be a good sport. I prefer this meeting between us to be private."

I watch her throat rise and fall as she swallows. I almost feel pity for her. *Almost.* She doesn't know who she is up against, but soon she will. Once she knows what this is all about and accepts it, there won't be room for pity.

Fuck does she look amazing. She usually wears tight jeans and t-shirts that press against her tits, but today she dressed up for me: a navy blue pencil skirt that smoothes over her tight ass, and a fitted white button down silk shirt that falls gently on the slope of her breasts. I wish she would've unbuttoned one more button up top so that I could get a better view as her cleavage rises and falls with each nervous breath. But I guess I'll have to use my imagination...or not.

Her full lips are coated in a reddish lipstick that I envision encircling my cock. Her dark brown hair is tucked back into a conservative bun, but the streak of purple lets me know she has a wild side hiding under that buttoned up shirt. Though I don't need a purple stripe to let me know that under that reserved exterior is a dirty slut.

"Who are you?" she asks again.

"My name is Tax Draconi. You can just call me Tax."

"What kind of a name is Tax?"

"It's the name of a person who always collects a debt," I say, watching her breath hitch in response to my words.

"This is inappropriate." *That's the fucking understatement of the century.* "I...I cannot work with you."

"Have a seat," I say, uninterested in her opinion.

"No," she says firmly.

She's feisty, and bordering on pissing me off. But I'll keep my cool. It's going to be fun to make her think she has a say in any of this. Then I'll take that shred of autonomy she thinks she has and crush it. I can't wait to destroy the look of fierceness she has in her eyes right now. I am going to piss all over her fire.

"If you are worried about your safety, I can assure you, I have no intentions of harming you."

Finally, emotion rips through the shock and her tone becomes indignant. "You broke into my house...you brought a knife..."

"It's what you wanted, isn't it? You begged me," I say, recalling that night. Aaaaand fuck, here comes the throbbing sensation of my cock hardening. I sit down to hide it, but also to put her at ease, to give her the illusion of control.

She sneers at me like she wants to slit my throat, and I know that's because every word of what I just said was true. She screamed *please* every time I thrusted into her pussy. If she didn't say it loud enough, I would stop and she would beg again. The globes of her tight, round ass quivered every time I slammed my cock into her, her tits jiggled as I pumped. She was made for fucking.

"Why? Why did you come to my house?"

"Because I wanted to."

"Are you even affiliated with those people?"

"That website? God no. Do I fuck like someone who's faking it?"

She goes silent. I am slowly breaking her will and piquing her curiosity. She wants answers, and she knows I am the only person who can give them to her.

"Are you...clean?" she asks, her cheeks turning red. Haha, THAT'S the question that makes her blush?

I motion my hands gesturing to my six-thousand dollar suit, fresh haircut, and body crafted through a finely-tuned diet and gym regimen. "I love myself more than any fucking thing in this world. I take very good care of my body. You've got nothing to worry about, doll."

"And how do you know I am?" she says, with a look of defiance. *Oooh,* this bitch has no idea who she's fucking with. *And why the hell did my cock just flinch?*

I stand up slowly, and walk over to her. She is standing against a wall, she doesn't even realize she's backed herself into a corner. As I walk over, her eyes expand in fear, but she puffs up her chest as a display of strength. How fucking hilarious coming from someone no taller than five-six and maybe 130 pounds, and I'd say a fifth of that is tits and ass.

I plant myself in front of her, and say nothing for a second. I want to remind her where she stands in this equation, who owns who, who has the power.

"Because I know everything about you."

CHAPTER ELEVEN

Mia

Fiona Apple – Limp

He stands just inches away from me and he may as well be a mountain. Everything about him is threatening, yet I don't feel like he's here to hurt me. At least for now.

My mind is filled with anger, confusion, fear...but my body, it heats up in his presence. I can't help but recall the connection we had. And I can see just below his belt, that whatever the reason is that he has decided to appear in my life, he feels it too.

Who is this man and what the hell does he want from me?

Maybe I should run, but my body, heavy with shock, refuses to flee. Where would I go anyway? If he really owns Alea, facing him is an inevitability. That is unless I leave behind the career I built over the past eight years.

I slide away and sit at a chair at the conference table, pulling out my laptop and opening it up.

"What are you doing?" he asks.

"I am typing up my letter of resignation." My chest hurts. I think I've gone numb because I am basically throwing my dream job out the window right now. I know later I will be crying my eyes out from the devastation.

"No, you're not," he says, leaning over me to calmly close the laptop. As if he has no reason to even commit to the slightest bit of extra effort, as if he believes there is no chance I will leave.

He leans against the table just next to me, close enough for me to catch his masculine scent. It's the scent I still smell when I dream about him, the one that fills me with lust, and right now, rage and confusion.

"Mia, you signed a contract to stay at Alea for a year, and with that, you received a handsome bonus—"

"I'll give it back."

"Don't interrupt."

Bastard.

"You have a non-compete clause in your contract as well." He walks back over to the head of the table, and picks up a small stack of papers. It looks like a copy of my contract. "But none of that matters," he says, tossing it into the nearest wastepaper basket. "Because if you leave, you will never work in this city again. And if you leave this city, I will make sure you never get another job anywhere else. Trust me, there are ways."

My chest tightens, fighting back tears. I won't give him my tears.

"What do you want?"

"A year. I want you to fulfill your obligation to Alea. Who knows? You might like it."

"So, you came here to taunt me? Don't you realize if you had just stayed away, you would have had me here for at least a year? If you had never shown your face here, I could have. I would have been none the wiser. But I can't now...I can't work with you."

"Mia, you don't want to make an enemy out of me."

"Enemy? Because I don't want to work under some predator?"

"Let's not pretend you were some innocent little lamb," he scowls. "You gladly swallowed my cock."

His words twist my stomach, the coffee I had this morning threatening to make a reappearance.

"Fuck you. No. I won't be held hostage. Fine, ruin me," I say. I am so scared, but I can't. I just can't stay. "You'll have to find someone else to run Alea."

I open my laptop again to type my letter, but my hands are so shaky I can barely open the word processing program. I look ahead firmly, trying to exude strength, but it's fear that drives me. Like a child hiding under her bedsheets, I hope if I can't see the monster, it won't see me.

Without saying a word, Tax pulls out his phone, taps the screen a few times, and the silent room fills with my pleading: *Please! Please! Please!* Even though the office is empty, I feel like everyone at Alea can hear me begging a stranger to fuck me.

Grunting. Groaning. Slapping. Moaning.

"Would you like to see?" he asks.

I look straight ahead at my laptop screen, grinding my teeth, seething with anger. Inside though, I crumble in defeat. He recorded us.

My lip quivers, using all its might to keep my emotions contained. My head, my chest, they feel like a pressurized container, ready to burst.

"I made sure my face wasn't visible, but yours is all over the footage. Let me make this clear: you'll lose everything. I don't just mean professionally. I will make sure everyone knows about your proclivities. About how you hire men to rape you. This video will be everywhere. Your online porn searches, your application to that website. I have it all. And I will make sure it will follow you for the rest of your life. And if there would ever be a slim chance of you getting a similar position elsewhere, well, no one wants to hire this kind of baggage." He slides the phone into my line of sight, and I turn my head away. I won't watch. He bends over, resting a hand on the back of my chair, and puffs of his breath graze my ear as he spews the rest of his venom. "You'll be bussing tables for the rest of your life. And even then, I will make sure everywhere you go, the people who work with you know. You're hot Mia. You know that. Men already look at you and imagine themselves shoving their dicks inside of you. Can you imagine working some shitty nightmare job, while your creepy male coworkers jack off to you? While they whisper behind your back? Because that is what your life will become Mia. You will go from executive, to minimum wage jack off material for your fat middle-aged boss. Really think about that. You can have a lifetime of humiliation and judgment...or you can give Alea a year."

"I'll tell the police," I say, thrusting my chair away from him to gain some distance.

"It won't make a difference, bitch. You do understand that once everything about this comes to light, it'll be you on trial, right? You don't understand who you are fucking with. Take me to court. Your lawyers will be giving my lawyers rim jobs by noon."

My stomach churns. Hot blood sears through me. *Bitch.* That word, in the throes of sexual heat, in what I thought was role play, feels so different than what it does now. Now, it's curdling with loathing. I clench my fists, so frustrated that he completely has the upper hand. There is too much to lose. I can't make a rash decision. He'll destroy my life if I do.

"Mia, use your head. Don't make an emotional decision. This is a business arrangement. That's all."

"Did you buy Alea to get to me?" I ask, realizing how ridiculous that sounds only after I utter the words. But it's becoming clear to me that this is personal, not some huge coincidence. He didn't just stumble upon the company of the woman he attacked. I don't know why, but I have become his target.

He laughs, in that cocky, self-assured way and leans into me. "I got you before I ever bought Alea."

His words burn through my soul. And yet, the warmth of his breath ignites something again. And it makes me so enraged with myself.

"What do you want!" I ask, a tear finally drips from my eye, and I am even angrier at myself for losing my cool. Something tells me this is what he wants. "Why are you doing this to me?"

He looks down at me with those cocoa-colored eyes, framed by long black lashes and simply says, "Because you owe me."

My head swells with thoughts, searching my life, trying to make any sense of this man in front of me. I have lived a good life. I grew up in a small town, I was good to people. I left to go to Marquette and started over here in Milwaukee. I don't ruffle any feathers. How could I have done anything to earn this predicament? I have always done the right thing, and the one time I take a risk, the one time I do something bad, it blows up like a nuke.

"Owe you? What the hell do I owe you? Why would I owe you anything?"

He crosses his arms, and just stares, his dark eyes hardened by burning rage the way obsidian is forged from lava. Whatever he thinks I owe him comes with a lot of anger.

"This is a misunderstanding. I have good credit. I haven't stolen anything. I don't owe anyone anything."

He almost laughs. "Good credit? This isn't that kind of debt. There's no refuge, you can't file for bankruptcy. This kind of debt follows you to your grave."

"I don't understand. Please just tell me."

"You know."

"I don't. Please maybe if you tell me, I can explain."

"I am done discussing this."

I let out an exasperated sigh.

"Can I think about this at least?"

"Sure. You have thirty seconds before I hit send on this video. You really should watch it. It's a fucking masterpiece. I'll make sure Dewey gets it first if you decline."

I look around the room, as if there is some hidden solution I am missing.

"25..."

"Stop! Fuckfuckfuck..." I say, trying to think, but the countdown only makes my thoughts messier.

"18...I am serious as fucking cancer Mia. I don't do bluffing."

In a last ditch effort, I try to snatch his phone away, but he jerks it out of reach without breaking his countdown.

"Please..." I beg with tears in my eyes. My anger hasn't helped, but maybe there is a merciful side I can appeal to.

"10...9...8..."

This can't be happening.

"4...3..."

"Stop! Okay! Okay!"

At least in this moment, I am done fighting. I am so tired, tired of looking over my shoulder, tired of wondering what happened that night. I have my answers now, at least some of them. Maybe I can just work under him, give him the year at Alea and move on. What really changes? I still love Alea, I still promised Dewey I would keep this company running. I just don't understand why this man feels the need to blackmail me to do something I already agreed to. Will he withhold my salary, like some form of indentured servitude? Something doesn't add up. I know what would make sense, but I can't allow myself to even think of that possibility. If I pretend it doesn't exist, then maybe somehow it won't.

"So you want me to work here? For a year? Fine. But you should stay silent like you promised. Things are fine here. I can run Alea and make her even more profitable than last year." I battle to disguise the complete loss of control I feel. "How is this repaying a debt? Are you not going to pay me to work here? How can I live?"

"Good," he says, smiling and walking back to the head of the table. I resent myself for noticing his beautiful white teeth and the way his smile highlights his features that look even better in the daylight. "And don't worry about your salary. My word is my bond."

Tax looks down at his watch and closes the conference room door. Then, *click.*

Oh shit.

I stiffen in my seat, but don't say anything. This time I watch him in tense anticipation. Tax sits at the head of the conference table and pushes his chair away.

In the back of my mind, based on our first interaction, I wondered if this "debt" I owed would be collected in other ways. But he asked me to give *Alea* a year. To me it seemed that he just wanted me to run his new company without leaving once I became privy to his identity. I am beginning to think that was wishful thinking.

"So, show me your product line."

"Excuse me?"

"As the new owner of Alea, I would like to hear from its best staff member about its product line." *Phew, okay this is still business.*

I clear my throat. "Um, okay, sure." The tension is still rife in the air, but at least now I can focus on my job and just get the fuck out of this room when we're done. *Please, just let this be business.*

I push myself up to my shaky feet and walk over the the glass shelves that proudly display the colorful and sleek sex toys.

My hand quivers as I display a vibrator. "Well, this is the Artemis—" my voice gets caught in my throat. "This model is small so that it can be discreetly hidden in an evening bag."

I look him over. His erection is still strong as his eyes bore right into me. The navy color of his suit compliments his tan perfectly. His dark hair is glossy and thick, shaved closely at the sides and much longer up top. I never got to see his hair that night, as it was covered by his mask, but it only adds to his physical appeal. Just looking at his faint stubble makes my skin tingle, like my nervous system remembers and is trying to remind me of how good he felt. And that neck tat, I don't know why, but it does something to me. It's like, despite how well he dresses, the tat reminds me who he really is.

Acknowledging his attractiveness makes me hate myself even more. My immoral lust got me into this mess to begin with.

"Bring it over here. I'd like to see it," he says.

My heart speeds up again, anticipating the change in physical proximity. I puff my chest and walk the petite silver and pink oblong vibrator to him. He takes it in his hand and turns it over, studying it.

"Do you like using this?"

"Excuse me?" I ask, as if this question is somehow beyond the bounds of our interactions thus far.

His eyes narrow. They have this quality to them, like he is always entranced, always in a state of pre-orgasm. They look like they are smiling devilishly. "I think you misunderstood me, Mia. I didn't want you to explain to me how the product line works. I want you to *show* me."

A lingering breath escapes my lungs and sinks my chest. *I am soooo in over my head.*

"I can't," I say.

"You will," he replies. "I guarantee you I am not bluffing. And if you so much as walk out of this conference room, the video goes out. That's it. You won't be able to take it back. Ever."

Public shame, or private humiliation: which is the lesser of two evils?

"Don't fucking act like you don't like this shit Mia. I know you want someone to dirty you up. I'll make you fucking filthy. Now, show me. "

"I never had a choice..." I say to myself, suddenly realizing that the entire debate thus far was an illusion. It was like breaking in a mare, only making the dissolution of my defiance that much more satisfying. He had me as soon as I spotted the serpents on his neck. As he glares as me with mixture of satisfaction and greed, his hard cock making me feel lusted for, my body betrays me as my pussy floods with sensation. *You traitorous bitch.*

"We all have a choice," he says. "You already know your options. I won't stop you if you walk out."

But he knows he's given me a false choice. I can have my career annihilated, my reputation sullied forever, or I can play with myself in front of a man who I have already had sex with. A man who I have fantasized about since he first had me.

In a way, there is a small part of me that is almost relieved I don't have a real choice. If I have no choice, then this is not my responsibility. Anything that happens between me and him is his doing, and I am an innocent victim.

I am so disgusted with him, but even more so with myself. Because right now, I hate this man. Hell, I don't even know this man. I can't control his actions. I know *me*, I can control *me*. But maybe I don't really even know myself anymore. Maybe around him, I can't control myself. Because I want to feel the way I felt two and a half weeks ago: Awake. Alive. Like a fucking volcano bursting.

Another tear drips down my cheek. He probably thinks I am scared or angry at him, but it's me. I am betraying myself. Because he's right. I still have a choice. I can still walk out of here. I may not have my career, or even my reputation, but I would still have my dignity.

But I'm not going anywhere.

"And I how can I trust you won't show the video anyway?"

"I keep all of my promises. If I say I will deliver, I do. Keeping my word is very important to me."

I want to laugh at his *oh so mighty* morals, but I have to believe there is an end in sight to do this. I think he truly believes in his very selective definition of honor. These honor codes aren't unheard of, it's the reason thieves and murderers look down on snitches. There is even honor amongst thieves.

"Okay," I say, my voice raspy with emotion.

His eyes hood even further, and as he rubs his hand over his bulge, his mouth curves into a smug smile.

I take a shaky breath and lean back on the table directly in front of him.

"Pull up your skirt," he commands. His direction actually provides a bit of relief. I am no position to self-direct.

I place the Artemis on the table just beside me, and bend over to grab the hem of my skirt, and then I pull it up.

I keep my knees together, barely exposing the white thong covering my mound.

He leans in slowly, putting his strong hands on my trembling thighs. There is a momentary hope for comfort as his touch is soft, but then his fingers dig into the pillowy flesh and pry my shaky legs open.

He softly pulls my thong over to the side, grazing my pussy lips as he does it. I feel a warm surge of wetness in response to his touch.

"Already wet, dirty girl," he says, biting his plump lower lip.

He leans back in his seat, nodding approvingly.

"Take out your tits."

My tremoring hands reach up and unbutton my blouse, one button at a time. I let the silky fabric slide off of my shoulders, then I unclip my lace bra and slide it off as well.

He licks his full lips at the sight of my breasts.

"Now show me."

I grab the Artemis, turning her on. The low buzzing is a pleasant distraction from the sound of my own nervous breathing. Holding onto the shivering device forces my own hand to still.

"Don't come. I want you to show me the product line, not just one."

I nod softly and put the edge of the Artemis against my nipple. The tight vibrations make it tingle, and I can't help but lose myself in the sensation.

His mouth remains closed, but a low grumble escapes his throat. He stands up and walks over to the shelf, pulling out a few more toys from their boxes.

"Show me how you would use this," he says, pulling out our best-selling Athena vibrator and turning it on. It's long and thick, like a nicely-sized penis, and it has an extension for clitoral stimulation. "Wait, I think I might know how this one works," he says sarcastically. Tax presses it against my lips so that I suck on it.

I purse my lips in defiance.

"Suck." He smashes it against my mouth. "Don't piss me off, Mia," he says, aggressively palming my dampness. "I know what you like. There are no secrets with me."

His words are terrifying, yet oddly assuring. He already knows my dirtiest secret. He is my dirtiest secret.

"Now suck, you little slut."

I begrudgingly open my lips, letting him slide the vibrator into my mouth. And then he thrusts it back and forth, forcing me to engage with it or choke.

Then Tax glides a few fingers inside of me to prime me for its insertion. I curse myself for getting so wet, making it so easy for him to enter me. He curves his fingers and a wave of relaxing pleasure consumes my insides. I can't help but lean my hips into his hand as he rubs my g-spot. I moan, and with every next level of pleasure, I get angrier. Another tear trickles down, then another.

But he is immune to my tears. In fact, he might even like them.

He takes the vibrator and slides it into me, slowly massaging it inside of me as the extension buzzes against my clit. I raise my feet up on the table so that I am spread eagle and I throw my head back in pleasure as tears stream down my cheeks in self-loathing.

But even our best toys don't match his god-given talent: that cock; that thick, hard cock, that curves just to the right spot. I want it in me so bad. I want my world to explode again.

And I know what he wants, I know what that son of a bitch wants. He wants me to beg. And with every new toy he puts to my body, he is wearing out my will.

He watches me with a predatory gaze, ire mixed with hunger. And I am taken back to the night he came into my house. How every spiteful word caused me to fill with desire, every painful grip triggered heat at my core. And now the pent-up wrath I feel towards this man has nowhere to go but out, and the only way out is through ecstasy.

I reach out to pull him close to me, to give me some sort of illusion that this is voluntary, but he swats my hand away and digs his fingers into my hair, pulling me forward so that my forehead meets his, as he continues to massage the vibrator inside of me. His warm breath caresses my lips, but I know better than to try and kiss him. I moan louder and louder, but I want him, not a fucking toy. If I am going to exchange my dignity for sex, then I better get some fucking sex.

"Do you want me to slide my cock inside of your cunt?" he asks.

I do. *How fucking demented am I?*

I look away, trying to avoid his dark glare. His fingers grip my hair tighter, forcing me to look at him again. He pulls the vibrator out, gliding it up and down my slit. Teasing, taunting.

"Do you want me to fuck you with my cock?"

I bite my lip so hard, I almost break the skin. Salty tears sting my lips.

"Your pussy is so wet. You're soaking your panties. You want me to fuck you. You're a good girl, and you want me to make you my whore."

He presses the bulge in his pants against my throbbing center, and I moan. Ironically, the only man who can release all of the frustration is the one who has caused it.

"Now say it."

"No."

He snakes his cock against my swollen clit, drawing an involuntary groan from my throat. Inside, I tighten, my pussy pleading with me to let him fill me.

"Say it, whore."

Through tears, I abandon my morals. "Fuck me," I mutter.

His lips curve up one one side. I hate myself for how easily he has defeated me.

"You need to ask me better than that."

He's not happy until I am completely humiliated, until I have not a single shred of dignity left. "Please," I choke out. "Please fuck me."

"More. Tell me how you want it."

"I want you inside of me. Please...don't make me beg again. I can't do it. You've won."

He unbuckles his belt and his hand reaches into his pants for his beautiful cock, and this time he's not gloved. His hands are large, strong, masculine, and yet well-maintained.

He presses his chest against mine. His lips graze my earlobe. "Beg, bitch," he whispers. "Say my fucking name."

Tears pour out of my eyes as I lament over my desire for this despicable human being. "Tax, please fuck me."

"More."

"Please don't."

"What do you want me to do?"

Each time he makes me beg, my arousal becomes more acute. "I want you to slide inside of me, come in me."

I am so fucked up in the head.

And finally, he slams his hips into me and presses me back on the table. I cry out with abandon. My hands find their way into my hair as I know he'll anger if I try to touch him. He bites my breasts, tugging my nipples between his teeth as he fucks me, snarling at me the entire time. It's almost like he feels the way I do, like he has to fuck me in spite of himself.

He grips the flesh of my ass so hard I growl with rage as his cock fills me in the way that only it can.

I moan his name as tears trickle down my face. My core tightens around his cock. At this angle, the base of his shaft rubs on my clit, while his head rubs against my g-spot, and the walls of my pussy begin to throb, begging for release.

He pulls my ass apart, hard. It feels like he'll rip me in half, but that sting of pain only adds to the range of sensations.

I come closer to release, my moans making it obvious. "Beg or I'll stop. Beg for my cum," he says cruelly. "Beg for me by name."

I am so close, so close to the explosion, I have no choice. "Tax, please come in me. Come," I plead, between quivering breaths.

And like a well-orchestrated symphony, every part inside of me that was threatening to burst, does all at once and I scream in impure ecstasy. Losing control, I try to reach for him, to clench him in my arms, to transfer the heat exploding out of me, but he grabs my wrists to stop me. His grip on my wrists triggers my instinct to fight, but my attempts to pummel him are pointless as his hold renders me powerless. I gasp for air as my entire pussy throbs around his surging cock. Tears trickle as I fight him. And again, I reach a height of emotional and physical intensity that I know is not possible without the conflicting feelings that only he can bring.

If I had any doubts of how this man made me feel that first night, the meeting that has just ruined my life has affirmed it.

Eventually, I dissolve against the immoveable strength of his grip.

He pulls out of me, grabs a box of tissues, wiping himself off, and oh so generously leaves the box beside me to take care of myself.

Though tears blur my vision, I watch him. The way the neck tattoo almost disappears underneath his crisp shirt. The way his luscious hair now looks freshly fucked. I want to hate him, but every time I look at him, my body swells with attraction and the hate reflects back on myself.

His warmth streams out of me and onto my thigh. Again he is inside of me, and under my skin.

Drifting in the current, so far away from who I was weeks ago.

He throws on his jacket and shrugs a few times to straighten himself out, cracking his neck once on each side.

"You will report to me the same time every week. I trust you will do an excellent job with Alea, but don't hesitate to contact me regarding anything I can help with."

I sneer at him, at how he can be so nonchalant about this whole thing. It's his way of rubbing it in and it's so much more infuriating than direct mocking.

"You should clean your face, your mascara is running." He heads to the door. "Oh and the products are excellent. You should be proud." He motions to leave and steps back again. "Oh, and you should move out of that motel. Go back home."

CHAPTER TWELVE

Tax

Garbage – Not Your Kind Of People

I slam the door to my penthouse, pissed at myself for giving in to her again. She was supposed to beg me, grovel, and then when she had not an ounce of pride left, I was going to leave her craving and unfulfilled.

But I fucking caved. I watched her with her legs open, her juicy pussy aching for me, her taupe nipples, round and plump, begging for me to suck, and I had to be inside of her. I had to feel her pussy clenching my cock as she came.

She still was humiliated, she still cried as I fucked her. Not because she didn't want it, but because she did.

The rapid clicking of heels approach me from behind. I can tell by their cadence that they are bringing hell. *Not now, not fucking now.*

"You fucking bought Alea?" Jude says, waving some paperwork in the air.

"How many times have I told you to stay out of my shit, Jude?"

"I was looking for a pen and this was carelessly splayed on your desk."

Suuuure.

"That was part of the plan all along. I don't know why you're so pissed about it." Only after I pour myself some scotch do I realize it's seven in the morning. *Ah, fuck it.*

"It was also part of the plan to kill that cunt. And she's still here."

"Oh, Christ Jude, I've gotten us this far, haven't I? Can you give me a little creative license? Can I just savor this one?"

"I just hope you haven't dipped into that pussy and had a change of heart. Is that why you won't show me the recording?"

I had a couple of cameras set up with the intention of making a snuff film for Jude. Knowing Mia was dead wouldn't have been good enough, Jude wanted to experience it. Of course, the video spontaneously turned into a porn, and there was no way I was showing that shit to my sister.

I snap. "Jude, for god's sake, just shut your fucking mouth. I can't believe you would even dare talk shit, after everything I have done for you, for us! This one is the most personal for me, she is the reason for everything!"

"It's personal for me too!" She shouts, her eyes watering. "We both have scars, okay?"

My sister can be such a bitch sometimes, but she's been through a lot. And unlike me, all of her scars are on the inside. She knows how to find the one spot of my heart, albeit tiny, that hasn't completely turned to jagged, black rock. "I just feel left out is all. We planned everything together, and when you came home that night you were supposed to break into her house and end her, you didn't say a word to me. You won't talk to me about what happened. All I know is she is still alive, and now you've moved onto part two of the plan without completing part one."

I take a sip from my glass, letting it burn my throat and cool my heated blood. "I made an executive decision. Both parts are running simultaneously." I put my arm around my sister's slim shoulders, knowing despite the aura of anger that shrouds her, she just wants to be loved. "I decided killing her wasn't good enough. I want to destroy her slowly, the way she's done to us. We've lived with the aftermath of her cruelty for so many years, and her life has been far too kind to her thus far. She has to suffer before her world goes black. Trust me."

Jude sighs. "I do, lord knows I do. But we're getting too close. If something happens to her, now that you've bought Alea, now that you have a known connection to her..."

"Has that ever ruined our plans before? This is what I do. This is how I got us all of this. I make things right. I make people pay up."

"Fine," she says, resting her head on the space between my chest and arm. "I love you Tax, my *wombmate*." Our attention is diverted by the sound of the front door opening. "It's Rex," she says.

Rex has been a fixture in our lives for years. We met him when he was just 13 after we left home. He was a homeless runaway and looked up to us, followed us around like a little puppy dog, and he's never left our sides since. Like any puppy, he loves one family member more than the other, and I'd say he's pretty much obsessed with Jude. She popped his cherry and he's only had eyes for her ever since. Of course, he's loyal as a golden retriever and he's been the one keeping tabs on Mia for years while I took care of other business.

But I took him off Mia's detail a couple of weeks ago when I decided that now it was my turn to step in. If I was going to do this right, I had to involve myself in all aspects of the mission. I had to be the one with eyes on her.

"Close the door," I tell Jude as she leaves to greet Rex. "Give me some time alone, okay?" The closer we get to finishing, the more Jude breathes down my neck. She practically lives at my place even though she has one of her own. She doesn't like to be alone. She never says that, but her actions make it clear. We have always lived together, we've never really spent any substantial time apart since we were born. Actually, since we shared a womb.

The door closes and I let out an exasperated sigh, threading my fingers through my hair and massaging my temples.

I fucked up, but I am going to fix this.

I have been watching Mia for years now from a distance. Jude and I have waited patiently for the right time to end her. But we had other people to take care of first, and there was a good amount of people. Mia is the most important one though, she put everything into play, she is the reason it all happened. Her betrayal stung the most. So we wanted to save her for last, to end it all with the person who started this.

I waited for the perfect time. Sure, I could have rigged her car, or poisoned her, but I wanted this to be personal. I wanted her end to be custom-made, tailored specifically to Mia. Besides working at a dildo factory, she seemed to live a perfectly tame, normal existence. We monitored her communications and her computer always had the usual crap: work, kitten videos, Facebook, twitter. Though she did watch some interesting porn...turned me on to a few good videos. *Thanks Mia!*

So, I guess I shouldn't have been entirely surprised myself when Rex came into my office, snickering about something I *had* to see. Some form she filled out at a website called Happy Kitty. The name and the service did not add up. I was intrigued though, very fucking intrigued.

Rex did what he's so good at, what we have trained him to do: dig. He is a regular at the bar Tiff owns, his way of seamlessly threading himself into Mia's life from a distance. He actually knows Tiff pretty well, fucked her a couple of times in the storage room of her bar. But Tiff has no idea who Rex really is or that he even knows Mia exists.

Anyway, he knows one of the high-priced whores that hangs there, and got out of her more intel on what Happy Kitty is. I have to admit, I was pleasantly surprised to discover Mia had this side to her. On one hand, it made her far more interesting; on the other, it reminded me that she's not innocent. She's a deviant like the rest of us.

So I had an in. I was going to show up at her house, and she was going to think I was the guy she hired. She wouldn't think she was in any real danger, but I had something for her. Something I knew from the form she filled that she really feared: a 9" serrated hunting knife, sharpened to perfection. I was going to throw her around, make her think she was in a twisted gigolo's hands, and then I was going to pull out the knife, hold it to her throat, and remind her about everything. Remind her who I was, what she did to me…what happened to my sister. I would relish the moment as her eyes shifted from lust to horror, savor her confusion, drink up her helplessness.

And then I would dig the knife into her throat and slash.

Part two of this plan was to buy Alea, and then close it. Yup, just shut that shit down. Why? Because I know she loves working there. It was something she helped build and I wanted to remove any trace of her legacy. I wanted her to be responsible for the pain of the people she cared about the way she made me responsible for Jude's suffering. Vindictive? You bet your motherfucking ass I am.

Except, I fucked up.

It started with her pathetic drunk dancing. I'll admit it, it was cute. It humored me.

It was also the fact that she is even more beautiful than I remembered. In pictures, I could distance myself, but in person, up close, she makes my dick rock-hard.

When I pressed against her, felt the suppleness of her curves and her velvety skin, my cock ached. Something about her scent, and the way she arched towards me as I grabbed her, made me lose focus. She melted into my arms, she just gave into me. She craved me.

And then she begged. That wasn't part of the plan, I wasn't going to give her my cock. But in that moment, having complete and total control of her, the way she looked at me like I was the only person in the world who could give her what she needed, I caved. I wanted to make her scream my name like the slut she is. I wanted to come inside of her as she pleaded.

And goddammit it felt incredible. Her tight, wet pussy clenched around my dick, her body shaking as I came inside of her. I'd never come that hard in my life, and I've done a lot of fucking. I almost fucking fell asleep in my car on the way home because her pussy sucked the life force out of me.

The truth is, I haven't stopped thinking about her since that first night we fucked. But now I know I can have her for a while and proceed with my plans. I am adapting like I always have.

When I finally acquired the resources, both financially and physically, to transform my body, it became an obsession. Just like my dad claimed, in my very late teens, I sprung up a few more inches, my flat arms and chest curved with the first signs of muscle, and my smooth face sprouted with stubble. Jude never really blossomed in the same way. Sure, she developed, but she stayed tiny. I could only assume that she took after our mother's side of the family. We had a couple of pictures of her, and Jude looked a lot like her. We both did. Our father had lighter features that seemed to be overshadowed by my mother's raven hair and dark eyes. But I got my father's build. The one good thing he did for me was pass those genes down.

Those physical changes triggered an obsession with fitness. My entire life girls looked past me like I didn't exist. Hell, most seemed repulsed by my tall, gaunt frame. Then, what seemed like overnight, women were throwing themselves at me. In a way, this was a good thing. I had learned not to attach myself to the need for female attention since I never received it. In fact, seeing how differently I was being treated made me resentful. Now I was worth something. Now that I looked good I was a person. Now they saw me. So sure, I took the pussy being flung at me, but they could never have me. I used them and disposed of them. My physical advantages became another tool in my arsenal. I could get women to do what I wanted.

I am a big believer of sport translating into life. Combat sports, like boxing and muy thai, are my favorite for this very reason. I learned in my years of training that while aggression was important, timing was critical. So many fighters jumped into a match already swinging, wasting all of their energy and effort. A smart opponent would watch them flail and tire themselves out, patiently observing their weaknesses and awaiting the opportune moment to land a single, decisive blow. I learned to be patient, to be quick on my feet, to adapt. Yes, I was strong – stronger than nearly any of my opponents. But I was also smarter than my opponents. The ability to pivot, both physically and mentally, when facing an obstacle was a far more effective strategy than mindlessly plowing through.

Pivot. That's what this change of plans was: I was pivoting. I could fight my desire to fuck Mia, or I could use it to my benefit. *Pivot.*

So, onto Plan B: I will suck her dry, I will fuck the life out of her, I will ravage her until she is hollow and used, and then when she thinks things can't get any lower, I will destroy the company she loves and kill her.

———◆———

A presence stirs me in the middle of the night. There's no noise, but I sense someone is in the house. *Jude.* That sixth sense we have about each other is what we refer to as *twinstinct*.

I sit up, rub my eyes, and rise to my feet, stretching as I check my phone for the time. 2:47am.

"Jesus!" I call out, when I glance over and see Jude's tiny silhouette in the threshold of my bedroom.

"I thought you knew I was here."

"Obviously I did, I was just trying to wake up. If I thought you were an intruder, I would have been a little less relaxed. Don't you think? And for shit's sake, can I get some fucking clothes on?" I ask, cupping my junk. I've always been a fan of sleeping the way nature intended and she knows this, but the whole concept of boundaries is foreign to her.

"Oh, like I haven't seen all that before," she smirks, waving her hand at me dismissively.

Thankfully, it's dark. I snatch the nearest pair of sweats and throw them on.

"You having a bad night?" I ask, still groggy. I sit back down on the bed. Jude sits beside me and rests her head on my shoulder.

"Yeah," she confesses, it's then I notice the stuffiness in her throat. It's a really bad night. She's been crying.

"Rex wasn't there?" I'm not trying to pawn my sister off on him, but he spends the night at her place sometimes and knows about her issues too.

"He was asleep. I didn't want to wake him anyway. And he's not you." Her words reverberate along my shoulder.

This is the Jude most people don't see. The side that is secretly always afraid, though she would rather fight to the death than be victimized again.

Jude lashes out and snarls like a fox in a trap, but it's all out of a pervasive fear. Don't get me wrong, there's anger there too, and fear and anger make for a hell of a cocktail. Jude will never allow herself to be hurt again. But it's exhausting work, always growling and showing your teeth. Occasionally, you have to give it a rest. Rex can be that for her sometimes, a person she can rest with, but Rex wasn't always there. I have always been there. I knew Jude when she was innocent. I am the only person she trusts enough to expose her belly without fear of being ripped open.

"That's a good thing," I say. Rex is a solid guy. I know she can't love him like a normal person might, but there's no one else I would trust with my sister.

"It can be," she says. She sits there in silence for a while, threading her fingers through mine. I'm not a fan of physical affection, but I let Jude steal it and sometimes I use on her it as a way to keep her level. It doesn't do anything for me. After her delicate fingers make a home in my thick hand, she sighs out: "I had the dream about having a baby and them taking it away."

There are a few recurring dreams she's had for the past fourteen years. This one is the most rare, and it's the most painful.

A bad night for Jude can be a number of things. What happened to us happened in the dark. I think that's why it's always nights for Jude. They used to be frequent. Nearly every night, she would wake up from a panic attack. Once every few months or so, she would have a vivid night terror, like the one she had tonight. We've lived in a lot of places, including on the street, and the tradition was for her to crawl into bed (whatever that might have been at the time) with me and cry or talk, whatever would get her mind off of things, and fall back asleep. When Rex got older, eventually some of that burden lifted off my shoulders and she would talk to and crawl into bed with him. But the really bad episodes, those always came to me.

Now that she's a woman, the nights are rare. Because Rex is usually around, I am not privy to the panic attacks when they still happen. Sometimes I forget she still has them, she even fools me with her show of toughness. But when it's a nightmare, she shows up at my place, quiet and weak, expecting me to put her back together.

"Rex didn't wake up?" I know from personal experience, she usually wakes up clawing and crying for the baby.

"You know he sleeps like a corpse. And we had a few drinks before bed. Well I had one, he had like seven."

I huff a silent laugh under my breath about Rex.

"It's almost over," I say to her, at the same time reminding myself of the vow I made.

"It's never over," Jude sighs. Her voice is raspy with fatigue.

She's right. Some things that were taken can never be reclaimed.

She inhales deeply, shrugging her shoulders, and then drops them with a lingering exhale. "Your smell...it always makes me feel safe. Have I ever told you that?"

"I don't think so," I say evasively. There's no one in the world who I am more comfortable with, but even she sometimes gets too close. Sometimes I don't want the pressure of being her hero.

"I don't mean your cologne or soap. It's the smell you leave on things, like pillows or clothes. I think it's because we've always been a team, and at home, when dad was being a dick, I knew I always had you on my side. Dad's smell always made me anxious. Yours made me feel secure."

"Thanks, I guess."

"Don't let it get to your head."

"You would never let that happen," I say. "Let me make you a drink."

I stand up and she follows me out to the kitchen. I make a warm liquor and milk concoction, sure to knock her right the hell out.

"Sorry I snapped at you earlier," she says, blowing steam away from the lip of the mug.

I nod.

"I just...we're so close. We're almost there...and Mia...she's so important to me because she hurt you. And you are the most important person in my world. It's something about her and what she did that sits the worst with me."

"Trust me, Jude. I'm finishing this. And you're right. Everyone else, I did for you. Now this one is for me. So you need to let me do it the way I want. She's mine."

She nods, brooding.

Jude sips her drink as I walk over to the floor-to-ceiling windows that embrace views of downtown Milwaukee and Lake Michigan. The black water seems to stretch out infinitely and I wonder how we can tell ourselves that Mia is the end while at the same time acknowledging that it's never over.

"It's been a while since your last bad night," my voice breaks through the ultra-silence of the dark hour.

"And you, you still have a perfect score," she says, alluding to the fact that I don't suffer from the same affliction. Sometimes I wish I did. Jude got the worse of it all, even though it was really about me to begin with.

"How much booze did you put in this? I'm feeling really woozy."

"That's the secret to my recipe, you can't taste the alcohol. This has been the key to shutting you up and getting me a good night's sleep for years now."

"Asshole. Well, I think you put a sedative in here or something because suddenly I am about to conk out. Bedtime." She stands, leaving the dirty mug on the counter (she knows that shit makes me twitchy) and marching over to my bedroom. "Slumber party," she says, pulling me by the wrist over to the bedroom.

"Fucking great. I have to sleep next to someone who somehow defies the law of physics by occupying more space at five feet and a hundred pounds than I do at six-four and two-thirty-five."

"What are you doing?" she asks, as I organize some pillows.

"I'm allocating your space and also blockading you from flailing your boney limbs at me all fucking night."

Jude flips me the bird and slides under the covers on her side of the bed. I lie on my back and cross my hands behind my head. In less than a minute, she's snoring her tiny munchkin drunk snore and I know I don't have a chance in hell of getting any sleep.

I sit up and look over at my twin. The fierce lioness is nothing but a snoring cub enveloped in a makeshift pillow fort. And for the first time in all these years, I allow myself to resent the responsibility she's put on me. Not of the vendetta, I gladly take up my sword and shield for that, but as her personal savior.

I'm not her goddamn hero. I can't make it all better. I can't always be around to keep the nightmares at bay.

CHAPTER THIRTEEN

14 Years Earlier

<u>Radiohead – Creep</u>

The bell rings, and the murmurs of chatting die down as everyone takes their seats.

"Alright, alright kids. Pull out your textbooks and open them up to twelve," Mr. Carthy says as he writes the word "Electricity" on the whiteboard.

"So we've been studying this amazing feat of nature for the past couple of weeks and this will be what we cover for your final project this semester. It'll be a partner project."

I see a couple of people smile and mouth *yes*, excited to use this assignment as time to hang out with their friends. But me, I hate this shit. I am alone. I am always alone. I've got my sister, but she's not in this class, or any of my classes. She doesn't take her studies as seriously.

"That being said, you will NOT team up with your usual partners. You need to pick someone you have never worked with in this class. This is not an excuse to chat with your best friend during class. I mean it."

A collective *AWWWWWWW* of disappointment rises from the class.

Mr. Carthy's instructions drone in the background as my eyes drift to her: her brown hair, her tanned skin, her pouty lips. She is the vision of perfection and to top it off, she's smart.

But she can have anyone she could ever want. She would never date a poor, skinny, piece of shit like me. In fact, she dates the richest kid in our tiny shit-hole town. His dad owns a bunch of factories all over the country, including the only factory we have in town. Almost everyone around here is employed by his father save for a handful of small business owners. Sure, we're in America, but in this town, the Pettits are royalty. And if Tripp's dad is the king, then that makes Tripp the prince of Clint, Iowa. The rest of us are just fucking serfs.

The scraping of sliding chairs and collective movement jars me out of my daze as I realize people are looking for the last person on earth they would want to partner with. People zig zag around me while I stay in my seat in the back. I'll just partner with the other leftover outcast. There's no point in trying.

Then I feel her eyes on me and my heart races. No, I must be imagining this. She swallows, smiles and makes a beeline towards me.

"Hi, do you have a partner?" Her voice is as sweet as honey. She's wearing a tight blue t-shirt and jean mini-skirt that shows off her perfect slender body. Her hair drapes down over one shoulder, stopping right above her tit. Her nipple is hard. *Thank the lord for air conditioning.*

"I, uh...not yet..." I say, correcting my slumped posture.

"You wanna?" she says, wagging her finger between the both of us.

"Uh, sure...yeah, sure," I say. *This cannot be fucking happening. Why would she ask me?*

"Sil, right?" she says, plopping her bags on the table just beside me. *She knows my name?*

"Yeah, Sil."

"I'm Mia," she smiles. *Like I and every other guy in this school don't recite her name as they jack off.*

"Yeah, I know your name."

"Oh," she laughs a little, and her smile is just...*fuck.*

The room buzzes with activity as the partnerships start working on their project.

"Is Sil short for something?" she asks, while unloading her books on the table.

"Silvio." I hate my name. It reminds me how different I am, how I don't belong.

"What kind of name is that?" she asks, without judgment.

"Romanian, I think. My mom, she's from there."

"Oooh, cool. Have you ever been?"

"No, she's dead. She died giving birth to me and my twin sister."

Mia's face sinks. I have issues with blurting things out that make people uncomfortable, I don't soften it for them. I guess it's because no one's ever softened anything for me. So I just stay alone most of the time and save everyone the awkwardness.

"I'm sorry about that..." she says. I never expected her to be so...nice. I had stared at her semester after semester since middle school. I watched her like a painting from a distance, but I always assumed she was the female equivalent of the big guys who slammed me into lockers and tripped me in the hallways.

I shrug. I never knew my mom, so whatever. I heard she was really nice though, that my dad was a different person before she died. He blames me and Jude for killing her.

"So, I don't have anything after school today, do you?" she asks.

"No..." I say. Usually I meet up with Jude and we go to the library to do our homework, the park, anything to stay away from home for as long as possible.

"Well, you can come over and work on the project with me, if you want. We could get a head start. This thing is complicated."

Holy shit! Mia Tibbett is inviting me over to her house. If there is a god, thank you!

"Okay, I just need to tell my sister that I'll be going with you."

"Okay," she shrugs and smiles.

I know I don't have a chance in hell, but just getting to talk to her, to be close to her like this, it makes my awful life feel just a little less shitty.

CHAPTER FOURTEEN

Mia

I sit in the parking lot of the office building, my stomach queasy, swimming in anticipation of my second weekly meeting with Tax Draconi. This past week has been hell on wheels. When he left me in that conference room with a smug look of satisfaction on his face, I locked the door behind him and slid down to the floor and cried.

I cried so hard it hurt. I wailed. I let it all out: the fear, the confusion, the isolation, the anger.

Who is this man and what does he want from me?

I wracked my brain for the name Draconi, but it rang no bells. I honestly think he might have mistaken me for someone else. I just don't understand. Maybe he's delusional, and he has concocted some sort of shared history that never happened? My week-long investigation has turned up nothing. His business seems totally legit. And I can't find a shred of info on his personal life. I thought about hiring a P.I., but then I realized that would likely somehow lead back to the unsavory things I am trying to keep secret. And I don't care how professional said P.I. is, I don't want him or her to know that I hired someone to "rape" me.

I am so screwed. He has me by the figurative balls and I don't know what to do other than grin and bear it until I can figure something out.

I've deliberated going to the cops, but what can I tell them? There is no sign of forced entry into my home. I solicited an attack on MYSELF. I begged him to have sex with me two times now...They would think I am certifiable.

And that brings me to the other thing that is scaring the shit out of me: *What the hell am I doing?*

Why is it that I hate him, that I fear him, but then when he touches me, all I want to do is touch him back?

That my body explodes with passion when he makes me beg for him, when he bites me, pulls my hair, and purposely demeans me?

I was never abused or mistreated. I don't have an excuse. I just have always kind of desired that extra stimulus sexually. And I kind of enjoyed the fact that I had my shit together as far as a good job, good friends, and stability while having a secret "freaky" side. But that dirty side never went as far as my imagination had wished. Some guys I dated dabbled in that with me, but that's all it ever was: dabbling. This was real, frighteningly real. It's like some karmic force is punishing me for my sick desires.

In the short time since our first encounter, I don't even know who I am anymore. He makes me become someone else. Or even worse, he brings out who I truly am.

After I let the tears flow, and wiped the remnants of him from between my thighs, after I questioned my sanity, I stood up and dried my eyes. I had a job to do. I had fucked everything else up, but I was not going to do that with Alea. I had been entrusted with a company that was run brilliantly and provided jobs for twenty hard-working, good people.

They didn't deserve to suffer because of my personal bullshit.

And that's what I have done all week, bury myself in my work. Spent as little time alone as possible. Anything to keep my mind off of the inevitable reunion with Tax.

I also made a declaration to myself. It was clear that Tax was getting a rise out of having the upper hand, the element of surprise. I think he got off on my confusion, but if I didn't give him that, then he couldn't win. If he wanted to kill me, I'd be dead by now. He wants to take something else from me.

So I won't cower in fear. I will meet him head on. I don't have much left when it comes to him, he's taken it all, but he won't get to enjoy my uncertainty.

I walk tall into the conference room, where he is waiting for me, just like the last time. I emailed him some reports, and I am surprised to find him scanning copies as I walk in. But I am pretty sure that's not why he's here.

"Good morning, Mia," he says with mock cheerfulness.

"Good morning, Tax," I say, placing my laptop bag on the table. He looks damn good, with his neck tat peeking out of a well-tailored grey suit. It looks like he has a fresh haircut, but the neatness of his hair contrasts sharply with the stubble on his masculine jawline. Before he can say anything else, I walk over to the door, close it, and lock it myself.

I feel his eyes on me. I think I might have thrown him slightly off kilter.

"So are we going to work, or are you going to fuck me?" I ask defiantly.

Tax hastily stands up from his chair, and I'll admit, a bolt of fear strikes my chest. He is so tall and dark. Not just his features, but his aura. His neck tattoo moves with the motion of his muscles as he swallows. The sinew along his jawline snakes as he grinds his teeth.

"Are you trying to give me sass, Mia?" he says, standing an inch away from me, looking down on me like a bug he could squash at any moment. "Because I promise you, you will fucking regret it." Heat from his body envelops mine, and wraps it in a suffocating embrace.

"Isn't this what you want?" I say, trying not to give in to the fear, but my voice wobbles.

"I'll tell you what I don't want," he says, the fragrance of his skin and musky vanilla scent of his cologne flooding my nose and violating my desire. "I don't want to deal with your sudden streak of confidence at five in the fucking morning." He presses me up against the closed door with his chest. "I fuck you when I want, how I want. I own you. Period. Don't pretend like you have any sort of say in this. Don't convince yourself that you can play mind games with me, because you will lose. Every. Single. Fucking. Time."

His breath tickles my nose, his chest presses against mine with each angry heave. And like the sick fuck that I am, I worry for a moment that he might not fuck me, just to prove a point.

I stare back at him through moist eyes, desperately trying not to let them hit their saturation point.

"Why are you trying to torture me?" I ask.

"Because you owe me," he says. The same damn answer he gave me last week.

"What? What do I owe you?"

"Your pain." His brown eyes, which at times can be deceivingly warm, go chillingly dark.

"Is there anything other than cruelty in there?" I ask.

He smirks. "You don't know me, Mia," he says, flatly. "Don't for a second convince yourself that what we do means you know anything about me."

He has to remind me at every moment he can that I am worthless to him, a piece of meat he can fuck and leave without even saying a single kind word.

"I'm a good person. I know you think because of the service I bought, I'm not. That I am some immoral whore. Maybe that's what you're punishing me for. But I am a good person."

"Take off your clothes, but leave on your heels," he commands.

Admittedly, I dressed up for the occasion again—I never said I wasn't fucked up.

I don't budge. Despite my attraction to him, I don't want to give him the instant gratification. I want to defy him. And yet, there is a great chance that he prefers my defiance over my submission. Maybe my resistance is the source of his greatest pleasure.

"You can take it off, or I can rip it off," he says. "Better yet, I can just leave and send the video out. Your call."

I tremble with frustration, never letting my angry stare leave him as I hesitantly motion to unbutton my blouse.

"You don't have to make it so fucking hard on yourself, you know?" he says with a smirk. He's not trying to comfort me; he's mocking the inevitability of my submission.

Tax doesn't give me space to undress. Instead, he stays close, hovering over me, one arm pressed against the door behind me, grazing my body with his as I disrobe. Slowly, I pull off my blouse like someone undressing in confinement, trying not to impose on Tax's space even though it's him who's imposing on mine.

Finally, I stand naked, my back against the cold door, only wearing a pair of black pumps. The cool air of the room strokes my skin, making me feel exposed and alone. Ironically, Tax is the only warmth, and my body craves his heat.

"Touch yourself," he says, just as he grabs my fingers and slides them between his full lips. It's oddly soft. And it's almost crueler than being rough, because he's playing with my head.

I slide my wet fingers onto my clit and roll soft circles, closing my eyes and tilting my head back.

"No, don't close your eyes. Look at me," he says. But I don't want to, I don't want to be reminded of what I am doing, how I am surrendering my body to such a heartless person. I'm trying to let my mind go somewhere else and he won't let me. "Do it."

I open my eyes and his are right there staring back, challenging me, overwhelming me. They are a chocolaty brown hue, the irises ringed with a darker brown that makes them pop, framed by long, dark lashes. His glare, it's like he wants to ruin me just by looking at me, but the longer I look, the more I realize there is something else. It's pain. Maybe even vulnerability. It's in there, I just have to reach for it. If I can access that part of him, maybe I can work my way out of this situation.

I touch myself as I stare into his eyes, biting my lip, gyrating my hips against my hand. My nerves course with anxiety. Looking into someone's eyes while touching myself should be intimate, safe, but this is an invasion. It's another way to break me down. I want to end the eye contact, I want to close my eyes and melt with him. I want to know he wants me back and this is not all just some act so he can torture me. Getting Tax to want me beyond this may be the key to getting some power back. Stubborn rebellion only fuels his cruelty.

"What are you thinking?" he asks.

I say my honest answer. "That I want to close my eyes. That I want to kiss you."

He doesn't say no, he doesn't flinch, but his eyes, the eyes I have so quickly learned to study, they become just a little bit softer. There might even be a hint of surprise in there. *Keep reaching.* I make my move. I have wanted to kiss those full lips since he broke into my house. I need to feel him wanting me back. And maybe if I can get him to put his guard down, just a little, I can get my life back.

I suck on his bottom lip, tugging it gently. I do it again. He doesn't stop me, and then I commit, kissing him passionately as I play with myself, feeling his hardness press against the backside of my hand. He doesn't kiss back, his lips remain dead like his soul.

Then for a second, maybe even a fraction of a second, he lunges his face forward, and sucks on my lip. The taste of his kiss makes goosebumps erupt all over my body. Their plump softness contrasts everything else about him.

There is a moment of hope, of connection. But it is only a moment, and moments are fleeting.

I reach my arms up to try and unbutton his shirt and he catches my wrists.

"Knees."

That's all he says, like someone commanding their pet. I hesitate, dazed by the almost-kiss from him.

He grabs my hair forcefully and pushes me down to the floor. I gasp in fear, at the sudden change in his demeanor, which up until this point had been only slightly less than savage.

I fall to my knees with a painful thud. Without releasing his tight grip on my hair, he says: "Pull out my cock, whore."

I unbuckle his pants as I take quivering breaths, and he pops out.

A wave of heat rolls through my belly as I think about him being inside of me.

"Suck it like you mean it. Suck it like a slut who hires men to rape her." His comment stings at my heart, more than any other insult he's ever said.

But the sting dulls quickly, and there is a part of me that wants to make him weak with my mouth. It's the only power I have.

I pool saliva in my mouth, spitting it onto his tip as I push my lips over it and down the shaft, coating his cock with slickness. His grip on my hair tightens. His hips move back and forth as I take one hand and glide it over his wet balls, while the other slick hand glides over his shaft in accord with my mouth.

Throaty moans escape his lips, but for once, he has nothing cruel to say. Maybe I found his Achilles heel. I look up at him as I pull my mouth away from his dick, and lightly roll the tip of my tongue on the slit of his head. His eyes look back down on me with a hooded gaze, full of lust and pleasure.

I resume twisting my slippery hand up and down his shaft, sucking with my lips, and pressing his slick balls as I massage. He grows even more in my mouth. I listen for him to tell me to stop, to rip me up to my feet and bring me with him to ecstasy.

But instead he says, "don't bite down, or there will be hell," in a low grumble.

Before I can make sense of what he says, he pinches down on my nose and shoves himself deep into my throat. I cough around him, choking on his length, panicking as I try to gasp for air. My hands claw at his trousers, instinctively fighting back, like a drowning person flailing in the ocean.

And then he shoves himself into my mouth, over and over, relentlessly, and I relax enough to let him choke me. He releases my nose just long enough for me to get a breath, and then he pinches it again, pounding into my face. His dark eyes stare down at me as he pumps and pumps, growing in hardness, my throat muscles squeezing around him as they clench for air.

"You see what happens when you act like a little bitch..." he says to me. "Then you don't get yours."

And he pumps and pumps and fills my mouth with his cum as I cough and choke on his pulsating cock.

He pulls out and I jerk away, falling over onto my hip, tears trickling down my face from the gag reflex. My lips and chin are stained with his cream.

"Lick your lips."

He hovers over me, enveloping me in his authority as I obey. Then he calmly kneels, and cups my chin in his hand, grazing his thumb against it, swiping off the trail of his release that escaped my mouth.

He offers me his thumb. "Suck."

I purse my lips around it and clean it off for him.

"Open your mouth," he says, as I gasp for air.

I comply hesitantly as he examines.

"Good, every last drop," he says with satisfaction. "I think you are getting the hang of how this works. And if you act how you are supposed to, then you'll get yours too."

I remain seated on the floor, naked, used, and unrelieved. My pussy pulsates with heat that has no way of escaping. But I won't beg, I won't give him the satisfaction today. I know it's pointless anyway. He's making a point, just as I had feared.

After tossing the box of tissues back on the table, he zips up his pants, straightens himself out, cracks his neck, and does a double take at my defeated posture on the floor. He keeps winning at a game that I don't even know the rules of.

I fucking hate him and I want him so bad.

He sighs and shakes his head, like that teeny piece of humanity I thought I saw in him has come to the surface. Maybe he'll take pity on me and show me a hint of kindness.

Instead, he walks back over to me, so that his crotch stops right in front of my face and he grabs his package with his masculine grip. "If you want it, all you have to do is beg, Mia," he says tauntingly. How cruel, to make me think he was about to show mercy, and instead use this moment to run up the score on me. I break my promise and the tears burst, because I am sitting naked on the floor of the company I run, and I have been reduced to nothing but a fucking cum receptacle by a man who hates me for reasons I don't understand. And yet, I am terrified he might disappear one day as quickly as he appeared, like a ghost, and I may never understand why. And I am terrified because if he vanishes, I will feel more alone than I ever have.

I have held it in for so long. Sure I have given him tears, but this time I lose it in front of him, the way I lost it when he left the last time. And I don't even care. There is no shame in front of this man, not after the things we have done.

He watches me quietly as I sob uncontrollably, my chest quivering, my breathing choppy. I thought I could stand toe to toe with him, but he doesn't give a shit, and that leaves me with no weapons to use against him.

I feel his shadow encase me. And then his deep voice.

"Give me your hand."

I shake my head, looking down to the floor. I am angered by my weakness and I don't want or need his fucking help to get me off the floor.

"Come on." This time his tone is gentler. "Just give me your hand."

I look up slowly, and he looks down on me with an unreadable face. But I obey, like he has so quickly trained me to do, and he brings me to my feet, and gently backs me up against the door, rubbing his massive body against mine.

"You don't have to beg today," he whispers in my ear. I rest my face onto his chest, fully expecting he'll push it away, but he doesn't. And I sob into his white shirt, as he slides his fingers into me and rubs.

His commanding fingers grip my g-spot, curling over and over again. I moan into his ear, my anger and hopelessness dissolving as he fucks me with his beautiful hand.

His other hand reaches for my hair and pulls it back, but not as angrily as before, and he dives into my neck, biting and sucking fiercely, his mouth singeing the sensitive skin.

I choke out weak mews, as I build closer and closer to climax.

The hot, fully clothed man in front of my cold, naked body so clearly outlines the power dynamic between us. And yet, I have never felt more connected with him than after I just let him see me fall apart.

"Say my name," he says, as I moan louder and louder.

"Tax..." I whimper between gasping breaths. As his name leaves my lips, there is a burst inside of me, my chest constricts, my body convulses as I recite it over and over. I clench my fists, so badly wanting to feel the warm skin of his chest, the stubble of his chin against my palm. But he won't let me get that close.

Because he hates me. Well, these days, I hate me too.

Tax

Fuuuuuuuuck. I let her kiss me. It was only for a second, but I let her lips touch mine. Dreaming about those lips got me into this clusterfuck in the first place.

Something is off. The way she crumbled today, she wasn't supposed to break like that, she wasn't supposed to be vulnerable. She was supposed to be cruel, like a delicious piece of fruit you cut open only to find a worm festering on the inside. Mia melts under my will, and even when she tries to be vicious, I don't see any malice in her eyes. After all I have done since I showed up, she still doesn't want to hurt me.

In fact, all she wants so desperately is for me to kiss her, and for me to allow her to touch me.

Despite her vulnerability, there is a subtle strength in how she has been able to handle Alea through what I imagine might be the most personally difficult time of her life. She shows up to work every day, puts on a smile, and keeps her tears private. That's either a sign of great character or the ability to put on many different faces. I assume time will tell.

Today, I broke again. I became weak and I gave her relief after I was so close to walking away without giving her satisfaction, after I had crippled her newfound will so artfully.

But she just sat there, limply, weeping against the door. Naked. Alone. Helpless.

She was like a pulp, I had beaten her will down too quickly. I needed to rebuild her so I could have my way with her for a while longer. She enjoys my ruthlessness, but not if I just take. I need to give too, otherwise she goes hollow and vacant. I can see the fear when she's left alone and used. But I can keep using her, as long as I give her just enough to latch onto. Plan B was a slow burn, destroying her bit by bit, savoring her destruction. I thought she was like me on the inside, made of stone, so I came in hard, but she's not like me. So, I need to dismantle her slowly or she'll be fucking catatonic in a week or two. I want this pain to linger.

So I did the only thing I know how. It's what I do when it comes to women. I can't give them affection, or love, or intimacy. That all died in me long ago. So I give what I can: Relief. Pleasure. Abandon.

I watched the life come back to her eyes behind the tears as I fucked her with my hand. Her tears are a shield, to allow her to believe she is a victim, but she knows she wants it more than she's ever wanted anything. I brought her back, so I can tear her down again. I'll keep doing that until she's got nothing left to give.

Every time I have a plan with this bitch, she throws it off even by just a hair.

I shouldn't have allowed her to come though. Her pleasure should only exist if it's in the process of pleasing me. I gave her that relief after I had already been sated.

Problem is, after I fuck her, I never feel sated. I get the fuck out of there, because I always want her again. I want more of her. And something about when I gave her her own relief pleased me, and it had nothing to do with keeping my cock happy. I'll admit, that's concerning.

I don't know what happened over the years, but she's different from the image I had of the person who so cruelly took whatever good I had left in me and burnt it to a char.

But, the damage from what she did still lingers to this day. And everyone has to pay their debts.

It's only fair.

CHAPTER FIFTEEN

14 Years Earlier

<u>Backstreet Boys — Everybody (Backstreet's Back) - Extended Version</u>

Mia said she had to run home right after school, but she gave me her address so that I could stop by after I found my sister. I pretended I didn't know her address. I'm not a creepy stalker or anything, but we live in a small town. That information just kind of falls on your lap, especially when that address belongs to the most beautiful face you have ever seen.

After some teasing and a small guilt trip from Jude, I walk over to Mia's house. My stomach sinks with nervousness as I ring the doorbell. That's not just because I am about to be spending one on one time with Mia, but because her dad is the sheriff. He is well acquainted with my household and it's not because we have invited him over for dinner parties. My dad has been put in the drunk tank more times than I can count and the cops have been to our home plenty of times. I always tell the police everything is fine at home. I know if I say what really goes on, they'll separate me and Jude.

A dog goes on a hysterical barking frenzy and shortly after, she answers the door, holding it by the collar.

"Come in! He's friendly, but he's a bolter and I reaaaally don't want to spend the afternoon hunting him."

She's changed into more comfortable clothes, a light blue tank top and black leggings. Her tits are small and perky, and her nipples harden from the draft when she opens the door. Her hair, which was loose earlier, is braided into two pigtails and there's something really hot about that. When she turns, I adjust the waist on my pants to hide my enthusiasm.

I follow her through the foyer and it's really hard not to stare at her ass, but I try to look elsewhere.

"I figured you might me hungry, so I put a pizza in the oven."

She has no idea, but some nights I don't know if I'll come home to a meal. And I am always hungry, apparently it's because of my recent growth spurt. I shot up from 5'8" to 6'0" this past year. I'm thinking I have another three to four inches of growth, my dad says that's what happened to him. You'd think that the height would stop assholes from fucking with me, but I only got lankier. 6'0" isn't intimidating when it comes in a 155 pound package.

"That's great, thanks."

"I figured we could just go to the den. My mom is resting upstairs, so we try to keep the main areas quiet."

"Yeah, sure," I say, still wrapping my mind around the fact that I am in Mia Tibbett's house.

We take our soda and pizza to the den and pull out all of our assignment materials. We spend a few minutes planning out the electrical grid we are designing for our physical science project. But while eating, Mia turns the conversation off the topic of schoolwork.

She's resting on her stomach, giving me an unintentional view down her shirt. This is fucking awesome. "Sil..." she looks uncomfortable, her brown eyes gaze down to the floor.

"Yeah?"

DEBT

"If this is too personal, you can tell me to shut up. I know I can be a little well, too open for some people. My dad's always telling me I shouldn't be so quick to say what's on my mind...but...I know you said she died during childbirth, but do you miss her, wonder about her, your mom?"

The question really throws me back. No one ever really has asked me how I feel about my mother's death. Jude and I used to play games, where we would "cast" an actress as our mother or pretend what she would be doing at the present moment if she was still here, but those games faded as we got older. And my dad, well, it was in our best interest to not remind him of her.

"I'm sorry, that was rude. I shouldn't have asked that," she says, shaking her head in embarrassment. "I talk too much."

"No...it's okay." Yes, it was intrusive, but no one has ever cared about what I thought. And she really put herself out on a limb to ask. "Yeah. I think about her. How about how my life would have been different. But I can't say I miss her. We don't talk about her much. I think my dad resents me and Jude for killing her."

"You didn't kill her!" Mia says in horror.

"We did. She bled to death because of us." There goes that morbid mouth of mine, she's going to tell everyone I am a freak. But to my surprise, Mia doesn't seem to be weirded out.

"Don't look at it that way. I am sure she would have wanted you and your sister to live over her. That's what moms want." Her eyes turn sad, like her words brought something to the surface.

"Why are you asking?"

She hesitates for a second. "I never knew anyone who didn't have a mom. And my mom, she's sick. Really sick. And...I don't know why I'm blabbing over here."

"No, it's okay. I know it's probably hard to mention it to people who might not get it." *Story of my life.*

"Yeah...I mean my friends care, but..." she chokes up. "Nevermind. I don't want to talk about it anymore."

I nod.

"Okay, let's change the mood in here!" she says, getting up to her feet and putting a cd in her player. Backstreet Boys booms throughout the den.

"For the love of god," I say.

She starts dancing, in a purposefully goofy way, and I can't help but smile. I always imagined she would be serious, or afraid to look silly. But nope, she looks incredibly stupid right now, and I wonder if she can be any more perfect.

"Okay, Mr. Music Snob, what would *yooooou* like to listen to?"

I pull out a cd I shoplifted a few weeks ago.

"Radiohead? What kind of a name is that?"

"What kind of a name is 'Backstreet Boys?' Those 'boys' hardly look like they come from any backstreet."

She laughs hard, plopping down beside me and starts singing the awful song loudly in my face. I roll my eyes, but this is the most fun I have had in a while. And her house, it's so nice, and clean, and safe. And I wish I could just stay here with her and never leave.

CHAPTER SIXTEEN

Mia

Fiona Apple – A Mistake

It's week six and my "arrangement" with Tax is becoming something of a routine. It's my dirty little secret. Every Tuesday, I come into the office at five am, and I have the ever loving shit fucked out of me by a vicious, mysterious, and gorgeous demon.

I ask the same questions, and I get variations of the same answers.

I try to get him to let me kiss him, or even take off his clothes so that I am not alone and naked when we are together. And I keep failing.

I still scream, beg, howl, and come so hard that it feels like I swallowed a fucking sex grenade. I don't cry as much anymore. My crying was an act of rebellion, a protest, both to Tax and myself. And it's too exhausting to keep putting myself through that. It's easier to accept my situation than endure the pain of crying about it. Eventually I will get through his hard shell and convince him to give me back my freedom of choice.

My feelings are still conflicted, yet the shock of my predicament is starting to wear. It's becoming a part of my life, just like my job at Alea, or taking my clothes to the dry cleaner. And while I feel helpless, there is a side of me that looks forward to Tuesdays. I never say those words in my head, but I feel it in the way that my skin tingles with electricity, my heart races, and my entire sexuality aches in anticipation of our next encounter.

I want him, and I don't want him to leave. These have been the most trying weeks of my life, but I have never felt so connected to anyone before. I have never liked or even loved anyone the way I hate Tax Draconi. But that hate is so strong, it sometimes morphs into other feelings. Hate can become so ingrained in you that it becomes part of your identity, your psyche. You define yourself with that hatred, so that if it leaves and there is nothing else to replace it, you lose a piece of yourself. I think when you feel anything strong enough it becomes its opposite. I think you can love someone so hard that you hate them. And I think you can hate someone so hard you grow attached. That's why some people spend their whole lives hating someone they repeatedly invite into their lives: they don't even know who they are without it.

And with Tax, I think I am starting to hate him so hard that I...I think you can't truly loathe someone unless you care. Because not to care is indifference.

Indifference is truly the most evil of emotions.

Tax is my rival, and there is something about me that enjoys our rivalry, even if I am always on the losing end of the battle.

Tax and I have a secret world. We are on this earth surrounded by billions of people, and yet, this thing we have, it's just us. It's fucked up, it's insane, but it's something I can only share with him. Only Tax can get me out of my head, turn me into pure wanton sex. With Tax, I am stripped, both literally and figuratively. It's nice to let go like that when sometimes my job and having no family to fall back on makes it feel like the world is crumbling on my shoulders. Our thing, it's becoming part of me, and I am beginning to feel possessive towards our unique relationship.

But I keep those sentiments inside. On the outside I always approach him scornfully. I snarl, I sneer. Then he fights back, reminds me of his power, and I relent, and then I beg. It's a ritual at this point. One where we both accept these bizarre circumstances by convincing ourselves that we are still only doing what we originally agreed on. I am his sex slave. Period. He's doing this to make me pay for something he won't disclose, and I am only doing this because I am being blackmailed. That's all this is.

It's always a battle in that conference room and it always ends with both of us coming.

But every week, things become more familiar, he holds me a little closer when we fuck, his eyes are a little warmer when he greets me. The shifts are minuscule, but I feel them.

That's what I am relying on, those small hints of humanity. Over time, if I can get him to grow fond of me, I can find a way out of this. But I learned early on the process will be slow, and if I try too hard, he recoils even more. It has to happen on its own time. It's possible that the only way back to autonomy is by allowing myself to develop feelings for him.

So today, as I walk through the parking lot, there are butterflies in my stomach, my heart does race, my pulse does fire, my inner thighs do heat up and it's because I am looking forward to seeing Tax on the frontlines this morning.

The door to Alea's office is locked. That's a first. I fumble through my purse, looking for my keys, and that's when a hand comes over my mouth.

"Don't say a word, bitch."

I drop my purse, its contents explode all over the floor. But just as soon as fear hits, I smell him, his signature aroma, his musky cologne, and I feel...relief. Relief because he is the devil I know.

But the rage that bleeds from his body into the air around us feels as fresh as the first time he fucked me at knifepoint. It's like we are back at square one.

His hand presses hard against my mouth and the other wraps around my waist. He lifts me off the ground and drags me to a bathroom, locking the door behind him.

He pulls my skirt up past my ass and pushes me over the sink. I look up at the mirror and this time, unlike the very first surprise attack, he's not wearing a mask. His eyes stare back at me in the mirror, but they are hollow, entranced with arousal.

He pulls my hips out angrily and tugs my panties to the side.

My pussy blooms with warmth and my juices spread out of me in anticipation of his brutality.

He reaches forward and rips my blouse open. I learned on week three to always pack a spare.

He rips my bra down, so that my breasts bulge over the tops of the cups. And my breathing turns staccato as I view the show in the mirror: the tall, incredibly striking, sexual beast behind me.

My dad used to warn me that the devil doesn't have horns and a pitchfork, he'll appear as the most beautiful thing you've ever seen. He'll make you laugh. He'll make you feel good. You'll do things you never thought you would, but he'll tell you it's okay. And before you know it, you've sold your soul to him. That's how I know Tax is my devil.

My breasts are propped out, my body bent over, waiting to be used by the beast however he pleases.

To my surprise, he sinks out of sight, and I feel his long tongue slide inside of me, his mouth embracing my pussy. He hums with arousal as he laps up my wetness, navigating the flesh with his tongue. Discovering, conquering, giving.

If he just wanted to use me, he wouldn't do this. He does this because this is about my pleasure just as much as it is his, even if he won't ever admit that.

It doesn't take long before I am exploding all over his mouth, clenching the sink as my legs dissolve under me. My high heels slip out from under my legs as they shake from the quake of my orgasm. I call out his name in thanks over and over.

I tremble in front of the mirror, as he rises back in sight, like a predator rising out of the brush. He pulls my ass out again with one hand, while reaching forward and squeezing the soft flesh of my breast so hard, I yelp.

"Shhhh..." he whispers into my ear.

His curved hardness presses in between my cheeks and I silently plead for the chance to fuck him today.

"I gave you something, now it's my turn to take," he says. I expect to take him in my mouth, but he reaches over my shoulder and pumps the soap dispenser several times as an aqua-colored gel pools in his hands.

I watch in confusion and he brings the hand down and rubs it in between my cheeks, right to the spot that he has only toyed with thus far. I gasp as he slides two fingers into the tight space, and my curiosity immediately turns to fear. Fear of him forcing his thickness into the tightness. Fear of the unknown.

I grimace as he reaches his long fingers deep into me. And he holds them there for a while. Another finger, swirling, moving, stretching me out.

"Breathe," he commands, and I let out a huge exhale. I didn't even realize my chest had become so tense.

He glides those fingers in and out of me, with each thrust, the strange feeling becomes more familiar, more pleasurable. And then he stops.

I look up at his eyes in the mirror, he tugs on his lower lip as his body pushes forward and I feel the intense pressure as he forces into me. He lets out a huge sigh as soon as his head is in. It's unforgiving, and so tight. It hurts and I am scared I won't be able to handle it, that I won't be able to please him.

Once he is a quarter in, he reaches around and covers my mouth. "I'm going to break you in. It's going to hurt like hell, and then it's going to feel good. Don't fucking scream. Understood?"

I nod, but I am so terrified I won't be able to comply.

And then he pushes the rest of the way in and I let out a gravely groan into his hand. It's so harsh, I shiver in his grasp. The feeling of his cock in my ass is so violent, such a violation.

"Fuck, Mia," he says, every muscle in his body sinks as he sinks into me. *He never calls me by my name when we're fucking.*

A tear trickles down my cheek because it's so intense, but I breathe like he told me, into the security of his hand.

He pulls out slow and pushes in slow. Each thrust picks up a little more speed. Suddenly, there is a sharp stabbing pain. I jerk violently, but his arms around me firm up and he pins his wide chest to me. "Shut up," he says. "Just breathe. It'll feel good if you relax." His tone is unusually assuring.

DEBT

The searing pain dissipates as a couple of tears run down my cheeks and rest on the hand that covers my mouth. I take a few deep breaths and Tax continues to pull out and push in, pulling me up to a standing position so that I rest on his chest behind me.

He fills me, taking me in the last place that was free of his ownership. With each thrust, I learn to enjoy this new sensation. I watch in the mirror as Tax stares into my eyes, his towering frame swallowing mine, his huge hand nearly covering half of my face. The collection of serpents on his neck dances as he tightens his grip around me.

This man is my stalker, my terrorizer, my lover.

His eyes roll up as he sighs, and I feel the tightness around him become a little tighter, and then he lets out a primal groan as his cock pumps in me. "Mia...fuck, oh fuck..." he says, releasing himself inside of me.

He pulls out of me and shakes his hand through my hair, an almost friendly gesture. But I understand that in this case it's like someone rewarding a pet for a job well done.

He stumbles over to the sink, and turns on the tap.

I watch him quietly as his mark on me slowly trails down the back of my thigh.

"Come here," he says, not looking over to me.

I wobble towards him, sore from the invasion, uncertain of what he wants from me now. He wets a stack of paper towels and reaches down my leg, lapping up the fluids that he left behind. "Here," he says, positioning them in front of me. I look up, the simple act triggering both gratitude and hesitation, and grab the towels from his hand to finish the job he started.

"Thank you," I say, confused by the less than mean-spirited gesture.

He doesn't respond. Instead, just like he always does: he puts himself back together, cracks his neck, and leaves the room like he didn't just set off a sexual nuke in here. Like he didn't just tear me into thousands of little pieces, like he doesn't take a little part of my every time he leaves.

CHAPTER SEVENTEEN

Mia

[Radiohead – Karma Police](#)

After a very long day at the office, I arrive at my house, kick off my shoes, and dump my bags on floor. Tuesdays are always exhausting. Thanks to Tax, I have an extra early wake up, and I find myself always staying later than I used to. Dewey was always the last to leave, and to me, it always spoke of his commitment to Alea, and it's something I would like to emulate.

I knead the tense muscles in my neck, letting out a deep sigh. There is a moment of refuge when I enter my house, a moment where I don't have to pretend my life isn't a self-imposed mess. But after that moment of relief, intense loneliness follows.

I think about him a lot when I am alone. How I wish I could understand. How I wish he would talk to me and tell me why. Maybe then I could explain myself, tell him I can't possibly be guilty of whatever he thinks I did. Maybe then, I hope, I would learn he's not just a monster. I see glimmers of it. Glimmers that he might see me as an actual human being, but it's usually followed by him being even colder as a backlash.

I've come to terms with the fact that I like the roughness. And it's genuine pent-up aggression that only he can provide. But I still need more. I want the roughness to come from a place of desire, possession, not hate. I can get through this if he gives me more. And maybe he might release me, give me a choice in this whole thing if I can get to that part of him, the pain that lies behind his dark eyes. I want to believe his word is his bond, but as long as he holds the video over my head, I live in fear. What if, after the year is up, he extends it to another year, then another? I could become his to do what he wants with forever. My life would revolve around this arrangement, it would ruin any chance I could have at a relationship, marriage, family. I doubt any potential suitor would be okay with my weekly sex meetings with Mr. Draconi. Yes, this is about sex, but it's so much more: Tax owns my life.

Despite these worries (or because of them), I have to stay focused. My only way out of this is to get through the storm that is Tax.

I only see him once a week. We have no contact outside of that conference room every Tuesday, and yet, his presence permeates every waking hour of my day.

During our time together, I sense Tax battles with himself much like I do. He wants to be unrelentingly brutal, but he'll break and do something almost kind. He'll lick a tear, or clean his cum from my thigh. If I embrace the tenderness, he whips it away and lashes at me, like a scared dog who bites a hand that tries to pet him.

DEBT

This stranger has become the center of my world. A puzzle I have to solve. My greatest pleasure and my deepest pain.

The truth is I don't want to date. Because in some fucked up way, I feel like I already am dating someone: The guy who I see every Tuesday morning, who hates me, or maybe he doesn't. I don't know.

I can't tell if I am losing it, maybe developing some sort of Stockholm Syndrome, and I don't have a sounding board. I am too ashamed to tell Tiff. In fact, I have avoided any substantial conversation with her since our last phone call, using my new job as an excuse. My situation has only gotten more bizarre since the Happy Kitty mixup. I don't want to deal with her looks of pity or disappointment. Even worse, I don't want to lose her respect. There is a space in my world where only Tax exists. And he takes up all that space, there isn't any room for others there right now.

Letting out a deep sigh, I flick on the lights in my living room. The tall figure just feet away startles me as I jump and holler. I'm not sure if I should be scared or not. Unlike our Tuesday visits, Tax is not wearing a suit, but a fitted heather grey t-shirt, and a pair of jeans that hug his athletic physique.

He's facing my bookshelf, full of books and knick knacks. I don't understand what he's doing here. He's not in his space; I think he's beginning to grow too large for the space he has already stolen.

I wait in silence, I expect him to turn and grab me, throw me to the floor, do whatever he feels. Maybe taking my ass wasn't enough this morning. Sometimes I feel whatever I give just isn't enough.

"Backstreet Boys?" he asks, without turning, looking at the case that's on the top of the small pile of cds I've had since high school. It's also the same cd and player I have had since then.

Keep reaching. He's seeing you.

"What? You didn't have enough time to snoop through my stuff when you broke in?" I ask, shocking myself with my cavalier tone. *What the hell is going on?*

"As a matter of fact, I did not," he says, turning to face me with a smirk. My heart flutters with attraction and a new type of excitement. He's...talking to me.

I try not to overreact by interrogating him, afraid he might push back like he always does. Like dealing with a scared dog, one waits patiently, for it to know you are not one of those people who will hurt it, and in time it will come and nuzzle against you. "Well, I don't know about you, but I am starving," I say, heading towards my open kitchen. "I am going to put a pizza in the oven. You are welcome to have some."

He nods.

Suddenly, music plays. And instantly, I recognize it as one of my cds from high school, a song called Karma Police by Radiohead.

"I don't know if you know this Tax," I say, ripping open the pizza box. "But gentleman callers usually call, or ring a doorbell."

"Gentlemen callers? I'd hardly call myself a gentleman."

I can't believe we are having a conversation that has nothing to do with sex or coercion.

"I suppose I was being polite."

He laughs softly to himself. It's such a rare sight, to see that smile that lights up his darkness.

Why is he here?

He picks up a picture from my bookshelf.

"Who's this?" he asks.

"I thought you knew everything about me."

"I do. But I want to hear it from your mouth like it's the first time."

His words spark a mixture of excitement and trepidation.

"That's my dad. He died a little over a year ago," I say, trying not to let my emotions come to the surface.

"Were you close?"

"Very. My mother died when I was in high school and I am an only child. So we spent a lot of time together. He was a really good dad," I say, feeling a frog in my throat.

"I bet," he says.

"What about you?" I ask, taking a huge risk that he'll snap at me.

He puts the picture back in its spot. "They're both dead."

"Oh, I'm sorry for your loss."

"It's better that way," he says. But when I look at his eyes, the ones he has trained me so well to look into when he takes me, I see something is not better. Something aches. And he's here because he wants more. I don't know what, but more.

"Tax..." but I stop myself. I am on the verge of asking too much, pulling him too far out of his comfort zone too fast. He guards his words ferociously, but with his body, he is more generous. I think he would give that before giving me his words.

So, I walk over to him softly. Maybe it's the fact that we are in my home and its warmth and security gives me confidence, but I want to feel him.

Keep reaching...

I approach him in my shadowy living room. I want him. And this isn't about him forcing me, or an expectation to give because I owe him some debt I don't even understand. Or even the excitement of him ravaging me as I wallow in a mixture of lust and loathing. I just want him.

"Tax..." I whisper, as I step in the narrow space between him and my bookshelf. "Can I...?"

I gently raise my hand to touch him, expecting him to swat me away, to grab my wrists and violently rage-fuck me. But he doesn't say anything, he just stands there in silence. I reach up to his terrifyingly elaborate and beautiful neck tattoo, and I softly run my fingers over the tangle of snakes. I have so wanted to do that since he first took me on this floor.

"It's beautiful," I murmur.

His chest rises and falls more deeply in response to my touch. I run my fingers down his muscular chest, the firmness of his abs, and I reach my fingers under the hem of his shirt. I begin to lift it.

"No," he says, grabbing my wrist. This time it's not painful.

"Why do you keep hiding?" I ask. "I don't want to hurt you. I just want to see you."

I just want you to want me back, Tax.

I look into his eyes, and they express a myriad of emotions: anger, appreciation, desire, mistrust, pain.

"I know you want more Tax, that's why you're here. You don't have to say it. But I can't give it if you won't let me," I plead. "And I can't keep giving if you don't give anything back. I won't have anything left in me."

His grip on my wrist disappears, and without warning, he pulls his shirt up overhead. His tattoo works its way down his neck and over his shoulder. It's even more gorgeous than I anticipated. His body is as sculpted and muscular as I thought it would be; the beauty of masculinity personified.

As my eyes admire his torso, they come upon the physical manifestation of severe pain he must have endured long ago. His torso is covered in scars, lashes of some sort, some big, some small. They are peppered throughout, forced memories of a trauma he won't be allowed to forget. I trail my fingers gently over the network of scars, and I walk around to his back, which is covered in them too.

I rest my cheek against the warm, smooth skin of his back, and I kiss each scar, one my one. His body tenses underneath my lips. "It's okay," I whisper.

He turns and grabs my shoulders, stopping me. His eyes are filled with confusion and frustration. "It's okay," I say softly. "Please Tax, just let me have more." I say, reaching my hands up toward his face. "I'm begging you." And I rise on my tip toes to kiss him, closing my eyes, hoping he'll meet me halfway.

Tax

I don't know what the hell I'm doing here. Every week it gets a little worse. I think about her, about her soft lips, and what they would taste like if I just let her really kiss me.

Every Tuesday, I walk out the door after fucking her, and I want to turn around and have her again, or just...stay. And each time I find myself cracking, having a moment of weakness, I collect myself again. I remind her that she is worthless, that she is a slave, that she owes me. I am starting to think I do it to remind myself.

Tonight, I find myself in her living room, shirtless, with her lips pressing softly against my back. I watched her today, like I always do whenever my schedule allows. But this time, I crossed that invisible wall. I'm so sick of fucking watching. I don't just want her Tuesday mornings. I want her all the time. There's no reason I shouldn't have her whenever I motherfucking want.

Mia's lips graze against the aftermath of her handiwork. I promised myself I would never give her the satisfaction of seeing these scars. The sting of each kiss against each one brings flashes of belt buckles trashing, boots kicking, bottles breaking, the taste of blood, screams, laughter. I flinch under each gentle touch of her lips.

How can she kiss them like some sort of healer, like she wants to make it better? She's the reason for these scars, she is the creator of my pain. She took the gift of life away from Jude, and so, we have to take it away from her.

"It's okay," she says softly. But I can't take this. It makes me feel. I hate feeling. I thought I was over that shit. The only feeling I allow is wrath, because it fuels me, because it makes me stronger than everyone in my path. Having nothing but wrath makes me invincible.

So I turn and I grab her, to stop the pain, the fear, the sick feeling rising from the deepest pit in my stomach and up to the surface.

"It's okay. Please Tax, just let me have more. I'm begging you."

She's begging me. There's something about when she begs that makes it so hard to resist her. It's the look in her eyes, she just wants me to give something back. *How can this be the same person who destroyed me?*

Her brown eyes gaze up at me; she is vulnerable, exposed. It's a trap, if she was a bitch, this would be so easy, but her openness, her ability to be so fearless with her emotions draws out deeply buried emotions I haven't felt in 14 years. I know the safety is an illusion, but the heart is the biggest fool, all it takes a little kindness to trick the heart. I should know, I've done it to others.

But no one has ever done it to me since Mia, and she's doing it again. Every time I dig deeper, looking to find that black spot on her heart, I only find more tenderness. Every time I dig deeper, I find it harder to crawl back out.

She should hate me, she should want to stab me in the back, not kiss it. But, that's what I once thought of her: a girl who looked at a skinny, piece of trash loner and saw more. And that all turned out to be a lie. So maybe she's playing me again, and I won't allow myself to be played a second time.

I'll give into her begging, I'll let myself feel, but this is for me. This is to let her think I care, so when I pull it all back, when I finally look into her eyes while ending her existence, she will feel the depths of betrayal that I felt.

She leans up to kiss me, and I wrap my arms around her fragile frame. She feels so small, so harmless. Mia's arms wrap around my neck, and she rakes her fingers through my hair. Her kiss is full of passion and pent-up desire. She's been working towards this since the first night I fucked her. She sucks on my lips, sliding her tongue against mine. And she tastes even better than I ever dreamed she could.

My dick pulses with desire, and flinches in pleasure every time it rubs against her stomach. And for now, here in this living room, I forget about the vendetta, and I just let us be: Tax and Mia.

I grab the soft, firm flesh of her ass, and lift her off the ground as she wraps her legs around me. She clenches me, like she doesn't ever want me to let go, like I might never return if she releases me.

I carry her over to the kitchen counter. She's wearing a skirt, like she always does for me on Tuesdays. I already took her once this morning, her asshole felt so incredibly tight. In fact, I think that's what brought me here. This morning, having her in that way, felt so fucking amazing, that it left me wanting more.

I push up her skirt, shoving her panties to the side. In between gasps, she reaches down and frantically unbuttons my jeans, shoving them down just enough to access me. She reaches into my boxer briefs and grips her small hand around my cock and I grunt with pleasure. She tugs, back and forth, moaning into my neck as she slips my head up and down the opening of her soaking wet pussy.

Fuck that feels good.

It throbs, it aches to feel the warm tightness of Mia around me. And so I push, her little gasp as I enter her makes me even harder.

"Tax," she whispers in my ear, swallowing air as I thrust deep inside of her.

Her pussy is so wet, so ready for me, that I groan and grunt, unable to pretend that this isn't the most incredible feeling on the fucking planet. Her soft, flowery scent, the one that clings to my clothes every Tuesday, fills my nose.

She moans and moans, whispering my name against my lips with each thrust.

She runs her fingers along the ridges of my flexed muscles, and along the welts and scars that I have carried on my body for fourteen years.

Her touch singes those spots. *Boots. Buckles. Shards of glass.*

I close my eyes and bury my face in her neck, I just want my thoughts to go dark. I don't want to remember. I wish she would stop making me remember.

I bite her neck, so she can feel the pain I feel now. The pain she has made me feel all these years. But instead of recoiling, she dips her head back, receiving my angry bites with a guttural moan.

I run my hand up the soft flesh of her breast, squeezing so that her tanned nipple perks up, and I run the tip of my tongue along the puffy flesh. Her tits are so supple, round and pure, I just want to make them dirty with my bites or cum.

Mia chokes out gasps from the back of her throat and my cock grows tighter, tenser, getting ready to explode.

The warm flesh of her cunt hugs my cock, and her breathing becomes shallower and faster. "Tax!" She digs her nails into my back, pressing her lips against mine as she swerves her hips against my thrust, becoming an active participant in her orgasm.

"Oh god!" she calls out. "God!" she cries, as her thighs squeeze my hips, and every muscle on her helpless frame tenses and then relaxes as she trembles, murmuring my name over and over again.

As her tight pussy contracts, I thrust and thrust as the pressure builds in my cock, my own breathing becomes heavy and the sensations of her slick pussy around me hit their apex.

"Fuck..." I breathe into Mia's lips as an eruption of pleasure pulsates out of my cock. "Mia...fuck..." I sigh as all the tension melts out of my body. I pump my cum inside of her, claiming her again. We both collapse in each other's arms out of exhaustion.

But I came, and all the feelings went. My head is clear now, at least for a few minutes, until that nagging feeling of wanting more returns.

I pull out of her, yank a few paper towels, and quickly clean myself off. I sense her watching me, her eyes questioning, insecure.

And I won't look. I can't.

I pull up my pants and head over to the living room, picking up my shirt from the floor.

In my periphery, I watch her slide off of the counter. I can feel her befuddlement, she's dazed.

This is good.

I slide on my shirt.

"The pizza," I say.

"Oh shit..." she says, running to the oven. "It's fine, just in time."

She thinks I'm staying for dinner. *Poor fucking thing.*

After placing the pizza on the range top, she looks over to me and her eyes grow sad when she sees I am headed towards the door.

And as usual, I make sure to remind her, and myself.

"This changes nothing, Mia. Do yourself a favor, don't convince yourself that I am a nice guy, or that I can receive love. I am not a good person and you will be sorely disappointed. I'm only using you. I don't care how you feel."

I turn and walk out the door before I can see the hurt spread across her face.

CHAPTER EIGHTEEN

Tax

I get home to find an unusually decadent dinner spread waiting for me.

Jude wants something.

"Where have you been? I've been calling you."

"Around," I say. I am not in the mood for discussion. I feel like a huge fucking piece of shit right now, for hurting Mia when she tried to reach out to me, but even more because I actually care that I did.

"Well, I had a nice day, thank you very much. I was in the mood to cook, so I made us dinner."

"I noticed. Thank you."

"Have a seat before it gets cold," she says, far too nice. This feels like a fucking ambush.

"Where's Rex?" I ask. If she's around, there's a 95% chance he's lurking somewhere near.

"He's coming later. He's out with some friends."

I take a seat and shovel some food on my plate. Fucking Mia runs up my appetite, and today I did it twice, so it's time to chow. Also, these self-imposed four am wake-ups are killing me. I am ready to crash after this meal.

As I eat, Jude just watches me, not even picking at her plate.

"Just fucking say it. What is it?" I ask.

"I was just wondering how you've been, twin brother." I hate when she does that, throws "twin" in there to emphasize how we are even closer than typical siblings.

"I've been fine. Perfectly fine," I say, stabbing my fork into a potato.

"You've just been...distant."

"Distant? You mean I've been myself?"

"Oh cut the shit Sil, this is me you're talking to."

"Don't call me that, Judith."

She rolls her eyes. We both hate our names, me because it only made me stand out more, and Jude because it was old fashioned. Apparently since we are half American and half Romanian, our parents split the names accordingly. And they went overboard in both instances.

"Fine, sorry. But stop acting like I don't know you. It's me. We're fucked up, but we get each other."

She's right. It's that twin psychic voodoo shit. *Fucking twinstinct.*

"I just want to eat in peace. I'm hungry and you know better than to fuck with a hungry Tax."

"And I want nothing more for you than to fill your belly. Can't a girl just talk to her big brother?"

She also likes to remind me that I am four minutes and thirty-two seconds older than her. And that I am 6'4" and she barely breaks five feet.

"Talk then, but I'm eating."

"Okay, I'm just concerned about the plan."

I roll my eyes. *Not this shit again.*

"It's not that I don't trust you'll take care of it. I just wish I knew more. For the past ten years, we have done this whole thing together. We confided in each other every step of the way. We are a team. And now, when we are so close to finishing, you're shutting me out. It's been months since Mia was supposed to be gone. You haven't even mentioned her since you bought Alea. I think I have been pretty patient."

"No I'm not." *Yes I am.*

"Then tell me."

"It's shit I don't really feel like sharing with my sister. Nothing personal."

"Are you really trying to pretend like there's anything that's off limits between us?"

I sigh, already exhausted from fighting my constant craving for Mia, the last thing I fucking need is my sister piling on. "You want to hear the fucking details Jude? You really want to hear them?" I ask in a raised voice.

"Yes!" she pleads, with a tone of relief.

"Okay," I slam my fork and knife down on my plate. "The night I went to the house to kill her, I fucked the living shit out of her instead. I fucking came in her and everything!" I pause almost imperceptibly for a disgusted reaction from Jude, but she doesn't even flinch. "Then I bought Alea, because I wanted to make her my whore. I have been fucking the shit out of her right in the middle of Alea. Making her suck my cock, fucking her in the ass, degrading her, calling her a slut and a bitch. She loves it and she hates it. I am slowly sucking her soul out of her body, making her fall in love with me. I keep taking more than I give. I am slowly showing her a little more tenderness each time I see her so she'll fall hard for me. So she thinks she can save a broken man. And when she does fall all the way, when she can only see a life with me in her future, then I will tell her who I am, and when she's crying, when she realizes who I am, remembers what she did to us, I am going to look her in the eyes and kill her. Then I am going to burn Alea to the ground." Jude sits taller in her seat, drawing in a slow breath. If I didn't know any better, I would think those words just turned her on. "Those are the specifics of the plan. Getting someone to fall in love with you this hard, in this complicated of a fashion, takes a lot of time. So please get the fuck off my ass and let me eat my dinner in peace!" I say, pushing away from the table so I can take my plate to another room.

As I say my new plan aloud my stomach grows tight with anxiety.

Jude smiles, "perfect," she says, impressed with my *Plan B*.

CHAPTER NINETEEN

14 Years Earlier

"So, I think you're onto something with this Radiohead and Tool you've suggested," Mia says to me, smiling.

The thought of this perky, pretty girl singing about wanting people to die and wash away into the Pacific Ocean makes me grin from ear to ear.

"Well, maybe, just maaaaybe, I might understand why Backstreet's back, alright?"

She shoves me playfully. "Now I know you're full of shit. Snacks!" she declares, spilling a bunch of bags onto the floor of her den. It's been a few weeks since we started this project together, which is due at the end of next week. During that time, we have hung out at least two evenings per week, usually when her dad is working late.

I get the sense that she doesn't like to be at home alone with her mom because it makes her sad.

In that time, I've learned she is honestly the most amazing person I have ever met. And I know it's not her outer beauty that's blinding me. In fact, getting to know her has only made me more attracted to her, and I didn't think that was possible.

She doesn't treat me like a weirdo, she doesn't look at my long hair, gaunt face, baggy black clothes and chains and see an "other." She just makes me feel comfortable. I don't feel so different when it's just her and me. She's even nice enough to let Jude do homework in the dining room when Jude has nothing else to do while we work on our project.

I think I'm in love.

Well, I'm pretty sure I am. All I do is think about her, especially at night when I'm lying in bed. Jude can tell, she'll catch me smiling and say, "What? Ya thinking 'bout Miaaaaaa?" as she rubs her index fingers together in a *shame-shame* motion. It kind of aches a little, to think about her. I think that's why they call it love sickness, because you feel queasy and your heart feels like it weighs a ton.

Oh, and I jack off to her a lot. Like a lot.

I know I don't have a chance with her. In this den, in this small box, it's just Sil and Mia. But in the hallways of Clint High, she's got a football player boyfriend, hot friends, and all the other stuff that comes with being beautiful and well-liked. But I've thought about it, and...I'm going to tell her. I don't have the guts to tell her face to face, but I am going to write her a letter and give it to her after school next week. And if there is a speck of a chance that she might like me back, then it will have been worth the potential embarrassment.

And if she doesn't like me back, I trust her enough to be kind about it. And maybe she'll even stay my friend after this project is done.

"Well Mia, seeing as I have initiated you into some real music...I can't take it away from you now. You can keep the Radiohead cd."

Her eyes light up like I just offered her a pony or some shit.

"Really? Awwww, Sil...you jerk!" She says, and then she hugs me. She fucking hugs me. I try not to stiffen up as her breasts rub up against me, but my muscles lock up. People don't hug me. Just my sister, and that's only sometimes.

I think Mia feels the tension, because she pulls away quickly and then nudges me on the shoulder. "Thanks, music snob."

And now, I am even more certain I have to tell her how I feel.

CHAPTER TWENTY

Mia

It's been a week since Tax came to my house, showed a shred of his humanity and then said the cruelest thing he might have ever said to me. But I know he's doing it because he felt something. I know he's trying to pretend he only sees me as his victim. I get under his skin the way he gets under mine and he can't handle it.

So I'll play along, but he won't get all of me anymore. I'll lay there like a cold fish, he can take my vagina, my ass, my mouth, but he won't have anything else. I am tired of being sucked dry. If he didn't want more, fine. But I know he does, and while I can let him use my body as a toy, I won't let him use my soul as one.

So I march up to Alea with my poker face on, ready to be fucked by the world champion of fucking. But I am done trying to see any humanity in him. He doesn't want me to.

Maybe there really isn't anything inside of him. Perhaps he really has no empathy. Maybe I keep telling myself he's more than just a heartless psychopath to cope with the situation I am in. Because the reality, that he purely feels hatred towards me, that he sees me as nothing but a piece of garbage he can use and dispose of, that I did something to earn this treatment, that I am truly alone right now, is so much harder to bear.

Alea is locked again, this time there is no surprise attack. I enter the office and switch on the conference room lights. Then I wait.

5:15am

5:25am

5:30am

Where the fuck is he? Is this another one of his games?

My façade of indifference starts to break down. Maybe he's done with us. Maybe he's not coming back. He'll just leave me a hollow shell because I know I will never feel the way I feel with Tax with another man.

Maybe that's not such a bad thing.

Am I broken? Is that why no matter how many dates I went on, no matter how "together" or handsome the guy seemed to be, they could never hold my interest? Do I require someone to brutalize me in order to feel an attraction to them? And does this make me destined to suffer?

I try to imagine what I would want from Tax. If he could just give me more, if he could keep the intense and angry side, but show me something else, I could deal. I might even be happy. But his hardness only works if there is some other softness. It's one thing to bend me over and fuck me like a gutter slut, it's another thing to really see me as one.

I don't have Tax's phone number. I have been fucking this guy for seven weeks now, and I don't even have his phone number. But I do have his email, so I send him a message:

Was our meeting cancelled this morning?

As soon as I send the message, I start to fume. Everything Tax does is deliberate. He knows I am sitting here waiting. In some ways, this blatant lack of consideration for my time makes me angrier than him blackmailing me for sex. I could have used the extra sleep. This is just another one of his games.

I send the email, not expecting a quick reply, but my text box pings with a message.

I am rescheduling to Friday. 5 am. See you then.

Well, I guess I have his phone number now.

It would have been nice for you to tell me this last night so I could have slept in. But I guess that would require a modicum of consideration.

My sincerest apologies, Mia. See you in a few days. And watch your mouth.

Ugh, his smartass response makes me want to punch a puppy.

I can't help but snicker at that last line, but I still want to kill him for being such an asshole.

Friday comes along, and I trudge my way through the parking lot. Today is going to be a loooong day. Tiff is throwing a party at the bar, a grand reopening of sorts to celebrate a major renovation. And partying with Tiff means a very late night.

This morning, out of spite, I don't wear my sophisticated and sexy getup. Instead, I wear my usual jeans, boots and a white t-shirt. I don't apply an ounce of makeup and I throw my hair up in a topknot. Serves him right. It's not like he doesn't make me get completely naked 95% of the time anyway.

The door to Alea is locked. Again, no surprise attack as I go for my keys. I enter the office; all the lights are off.

5:10am

5:20am

5:35am

He's stood me up AGAIN.

And I hate to admit it, but I am disappointed. Of course, I am livid too.

This time, I text him. I don't know if the fact that I have his phone number means anything. But I like to think with him, everything has meaning.

I am here. Alone. Again. You said Friday 5am.

I expect a quick response, but there is nothing. Complete radio silence.

Is he done with me?

I resist the urge to call him. To come off as some desperate wannabe girlfriend, but he's always showed up. Hell, the last time we saw each other it was twice in one day.

A sadness comes over me, wondering if this is really it. He's bored with me and has moved onto the next woman. There is also the possibility that I scared him off when he came to my house. That he felt something, and now he's running away like a big fucking coward.

I *should* be thrilled about this possibility.

Well, it's official: I am crazy, missing the guy who has made it his personal hobby to torment me.

Tax

I watched Mia leave her house this morning. She was wearing jeans and a t-shirt. She's either tired or silently protesting me. Little does she know, I think she's just as hot in a t-shirt and jeans as she is in a silk blouse and skirt. Win-win for me.

I made the decision not to see her this week. I need distance.

Jude's hunches are hitting a little too close to home. I told her my plan to shut her up for a while. It'll work, because I have always come through, and I know she's not interested in hearing any more details about her brother's sexcapades.

But things aren't adding up for me. I'm not an idiot, I read people incredibly well. That's how I have been able to destroy the lives of everyone else who destroyed mine and single-handedly take an entire town off of the map.

But I don't see it. I am just as baffled now as the moment I learned of Mia's betrayal fourteen years ago.

Could I be wrong? Impossible.

She's blinding me again, making a fool out of me like she did long ago.

I used to think of her and see blood, thirst for her painful end. But now, when I think of her, I start feeling...warmth. Motherfucking warmth.

It's her pussy, I think it's so good that it's making me soft. So this week, I'll fuck with her head, get distance, get focused, and then I am going to come back strong and make things right once and for all.

But there's one major problem with my ingenious plan: I am giving *her* distance, but I'm not giving myself any distance from her as I sit here in my car following her every move.

CHAPTER TWENTY-ONE

Tax

Stone Temple Pilots – Sex Type Thing

I am parked across the street from the bar that Mia's friend, Tiff, owns on Water Street. It looks like there is a big party as there is an unusually long line out the door, but Mia goes straight in.

I call Rex.

"Yo Tax."

"Hey, I need you to come downtown."

"Sure bro, what's up?"

"Mia's at Cuddy's and I need you to keep an eye on her."

"Oh, always a pleasure. Off all the people you had me tag, she was the most fun to watch."

My collar heats up. "I bet. How long are you gonna be?"

"I'm five minutes out."

"Good. Keep your phone close. And keep your distance from Mia. I just want eyes on her."

"Always, man."

I turn off my phone and wait. I get the feeling she knows I am watching, because the outfit she had on tonight was designed to taunt, to make me want to bend her over and remind her she's mine.

It's this tight black dress with spaghetti straps that stops at about mid-thigh. Basic, but designed to perfectly frame a tight body like hers without any distractions. Her cleavage was peeking out and she's wearing these red fuck-me heels with ankle straps. *Ankle straps.* Something about those things get me every fucking time.

She usually keeps her hair up in a ponytail or bun, but today it's loose and full and she looks so fucking...womanly. All thick glossy long hair, and tits, and legs and ass.

Aaaaand there goes my goddam trouser snake, missing her pussy. This guy is fixin' to get me in a world of trouble if he doesn't start getting interested in other women.

I have my set pieces of ass I can go to. These woman are fine as hell and down to do dirty shit whenever. They don't ask questions, they understand that there's not a chance in hell they'll get anything more from me than a great fuck. But whenever I get horny, which is pretty much all the time, I gaze at the contacts list on my phone and it's that feeling I imagine women talk about when they look at a closet full of clothes and have nothing to wear.

My cock keeps whispering: *"Mia's pussy. Mia's pussy, please."*

I thought that by giving her my number, she might break and call me or text me more than once. But I gotta give it to her. She's sticking to her guns. I haven't heard from her since that one text this morning.

I don't even realize I have spent the past twenty minutes thinking about Mia until my phone rings.

"Rex."

"Hey bro, I'm in the bar. It's bumpin' tonight, but I see her. She was with Tiff for a while, but Tiff is all over the place working. It looks like some dude is creepin' up on Mia. Looks like a total fucking knob too."

Fire. I feel like my fucking chest is on fire.

"Specify creeping."

"Well she's standing at one of those high top tables, and it looks like he bought her a drink. I can't tell if she's feeling him or not. Oh wait, he just put his arm around her waist, but she kind of side-stepped."

Atta girl. That still doesn't mean I don't want to break his hand, all five fucking phalanges.

"So, he's whispering something in her ear. And she just laughed."

Heat. Lava. In my veins.

"It looks like he's pleading with her. Literally has his hands up like a prayer and she's smiling...aaaand she's going to the dance floor with him. He's behind her..."

I am already crossing the street and heading to the bar before he finishes his sentence.

"I'm coming."

"Oh shit," Rex says. He knows me well enough to know what's coming next.

I walk right in, even though I don't go to Tiff's bar for obvious reasons, any bouncer who knows a damn thing in this city knows not to stop me.

It's like I have radar for Mia's pussy, because in the dark, bustling crowd I spot her, rubbing the ass I own against that douchebag's crotch.

Mia

This guy doesn't have a chance of going home with me, and I have made that abundantly clear. But he bought me a drink and begged me for a dance, so I'll have fun with him. He seems nice enough. Hell, I'm not in a relationship, at least not anything that could be considered as such by any normal standards.

I am going to have fun tonight, the way any normal American woman would, because I am so over feeling conflicted. Tax has abandoned me, and I really should be thrilled about that. I take two quick Jager shots before heading to the dance floor with this guy. He's cute, but mildly douchey. I don't mind the company though. Tiff's got a lot on her plate tonight, so it's nice to have people to mingle with.

I start playfully shaking my hips and the guy slides behind me, moving his in sync with mine, and rubbing up against my ass. He's pushing his limits, but he's smart about it. I'll let it slide for now. If I feel any poking, we are moving to the face-to-face sidestep.

I look up at the huge crowd and smile. I am so happy for Tiff. The bar looks amazing. She has wanted to renovate since inheriting Cuddy's a few years ago. It still has a homey feel, the kind of place you could hang with friends after work on a workday, but can quickly become a trendier weekend spot with some creative lighting.

And that's the vibe that is going on right now: it's dark, there is club lighting and the dance floor is full.

The crowd is like one lively organism: swaying, bouncing. I can hardly tell one person from the next. But then as I look off into the distance I spot a tall drink of water: he's wearing a perfectly tailored black suit with a white shirt and no tie, his shoulders are broad, and my eyes travel up to his masculine jawline, his perfect tan, his hair shaved at the sides, long up top and his...neck tattoo?

Oh shit.

After the millisecond it takes for me to realize Tax is in the club, I notice he is making a beeline towards me. His nostrils flare like an angry bull's. He is massive and intense and it freaks me out to see him outside of my house or the office building. Until this point, it's almost like he might not have been real because no one else saw him.

But he's real. He's definitely fucking real.

His eyes are black like coal, and I worry for the guy winding his hips against me. But Tax is in front of me too quickly for me to shoo him away.

"Let's go," Tax says. *The nerve.*

"No. I'm here for a friend," I protest.

"Then you'll be here for a friend, but you will come with me."

"Dude, chill the fuck out," the guy says.

Dude, that was stupid.

If laser beams actually shot out of eyes, Tax would have incinerated the guy the second he looked over to him. "Back the fuck up," Tax says.

"Fuck you—"

Aaaand Tax drops him with one perfectly connected punch on the nose. He pulls the guy back up and slams his face down on the high top, making the glasses on the table jump, and twists his arm behind his back. Blood drips down his nose and onto the tabletop.

"Listen..." — he pulls out the guys wallet — "Paul? Get the fuck out, and drive straight home. You don't know who you're messing with."

"My dad's a lawyer!" he says. I knew he was a douche.

"Get the fuck out of here," Tax says, shoving him towards the bouncers

Apparently the bouncers know Tax, because they drag the poor guy out and leave him alone. Some guy with spiky hair and a black leather jacket comes up to Tax, who nods and says something back. Then the spiky-haired guy follows the bouncers and this Paul guy out.

"Tax, are you out of your damn mind!" I yell. I should try this seeing him out in the open thing more often, it makes me a lot ballsier. "He wasn't doing anything wrong."

"I'll decide who's doing me wrong. Don't worry, my friend is making sure he gets his ass home without bringing any cops into this."

"Is everything alright?" Tiff comes over. "I did not expect to see you in the center of the shennani—well, hello..." She says, immediately noticing the stupidly gorgeous, tall, tatted guy standing next to me.

She gives me eyes. *Fuck. Worlds colliding. This can't be good.*

"Ummm, this is Tax, my friend." *My serial fuck buddy— blackmailer.* "Tax, this is my friend, Tiff."

I omit the word *best* because I am sure he's some version of a sociopath and I don't want him to know how important she is to me. Just as quickly I realize he probably already knows who Tiff is because he's a psycho stalker on some personal vendetta to fuck me to death.

"Nice to meet you," he says. "Sorry about the commotion. Buy everyone a round on the house." He hands her his credit card.

She looks around the room. "Seriously?"

"Do your damage," he says.

"Ooookaaay," she says, turning away. Then she turns back sharply to me and leans into my ear. "Bitch, we need to talk, and he is fucking HOT."

This is a terrible, terrible turn of events. He's moving out of the space in my life where only he inhabited and is now parking his tight behind in other spaces. This whole thing worked because it was a Tuesdays at 5am thing, but this crazy arrangement can't work if he starts mingling with the rest of my world.

As soon as Tiff is out of earshot, I yell: "What are you doing here?"

"You can't see anybody else. I thought that was clear."

"See? You are implying we 'see' each other. We don't see each other, you get to have me as you like and then remind me how much you don't care. You stood me up twice this week. You didn't even bother to reply to me today. Remember? You're only using me? You don't care how I feel."

"This isn't about feelings."

"This is exactly about feelings. What just happened, just there? That's jealousy. That's a feeling. You can lie to yourself and say you don't have them for me, but if you didn't care, you wouldn't be standing here. If you didn't care, you wouldn't have come to my house! You are such an asshole!" I shout.

"Enough," he says in his booming low voice. "Come on."

"I can't leave, this is my friend's event. She's important to me."

"We're not leaving, we're getting some air."

He grabs my hand, and it's an unfamiliar feeling. I am used to being dragged, shoved, yanked, but not taken by the hand. And instead of pulling me to the front, he takes me down the hallways that lead to the back of the bar and out to the back alleyway.

It's empty, save for a trash container, and a few distant voices echoing from the main street.

"What do you wa—" Before I can get the question out, his lips are violently colliding against mine.

He's let me kiss him, and only really once before, but never has he initiated a kiss. And this is not just a kiss, it is a *kiss*. It's filled with the range of human emotions, it sends me a message without saying anything. He feels something for me. Maybe he can't articulate it, maybe he doesn't understand it, but he feels it. And this is the only way he knows how to tell me what he feels without saying it.

He presses me against the brick wall of the exterior of the building. It scrapes my bare back, the burn contrasting the smoothness of his lips. We are shielded from the main street by a dumpster about 20 feet away, but that doesn't save us from the possibility of a club employee or random wanderer coming upon us.

And I don't care. In fact, I kind of like the idea.

Tax tugs my dress up past my waist, sliding his hand down between my legs.

"No underwear," he grunts.

"I think it was wishful thinking you might come around," I admit.

"You're the perfect little whore, but you're my fucking whore," he says, pushing me down in a deep squat position and pulling out his rock-solid hard on, pent up due to his own stubbornness.

"That means no other fucking man touches you but me. Spit on my cock. I want to hear it," he commands. I follow his orders by pooling my spit in his mouth and spitting on his tip, then using my hand to smooth the wetness up and down his shaft. He slams his hand against the wall behind me and throws his head back with abandon as I take him all the way to the back of my throat, choking on him.

I reach a steady rhythm with my hand and mouth, sliding up and down. His groans fuel me to fight the ache in my jaw from sucking on his thickness.

He swells in my mouth, but before I can take him all the way, he pulls me up to my feet, slams me up on the wall, and wraps one of my legs around him.

Someone comes out to the alley from the kitchen for a smoke.

"Get back inside!" Tax's voice booms. I watch the person's shadow jump and run back into the building.

I laugh, and then he laughs when I laugh. It's such a rare, beautiful sight. The brightness of his smile overwhelms the shadow of darkness in his eyes.

He pushes his wet dick into me and I gasp carelessly as his curved cock lands right against my g-spot.

"Tax, fuck me," I beg. He's fucking me, but I want more. I want him to hurt me, I want my body to reflect my mind with conflicting feelings of pain and pleasure.

"Mia...Mia you are so goddamn beautiful," he murmurs so low, I almost miss it. He says it like he begrudges that he feels that way. "I hate you...I fucking hate you," he grumbles in a much clearer voice.

"Hate is a feeling too," I whisper through a moan.

"I don't want to feel anything anymore."

"Feel yourself inside of me," I plead. "That's all you need to feel right now."

"You ruined me," he growls, thrusting forcefully, snarling at me.

"You ruined me," I reply.

He flashes his teeth as he grips his large hand around my throat, squeezing, slowly cutting my airway. He looks me in the eyes and I stare back, just like he has trained me to do.

I clench around his cock as it stabs me, a weapon he uses to hurt me that is far greater than any knife or gun. He grips at just the right pressure so that if I suck fiercely, I can get enough air to stay conscious.

The dull thudding of the club music, the chatter from patrons on the street, the steady dripping of a drainage pipe on the far side of the alleyway, it all disappears behind the sound of my own sharp gasping.

And I erupt around him, frantically clawing at his hair, his jacket, the waist of his pants, as my vision goes bright for a millisecond. I hear him call my name into my neck, but he sounds distant, like he's somewhere far away. Again my senses are dampened like I am underwater. It's like my orgasms with him are traumatic and my body shuts down to cope with it.

I dig my fingers into the fabric of his suit and grip, afraid of this feeling, like something inside of me has jarred lose. Afraid he might just leave me in this alleyway used and alone.

But he doesn't pull away, he doesn't yank my hands off him. He lingers for a few extra seconds. And then he pulls out a fresh pocket square from his jacket, pulls out of me, and wipes me between my legs.

"That should do. I want you to keep my cum inside of you all night."

DEBT

I nod in silence, as I collect my bearings. I pull my dress down, and smooth out my hair, waiting for him to insult me, to make it clear that I am garbage, that I mean nothing, that this means nothing.

"Alright, let's go fucking party," he says.

CHAPTER TWENTY-TWO

Mia

<u>Garbage – #1 Crush</u>

Tax takes me by the hand and leads me back through the hallways and into the commotion of the bar. I am surprised to see Tiff at the high top table I was using earlier, chatting with the spiky-haired guy who was talking to Tax earlier.

She spots us walking in, smiles and waves us over.

"Mia, you left your purse here. What's gotten into you?" she asks jokingly. *More like who.*

I am still in a daze, and the loud music and club lighting aren't helping, so I just smile and my eyes dart over to the guy she's with. "I assume you two know each other," she says. One would think so since I know Tax, but I know nothing about Tax, let alone his acquaintances.

Before I can say anything, Tax says: "This is my brother, Rex."

Brother? They don't have an inkling of family resemblance. Rex has green eyes and he's fit too, but much smaller-framed, maybe 5'10" or so. And his hair is dyed black, but he is very fair, with freckles, like he could be a red-head underneath the dye.

"Step-brothers," Rex says, noticing my confusion. "That's why I'm not jacked like him." He winks.

"Do you two know each other?" I ask Rex and Tiff.

"Oh yeah! He comes here all the time. We've known each other for years now. Maybe you should stop making dildos and party where the real dicks are," she says. Rex erupts with laugher, Tax smirks.

But I shudder a little bit. Tax has a friend who knows my friend. Is that a coincidence, or like everything he does, some sort of calculation?

"Yoooooo dude! You're the man." Some drunk guy says, walking by and pointing at Tax, who is obviously not thrilled with the attention.

"You fucking rock man!" says someone else.

Tax leans across the table towards Tiff. "You could have gone without telling people who bought the drinks."

"Badass motherfucker!"

"Oh no, you're getting credit for it bud," she says, leaning in, with a wink. She thinks he's hot. Who doesn't? But I know that's just how she is, she's not trying to take him away or anything.

"So," Tiff motions the beer in her hand to my direction. "Mia is soooooo in trouble with me. She has never mentioned a guy named Tax. I thought we told each other everything."

"I wonder why that is..." Tax muses aloud. *What a bastard.*

"It's nothing," I say, going overboard on trying to downplay our "relationship."

"Nothing?" Rex says, calling me out in jest.

"Mia, he's right there! How cruel!" she says.

This is unbelievable. *I'm the cruel one.* How does he do this? How does he stand there and do nothing and make me look like a jerk?

"I didn't mean it like that! I mean, it's new. And I'm just trying to keep things private."

"Well fine then," Tiff says. "So...now that it's not private, how did you two meet?"

A round of shots come to the table. I freeze. I was so not prepared for this. Tax's hand rests on the small of my back. I think it's part comfort and part *shut the fuck up and I'll take this one.*

"I purchased Alea and I took a silent role. So I work with Mia while she runs the company."

Tiff's eyes widen. "Oooooh, so I get it. Private because of the whole working thing!"

"Yes!" I say, thankful that this whole thing is coming together so much better than I had imagined.

"Well, Tax, be good to my friend. She's the best person in the world."

"Awwwww," I say, knowing it's already too late for that request.

"She is something," he says, his hand rubs my back and I stiffen more. That statement is so loaded. And this touching without sex thing is throwing me for a loop.

"So what do you do, Tax? Besides buy vibrator companies?"

"Hey," I butt in, "they are intimate devices for female pleasure."

"They are amazing is what they are," Tiff says. She turns her attention back to Tax. I am so envious she can ask him the questions I am not allowed to, but I intend to take full advantage of her nosiness.

"Well, I do a lot of VC, stocks, it's all boring. I rarely do any acquisitions unless I see something I really want, something that has a lot of potential."

His hand is still on my back, making my spine tingle.

"I know I sound like I am gushing over my friend here, but keep her around. She loves Alea and no one will work harder than she will."

"She has a place at Alea as long as she wants. With her at the helm, I feel like it's in good hands. Everyone always has kind things to say about Mia," Tax says. "And I am inclined to believe them."

Okay, is he talking to me indirectly? Like is he trying to mind meld, or is this all bullshit?

We all take a round of shots together, then another. I am both excited and terrified of finding out what a drunk Tax will be like.

"So, Rex, do you work with Tax?" I ask.

Tax gives me a look out of the corner of his eye.

"Me? Yeah. I do research, tech, I'm kind of a jack of all trades," he says with his youthful smile. He's a cute one. Something tells me Tiff has pounced on him already.

"Come dance with me Mia," Tiff says.

"Uh, okay." I don't know why I feel I need Tax's approval, but I do.

"She's in good hands Tax. Please don't try to kill another customer of mine!" She pleads, already three sheets to the wind.

"Go on, I'll be here with Rex." Tax leans towards my ear, slides his hands down and cups the crook of my ass, hooking a finger close to my pussy and clenching. "Remember. Mine."

Tiff lays her forearms on my shoulders, pulling me in close as we dance.

"Jesus Mia, what the fuck? He's gorgeous!"

"I know..." I lament.

"Girl, that neck tat under that suit!"

"I know..." I mope.

"I know you two just fucked in the alleyway," she winks. "Julio nearly shit himself when went out there for a smoke."

"Oh shit," I say, burying my head in embarrassment.

"No...this is great! This is what you need. This is what we were talking about! You need someone who is strong enough for you. No one has ever kept your interest. You need that guy who is going to give you a run for your money. Someone who keeps you on your toes. You never needed a man to define you, but it's nice to have someone you can lean on and be vulnerable with. You are a strong, successful woman, but sometimes it's nice to have someone equally strong to take you on."

That's not exactly how I would describe our dynamic. I feel anything but strong around Tax. From the very first moment we met, he has dismantled my independent, strong persona and has reduced me to a weeping, begging, mess.

"Anyway, we have to catch up. You've been like a ghost. I was afraid you might not even show up tonight."

"You know I would never leave you hanging!"

"I know, I know. But that new position at Alea has you really busy, just don't forget to live."

Oh, I've been doing enough living for a lifetime.

Of course I have been avoiding Tiff, but it's not because of work, it's because I am afraid if I see her alone I will burst. I've trusted Tiff with everything, but this secret, this is a monster. What I have been enduring is vile. What's even more vile is how I have allowed myself to enjoy it. What would she think of me? She's never judged me and I have never judged her. Tiff lives a wild life: long nights, sleeping until 1pm every day, multiple partners (sometimes at the same moment). I've sat in the waiting room as she had an abortion. She cried in my lap when Blake, the only guy she ever loved left her and argued with her when she took him back. We have been through so much and loved each other unconditionally and without judgment. But this predicament is different. I am willingly subjecting myself to some phantom debt. I don't even know why Tax wants to make me pay. I ask every week and I get the same bullshit answer. It's gotten to the point where my curiosity is starting to dull because it doesn't even matter anymore. He's here now, and whatever the reasons may be, he has already made his stamp on my life.

A cocktail server brings us some shots and I gladly swallow the liquid courage. We make our way back to the table where there is another round of shots. The alcohol is starting to hit me hard. Drinking makes me talkative and touchy. Oh, and horny. And there is a tall, muscular guy with a neck tat, and perfect hair, and lips, and he smells amazing, and all I want to do is put my hands all over him.

I start feeling the music and swaying to the rhythm. I turn to face Tax and pull him to face me, wrapping my arms around his neck. As I grind my hips against him, his hands slide down to my ass and he bites his inner lower lip.

"Dance with me," I plead.

"I don't dance, babe." *Babe?*

I pout and he grins faintly, but he's not budging. This might be one area where begging doesn't work with him.

The bizarreness of all of this is not lost on me, but it's something about being in the real world, and maybe the alcohol is helping too, but I almost forget about the circumstances that brought us here. At the very least, I can ignore them.

"You can dance *on* me if you want to though," he says. That is a tiny concession, but for Tax it's like he's the UN right now.

"I'll take what I can get," I say, pulling him away from the table and pushing him onto to a wall.

I turn around and sway my ass into his groin, snaking, popping, rubbing, getting as close to sex with him as I can while clothed.

I spin back around and look up into his eyes, they are hooded, he's feeling the alcohol too. Maybe I can get through to him, maybe his defenses will weaken. Hell, being here, right now, like this, clearly they already are.

I snake my hips hard, my spine arching and cresting like a wave, as I run my hands under his suit jacket and up the crisp white fabric of his shirt. The firm ridges of his abs underneath my fingers incite my greed. I stare at him the way he stares at me: with hunger. And he looks down at me with smoky eyes and a pleased smirk as I rub myself against him and his bulging greed pressing against me.

I smile and spin while keeping my eyes on him, circling my back against his abs, and dropping down, piking my ass up, flipping my hair, and driving my ass up the length of his leg as I bite my lower lip. My body feels like it's on fire and he's rushing river of cool water.

I spin again to face him, and I hike my dress up just under my ass, while straddling one of his legs. His eyes are affixed on mine, like we are only two people in this crowded club. I ride his thigh, rubbing my bare pussy against him, as I lick my lips and run a hand through my hair.

My chest presses against the firmness of his torso, my nipples stiffening from the contact.

"Please, dance with me," I beg in a mewl.

His hand threads through my hair, the other grabs my ass and pulls me up and against his thigh, applying more pressure against him.

Brick by brick.

And we move in sync: slow, rhythmic grinding. Eye to eye. Lids barely parted. Sweat beading. Low moans vanish into the air. The deafening music drowns out any conflicted feelings that remain. He tugs my hair and extends my neck, grazing his teeth against my chin, the tip of his tongue awakening the sensitive nerve endings. His hand squeezes my half-exposed ass, and everything lights up. My nipples and clit, a partnership of arousal, tense in ecstasy as they stroke against the man who sets me on fire. He is also the only person who can put me out.

My moans grow louder, but they are drowned out in the safety of the music. And like the flashing lights in the club, I become ablaze with flickering energy, throwing my head back, arching my spine as he supports me, as he lets me use his body, his smell, his taste, his overpowering masculine energy to put out the blaze that he ignites inside of me.

I collapse onto him, grasping his shirt, taking in his smell, the warmth of his broad chest, completely lost in the sensory experience that is Tax Draconi. I smile as I burrow my face into his chest, drunk off the mixture of alcohol and lust.

Tax strokes my hair and slides his hand to the curve of my lower back. I look up at him hesitantly, afraid that at any moment this will all end and he will have erected the wall I managed to crumble just now.

His eyes are dark, but it's with desire, not hate this time. They almost smile at me.

"What do you say we get the hell out of here?" he says, generously displaying a hint of his incredible smile.

Radiohead – Paranoid Android

Radiohead – Karma Police

"I think you might be tipsy yourself Mr. Tax," Mia says, stumbling into the darkness of her house.

I am, but I won't let her know that. She kicks off her shoes and drops a few inches closer to the ground. In true Mia fashion, she immediately heads for her shitty pink and silver boombox. I know how much she makes, she can afford a goddamn modern stereo system.

"You want water?" she asks, haphazardly walking into the kitchen. She's so happy because I'm here. This piece of shit who has left countless stories of devastation in his wake. She somehow thinks she's safe with me. She trusts me. No woman lets you into their house when they are drunk unless they trust you.

"I'm fine," I say, scanning her living room. I don't know why I do that, I never do it anywhere else, but I think it's because I am looking for clues. For some explanation as to how the fuck she can be the person I know she is. A person who is cruel and who toys with emotions, but there's nothing. All I see is someone who wants approval, who wants me to care about her, who tries to find the good in me. She meets my rage with a weapon more powerful: acceptance.

If she can find it in herself to be kind to me now, how could she be the same person who years ago met love with cruelty?

I don't know what happened in the club. I honestly have no explanation for it. I don't want another man touching her, that's for sure. But I could have stopped at that, and I didn't. I'm telling myself *this is part of getting her to fall in love with you*, but I'm starting to think that kind of stuff happens both ways. Tonight, we weren't locked in a room beholden to some set of rules, we were out in the world, just Tax and Mia. Holy shit, it was a lot of fucking fun. *She's* a lot of fucking fun. And it's hard enough staying the course sober, but with the alcohol in our veins, things have taken some unexpected turns.

Kissing her is the dumbest thing I have done so far. Yes, I have let her kiss me in throes of heated fucking, but I have never initiated. It was always clear I was doing her a favor, that I never really wanted or needed it. Staying away for over a week backfired. I just wanted her in every way, I couldn't hold back, I wanted to take every part of her I could, including her delicious lips.

"It's not 1999, Mia," I say, referring to the Backstreet Boys playing on her cd player.

"No, but I remember how thrilled you were to see it in my stack of cds, so I thought I would play it for you."

She slinks over to me. "Take off your jacket, get comfortable!" *Mia Tibbett: world's giddiest drunk.*

I slide my jacket off and place it on the couch. I remain standing, this night has taken so many turns, I can't get too comfortable in her house.

She starts dancing. Yes, apparently she dances to this crap in the presence of others in her house, not just when she is alone. She doesn't even realize that the last time she danced alone in this house, she was potentially minutes away from her gruesome death at my hands.

"Whoops!" she says, as she spills water on me. "I'm so sorry!"

"Don't worry, I'll send you the dry cleaning bill. Water wasn't the only thing you got on my pants today," I say, recalling our bodies, hot and sweaty, grinding in the club. And her fragile body in my arms as it quaked on my thigh. *Fucking-a that was hot.*

She looks down coyly. "Sorry," she pouts.

"I was kidding, Mia."

"I know," she says, putting her glass of water on the kitchen counter. "Dance with me," she pleads, doing the running man.

"I already told you I don't dance," I reply, standing firmly in front of her swaying body with my hands in my pockets.

"What about what we just did at the club?" she asks.

"That wasn't dancing, babe."

Her cheeks burn bright.

Fuck. Shit. I keep calling her that. It just rolls off the tongue. I feel possessive towards her, and it's bordering protective. That is not the mindset I should have with someone I need to kill.

"Oh, come on, what's that saying? Dance like no one is watching? I'm no one to you, right?"

Her words unexpectedly punch me in the gut. Because I can tell she's not fishing for me to assuage her. She truly believes it. I have succeeded in making her believe she is worthless to me. And that was the point of all this, but feels wrong.

"You're not no one." Mia isn't nothing, she is all I think about. And for the longest I meant that in the worst possible way. I dreamed for years of ending her life brutally. The others had mostly peaceful or quick deaths, but with her I wanted her to know, to understand, as she died in terror.

But now, she's becoming something else to me. And I keep fighting it, I keep trying to convince myself that all I feel towards her is bitterness and vengeance, but I am lying to myself. So I either need to end her soon, or start figuring out a Plan C. Because I am really starting to like the idea of keeping Mia alive, and it's scaring the shit out of me.

She doesn't say anything. I brush past her, picking up the old Radiohead cd, in its original cracked case, and slide it into the player. This time, I play Paranoid Android.

Mia's right, I am tipsy, and I do kind of feel like dancing. Only with her though.

I walk up to her wrap my arms around her slight waist. Her eyes smile at such a small gesture from me. I give her so fucking little, that just agreeing to this makes her feel like she's having some sort of victory.

"This old music reminds me of my hometown," she says, resting her hands on my shoulders.

"Where's that?"

"I think you know Tax. You know everything about me," she says, cocking an eyebrow.

"Refresh my memory," I say, gently drifting side to side with her.

"It's a small town in Iowa called Clint. Well, was. The main factory closed down there like two years ago and it pretty much turned into a ghost town. I inherited my dad's house when he died, but it's worthless now. I'm not kidding. The town is full of either people squatting, or a proud few who refuse to leave. The place is a mess. Boarded-up shops. Houses falling apart with overgrown lawns." *Don't I know it.*

"Do you miss it?"

"Honestly? No. I never felt like I belonged. People there were so judgmental and nosey. I left and never turned back. If I went back and told them I worked at a sex toy manufacturer..." she laughs. She has a way of making everything lighter, even when she talks about the things she hates.

"How did you feel like you didn't belong?" It's like I am talking to another person. She was popular, loved, envied. Her dad was the sheriff of the tiny town. If the Pettit's were royalty, then Sheriff Tibbett was a knight.

"Well, I guess I did on the exterior, I had all the right friends and such. But everyone was so obsessed with the dumbest things. Like football. You know that show Friday Night Lights? Yeah, that times a thousand. Those kids could have gotten away with murder. They didn't have to do homework, teachers had to pass them anyway. I had even heard of some girls who had been assaulted and their own parents told them not to press charges. How ridiculous is that?"

Heat snakes up my collar.

"I felt like I had to be a certain way to fit in, but as soon as I had a chance to leave, I did. And I never missed it. The only person that connected me to the town was my dad. But he'd come here to visit because I think even he wanted a break from that place. I miss him a lot," she says, her eyes drifting away with her thoughts. "We were all we had for so long, and now...I guess I'm alone.""

"You're not alone..." she looks up at me expectantly. "You have Tiff." She looks down again. *Give a little, take much more.*

"This song reminds me of you," she says, referring to Karma Police, which now plays.

"How so?" I ask. *Is she onto me?*

"It's a song about comeuppance...and you're taking out your revenge on me...right?"

The way she said it, the way she has accepted this fate she doesn't even understand: that is the saddest thing anyone has ever said to me.

I look up, dismissing her question.

"Tax, when are you ever going to tell me what you think I have done to deserve this?"

What you did, Mia. It's what you did.

"I'm not sure anymore." I don't want to want to tell her, because if I do, I'll have to kill her.

She looks up at me with sad brown eyes.

"Sometimes I look in your eyes and I see something familiar, something kind. And it makes me wonder if I did do something to you, if I hurt you in a way I didn't even realize. And if I did, I am so so sorry that I hurt you so much that you felt I deserved this. But whatever it is I did, I really hope you think about it and ask yourself if it's worth it. Because whatever I did, I never meant to hurt you. I don't like to hurt people, Tax. Even now, I should hate you, but I can't. I don't have that in me."

How can she say that to me? How can she experience the putrid hate I exhale with every breath, and yet apologize to me? I live off the misery of my violators. My life force is vengeance. My fuel is their blood. Whatever she thinks she sees, there is no good inside of me. That was taken from me when I was 15.

This woman in my arms, those words, I almost don't even care for a moment about what she did. Because I want to have her. She is the only person who makes me feel something that isn't anger or a retribution. Maybe the way she makes me feel is her penance. But that's not enough, because I wasn't the only one ruined that night. Jude won't accept anything less than death, and Jude is the one person who has ever given a shit about me my entire life.

But I am selfish, and I want to feel Mia's warmth. I want to reward her for her kind words the only way I know how: with sex.

I kiss her on her velvety soft lips; her fresh taste instantly makes me hard. Her scent, the flavor of her pussy, everything about her makes my blood churn, so that I have to have her.

"Are you in a rush?" she asks.

Woah, I always take care of her needs, so I don't know what kind of question that is.

"Why do you ask?"

"Because, I'm not...in a rush. I mean, we're not in the office, you don't have to go so fast when you're done with me."

Done with her. Like a piece of trash. It's me who's the piece of trash.

"I'll consider taking my time then," I say, pressing my lips back onto hers, feeling her melt into my arms with need.

When I preyed on her, I wanted to break her down. I wanted to make her weak. But her openness, her willingness to bare herself to me, no matter how harshly I reject her, that's bravery. To know someone like me, and to allow your heart to feel anything at such great personal risk, I don't think that is weakness at all. Guarding the heart is a fucking cakewalk compared to the pain she faces from me.

Mia stops, looks up at me with her penetrating eyes, hooded with need, and then they widen. Her cheeks puff up, and she kind of jerks forward a few times.

"Oh god, I think I am gonna be sick."

"Shit," I say.

She scurries away, lunging through her bathroom door like a damn linebacker and I hear the god awful sound of her retching.

This night keeps taking turns.

I should walk out, right now, in her time of need. In fact, I should pull her dress up and fuck her while she keels over the toilet in suffering. That is the reminder we both need. But part of what connected us that first night, the thing that makes my cock throb every time I think about it, is the fact that she liked my sexual rage. She likes to beg, to scream, to absolve herself of all the responsibility she faces every day. To play the victim for once, while she maintains control over everything else in her life. With me, she's not in charge of a ten million dollar company, or responsible for the livelihood of 20 people and their families. With me, she's not alone in this world, with no family. Even though she knows I know everything about her and she knows nothing about me, I think knowing that I am always there is a comfort to her. She believes the debt she owes is repaid in sex and subjugation, and so she feels safe in that because she gets something from it too.

She doesn't understand the full repayment of the debt is in her blood.

So for me, there is no pleasure in fucking a girl puking over a toilet. She's probably in agony, she won't give me that pained look of need I thrive on. And I don't want to treat her like a fucking dog. That doesn't do it for me. I fuck her because

I want to and I know she wants me to, not ever because I have to.

So, something deeper than vengeance drives me to peek into the dark bathroom, and switch on the lights. She's resting her arm on the toilet, her body limp and weak.

"You're still here," she says, before hurling again.

"Yes, I am," I sigh.

I am. This is usually the time I check out with *any* chick. If I can't get what I came for, I don't have time for this shit.

Her limbs are sprawled along the white tile of her bathroom floor, and that uncomfortable feeling of protectiveness kicks in. *Fuck me. When did I become such a giant pussy?*

I undo my cuffs, unbutton my shirt, and throw it onto the living room couch, so that I am in just a white tank.

I kneel in front of her and brush her sweaty hair from her face. "You want some water?"

She nods her head lethargically.

"Alright, I'll be back."

I head to the kitchen, and pull out a glass from a cupboard. In the quiet of her kitchen, I become hyperaware of the hunting knife I tuck into a holder in my pants between my undershirt and dress shirt. You know, just in case the moment strikes where I decide to go through with the plan. How fucking sick am I? That I can slow dance with this girl in her living room while keeping that whole assassination option available to me?

I realize now that I have taken the shirt off, she could see the knife, though she was resting her head with her eyes closed on the toilet bowl as I left. I don't want to freak her out, as I have no intentions of using it tonight, so I remove the holder and wrap my jacket around it, tucking it away on the seat of a dining room chair.

I reenter the bathroom with a glass of water. She looks miserable.

"Hi," she says, trying to downplay how sick she feels. "I probably should have eaten more before taking all those shots, I think."

"Happens to the best of us," I say. She did almost drink as much as I did. I am amazed she's conscious. "You need to stay in here?"

"I think I might be done for a while," she says, pushing out a smile. She takes a sip of the water. "Bad idea." She puts her head back in the toilet bowl. I stand over her and hold her hair back as she finishes purging. Mia flushes and fumbles to get back to her feet, so I pull her up. She gargles some mouthwash and then pauses at the sink for a second, like she's trying really hard not to puke again. "Thank you," she mutters.

Mia's pale and shaky so instead of slowly walking her out of the bathroom, I pick her up. It's easier for both of us that way. She makes a throaty purr while nuzzling to my neck.

Warmth. That fucking warm feeling is happening again.

"You probably think I'm gross," she grumbles into my neck.

"I may think a lot of things about you Mia. Gross is definitely not one of them."

The breath of her silent giggle tickles my neck.

We end up at the couch instead of the bedroom since it's a shorter distance to the toilet. Also because the bedroom is just not a good idea, I think. It'll be easier for me to slip out from here. I'll stay until she falls asleep and then I'll slip away.

I stand her back on her feet and sit on the couch.

"Come on," I say, patting my thigh. She plops on the sofa and rests her head in my lap. I pull a throw from the back of the couch, the same couch that I bent her over the first time we met, and I cover her.

"Tax, thank you for taking care of me. For staying."

"It's all good, babe. Just rest up." She nuzzles into my lap, and then the house is only filled with the sounds of Radiohead.

CHAPTER TWENTY-THREE

Tax

A vibration on my hip awakes me. My head feels foggy from drinking and as I try to blink away my blurry vision, I spot Mia's head in my lap. I feel for my phone in my pocket. It's Jude. *Fuck it.* I ignore the call and check the time. Shit it's almost noon, and SHIT, I spent the night.

Mia stirs and lets out a moan of discomfort as she wakes. "I feel like ass," she says, with a smile on her face. "Good morning."

"Morning," I say tensely. "Hungover?"

"Yeah, my head, my body. It's awful."

I run my fingers along her purple streak of hair. "Sorry to hear that."

"I feel really stupid," she says. "I made a fool out of myself last night getting drunk like that. Puking...ugh! How juvenile!" She rolls towards me and buries her face in the crook of my lap.

"No need. I think everyone needs those nights every once in a while. It reminds you why you should mind your alcohol.

You almost drank me under the table last night." She sits up and I stand, heading for the dining room table where my jacket lays.

"You kind of have that effect on me," she smirks.

"Alcoholism?"

"Not yet. But when you unexpectedly beat the crap out of a guy who...wait? How did you even know I was there?"

I look at her disapprovingly and run my hands over my face and hair. "Too early for questions, Mia."

"Coffee?" she asks.

"No, I'm leaving," I say as though last night never happened.

"Okay. Well, you probably know this from my shared calendar at Alea, but I'll be out of town next week. I'm going to a convention."

"I didn't look yet."

"Well, I won't be around Tuesday is what I am saying."

"And where will you be?"

"It's a convention for the adult entertainment and products industry."

Mia, Mia, what a career you've chosen.

"A dildo convention?"

She lets out a pained laugh. "No!" Then she laughs again. "I guess you could call it that."

I grab my jacket and remember the hunting knife I have tucked inside. Taking it off last night was like removing 14 years of baggage from my body. Seeing it separated from me, as its own entity, with no intention of being used, I realize how fucking sick our plan for Mia is.

I turn away from Mia and brace as I shift my tone towards her, trying to regain some ground from last night.

"You belong to me. You understand? Even when you are out of town, no one touches you."

She watches me, stunned. I think she thought we were on some sort of equal footing for a moment. But now she remembers her place in this relationship.

"Tax, I am a professional, I don't look for fuck buddies at business conventions," she says. "And as I recall, the deal was I give you sex. Not a monogamous relationship." She has to know how ridiculous her logic is. She fucks the owner of Alea in a conference room every Tuesday. She doesn't think she has a choice, but still, I wouldn't call that professional.

And I'm not sure if I like her boldness.

And I don't give a shit what the agreement was, no one else will touch her.

"Don't test me, Mia," I reprimand.

Resisting the uncomfortable urge to kiss her goodbye, I exit the house.

———⋄———

I can sense Jude is in my place before I even open the door.

Before I can take a single goddamn breath, she's on my ass.

"Where have you been?"

"Out," I say, desperately needing a hot shower.

"Maybe you forgot we had plans for brunch today," she says glaring through me.

"Aww shit, sorry. We can go after I shower."

"Tax, this isn't about breakfast. I know where you were. So what? Now you're spending the night?"

"I'm done having conversations about this topic. You need to get a life outside of this whole thing," I say.

"This whole thing? *Thing?*" she says, stretching out the last word.

"All I am saying is this is coming to an end soon. What do you have, Jude? Your whole life has revolved around this. Every goal we ever had was about looking back at that night. Who are you going to be when this is done? You need to start living a real life. And I need my own space."

"*What?*" she says, her voice quivering in disbelief.

"I'm saying I don't want you just coming to my place unannounced."

"I cannot fucking believe you!" she snarls. "Now you're suddenly a life coach? What about *your* future? Have you planned yours?" she asks, mockingly. "Oh, does it involve Mia?" she asks in a syrupy sweet voice.

"Shut the fuck up. I don't know what's gotten into you lately but I am getting sick of your interrogations. I have one mother and she's dead."

"What's gotten into me? What about you? You're different. You ignore my phone calls, I don't hear from you for days. I have to pry everything out of you. And now you don't want me coming over? You're shutting me out. I am your fucking twin, your best friend, your only family, Tax!"

"And maybe it's time your start branching out. We have to start living! That means you maybe finding a guy you like or other friends or a fucking hobby that doesn't include revenge...fuck this. I'm not Dr. Phil. You need to start living at your own place and start minding your own life. You think once this is over anything is going to change? You think you'll be happy, Jude? It'll never end! You don't even know who you are without this vendetta!"

"Are you growing soft on me?" Her eyes narrow as she leans close. "She's doing it again, isn't she? Bamboozling you.

You get a little pussy from her and you want to be her knight in shining armor."

"Oh, fuck you," I say, dismissively.

"It's never gonna happen Tax. We are not her kind of people, we never were. And if she finds out what you've done, she'd hate you. And she's not the person she pretends to be."

"Because we're any better."

Her eyes well up, holding in tears of frustration. Her voice begins to quiver with fury. "Maybe you need to remember Tax, because I think you are forgetting. Remember what they did to us! Time softens people, they all soften. Everyone moves on, has a chance to grow and become better people. They magically develop morals, and they try to forget the things they did that they never paid for. They think time is an escape, that it makes things better.

"Didn't Huck have a wife, children...*a daughter*... a daughter, after what he did to me! How could he ever even look her in the eyes? Having a daughter and being a dad doesn't make what he did go away!" Jude growls.

"And now those children don't have a father."

"And I will forever be childless!" she screams, tears pouring down her cheeks. Reminding me of the debt, of what they all owe Jude, of what I owe her.

"You want me to move on, Tax?" she cries. "They took my life from me. They took my innocence. They took my future." Her mascara runs down her cheeks. "They destroyed me. You're right, I'll never be okay, so the only thing I have is to make them feel the same. And don't fool yourself Tax, you are just like me. You've been elbows deep in this shit, just as committed as me, until now." Jude grabs my hand, pleading, her face stained with desperate tears. "Tax, it's you, and me. I love Rex, but he wasn't there. He doesn't understand what it's like to go through what we went through. He doesn't understand the level of humiliation and injustice. We were just kids..." her pleas turn to sobs.

I watch my sister and I am reminded there was a time she was innocent long ago. But now, she is a shell. She is hollow, barren, and she won't stop until every last person who took her past and her future away is gone. And Mia is at the top of that list.

Jude has always been focused on getting revenge, but she's never been as bitter and rotten as she has become since I failed to kill Mia. I think she never previously doubted my commitment, but now that she does, it's making her desperate and ugly. Jude and I used to have fun, we'd laugh, we'd talk, we'd confide in each other. But, this delay in killing Mia has driven her to a much darker place, and the more she insists I follow through, the more doubtful I become. Seeing my twin so desperate and blind for revenge is like putting up a mirror to my own motives. That is who I am. It might hide under calm demeanor, but that black hate is exactly who I am.

But I know my sister is still in there. And the reason she is so loathsome is because long ago, my naiveté put her in harm's way. I need to find a way to make this right for us all.

"I promised I will take care of it. I will make it right." I let her rest her face on my chest. "And this isn't just about you. You were a bystander and I will never understand your pain, but for me, with this one person, it was personal. I am working on it, just like I promised, but you should know me enough to know that being on my ass doesn't fucking work. You need to give me some space. Now, give me your keys to my place and go home," I say.

She whips her face away from me, hardening again. "Fuck you, Tax!" she shouts, pulling her keys out of her purse and hurling them at my chest. She flings the front door open, and I spot Rex standing out in the hall. He stays out of our epic twin fights.

I head towards the open front door to find Rex pulling a drag of a cigarette.

"How many fucking times have I told you not to smoke out here?"

"I was hoping for the balcony, but I heard shit going down when I got up here and I am not going to get in between you and Jude. You know my policy on that. You two are too fucking intense for me. And I don't pick sides in your insane evil-twin battles."

Jude and I get each other. That's why she could sense from the very beginning something was off. I worked on one mark for two years and she never got impatient, but she just knows now. We love each other, we've done horrible things for each other, but when we fight...wow, people would pay good money to see that shit. I think it has a lot to do with the fact that Jude is fiery and emotional, and I run cool. She puts on a huge dramatic show, and I just don't respond the way she wants. I know she wanted me to chase her out of the building. Not gonna happen. I don't have time for these games. One of us has to have a level head. If this vendetta were up to Jude, there would be decapitated heads all over the place and we'd long be in prison. We definitely wouldn't be rich as fuck either. I planned all this shit. I got us the money, I meticulously set up the kills. Sure she helped, but I led and planned it all. And yet she has the nerve to question my loyalty. No fucking way am I chasing after her.

"Get your ass on the balcony then," I say to Rex.

We walk out to open balcony overlooking Lake Michigan; I rest my elbows on the railing and let out a deep sigh.

"She's pissed huh?" Rex asks.

"When isn't she?"

"Especially these days," he says. "All I heard about since I met you all was this shit, and I thought she would finally relax, but she's getting worse."

Rex blows out a trail of smoke. His neck is covered in scratches. I try not to think about it, being she's my sister, but I know that's Jude's doing. I am not the only one with the penchant for rough sex. She was sixteen, I think, when she popped Rex's 13-year old cherry and she pretty much has used him a personal sex toy ever since. He's happy to oblige, they have some weird maternal-like relationship thing going on. We're all so fucked up, I never really gave it much thought. But Rex has always really cared about Jude, and for him to be saying this shit about her tells me he's even beginning to see through his Oedipal shit with her.

"Yeah, I just need to figure some shit out."

"You don't want to kill her, do you?"

I don't say a word.

"You don't have to worry about me telling Jude. I've actually grown to be real friends with Tiff and she really loves that girl. I've been watching Mia so long, I feel like I know her. I was never really thrilled about your plan for her, but I understood it wasn't my call after what she'd done. But, when I saw you two last night...Man, I wouldn't want to kill her either."

"She's done some fucked up shit, Rex."

"Well, so have we." He throws his butt onto the floor and steps on it. He immediately moves onto a second.

"Jude's my sister. All that fucked up shit we see, all that pain she's in, it's because she got pulled into my shit and the shit we grew up in. She's always had my back. Our anger has fueled us, I can't just turn my back on her because now her anger is inconvenient."

"And man, has that anger been good to us. Look at what we have because of it. You have the brains, and the wit, the brawn, and the fucking balls, but it's always been Jude who lit that fire under you. That shit is slowly killing her, but it's also the reason you're rich. It's the reason we're off the street and she doesn't have to turn tricks and you don't have to scheme. But, just because you don't give her Mia's head on a platter, doesn't mean you are betraying Jude."

"Maybe we should have stopped at the getting rich part," I say.

We have collected on nearly every debt owed to us: Tripp's NFL dreams were shattered after we rigged his car and he got into a bad wreck in college. Tucker died as a passenger in that accident. Due to Tripp's subsequent depression, no one even questioned his later "suicide." His piece of shit dad died of a heart attack we gave him with an injection of succinylcholine. After both her son and husband tragically passed, I seduced Tripp's mom. She was too devastated and lost to run Pettit Metals on her own, so slowly, I took over the company and eventually convinced her dumb ass to make me sole heir to her fortune and give me power of attorney. That took two miserable years of my life, fucking that old bag so I could get her millions. When she died, also thanks to my favorite heart attack in a syringe, I sold the entire network of Pettit factories, except the one in Clint. That one I liquidated and shut down just out of spite. I single-handedly destroyed that shit hole of a town. Huck and the other guys, we picked off one by one in various subtle ways. Ways that couldn't be connected. An unfortunate accident here, an illness or disappearance there. A decade of my life has been solely dedicated to avenging one night.

But Mia left Clint, escaping all the misery. She made a great life for herself. She had no real connection to Clint that would even make her wince at the factory closing. She has always managed to be unscathed by everything we did. I was saving the best for last. And I had to make sure she got a personal delivery from me.

I'll be honest, I have had no regrets. I left a trail of misery, and I have slept very well at night. That is, until the night I reunited with Mia, and now there's one thing I wish I hadn't done.

I haven't been sleeping as well these days.

"I know it's not my place. I get it, I am not really your brother, and I wasn't there, but whatever you want to do, I support."

"Rex, you are my brother, don't say stupid shit like that."

Rex smiles, drinking up that approval he has always thirsted for from Jude and me.

"All I am saying is, you've proven your point, right? Think of all the stupid shit we did when we met. We robbed people, stole shit. What if someone came back for us for the things we did? Mia set it all off, but she wasn't there. You really think she thought all that shit would go down?"

I want to tell Rex to shut up, I don't need any more conflicted feelings than I already have. But, all this time, he has taken orders without question. My only real sounding board has been Jude, who is a growing ball of rage and bitterness. Maybe it's time I open up the floor to some other points of view. "I get what you're saying, but we stole because we were homeless kids. The high level shit, the millions of dollars, that was because the Pettits did us dirty first. They owed us. But what Mia did, what they all did, that was pure cruelty. There was no reason other than to inflict pain for personal pleasure."

"You know better than me. But do you think she's really that cruel? I have been watching her for years, following her, looking through her shit. I never felt like I was watching some cold-blooded bitch. She's quiet, she works hard, she is loved."

"I fucking know," I say, shaking my head. *It doesn't add up.*

"I'm just giving you my two cents. Do what you will with it. But Jude's chompin' at the bit. So, if you are going to make the call, make it soon, or shit is going to blow up. She's like a powder keg," Rex says, tossing his half-smoked cigarette to the floor. "Alright, I am going to find Jude and talk some sense into her."

A.K.A. fuck her brains out.

It works though. Whenever she's pissed at me, Rex helps calm her, convinces her to give me space. He reasons with her. Shit, I guess he does that for me too.

Rex exits the balcony without saying another word, leaving me alone to contemplate my next move. I need to buy significant time.

Jude is a pain in the ass when she gets in these moods, but she is my sister, my ally. No one understands what we went through. They can try to imagine, but they will never understand. Jude will always be a part of my life. And who she is today is because she had my back fourteen years ago. I owe her something. But maybe it's not death, maybe it's life.

Maybe there is a way I can have Mia *and* Jude.

Tax

I slip into Mia's dark, quiet house. She has been running errands all day today and yesterday, in preparation for her trip, leaving me with plenty of time to slip into her house to do a little recon.

I know what I am doing is fucked up on so many levels. But, I see no other way to save her life and cool down my sister. I can keep delaying things, telling Jude I am working on the long game, but it'll always be a temporary solution. I need something to snuff Jude's anger and she only has one weak spot.

Mia might hate me forever, but I have already dug a hole so deep that she will hate no matter what when she learns of all the things I did. This is a long-term plan to keep her alive, even if I lose her in the end.

I enter her bathroom and open the drawer where she keeps her disc of birth control pills. I count the number of empty pill bubbles, and take the replacement one I brought and pop out the same number of pills. The perks of formerly being a hustler: plenty of connects in illicit pharmaceuticals.

I slide the new disc of one-hundred percent placebos into her vanity and pocket her pills. *Pivot.*

Now we wait.

CHAPTER TWENTY-FOUR

14 Years Earlier

Everything seems fine on the outside. Every day I sit in the cafeteria and listen to my friends talk about their huge problems: who's going to make the cheer team, does Huck like Jessica, or how much they hate whatever the fuck Sara Toms is wearing. On the exterior, I am my usual self. I don't like to drag people down with my personal issues, but this week has been really hard. My mom has gotten really sick. This has happened before, she has taken a bad turn and then had a miraculous recovery, and I am sure it'll happen again, but I can't help but think about her when I am at school.

My parents insist I don't miss school. They don't want my life to be constantly disrupted since mom's always in and out of the hospital. Mom's illness has put a lot of things into perspective. From my relationship with Tripp, which seems to be more about him being interested in what's in my pants than my head, to my friends who seem to think life begins and ends here in Clint. I just feel different.

Anyway, I've decided one day I am getting out of here. Only a couple more years and then I am going to college out of state and leaving this town behind for good.

I walk towards my locker after last period, anxious to get home and see how my mom is doing. Walking in the other direction is Sil, my physical science project partner. Well, he's more than that. Over the past few weeks, we have grown to become friends. It's been refreshing. He doesn't give a shit about what people think, he's introduced me to new music, and we laugh a lot together. I'll admit, I asked him to be my partner because I was curious. He stares at me a lot in class, and I wanted to know more about him. He's not my type, he's so thin, and he has long hair and wears all black, but there's something about him...his eyes, I think.

I'm glad I did, because despite all the darkness on the outside, he's fun and he's a good guy. We don't talk much outside of class or my house. In school he keeps his distance, and we don't run in the same circles. But I always say hi whenever I see him. I want him to know I am not ashamed by our friendship even if some of my friends are kind of assholes towards him.

But today, it seems it'll be more than a passing hello as he comes towards me with purpose. He must want to ask me something about the project.

"Hi," he says. He seems tense, but, that's usually how he is in school, when it's not just us in my house.

"Hey," I say with a smile. "What's up?" I ask, opening my locker.

"I wanted to give you this." He hands me an envelope.

"What's this?" I ask. "Is it for science class?"

"It's...uh..."

I feel a smack on my ass and jump. It's Tripp. "I hate when you do that!" I say. He leers over at Sil.

"Have you met Sil? He's my partner," I say, shoving the envelope in the pocket of my denim jacket.

"Oh, yeah. I know Sil," he says, roughing his hair up. Sil jerks away.

That shit pisses me off.

"Come over here," I say to Tripp.

He sighs. "Whhhaaaat?"

I pull him away from my locker. "Don't be rude. He's nice. I don't like when you act like that."

"Whatever Mia. That kid is obviously in love with you. You think I am just going to let him be all up on your ass?"

"Don't be ridiculous. We're lab partners."

"He just better watch his back. I don't trust him."

"Whatever."

"Anyway, I came by to see if you wanted me to walk you home."

"Fine. Let me grab my things."

I go back to my locker and Sil is long gone. I feel bad that Tripp had to do that stupid show of dominance. Tripp isn't always like that, but around other guys, and especially when they are with me, he has to find a way to puff his chest.

I've been thinking about breaking up with him for a while. Actually, I tried a couple of months ago and he cried like baby, begging me to stay. I relented. I don't like hurting people and he just wore me down. So I thought I would give it another shot, but, it's crap like the way he just treated Sil that reminds me some things never change. Tripp has always gotten what he wants, and maybe I am part of the problem for giving into him too.

Tripp and I walk to my house in silence. My mind is on my mom and I don't really talk to Tripp about her. Actually, Sil is the only person who I talk to about my fear of losing her. He lost his mom as a baby, and I don't feel pity or awkwardness when I speak with him about it.

"Alright, I'll see you tomorrow," I say once we arrive at my front door.

"You're not inviting me in?"

"I have a lot of homework and I'm tired. I'll see you tomorrow." The truth is the house is glum and sad. I just want to sit by my mom and read to her. And I know Tripp wants more than just to hang out. Hooking up with Tripp is the last thing on my mind right now.

"What's your deal lately?"

"What are you talking about?"

"You've been acting all fucking snotty."

"I am not in the mood, Tripp."

"You fucking Sil?" he leans in and whispers.

"What? Are you kidding me?"

"I know he's been coming over, Huck told me." Huck, his nosey friend who lives across the street. "You think because I'm at my tutor's I wouldn't know?"

"We're doing a project together like I said! You are being ridiculous. I am done having this conversation." I fumble for my keys and drop them on the floor. Tripp waits with his arms crossed as I grab them. I unlock and pull open the door and stick out my hand, signaling for Tripp to pass my book bag that he had been carrying.

He shoves it over to me and I walk into my house.

"Mia—"

"What?" I ask petulantly.

"Uh, nevermind," he says. "I'll see you tomorrow."

"Yeah, bye."

My complete lack of curiosity about what Tripp wanted to say only confirms that I need to end things with him soon. I drop my bag on the floor and hang up my jacket and peek into my mother's room. My neighbor is there, she has been helping while my dad is at work.

My mom smiles, she looks better. I knew she would. My neighbor steps out and I grab the copy of Romeo and Juliet on the nightstand. I have been reading it to her, acting out the various parts of the play. She loves it.

Eventually, she doses off and I grab my bag so I can start on some homework. That's when I remember the notes Sil gave me. I reach into the pocket of my jacket, and there is nothing. Then the other. I could have sworn I put it in there. I rummage through my bag and open the front door to see if I dropped it when I bent over to grab my keys. Still nothing. Crap, I might have lost some notes, but I figure I can ask Sil tomorrow when I see him during last period. With any luck, maybe it'll magically appear in one of my notebooks or something.

CHAPTER TWENTY-FIVE

Mia

"Welcome to the Shore Club. How may I help you?

"Hello, yes. I have a reservation under Tibbett, Mia."

It's been a few days since I have seen or heard from Tax. I thought that the night at the club might have changed something, but he has recoiled back to his hiding place. I feel so stupid for thinking that that night meant anything. He just saw me as a possession that needed to be reclaimed from some guy. He drank, and when you drink you do things you normally wouldn't. As soon as he sobered up, he went back to his role as my blackmailer, my master. To top it all off, my nerves got the best of me. I drank way more than I usually do, and puked right in front of him. Awesome. That's exactly what you want to do in front of an egotistical anti-social narcissist: give him a reason to look down on you.

After all these months he is still a stranger to me. It doesn't feel that way because we have become familiar. But familiarity is just an illusion. It actually tricks me into thinking I know more than I do, that I mean more to him than I do.

I don't even know where the guy lives. I don't know where he's from. It took about two months to get his phone number. The little I do know has come from the occasional slip in conversation or the circumstances of our arrangement. I must be delusional to think that he has sincere feelings for me, and I am an even bigger idiot for having anything other than contempt for Tax.

I keep thinking that, somehow, I am getting through. That I can get him to care for me enough to see me as a person and give me my freedom back. But, sometimes, I feel like I am right back in my dark apartment, getting grabbed from behind by a masked intruder. The only thing that has changed is the weapon he uses against me.

Tax tried to hide his drunkenness, but based on his openness that night, it was clear he was wasted. I think that's why he stuck around after I got sick too. That part of him that he tucks away so deep, the one that isn't hard and cold like steel, was given a free pass to reveal itself after a couple of drinks. But the next morning, sober Tax quickly reminded me that this is an arrangement, nothing more. Whether or not he feels anything doesn't even matter, because he is determined to shut me out.

"Okay Ms. Tibbett, I have you all set for the penthouse suite. Do you need help with your bags?"

"Thank you—wait, did you say the penthouse?"

"Yes, it says right here you reserved the penthouse suite."

"That's not possible. I am traveling on business, that's too extravagant. Wait a moment, the person who makes my arrangements is here." I tiptoe and look across the long counter for Laney, who is traveling with me and a few others to represent Alea. "Crap, I think she already went to her room."

"Ma'am, I am sorry, but there are no other rooms due to the convention. This is all we have."

"Ugh, really?"

"Yes. I am so sorry, but someone did call in these reservations. I can see it in the notes. Maybe someone else in your party needed a room, so the person who did the booking upgraded you?"

"Can I cancel and double up with someone else?"

"Ma'am, I'm sorry, but the cutoff for cancellation has already passed. You'll still be charged for tonight."

Dammit Laney. Maybe Laney thought I wanted the penthouse because of my new position. Or maybe that's all that was left. I would just remind her later that I want to run a tight ship at Alea financially and that includes no penthouse suites for my future business trips unless first approved by me.

"Well, I guess I have no choice then," I say, handing her the company credit card.

I make my way up to the extravagant suite. Despite feeling wasteful, I have to admit feeling giddy as soon as I walk in. The room is wrapped in floor to ceiling windows with views of the ocean and downtown Miami. The room is furnished with crisp white linens and upholstery, the floor tile is a muted grey. I open up the sliding doors to the enormous deck, letting in a soft ocean breeze. The sound of crashing waves and the stroke of the breeze against my skin is nature's therapy. Maybe I should thank Laney instead of correct her. She knows I've been stressed. Of course, she only thinks it's from transitioning to the new role. But maybe she was doing me a favor. For the first time in months, my mind is quiet.

Tonight's big event is a black tie banquet, so some of the Alea crew head to the pool, but I opt to take a nap on the deck before getting ready.

The mental tranquility doesn't last very long once I lie down, and I regret not distracting myself at the pool. My thoughts drift to what Tax is doing: Is he thinking of me? Did he have as much fun as I had at the night of the club? Is he seeing other women? *Shit—I need to ask him if he is since we still aren't using protection.*

It's only been a couple of days, but I crave his forceful touch, his pliant lips, his warm breath against my neck, his masculine scent. I think about his body, rigid with muscle and how he often hides it from me, only making me want it more.

His scars. Remembering them softens my feelings for him again. He's not only expressing that angry sexual domination — there is something else. I felt him flinch under my kisses, and I remember how he took me in the kitchen to make his pain stop.

He told me in the alleyway of Cuddy's that he doesn't want to feel. He hates me. I think it's because I make him feel.

Why do I do this to myself? Despite this man making it a point to dehumanize me, I continue to seek humanity in him.

There's something that happens when I am with Tax. I don't have to be so perfect, or have all the answers. Everyone thinks of me as the person who has it all together. When my mother died, I was so concerned with appearing perfect, that I hardly even mentioned to my friends that she was sick. I have always maintained an aura of stability, afraid to be seen as vulnerable. But I know I need someone who breaks me and allows me to be weak. Tax gives me no other option. With Tax, I can be a broken mess. Just as I force Tax to feel, he forces me to embrace my flawed nature. To be perfect requires a shutting down of extremes. I can't be too excited, or emotional, or sexual. And that means a life of internal monotony. When I am with Tax, I am an imperfect mess, and no longer shut down anything. I become a live wire. As much as I hate it for being true, I am my most honest self when I am with him. His domineering aura takes up all the air in a room, suffocating pretense.

I close my eyes and try to evict thoughts of Tax from my head. Romanticizing our relationship isn't healthy, even if it's my way of coping with the lack of control. What we have isn't even a relationship, it is a crooked business agreement. He doesn't care about how I feel, and I need to start doing the same.

Mia

I enter the ballroom and spot Laney with a few of the others, picking up their name tags from a long table. These events have the most interesting mix of people: adult film stars, producers, manufacturers, website owners. Tonight, though, this ball is specifically geared towards the physical product side of the industry. There will still be plenty of crossover, since many actors have toy lines or license their image, but we try to pretend at this particular event that we sell something other than sex. People dress up, they drink champagne, they talk about industry trends. One might look in and think we are at a medical convention or something. Okay, that's a lie, we are much hotter, and even at the black tie events, people dress far sexier.

Tonight, I have on a fire-red dress with a cross-over halter top and a low back. It stops a few inches above my knees. I leave my hair loose, but press in a few long curls here and there for some volume. I top off the look with black strappy heels that have a gold chain detail on the ankle strap. A few members of the group go to the bar for drinks, but Laney and I head over to our table. I don't even want to look at a glass of wine for the next month.

Laney and I take our seats, and she tells me about her afternoon at the pool. I listen attentively, happy to hear her spirits are finally up from her split with Luke. I laugh at the joy in her big green eyes as she tells me about all the hot male porn stars sunbathing in their tiny swim trunks. Laney's bubbly mannerisms when she's in a good mood serve as an endless source of entertainment.

When there is a break in the conversation, I use the moment alone with her to bring up her hotel booking snafu. I prefer to correct employees in person, since tone can be misinterpreted in text.

"By the way, imagine my surprise when—"

Laney's bright eyes suddenly shift. She looks up and over my shoulder, and squeezes my thigh.

"Hold that thought. Don't turn yet, but there is a guy whose babies I would have tonight. Without question. Calgon take me away."

I laugh and freeze. "Okay, okay. Is it safe to turn?"

"Yes—no—wait! Oh my god, oh my god. Act normal, I think he's coming over here. Act casual," she says, sitting up and tucking some hair behind her ear.

DEBT

"What? He's coming over here?" I ask, tensing in reaction to Laney's nervous excitement.

"Shhh!" she says, which means he's in earshot.

A familiar heavy hand rests on my shoulder and musky hints of vanilla and pine hit my nose. *Oh fuck.*

I spin around to look up at an impeccably dressed Tax, wearing a pale greyish-blue suit. *How very Miami of him.* I swallow hard, trying to reactivate my salivary glands.

I know this asshole is in no way interested in current sales trends for handheld vibrators, so what he is doing here?

"Mr. Draconi," I say, rising to my feet. "I didn't expect to see you here."

"I thought I should make an effort to learn more about the industry I am investing in."

I glance over to Laney, who apparently doesn't realize her mouth is completely agape, and make my introduction.

"This is my executive assistant, Laney Pulaski. Laney, this is Tax Draconi, the owner of Draconi Corp, the new owners of Alea. They maintain a relatively silent role, but he and I do meet from time to time." Tax fights to keep his lips from curling.

Laney stands tall, puffing out her chest and sticking her hand out for a shake. "Yes, we've spoken on the phone, I believe, when I first scheduled your morning meetings. So very nice to meet you, Mr. Draconi." Her cheeks blush. I silently smile at the fact that she just told me she would have her boss's babies.

"It looks like they're getting started," I say, relieved that I have some time to reflect on what the hell is going on.

The lights dim, and everyone takes their seats. There is a hushed round of introductions as the other Alea staff members arrive at the table.

Someone steps to the podium and welcomes us all, and makes some statements about the industry, but I can't focus on a single word. I look straight ahead, pretending that Tax's presence isn't stifling. I'm afraid if I look in his direction, everyone will instantly know we are fucking. *Worlds colliding again.* And I notice a pattern: while it's Tax who tells me I mean nothing to him, it is he who keeps initiating contact outside of the conference room.

My eyes dart in his direction, trying to gauge his facial expression without giving myself away. He seems to be looking ahead too, but it's hard to tell.

The host introduces the first speaker, who makes his way to the podium to light applause. Under the clattering of hands, a warm palm rests on my knee under the table. I become rigid and overcome with indignation. How dare he do this in front of my employees? He's taken everything, and now he wants to risk me losing the respect of my coworkers? I fidget, and his massive hand clamps down on my thigh, making me lock up again.

Electricity shoots up my leg in response to his commanding touch. I lick my lips and continue to look straight ahead, unwilling to give him the satisfaction of my discomfort.

Looking ahead at the stage, he leans in and whispers: "I came all the way from Milwaukee to see you, and this is the response I get?"

My chest sinks as I let out a uncomfortable sigh. *He came to see me?* I know, *no shit*, but he didn't say to fuck me, or something crude like that. He came to *see me*. His grip on my thigh softens and my muscles relax in response. The tips of his fingers trail up my inner thigh as warmth blooms between my legs. I lean forward to create the illusion that I am enthralled by the latest cock ring numbers, and as I do, his fingertips make it to my mound, lightly fanning against the fabric of my underwear.

He leans in, still looking ahead and whispers "so wet for me." As if on command, heat soaks my panties.

I exaggeratedly nod my head as if he has just made some insightful comment about the speaker's topic. He adds pressure and begins to stroke my clit through the lace, making it hard for me to keep my calm exterior. *God, I want him.* I don't care about anything right now other than the raging heat he inspires.

His touch ignites my body with arousal, and I begin to morph from disciplined president of Alea-Mia, into dirty, begging, sex slave Mia, wanting nothing more than for the man beside me to bend me over and take me. I believe Tax gets more than what he bargained for when I reach under the table cloth and put a hand on his bulge. He breaks his character and looks over at me, while I stare ahead and grin. His cock begins to swell in my hand and he leans in, "Mia, you are my perfect little slut."

I let out a gust of air that gets Laney's attention. *Shit.* "Mr. Draconi wants to discuss some matters with me," I say rolling my eyes, as if he is such an inconvenience. "We are going to step out for a bit."

I lean back to Tax. "I'm leaving to the hotel bar. I assume you might need a few minutes before you stand." I rise confidently, exiting with a sway in my hips.

Stone Sour – Wicked Game

I nurse a seltzer at the bar as minutes pass with no appearance from Tax. Waves of heat and cool throb all over my body as I stress over his whereabouts. Is there another bar? No. Did he change his mind?

Just as my doubts begin to take over, I get a text:

Go to our room.

Our room? Of course, *he's* the one who got the penthouse. The thought hadn't initially crossed my mind since Tax doesn't really exist in the real world, save for one cameo. I certainly didn't think he thought enough of me to take a flight down to Miami. I text Laney to tell her the meeting is turning out to be more serious than I thought, and ride the elevator up to the top floor.

I enter the room with my keycard. Not a single light is on, highlighting the light-speckled nighttime views of Miami hundreds of feet below.

"Tax?" I call out.

My skin tingles, like I am watching that part of a scary movie when the girl slowly opens a door into a dark room and her doomed fate. "Tax, I know you're here."

I gasp when I see his tall silhouette in the shadows of the living room. I watch him in silence for a few beats.

"What are you doing here?" I ask. He knows I don't just mean the penthouse.

He walks up to me, his gait measured. But when he steps closer to me, light glows against his features and the darkness no longer hides his passion.

He wraps his arm around my waist and pulls me in forcefully, the tips of my toes barely make contact with the floor as I land against his hard chest. "I'm here because I dream about you, the taste of your pussy, your moans, your cries, the way you beg for me..."

I instantly become wet as his warm breath, spiced with just a hint of brandy, caresses the shell of my ear.

"Because as soon as I leave after having you, I want you again. And then even when I have that, it's not enough. When I see another man look at you the way I do, I want to kill him. I want to swallow you. I want to consume you. I want to possess you. I want you." His other hand reaches around and cradles the nape of my neck. It feels so small in his grasp, like he could snap it with the jerk of his wrist. His lips brush against my collarbone as he whispers the last words with a rasp: "I want more."

The room goes silent. Our breaths, heavy with want, are the only sound. I swear he can feel my heartbeat as it threatens to purge itself from my chest.

Then there is an eruption. Tax turns me away and presses me against the glass of the penthouse windows to face the sparkling vista below.

The sounds of fabric rustling dominate the quiet as he wrestles off his suit jacket, and buttons rain on the floor as he rips off his shirt. Then his body pushes up against my back side. He slides his hand down between my legs. "This..." The other grabs a breast. "This...is mine."

I shake my head up and down. My mind spins with mild vertigo as the view of the several hundred foot drop threatens me.

"Tell me, Mia. Tell me it's mine."

"It's yours," I moan shakily.

"Say my name."

"It's yours, Tax."

He thrusts his hips into my backside, his dense cock teasing me with its power.

"Fuck, Mia," he says, clenching my hair and burying his face into its scent. "I want to damage you. I want to ruin you for anyone else."

"You already have," I mewl, arching my neck to receive him. Tax yanks up my dress past my hips and slides his hand down the front of my thong. "Your cunt is so fucking wet." He slides two fingers in, curling them, building more tension inside of me. I moan and gyrate my hips against his cock as his fingers fuck me possessively. "Only for me," he says.

"Only for you," I repeat back in surrender. He slides his wet fingers against my lips and without a command, I lap on them. His lips join mine as together we taste my arousal from his fingers.

"You taste so fucking good. I love when the smell of your pussy stays on my mouth. It makes me hard again as soon as I leave you."

I curve harder against his cock. Tax has done dirty talk, really dirty, but this...it's clear I am not just some interchangeable tool, he wants *me*. When he dreams, he tastes me, he smells me, he feels me just like I do him. He pulls the fabric of the halter top to the valley of my breasts, exposing them to the cold sting of the glass.

His bites against my shoulder assure me that whatever he feels towards me is still raw and undeveloped. He is still an animal of a man, a brute who shows his affections through conquering. His warm hand contrasts with the cold of the window as he grabs a handful of my breast, kneading the meat until he arrives at the peak and tugs on the nipple with his fingertips. I let out a husky moan from deep within my chest.

I can't wait any longer, I need him inside of me. I need him to put out the burn that spreads through every cell of my body, destroying the Mia who existed before Tax.

"Fuck me, Tax," I beg, reaching behind me and rubbing my hand against his own display of need.

In one swooping motion, Tax pulls the dress over my head. He kneels, grabs the thin strings of my thong, and looks up at me while sliding them off. He grabs one of my ankles and bends my leg at the knee, tugging at the ankle strap of my shoe with his teeth. I watch him over my shoulder, thriving on the thrill of Tax below me.

"You taunt me with these. When you wear your little tank tops, your tight jeans, your skirts. It's like you're trying to break my will." His teeth sharply snap at the smooth flesh of my ass, followed by his hands rubbing smoothing circles along its curves.

I purr at his words, because there is some truth in them. I never see him, but I have always suspected he watches me. Maybe not always, but at times, I can feel his eyes on me, as if the desire is so strong it sends out a beacon. There is security in his constant gaze, I feel wanted, adored, possessed. And yes, I often dress hoping he'll see me and want to rip off every last piece of clothing from my body.

I stand naked except for my heels, just as I have done so many times in the office. Though when he spins me to face him this time, I don't feel alone. His upper body is naked too, the ridges of his muscles highlighted by the shadows in the penthouse, the snakes on his neck heave in harmony with his chest. The slashes all over his torso remind me of his pain, and trigger my instinct to make him feel better the only way he allows.

He presses his bare body against mine, warmth against warmth, flesh against flesh, for the first time. His teeth graze and tug, his lips suck, his tongue tastes.

"Fuck me, Tax. Please."

"Mia..." he moans, pressing his cock onto my belly. "Beg."

"Please," I whisper breathlessly into his ear. "I need you inside of me. I need you."

And my confession, that this is becoming more than desire, it's becoming part of my identity, the fabric of who I am, sets him off. Tax unbuckles his pants, his belt buckle clinking against the tile as it hits the floor. He pulls himself out of his boxer briefs, stroking up and down my creamy entrance.

"Tax..." I whimper, thrusting my hips against him. What more can I do? He wants me, he wants me so bad, but he still teases. "Fuck me..." I plead, tugging on his neck tat with my teeth.

"No, Mia. You're gonna fuck me tonight." He grabs two hunks of my ass and tears me from the ground. I wrap my arms and legs around him and he brings us to a sofa, seating himself beneath me.

"Fuck my face. Fuck my face the way I fuck you."

My pussy throbs with need, and I am eager to relieve the mounting tension. I straddle his shoulders as he leans back, and softly lower myself onto his face. His dark eyes stare back at me, full of sexual energy and power, daring me. Even though I am on top, this is his doing. His mouth latches onto my pussy, like one of the venomous snakes on his neck tat, and he plunges his tongue deep inside of me. My hips thrust against his face, he groans as I call out his name like a desperate prayer.

"God, Tax," I gasp out. "Fuck!"

His tongue swirls along my hypersensitive clit. My hips sway on his face with abandon. "Goddammit!" I draw deep breaths of air, like I'm drowning in lust. His hands grasp the meaty flesh of my ass and dig in painfully, sending a shot of energy through me. I fuck his face hard, as if his tongue were a cock. My juices soak my thighs like Tax is biting into a ripe piece of fruit. With no shame, I loudly suck for air, as my pent-up desire explodes all over his mouth. I grab my breasts, my hands too small to palm them the way Tax does, but I mold them anyway, their softness contrasting the harshness of my grinding. *Grinding. Fucking. Creaming. Thrusting.* Tax's warm mouth drinks me, reveling in my juices. He grunts like a starving man consuming a feast.

My clit pulsates in shockwaves that ripple throughout my body, alternating between waves of euphoria and numbness, like my being is overloaded on desire. I grip my fingers through his hair and I ride his face like a raging bull rider until the intense ripples die down.

My core tingles with the aftershocks of Tax's work, but this isn't over. Still sensitive from coming, he guides me down onto his solid cock and I let out a choked cry of pleasure. His dick fills me, hitting so deep into my womb, it borders on pain. The full head of his cock rubs against the sensitive spot inside of me, like our parts were designed to fit perfectly.

I look right into Tax's hooded eyes, the way he has ingrained in me, but his are not on mine. Instead I watch him bite his lip, still glowing with my wetness, as he admires my body with a look of ownership. His hands run up my torso and each one grabs a breast, squeezing so that each nipple puffs up. He glides his wet lips along the tips, and I melt underneath the sensation.

"Mia, your tits are beautiful," he growls. Tax runs the tip of his tongue along a nipple then bites and tugs harshly with his teeth. I yelp as he follows up by sucking on it, like he's nursing away the pain. "Fuck me, Mia," he commands. "Hard. Dirty. I know how you like it."

Tax's eyes return to mine and he leans back, holding my waist, watching me as I ride him. I explore this new territory, running my fingers along his chest, his shoulders, his ripped abs. His breathing becomes harsh, the pain in his eyes battles to surface. He grabs my hands forcefully, and crosses them behind my back. His tone becomes serious, as if he is growing impatient. "Mia, I said fuck me."

This man who is so terrifying in and of himself, is petrified of intimacy. Anytime I get close, he bites.

He sits up, biting the flesh of my breasts, clenching my wrists angrily. I throw my head back, relishing in his control. "Mia, don't fucking test me. I'm still me. I will hurt you."

Something about his threat turns me wild. Even still, face to face, finally naked and exposed, he won't let me have all of him. Like a wild animal that has been tied down, I resist his grip in rebellion. It only makes him use another fraction of his strength to restrain me. I am hopeless in Tax's arms. He clutches both of my wrists in one of his large hands, the force of his grip bites into my flesh.

With the other hand, he slaps my ass so hard I wrangle against him. "Mia, fuck me. Show me who you are." I bounce up and down on his cock, growling in erotic pain from the depths he reaches. He spanks me again with no restraint. The spot where his hand lands pulsates with fire. "I know you want this. You like it when I hurt you." Another slap, so hard, I growl uncharacteristically.

"Fuck you!" I shout at him as I bounce ferociously on his dick. My breasts bounce up and down recklessly, and he slaps one hard. "Fuck!" I cry out.

"There you go. My good little slut."

I rise and rise, again going to a height where only Tax can lift me.

Tax grips my face, kissing me so hard I taste blood.

He rises up to his feet, still inside of me. His show of strength brings out a beast, and I bite his neck fiercely. He slams me down on a table, knocking over decorative vases. The clash of porcelain against tile makes me choke with excitement.

"You crazy bitch," he says with a smirk. "You wanna fuck like animals? I'll fuck you like an animal. You'll howl like a motherfucking animal."

He brings my legs up on his shoulders and leans forward, elevating my hips off the table. Using that leverage, he rubs his cock inside of me, and it only takes a few thrusts before I am howling as I grip the table. As I reach the apex of my orgasm, Tax pulls out and slams into me over and over adding pain to the incomprehensible pleasure as I let out sounds no human woman should make.

"Fucking shit..." Tax says, digging his fingers into the front of my thighs. He beats my pussy with his cock and shoots his warm cum inside of me, snarling like a savage beast.

CHAPTER TWENTY-SIX

Mia

Fiona Apple – I Know

Tax is still here and I think he's staying. He did call this *our* room. I sit on the sofa, wrapped in a blanket, as Tax stares out the window in all of his naked awesomeness. I drink up the view. Despite all the sex we have had, he's never stripped down to absolutely nothing before.

His body is beautiful. I never thought of using that to describe the male physique until I met him. It slopes and curves with muscle, a topography of masculinity. His shoulders are broad and strong, his back flares with ridges of muscle that cord down his waist to his hips. Those lines on his hips that lead down to his package...they tease my libido.

The tattoo on his neck and shoulder that seems to have a life of its own is a work of art in and of itself. Even his scars, they tell a story, like chisel marks on a statue.

We haven't really said anything, haven't even turned on the lights. We are just learning, I think, how to be around each other after sex.

"Shit. I should be downstairs," I think aloud.

Tax turns. I involuntarily bite my lip at the sight. "I'm your boss, and I say don't worry about it."

My comment seems to break the quiet. "Will you sit with me?" I ask.

Tax juts his chin up skeptically, as if I might be holding a knife behind my back. "Maybe I should open up wine or something." He sounds like an alien life form reciting the ins and outs of human behavior.

"Maybe a little. I'm still traumatized over Tiff's grand reopening."

He smiles, and my stomach quivers like harp strings.

"You had a lot of fun that night, didn't you?"

"I think you did too," I say with a smirk.

Tax comes to the couch with two glasses and a freshly opened bottle of Prosecco. He sits down beside me and pours us each a glass.

"Your feet are freezing," he comments.

I didn't even realize I had burrowed them under his thigh. It's an unconscious thing I have always done.

"They always get cold," I say apologetically. I have always had a habit of rubbing them against people. "My mom used to give me so much crap about it." All these years later, mentioning her still hurts. Tax looks at me and faintly nods like he somehow understands this. He hands me a glass, then puts his down and grabs my feet from underneath him, placing them on his lap and rubbing them in his large warm hands. "If you want me to warm them, all you have to do is ask."

The tone in his voice reminds me of the day he stood over me mockingly as I cried. *If you want it, all you have to do is beg, Mia.* Even then, the slightest hint of his softness towards me peeked through as he helped me to my feet and gave me my release.

"Seeing as you are already warming them, I guess I don't."

There is a lull, because we could go on about pleasantries, but this thing we have is the opposite of casual. It's loaded, full of unanswered questions and unspoken feelings. If there is anything I understand about this labyrinth of a man, it's that talking doesn't come easy. At least when it comes to anything other than anger.

He said he wants more, but I don't think he knows how to define that. I have to have to guts to show him what that is, even if he lashes out.

"Tax, what are we doing?" I ask. I brace myself for a harsh reminder. This is just fucking. You owe me. I own you.

He reaches forward for his glass and takes a sip. "I don't know."

I huff out a single laugh. What a casual response. It's honest though. Finally.

"You said you want more..."

His body language becomes rigid. Those words mean a lot to him. I reach out and softly put my hand on his shoulder.

"I do too."

He looks over to me, his brown eyes reflecting the lights of the city. "I know." He says it sadly, as if my words are tragic. "Why?" he asks.

Even he doesn't get it.

I chug the Prosecco. "Tax, I ask myself that all the time. I think about it a lot when you vanish on me for days."

His eyes turn away. *Could that be remorse?*

"I know you think I am just some stupid woman who did something really stupid by hiring someone to come after me. But I was trying to find something I couldn't find anywhere else. And I did."

He leans forward, digesting my words.

"Mia, I'm trying to fight this. I've been trying to fight this. I'm going to hurt you. Not because I want to, but because that's what happens. It's what I do. It's what I'm good at."

"I think you believe that about yourself. I think that's why you told me once you can't receive love. But I don't believe that about you."

"Mia, you don't know anything about me." He's told me that before with disdain, but now, it's full of regret.

"Then tell me."

"I can't."

"I'm still here...after what you—" I hesitate to say the truth and put him on the defensive.

"After what I've done to you."

I look down, but then I meet his eyes again. He did do horrible things to me, I shouldn't be ashamed to say it.

"Tax, we can't go on like this forever. Eventually, the truth will need to come out. I can't give you more if you won't give me more."

"Just because we want more, doesn't mean we can have it."

My heart plunges and my fiery side jumps from that low point. "Tax, maybe you haven't noticed this about me. But I usually get what I want."

He shakes his head at me as if to set me straight, but then he furrows his eyebrows in realization. "Actually, you're right..."

"What you're doing to me, holding back the truth, it's not right." I plead.

"You don't know that."

"I can't keep giving you more if you hold back. Eventually, I will have nothing left."

"Mia, I promise you will regret anything more than what we have." His honesty is so brutal sometimes it physically hurts.

"Bullshit." I say stubbornly.

"No," he says, firming his stance. "Not now."

"I've thought about it so much…I haven't hurt anyone. I don't owe anyone anything. My father, he was a cop. Is it something he did?"

"Enough, Mia."

"I deserve to know why you blackmailed me."

"Not tonight."

"Then when?"

"When the time is right."

I sigh.

"Mia, trust me when I say there are reasons you will understand someday. I'm trying to protect you."

"Protect me? Is someone after me?"

"No one will touch you. No one." His eyes grow black. What he did to that harmless guy at Tiff's club tells me it's an oath.

"I won't stop asking until you tell me."

"I know."

I look him up and down, my eyes outlining the trauma on his body. I reach out and run a gentle finger on one of the marks. His nostrils flare and lips purse as he looks ahead.

"What happened to you, Tax?" I ask tenderly.

"I was set up by a friend." He says, the hard sentence making it clear he won't say more.

"That's horrible. To have someone you trust hurt you." His jaw tightens, and the snakes on his neck stir.

"There's an easy fix for that: Trust no one." Tax has hardened again.

I stroke his silky hair, knowing that his hurt lies deep and no words I say now will change that.

"I guess I should ask you then..." *I blow at segues.*

"What?"

"Have you been with other women, since we—"

"No."

"Because we have—"

"The answer is no. I have only been with you. I very much enjoy fucking you raw, and I also very much enjoy my cock, so I keep him well taken care of."

If my pussy could smile, his comment about fucking me raw would illicit one. *I am such a mega perv.*

"I'm trusting you on that Tax."

"I know."

I rest my head on his lap, nuzzling into the scent of our sex that lingers on his groin. I bury myself, hoping that I'll get under his skin the way he has gotten under mine. That he'll go against his instincts the way he has made me go against mine.

His fingers stroke my hair. The room is silent, but not quiet, the volume of Tax's introspection is deafening.

"Tax," I say in a woozy voice. "I wish you would trust me."

"So do I."

CHAPTER TWENTY-SEVEN

14 Years Earlier

I almost chickened out and played hookie today because I was so nervous about Mia's reaction to the letter. She had to have read it by now. She officially knows how I feel about her, that I think she is a beautiful person, and I think she deserves better than the asshole she is with now, even if that means not being with me.

I chose to give her the letter yesterday because we wouldn't have any classes together today. If she wanted to talk to me about it she had a choice. And honestly, I could use the extra day before the awkward hell of facing her. There is no way her reaction would be anything other than: "I like you as a friend."

Our lockers are on opposite ends of the floor, but we usually see each other in passing a couple of times a day. Usually she waves and smiles, but has her friends flanking her on either side, like some sort of high school popularity guard. So while I might not have to sit with her for an hour, it's not likely that I will get through today without running into her.

As I rummage through my locker, the bell rings for second period. I make my way down the hall, and spot her walking in the opposite direction from the other end. We lock eyes and I swear I am going to hurl.

But before we can get close enough to say anything, Mrs. Strumbull, the principal, taps her on the shoulder. Mia turns around and follows her down another hallway, out of sight.

I don't see her for the rest of the day, and I wonder what would have happened if she wasn't called over. Would she have smiled? Spoken to me about it? Pretended it never happened?

It's pointless to guess. Tomorrow, we'll have to present our final project and have no choice but to talk.

I open my locker to grab some stuff before going home and a letter falls to the floor. I look around, to see if anyone is watching, but the hallway swirls with people going about their own business.

I carefully open the letter, which is written in Mia's handwriting, using big circles to dot her "I"s.

Dear Sil,

Thank you for your letter. It was so beautiful. I like you too. Ever since we started this project together, you are the only person I think about. Getting to know you this semester has been amazing. But, I'm with Tripp, so I would like to see you in private. Please keep this a secret and don't tell anyone. It's the only way this could work for now.

I want to meet you tonight at the old boathouse at 8pm. Please come alone. Bring swim trunks in case we decide to go for a dip. <3

Love,
Mia

I hide a smile as I fold the paper and shove it into my pocket, and gently shut my locker, like someone might notice my excitement if I close it too hard. This cannot be happening.

Girls like Mia don't like poor, skinny pieces of shit like me. But maybe that's not true, maybe there are people who see past the obvious, and are attracted to the good in others. Maybe I have finally caught a break.

I shoot another quick glance around and run out to meet Jude in front of school.

14 Years Earlier

As soon as I walk into Mrs. Strumbull's office and see my dad standing there, I know. The look in his eyes, like they each weigh hundreds of pounds, makes me so sad for him. I know dealing the loss of his wife is hard enough, but on top of that, he has to tell his daughter that her mother is gone.

"Dad?" I ask, my eyes welling up to the brim, my voice clogged with unshed tears. I don't even say the words. We've known this day was coming, but she seemed to be getting better again. I hold onto that last sliver of hope that maybe she's just in bad shape, and I still have a chance to say good bye.

"Mia, baby girl—" he chokes up. And I know there is no hope, that I'll never get to hold her warm hand again, or read to her, or hear her laughter as she tells me to stop warming my icy feet under her butt. "Mommy had a heart attack. She just got too weak from the cancer, she couldn't fight back."

I knew this day would happen, it had become clear my mother would never be cured, but like magic, every day she was still there. She would get sick and come back, and I guess stupidly, I thought she would keep fighting for me. I thought maybe she could will herself to live so I wouldn't have to be without her.

I try to stay stoic when I hear the news. All this time, I didn't want anyone to pity me. I never really talked to my friends about it. My dad was so stressed with work and my mom, that I didn't want to make him worry about me. And my mom, I cried once in her arms when she first told me she was sick, but after that, we tried to make all of our memories happy. We would go to the park on our bicycles, and then when she got sicker, we would take short walks and have pizza and movie nights. Eventually, when she couldn't walk anymore, I would read love stories to her. Sometimes they had happy endings, sometimes they were tragic.

Today I am living in one of those tragic books. There is no sunlight even though the sun burns bright, there is no laughter even though the hall is full of silly teenagers. There is a hole. It's a hole that can never be replaced. No one will be as wonderful and special as my mother. No one else stayed up with me at night when I was sick, no one else made my Halloween costume from scratch so that I was the coolest kid in town, no one else kissed my ouchies and made the pain disappear. No one made the best spaghetti bake in the universe because she made it with her special ingredient: love. Her love was gone. Yes, I still lived with it in my heart, but I would never feel it in her hug, I would never hear it in her words. She doesn't exist. It's so final. Nothing in life should ever be so final.

She's too young to be gone. It's not fair. Who will help me pick my dress for prom, or help me plan my wedding? It's not fair. She was too good to die.

I don't even realize I am collapsing until I my dad catches me in his arms. I sob uncontrollably as he whispers in my ear, "We're gonna be okay baby girl. I'm gonna take care of you. Daddy loves you."

CHAPTER TWENTY-EIGHT

Tax

I wake up to the sound of Mia fumbling out of bed. I look up at her, and her hair is a mess, her face swollen with sleep. It's clear she's not a morning person, which only makes me more of an asshole for requiring her to meet me for weekly fuck sessions at five in the morning. It's good to know I wasn't the only one struggling to get out of bed.

I glance over to the clock on the nightstand. It's almost 7:30. My sadistic side relishes in watching her scramble through her luggage.

"In a rush?" I ask, my head propped on my hand.

"Jesus! You scared the bejesus out of me!"

I watch her, while I battle with the fact that I just spent the night in bed with a woman I have spent the last ten years of my life plotting to kill. She's so harmless...but she's not. She's got me by the balls already and she doesn't even know it. There is power in her kindness and warmth. If she was a cold bitch, she'd be dead by now, but her vulnerability has been an impenetrable shield.

After talking to Rex, his words were like the gentle breeze that pushed my teetering body off of the ledge. After I swapped out the pills, I needed to get to work impregnating her anyway. But that reason is bullshit, it justifies me being here in the framework of "the plan," but I am here because I want to be here. I want to fuck Mia, to see her, to know her.

"I have to be downstairs by eight," she says, hopping over the clothes she tore out of her luggage on her way to the shower.

"It's not looking good."

"Thanks for the encouragement!" she calls out, disappearing into the bathroom.

For a moment there, it felt like we were a normal couple, that I don't constantly battle with wanting to punish her and fuck her. Or fight a battle more terrifying: wanting to punish her or wanting to spend time with her.

I sit up and crack my neck, grab the hotel room phone, and call room service. "Hi, bring up whatever breakfast food you can as quickly as you can. I have someone who needs to be somewhere in fifteen minutes. Thank you."

I walk past her things scattered on a table in the bedroom and my eyes catch her disc of birth control pills...Correction: placebo pills.

I am so fucked up. Such a piece of shit.

I am doing this for her. I can't live with Jude never getting her payback. I am responsible for who she is today. I made a vow to Jude. Even if I could break my promise, Jude would never accept it. The only way for Mia to be safe outside of getting her pregnant is to kill Jude. And that's not going to happen. There is only one thing that can make Jude look past the wrath she feels, the one thing she has fixated on all these years: a child.

Jude is infertile, due to massive internal injuries she suffered, and she always wanted a child in our family. Our family is just her and me, and so that leaves me having a kid to fulfill this fucking obsession of hers. I never had an interest in having children and it broke Jude's heart. It was like she was losing the ability to have children twice. We are fraternal twins, but she always considered us half of a whole, one complete person. And so, she would love my kids as if she had given birth to them. They would replace the rage her barrenness has left behind.

No matter how she begged, I refused her that. I could kill in the name of this debt, but I wouldn't bring a life into it. I never met a woman who I wanted to have my children and I never felt the yearning to be a father. The word "father" was like a curse word to me. I hated my own dad. I don't just mean that in the way most bitter children of asshole parents do. My dad hated us and we hated him back. Usually you learn how to love from your parents, I learned how to loathe. He taught me so well, in fact, that I killed him. Oh yeah, he owed us too. He was just as guilty as all of those other fuckers. Some could argue he was the most guilty, because he had an obligation to protect us. But he chose booze, and money for a lifetime of more booze, over his own fucking kids. *Father*, that word makes bile rise up my throat. Why would I want to be a *father*?

No woman ever meant anything to me, other than Jude, and that's different because she's my sister. I could never bond with a woman emotionally. It's as though a fuse was blown somewhere inside of me. I could fuck them, I could make them fall in love with me, but I could never return anything other than indifference.

When I had to fuck Tripp's mom for two agonizing years, I might as well have been fucking a waterbed. I didn't even care enough to dislike her, though fucking her was as about an unpleasant act as I could think of. Patiently seducing her was so much harder than killing people. Good thing it was the most lucrative of all debts we collected. Hundreds of millions when all of the factories and properties were sold.

That's what fucked me up about Mia. It wasn't just that the sex was great — I've had my share of beautiful women. No, it was what I felt during it...well, more that I felt anything at all. The fact that once I busted my nut, I still thought about her. She even tastes different, like her body chemistry draws me to her.

So, if there is any woman in the world who I would want to have my baby, it would be Mia. And I am lying to her so that she can finally be safe. I warned her, that no matter what would happen, I would hurt her. It's all I am good for. There is no way this ends without Mia getting hurt, but I can do everything in my power to lessen the pain. An unplanned pregnancy is far better than death.

Jude won't hurt the woman who is having my child. And she won't want that child to lose its mother the way that we lost ours. I know Jude well enough to know that. Children are her soft spot. My child is the only solution that will dilute her potent rage.

After a few minutes, there is a knock on the door. I throw on some boxer briefs and accept the room service, pouring myself a coffee and putting some in a to go cup for Mia. *See?* I can be nice when I am not focused on a 14-year vendetta.

Mia stomps out into the living area, stopping in her tracks when she sees the breakfast spread. She's wearing a white flowing sundress. It makes her look so pure, and I want to filthy her up while she wears it.

"Did you order all that?"

"Yes, I figured you might not have time to eat otherwise."

"Wow, thank you..." she says skeptically. I don't blame her, I've poisoned people before.

"Here, I don't know how you take it, so it's black," I say, handing her a to-go cup filled with coffee. I catch her give me the once over, and she so subtly bites the inside of her lip. I'm not going to lie and say I don't love the fact that she's as attracted to me as I am to her.

"Thanks again. Sorry, you have to forgive me, this is so...different."

"I got you some breakfast. I'm not Prince Charming."

"Still very much appreciated." Her phone chimes. "Shit, I gotta go."

"I'll see you for lunch."

Her eyes brighten, but then she sighs. "I can't keep stealing away. They're not idiots. They are going to get suspicious. Laney has already texted me three times about last night."

How cute...she thinks I take no for an answer. *How cute?* Fuuuuuck, I need to go wrestle a rabid bear or some shit.

"I'll see you for lunch. In fact, let your staff do the work. You aren't a Director of Operations anymore, you are the fucking President. You're taking the afternoon off. Don't forget, I still own your ass."

Yes, I am prick for bringing up the leverage, but I know it gets her wet when I exert power over her. So, yin yang or some shit.

"Fine! I'll see you later," she says, shoving a banana in her mouth. *Instant erection*. Mia snatches a bagel and heads for the door. Then she skids to a stop, turns, runs towards me and plants a kiss on my lips. She stuffs the bagel in her mouth and says "buuhhyeee," and disappears out the door. I kind of stand there like a stunned jackass. The things I have done to this woman, and it's a peck on the lips that makes me freeze.

I stare at the door for a while, and then realize I am smiling. In fact, I have been smiling since I woke up this morning.

Mia

I don't know what's gotten into Tax, but I like it. The coffee, I keep inhaling its scent, it smells like the best coffee ever because he poured it for me. This dry-ass bagel tastes like the most doughy piece of deliciousness because he ordered it for me.

Is it safe for me to put my guard down? For me to at least expect that he'll still be here later like he said he would? There is so much progress that needs to be made, but last night was a different Tax. He was still fierce, but fierce with desire, not just contempt.

I can tell his heart is heavy with some sort of inner battle. I don't have the slightest idea of what that could be. For all of the emotion I have wrapped up in this man, I still know almost nothing about him.

I know he has a step brother named Rex. His parents are dead. He owns Draconi Corp and thus, Alea. He fucks like a sexual demon. He thinks I owe him. Yup, that's about it!

Am I crazy? Has something snapped in my brain? How can I feel safe around this man? Why would I want to pursue anything deeper with someone who came into my life by sneaking into my house under the guise of a rape-for-hire prostitute?

But my heart doesn't give a shit of what my mind has to say. She wants what she wants. For all of the mystery that shrouds Tax, I live when I am with him. Everything is more potent. Colors are more vivid, food more savory, scents more aromatic. If I can just get him to trust me, then we can evolve.

I'm not an idiot. The scars on his body, the rage that always bubbles underneath the surface: I know there is a demon shrouded in a beautiful shell. Tax promises he will hurt me. Being with him is like mounting a phoenix, I can only hold on for so long before I am incinerated.

But, there is something I think we both realized last night. Neither one of us has a choice. When we are together the energy is cosmic: when we are apart all we can think about is the next time we will meet. Whatever will happen between us is inevitable. All I can do is brace for our impact.

I enter the convention hall, and though sex is on the menu, the energy in the room is almost silly: silicone-implanted porn stars pose with fans, bright booths show off the latest gadgets, men walk around in assless chaps. Yup, this small-town girl from Iowa has made a life for herself in this world.

I find the Alea booth, and I gleam with pride, admiring the modern metals against teals, pinks, and purples. Our models, all named after Greek goddesses, stand triumphantly in display cases. Thanks to Tax, I will never look at some of those models the same way again.

"Mia!" Laney calls out excitedly.

"Hey, this all looks great."

"I got worried when you never came back last night. You said the meeting was serious. Is everything okay with Alea?"

"Oh, yes. Sorry, I didn't mean to worry you. Mr. Draconi apparently came down because he wants to take a more active role with the company and of course he's springing all these meetings on me now. He can be really demanding. So I am going to have to have you steer the ship while I am gone this afternoon."

"Well, lucky you," she says with a smirk.

Shit. "I'm not catching what you're throwing."

"Are you blind? I'll admit I was a little thrown off when he came over, but how can that guy be the owner? I love Dewey, but Dewey was like a dad. Mr. Draconi..." she shudders.

"Yes, Laney, he is very good looking."

"Is he married?"

Step back, Laney. "No, but even though we don't have an official policy, fraternizing with owners is something Alea looks down upon."

Laney's eyes flare up, remembering that despite our casual friendship, I am now the President of Alea. "Well, of course Mia! I just wanted to know who the lucky beyotch was."

I smile a little on the inside. "Not sure, he's very private." *Don't I know it.*

The day seems to drag on as I chat with potential distributors, passersby, and the usual ilk that attend these events.

Just before noon, Tax texts me.

Meet me out front. You're done for the day.

I let Laney know I have meetings with Draconi Corp for the rest of the afternoon and to call me if she needs anything. I'm not being irresponsible, right? I'm delegating!

As soon as I step outside, the humid Miami air latches onto my body, making it glow with a thin layer of perspiration. I shield my eyes from the sun to search for Tax when a hand lands on my lower back.

"Oh, hi!" I say, trying to contain the shivers that his touch ignites.

"How was the dildo convention this morning?" He asks so seriously, that I burst into laughter.

"Please stop calling it that. I can't even take my life seriously when you call it that."

"Mia, I bought a sex toy company so I could be close to you. If there is anyone who shouldn't take themselves seriously, it should be me."

Those words should terrify me, but instead they shoots fireworks down my belly. To have anyone give you that much importance, good or bad, is thrilling.

"The place is just a short walk away," Tax says, pushing back a loose tendril of my hair. I fidget nervously and scan the perimeter to make sure no one I know sees us.

"My ponytail is a mess," I say.

"I like the purple." He smirks. "I also like when you leave it out. Only for me though." He runs a finger across the back of my neck.

This man.

"It's possible I am hungry for something other than food now," I say breathlessly.

"Aren't you always?" he whispers.

"Only for you." My spine shudders, realizing those are his words, and like everything else about him, they have gotten under my skin.

His lips graze my neck as he leans in. "Oooh, now I know you are trying to get fucked. But you have to know by now, I like to make you suffer for it. So you're going to wait a little longer before I give you my cock, Mia." Dear god, the way he says my name, he purrs it like a lion.

"You're going to kill me one day," I confess.

He stiffens, grabbing his phone to check for the time. The mood becomes heavier. "We should go."

It is sweltering today, and the breeze off of the coast is only a fleeting respite from the unrelenting moisture in the air. Even Tax, who is usually suited up, is dressed down in a pair of ivory pants and a relaxed navy tank that highlights his shoulders, pecs, and of course, his colorful neck.

Within minutes, we are walking down a dock, greeted by a man dressed just like you'd expect a ship captain to dress: in a crisp white uniform and a cap.

"Mr. Draconi, good afternoon."

"Afternoon," Tax replies, stepping aside so I can board the yacht first. I am dumbfounded. I thought we would go to a cafe or something.

Self-preservation instincts kick in. I don't really know this man. From this point, he could take me to any Caribbean island. He could leave me in the ocean. But as I have done thus far with any ounce of rationality, I ignore it in favor of the more powerful instinct that tells me to keep grasping for more. To follow this man into the depths of hell.

Tax leads me to an expansive deck. Beverages are stocked, and several picnic baskets wait for us.

"Tax, a yacht?" I scold. "This is too much."

"We're in Miami. How often do you get to enjoy the ocean? Besides, I can't fucking stand the people here, I prefer the solace of a boat. Trust me, it doesn't take much effort to put in a phone call and reserve a yacht. Think of it as a floating cafe."

There he goes, minimizing his gesture. It's his way of reminding me not to read too much into his kindness.

We pull out the food from the picnic basket and I take in a few bites, but being out here with him on these sparkling waters distracts me from my hunger.

"Are you done?" he asks, after I stop eating.

"Yes, it's good, I'm just not very hungr—"

"Take off your clothes."

"Sorry, what?"

"Mia, just because some things are changing, doesn't mean everything does."

My gut flinches at those words. He still owns me. He can choose to be nice, he can choose to stick around when he's done, but he still has my reputation in his hands. Though at this point, I wonder if he would even ruin me if I challenged him. I just don't see why he would do that after last night. There are moments of rawness between us, where we expose parts of each other no one else sees. I feel that he cares about me. Would he really want to destroy me?

"No," I say.

"Mia, don't make me regret my kindness."

"There is another man on this boat."

"He's at the helm, he won't be out here."

"And if I still say no?"

Tax's jaw muscles undulate as he grinds his teeth.

"It's nice to see someone love their career the way you love yours. I don't want to be the one to make that all go away. Now don't make me repeat myself."

"After all this, you would still do that to me?"

"Right now, doing this to you is what's keeping you safe."

I don't understand. I am so sick of his cryptic threats and unknown debts. I never felt like my life was in danger up until last night, I only thought my dignity was at stake. But this is the second time he has mentioned my safety, and somehow I do believe that this man who I thought was my greatest threat, might actually be protecting me in a way I don't understand.

"I doubt making me your sex slave is keeping you safe."

"Don't," he says, rising to his feet. His patience evaporates. "Mia, I give you just a little bit of anything other than my anger, and you start to become defiant. I cannot have that. Don't make me regret coming out here. If you want me to go back to my old ways, I can do it in a heartbeat. Don't for a second believe I can't shut this shit down. You don't know what I am capable of."

I choke back tears of disappointment. If I had just taken off my clothes, things would not have gotten to this. Lord knows I wanted to, but I had to challenge him. He's right, I began to feel confident in my place with him, but Tax does the ordering and he doesn't take kindly to defiance.

"Now take the dress off or I will fucking rip it off myself."

The boat stops to anchor, the humming of the motor dies and there is only the gentle lapping of waves against the boat.

The light ocean breeze licks against my skin, but not as powerfully as when the boat was moving. The humidity and sun begins to claw at my flesh again, covering me in a glistening veil of perspiration. I look at Tax through fierce eyes, like I could stab him right now, but inside, my body responds to his harshness. I want all of Tax, his ferociousness, his forcefulness, but I must have the other part. The part that wants more. I can't live with myself if I give in to a man who despises me, and uses sex only to hurt me. But if I know he cares, if there is more, this interaction is something else entirely. I like the violence, the abandon, but I need to know he won't leave me or hurt me every time we're done.

"You're just going to keep using me and leave me. That's what this is all about. I am a person, Tax. I have feelings. You can't treat me like this."

He lets out a deep sigh. "Mia, don't do that."

"I thought you wanted more."

"I do. Don't you?"

"Yes, but—"

"Then do as I fucking say."

I slowly slide off each strap of my dress, and let it collapse to the deck. Underneath the dress, I have on a white bra and cotton bikini briefs.

"White cotton panties?" he asks. Usually I wear lacy thongs.

"This dress has a tendency to kick up in the wind, so I'm just trying to cover up."

He grins subtly. "I like it. There's an innocence about it." I look down. Yesterday we were flesh to flesh, but today, we are back to me being stripped alone. "Your bra. I want to see your tits."

I unclip, my eyes darting past his shoulders to make sure the captain isn't around, but he hasn't made an appearance since he greeted us.

The sun heats my breasts as I let my bra drop to the floor. Tax lets out a hushed groan. His shorts expand underneath his waistline and he rubs a hand against the bulge.

"Let your hair down."

I grab the elastic and tug until my hair falls down my shoulders and back. I slide my thumbs into the waistband of my panties.

"No. Keep those."

He walks over to me, and slides his fingers through my hair. Suddenly, he is softly pelting one side, then the other. I haven't worn my hair into two braids like this since high school. My white panties dampen in reaction to his mixture of force and tenderness.

"Mia, you need to understand there are things about me that will never change. This being one of them." He doesn't have to specify what he means. I'd be a fool to think this beast of a man would ever lose that ferocity.

"That can be a good thing," I say.

He cocks his eyebrow.

"Tax, I told you I was looking for something. This is what I was looking for."

"Then why do you fight me? Cry? Why do you keep trying to see past this?"

"Because I want all of you, not just this. I fight you because I am fighting myself. Because I have always felt wrong for wanting these things, but you allow me to have these things without the culpability. If I always give in, if I don't fight, then that means it's all me. It means I am sick."

He runs a fingertip along the wet spot of my underwear. "You're not sick, Mia. You're the most alive you've ever been." The spot expands underneath his touch.

"I am understanding that now. I don't need you to blackmail me. I'd willingly give it to you, can't you fucking see that? But I need you to allow me to trust you. That means you can't just vanish when we're done. I know that you came here for me, that you spent the night, but I feel like once we get back, it'll happen all over again. Most of all, you threatening to expose my secrets doesn't make me feel secure or safe with you. I don't even know where you live. You can just decide to up and leave forever, you could still expose me after all this, and when you're done with me, and I'll just be broken."

"I keep my word. I would never go back on what I promised."

"Why should I have any reason to believe you?"

"Because I am here now, because I came here for you."

"And yet you hold threats over my head. I think you're afraid too."

"I'm not afraid of anything."

"Then why do you keep pulling away when I get close?"

His eyes shift away from mine.

"You have all the power. You know everything about me and I know nothing about you. If you're afraid of letting me in, can you imagine how I must feel? You came into my life, crashing like a meteor, and if you just leave me like that...I'll never be the same. I want to know that you'd fucking care if I died tomorrow. Because sometimes it feels like you could dispose of me at any moment. Like you could replace me in an instant. I like what we do, but what we do outside of that matters just as much. Let me do it willingly. Don't blackmail me. It's the difference between you being my lover and you being my..." I hesitate to say the word that has lingered in the air since we first met. "Rapist."

"Don't you ever fucking call me that," he snaps with fire in his eyes, darting his finger at me. "You always had a fucking choice. You begged me to fuck you the very first night." He circles away from me in anger.

"I didn't mean it. I mean, I don't want to mean it. But that means you have to show me otherwise. There's a reason you just snapped at that word, because when you are forced to face things you lash out. Clearly what I said resonates, otherwise you wouldn't have just gotten so angry."

"Mia, you have no fucking idea what you are talking about." The veins in his forearms bulge as he tenses his fists. "You have no idea what that word means to me."

"Then tell me."

His lips form a tense line, as if his life story would explode out of him if he were to relax them. His chest sinks with a slow exhale.

"Don't ever call me that again." His tone is still firm, but there's something softer underneath. It's almost as if he's asking instead of telling.

I soften my voice to a plead. "As long as you threaten me, then none of this is real. How can we trust each other's feelings? If you stop holding the video over my head, then you can trust I am with you genuinely, and I can trust that you aren't just here to hurt me. I want to know this is real. I'm just trying to say, I'm afraid you'll leave. No one else is like you, Tax."

I reach out to touch him, and he grabs my wrist, pulling me in close. "Mia, I'm not going anywhere. But I need you to promise me the same. I mean it when I say that this is to protect you. I don't want to hold anything over your head. There was a time when I relished the thought of humiliating you in that way. Not anymore. But I will do it if I have to. Only if I have to. For you."

"Tax, you never did," I say. He had me all along. If he had walked into that conference room without that recording, without his threats, it would only have been a matter of time before I was naked in front of him anyway. He bewitches me with his powerful aura. I would have fallen into his arms in spite of myself, no matter what. He had me the second I smelled his scent, felt his chest press against my back in my kitchen. The rest is just pretense.

"No one is like you, Mia. No one," he says, passionately colliding his lips against mine, biting my bottom lip painfully. My hips press against his forceful touch. "I don't know how to fucking do this. Don't you see that? I don't know how to be with someone. Maybe you should leave. I can put up the video and then this will all be over. You can start over somewhere far away. I'll let you start over." He says it the way two young lovers muse when they fantasize about running away together, knowing it's an impossibility.

"I don't want to start over. I like my life. And I won't go anywhere without you," I vow.

Tax

I look down on Mia's face, resting in my lap. Her dark hair is still in messy braids, like she so often used to wear them when I knew her in a past life. Her skin glistens with a golden hue under the afternoon sun. Her breasts lie beautifully on her chest, her bare pussy still glistens from our sex. She lies here in the vulnerability of sleep, trusting that I will keep her safe from an unknown fate.

I wish I had the strength to let her go, but every time I try, she begs, and I can't resist her. I should put out the tape, ruin her career and life. Then I can work to convince Jude that's payment enough. But I know Jude, that won't suffice. Just like Tripp's injury wasn't enough. It's either death or life. I choose life. Then I can finally have my sister back and keep Mia too.

Mia is not the person who hurt me years ago, just like I am not that kid who was a constant victim of circumstances. I am beginning to believe Mia never truly meant to hurt me. Maybe she thought it would be a silly prank, or she felt the need to protect her friendships. Perhaps she was scared of Tripp. She deserves to pay, but not with death. Killing her would only be punishing myself. For the first time, I can see a future beyond the vendetta. Jude can have everything she wants, but she can't have Mia. She can choose to accept the gift I will bring into this world with Mia, or she can go to hell.

CHAPTER TWENTY-NINE

Mia

Someone should nominate me for worst new corporate president of the year. Tax chartered the yacht for the entire weekend. We went to the Bahamas. Yeah. Did you know you can do that? Just hop on a boat and go to the Bahamas? Well, now you do. It was a weekend full of insatiable sexual appetites, amazing food, and lots of sleeping.

If Laney was suspicious, she hid her suspicions well and happily took on the added responsibility of representing Alea at the conference. I told her Draconi wanted to fly me out to talk about some long term plans for the company, but not to worry as this was a good sign. The truth is, the only Alea talk that happened is when Tax had me demonstrate the rest of the product line.

But now I am back, away from the fantasy world of an impromptu vacation. Things are already different though. As a matter of fact, I am sitting in Tax's penthouse condo, to which he invited me over for dinner before heading back home to face another workweek.

The sweeping open space is completely surrounded by floor to ceiling windows, with endless views of Lake Michigan and downtown Milwaukee. I look far out into the distance as the sunset glows around the Calatrava Pavilion of the art museum. Its white wings look majestic as dusk falls.

The condo wafts with the smell of garlic, olive oil, and roasted tomatoes.

"Are you sure you don't need help?" I ask.

"Nope. You'd probably fuck it up. It's not a frozen pizza," he calls from the other side of his enormous living space.

"That's not fair. Pizza is Italian too."

Frozen pizza is something I ate quite a bit after my mother died. My father tried, bless his soul, but I could not stomach his culinary efforts. It's still something I stock in my fridge regularly, as it's always been a habit to pop one in when I have guests over. I wonder if he knows that about me from that one time I tried to make one for us and he bailed, of if it's just one of the many things he knows from spying on me.

I make my way over to the open kitchen, a chef's dream with huge grey caeserstone countertops, various stainless steel sinks, and two commercial ranges with ovens. *I bet those ovens would make some kick-ass frozen pizza.*

"By the way, I DO know how to cook. I am just usually so busy with work."

I observe Tax as he chops up fresh herbs in a white t-shirt and grey sweatpants. I am standing on the side of his neck tattoo and it's hard not to bite it. There's something so hot about watching this man stand over a steaming skillet, intently prepping food in his casually sexy getup.

My eyes scan the modern minimalist apartment, and I notice something. For one, he has a ton of books. An entire wall is dedicated to a floor to ceiling bookshelf, brimming with books. The apartment is minimalist and spotless, except for the bookshelf, which is spilling over. It's clear they aren't just there for show, that he pulls books out regularly. It adds a human touch to the monotone and linear theme of his condo.

And I notice something else: There are no pictures. Not a single one, of himself or anyone else.

"So...Rex?"

His rhythmic chopping stops. "Yes? What about him?"

"He's your brother."

"I think we went over this already, or were you too drunk to remember?" he asks, snidely. By the way, I have picked up on this in the months since we have met: His humor is drier than the Sahara. I can pick up on the almost imperceptible changes in his tone that are the difference between a literal statement and a joke, but others might think he's just being a blunt jerk. And he is blunt, but that's part of his humor. I enjoy it. I like people who don't bullshit.

I roll my eyes at him. "No, I was not too drunk. He's obviously not a blood relative. You mentioned your parents are gone. How are you two related?"

I watch Tax make a series of mental calculations before he says anything. I expect him to dodge my question. He is giving me more of his time and attention. But as far as information about who he is, he has still been very greedy.

"We met on the street," he says, clearing his throat.

"The street?" I ask, looking around at the very expensive habitat. "You hung out on the street?"

"I lived on the street."

"Oh..." I say. I know he doesn't want my pity. It's probably why he is reluctant to mention it. "So you don't have parents in common, it's more like you're brothers because you are so close?"

He keeps his face down and ahead at the chopping board, but his eyes dart over to me a few times. "Yup, exactly like that."

"That must be nice, having someone you can be that close with. I'm an only child. My mother had me when she was young and she always promised me a sibling, but then she got sick."

"I know." Tax says it with the softness of understanding. I tell him snippets of my life all the time, forgetting I am likely telling him things he already knows. He looks up at me. "I didn't mean it's less important since you are telling me what I already know. Just that I understand. Losing people."

"Oh, I know you didn't mean it that way," I say. "You mean your parents?"

"Yeah. I lost my mother when I was young too. My dad died when I was older."

"I'm sorry to hear that," I say, kissing his neck. The softest peck of my lips makes his entire body flinch with discomfort. *I can't receive love.* I remember the words he told me after he first showed me his scars.

"Tax, I won't be mad, I just want to know...did you plant Rex into Tiff's life?"

This time he doesn't take nearly as long to think about his response.

"Yes, I did. But Rex is a good guy. He likes Tiff. He considers her a friend. Just because he was put there doesn't mean he doesn't care. We're all put into situations that we have to make do with."

DEBT

I take a deep breath, still trying to wrap my mind around the level of surveillance my life has been under.

"Rex likes you too Mia. He's the reason I ended up in Miami. He gave me some brotherly advice."

"Oh, wow. I didn't even know there were forces like that working in my life," I say.

"Mia, everyone who meets you falls in love with you." I watch Tax's eyes as they jump, realizing in an indirect way he just said that he's falling in love with me.

"Oh, I don't think you had those feelings when you met me," I joke, getting him out of his mental corner. "You hated me."

"Hate is a feeling." My words coming out of his mouth. I get under his skin too.

"So Rex is your only sibling?"

"I have a younger sister too. We aren't very close," he says.

"What's her name?"

"Judith Ann."

His responses are choppier when he speaks of her.

"Well, you have made quite the life for yourself," I say. "This is incredible. I am sure your mother would be proud." He slides the herbs from the cutting board onto a skillet. The skillet sizzles and pops as a billow of steam rises from the pan.

"I like this," I say, wrapping my arms around him from behind, taking in a deep breath of his smell, his warmth. "Learning about you."

"Mia..." he says, hesitantly, like he is bracing us both for a rejection. "Can you grab the white wine from the fridge?"

My heart sinks, he's asking me to let go of him, but he's just doing it in a less brutish way. It doesn't hurt any less.

"Sure," I say, sliding my arms away from his tense torso. I understand just that small conversation, that opening up his life, his family, is a leap for him. The very act of showing me his home is saying to me: *I'm staying, Mia. I won't vanish.*

I can't expect everything to pour out of him at once.

Within minutes the pasta, colorfully flecked with fresh herbs and vegetables, makes its way onto two plates. He pulls out the crackling golden Chilean sea bass from the oven and places a fillet on each plate.

We sit out on his expansive deck, with views of the lake twinkling underneath the moon, white sailboats perched along docks, and little orange and red glowing lights as vehicles cruise along Lincoln Memorial Drive.

"Thank you, this is amazing. I never would have thought you could cook like this."

"I'm not sure if that's a compliment," he says with a half a smile. Oh how I love when he shares his smile.

We eat in peaceful silence. For the first time, I believe Tax. He won't leave me. As unconventional as we may be, he won't just use me and discard me.

Tax

In This Moment – Sick Like Me

Contrary to what Rex might tell you, I do work. You just don't sit on hundreds of millions of dollars. You manage it, you grow it, you invest it. And I tried really hard to work today, but my mind is restless. I made promises this weekend, and I keep my promises. And now, all I can think about is how I can keep them all. I believe I have it figured out, but until *Plan C* is complete, I will be on edge.

I haven't spoken to Jude since she gave me her keys. We'll make up, we always do. I just need time, and I'm glad she's giving it to me. Hopefully she's thinking about what I said to her. I know my change of heart appears self-serving, and it is, but I do want my sister to build her own life. This past decade we concocted plans so complicated and risky, that it seemed like our mission of payback would never end. Well, the end is near, and I think Jude and I have different ideas about where to go from there.

My dominion over Mia has shifted from one of destruction to one of guardianship. She is willingly giving herself to me, and now I must make sure nothing happens to her under my watch. I have become her dark knight.

Mia's not trying to change me, and that is what is so incredible about her. In fact, she wants all of me as I am. I have never had that with a woman before. I have only used fragments of my identity to achieve my goal: sex, money, or domination. But Mia craves that dark side of me, a carnal side that devours as it fucks. And yet, she brings out a side of me that wants to safeguard, to share, to express. The more I do of the latter, the more she craves the former. The shadows cannot exist without the light. For fourteen years I have only lurked in the pitch black corners of my psyche. Mia pulls me out even if it's just to peer out of the dark and remember what it was like to bask in the glow of something good. And Mia gets to peer into her own dark corners with me. For so long, I kept to one end of that dichotomy, not allowing myself the full spectrum of heat that comes with someone who makes you feel safe enough to become truly dangerous.

Mia's affection doesn't change that I am a psychopath, but it gives my urges a purpose, a way to be productive, not just destructive. For the first time I have met someone who makes me want to be uncomfortable. It's hard for me to care about anyone enough to put myself in the unsettling position of growth.

In Jude's defense, all of my accusations towards Jude were just as much about me. We have the money, the satisfaction of revenge. And then what? None of us are even thirty yet. I couldn't just dissolve into everyday life. My life is revenge. My life is rage. I had nothing to look forward to. But now, for me, it's Mia. She has given me something to see beyond the singular goal of vengeance. When she has my child, she may ironically be the key to helping heal Jude. I can grow past this, become something more than a murderous con artist. She is a miracle: loving enough to care for an asshole like me, and yet she has dark urges of her own.

It's come full circle: the girl who set me on the path of destruction can be my redemption.

I wait in the darkness of Mia's living room. Some things won't ever change. She's been away at work all day, and the distance makes me crave her, and the cravings morph into something dark when she's not around to temper them right away. She was looking for this. She was desperate for it when I found her.

When I think about Mia, I start to feel something warm, and it makes me angry when she makes me feel. So I have to put that rage back onto her. Make her feel the helplessness I feel when I think of her and can't have her.

I know, I'm fucked up. There are times I can give it to her less than savagely, but there are days like this, when it builds up so quickly, like a flash flood, and I can only express it by tearing her to shreds.

Her keys jingle in the lock and I salivate, tasting her essence on my tongue, like a junkie about to get a fix. I rise to my feet and wait for her in the shadows. I want to feel her flinch in those first moments of panic, followed by her muscles melting in submission.

She sighs as she dumps her bag on the floor beside the entrance and kicks off her shoes. I inhale her flowery clean scent as she feels around for a light.

She turns on a small lamp that gives her just enough light to look at her phone and she types something, holding a small grin on her face.

My phone chimes seconds later. She whips her head around with a look of shock on her face and before she can let out a peep, I wrap my hand around her mouth.

"Shhhh...don't fight me," I whisper into her ear. *She melts.* My cock rages.

I slide my hand up her trembling stomach and squeeze her plump breast. "This is mine," I grunt. "Your cunt...is mine. I take it when I want. My perfect little slut."

She curves back into me, just like the first night I had her in this house. My dick pulses with need as I recall the images of my cock sliding into her pussy, like my own personal porn.

"I've been thinking about your pussy creaming around my cock all day."

I pull up her t-shirt, push her bra cups down and roughly twirl her nipples in my fingers. She lets out a deep sigh of relief. "I'm going to leave my marks on your tits tonight. So fucking round and pure. I need to ruin them. I want them to ache tomorrow. I want you feel my bites tomorrow and your pussy to cream when you remember how I'm about to fuck you."

"Tax..." she murmurs, rubbing her tight ass against my cock. It aches, pestering me to take quick relief in her mouth or pussy. But, I also take pleasure in drawing this out for her.

I whip her pants down and she groans from the burning friction. Her red thong screams *secret kinky whore* to me, and I slide my fat cock against the crease of her ass. If it was possible, I would put my dick in every single hole at once. I want to have every piece of her. My hips thrust against her ass, teasing her rear. I reach forward, exploring the creamy flesh.

"Fuck," she whispers. I slide in and then out, spreading her cream all over her pussy.

"You're always so ready for me," I say.

"Always," she whispers, craning her neck towards me. I reach up and slide her bun loose, her feminine hair unravelling along her soft skin.

My free hand grips a breast, the other hand fucks her, as I rub my cock against her supple ass. I grip her small frame tightly against me. If I squeezed hard enough, I could break her, ruin her. With such little work on my part, she cries out, convulsing in my arms. Her pussy soaks my hand. I love the way she comes, it sounds like she's crying.

"Your pussy is so fucking wet," I say, using her juice to slick my cock. "Mia, you've been teasing me all day and you don't even know it. It pisses me off to have to wait for you. And now you came too quickly, next time you need to wait."

I stroke my cock, layered with her wetness, against her ass until I have to stop lest I come before entering her.

"Lie on the floor." She bows in front of me and lies back, like a good girl.

I stand in front of her, pull off my shirt and kick off my pants and underwear, and her eyes flare with heat.

I roll the tip of my cock along her nipples, enjoying the look of surrender on her face as they harden.

A drop of pre-cum surfaces. "Lick."

She complies, running her sexy tongue at the tip of my head, taking in my taste. She licks her lips looking right into my eyes. *Fuuuuck.* She used to look away, full of shame, but I've trained her not to feel that. She loves being dirty for me, there's no shame in that.

I mount her, slapping my weighty cock against her entrance and clit, taunting her.

"Beg."

"Please fuck me, Tax," she groans.

That's all I need today. Shit, I am about two seconds from begging her my damned self. I plunge inside her pussy, the slick fleshiness is so tight, I roll my eyes back as my dick is overcome with sensation. Her fat tits beg to be brutalized, and I bite the pale flesh. Each of her gasps make my cock flicker with arousal.

She calls my name, her tone pleading for me to stop and continue. The way the smooth meat of her breast compacts under my teeth fills my blood with heat. I slap my pelvis against her, wanting to wound her with my cock.

"You're gonna feel me for days Mia. Whenever you shift in your seat, touch it to clean yourself, you are going to remember that I own your pussy. I own those fucking tits. It's my cum that fills you."

She calls out with abandon, her innocent face marred by the curse words that flow so effortlessly out of her flushed lips. I fucking love turning her into my filthy little whore. I thrust ragefully, her opening clenching around my swollen shaft with each exit and entry. I gnaw at her breasts, the flesh now covered in welts and teeth marks.

My instinct is to pull out and cum all over her tits, ruin them further with my cum, but *Plan C* is getting in the way of that. I'll have to save that for another time and enjoy the clench of her silky pussy around my cock.

She calls out for God, and I know she's close. I look down and watch my dick enter her over and over, and the way it glistens with her cream, thick from arousal. Being a voyeur to my cock plunging in her cunt, watching it bloom for me, like a pinkish flower, the swollen and battered lips receiving me so enthusiastically, takes me over the edge.

I grunt as I plunge into her as deeply as I can, my cock pulsating with violent pleasure, releasing into her pussy as its walls contract around me. I grip the rug underneath her, wanting to rip something to shreds as her pussy rips the cum out of my cock.

CHAPTER THIRTY

Tax

We lie on the floor on Mia's rumpled shag rug. This thing must have more bodily fluids on it at this point than a bed at the local Motel 9.

Mia traces her finger along my lips.

"You have the most amazing lips," she says in a woozy voice.

"So do you," I say, rubbing her soft pussy. "I think it's so fucking hot that you lie here with my cum still in you."

"I like having a some of you inside of me," she says with a smile. "I didn't expect you to visit tonight, but it was an awesome surprise, well, after the mini-coronary."

"My cock won't stop pestering me. It's really fucking annoying."

"I bet," she says lazily.

"I thought you liked the mini-coronaries."

"Oh, I do, Mr. Draconi. A rush like no other. Is it the same for you?"

I grin, thinking about the dark joy I feel in my sexual aggression. "I think the answer to that is obvious."

"Quite the match."

"Quite," I say, running my finger over a faint red mark on her breast. "How was work?" I ask. Usually as soon as I ask anyone that kind of question, I tune out, but I actually want to hear about her day. This whole giving a shit thing is so bizarre.

"It was good. Having Laney do a lot was a good idea. It helped me realize I need to delegate more or I'll end up burning out. Alea didn't go down in flames just because I stepped back for a bit. Dewey was good at that. He trusted us, so I am going to make sure I do the things I need to do and trust the staff enough not to meddle unless necessary."

"It sounds like you are getting the hang of it," I say. My original intention in purchasing Alea was to shut it down. I didn't care about the millions thrown away to do it. I considered it the purchase price for the satisfaction of destroying Mia's hard work. But now that I see a possible future with Mia, I want to see Alea succeed and grow with her as its leader. Strictly from a business standpoint, there is no one else I would want to run that company.

"Yeah, we even signed up a few new distributors at the convention. So that's makes the whole thing well worth it. More distribution, more profits." *Hell, that was kind of sexy, the way she purred that business jargon like a hot little shark.*

"I believe I made a wise investment."

"Yes you did, Tax. I may be a fuckup in my personal life, but if there is one thing I am great at, it's my job." *That's one thing we definitely have in common.*

"I don't believe I have told you this all the time we have been seeing each other, but that's something that impressed me about you. No matter what was happening, you were resilient.

You showed up to work every day and ran a multimillion dollar company. No one would have even noticed you might be going through something. That takes an enormous amount of poise."

"Wow...thank you. That means a lot to me."

She traces her finger down my torso, along my scars. *Blood. Boots. The stench of piss. Mocking laughter.* Anger towards Mia starts to form, and I thread her fingers in mine to divert her attention away from the rejection.

Eventually, I will have to tell her who I am. There is no way around it. I don't want to tell her, because I don't want to hate her. But when I think about that day, no matter who the Mia is in front of me now, no matter what her intentions might have been by setting me up, that dark hate, finely cultivated over fourteen years, petrified and dark, outweighs and overshadows anything good. I am afraid depending on her reaction, I may snap. I could lose it all. I wish I could go back and never mention the debt. I could have done this all without rubbing that in, and I could just be Tax Draconi, sadistic asshole turned not-as-sadistic asshole. But it's too late, she won't tolerate not knowing forever. Especially, if Plan C comes to fruition.

The only way I can enjoy Mia is not to think about that day, to think about her as a separate person than the one I have been scheming to torture and kill. But once I make it known to her who I am, and I remind her of what she did, I won't be able to shove that image of her into that dark crevasse of my memory. She will have to answer for it. The present Mia and the past Mia will become one and can never be separated again.

"Thank you, for taking care of Alea, babe," I say, trying to combat my own seething anger clawing its way through my chest.

"Mmmm, I love when you call me that. And I love the way you say my name when you're horny. *Miiia*," she says in a mock-husky voice. The boil turns to a simmer. *Just stay present*, I tell myself.

"I'm a fan of you saying my name when I'm fucking you. But, I think you already know that..."

"Oh yes, you make that abundantly clear you kinky bastard. And it's my pleasure to say it, Mr. Tax Draconi... Draconi? What is that?"

"Romanian."

"Romanian? How exotic! I am lying on the chest of a hot Romanian guy? Hmm..." She kisses my chest. "I knew someone who was Romanian..."

"Oh?"

"Yes, but I think he was only half, because his last name was boring. It was James I think."

She remembers.

"Doesn't sound Romanian to me."

"No, I think it was just his mom. His first name though...it was something more exotic...well it was Sil...but it was short for something. Sil...Silvo...Silvio! That's it: Silvio James. He always went by Sil though. We were lab partners."

I take a deep breath to keep cool. She doesn't sound like someone who holds any guilt for hurting Sil—me.

"Lab partners? Fucking nerd."

"Shut it. Yeah, well, we were becoming friends but...yeah now that I think about it, it was really weird. He just up and vanished one day."

"Vanished?" My tactic right now is to get her to confess, and the easiest way to do that is to let her keep talking. If she can show me true remorse, I can work with that.

"I'm remembering now...It was really weird. We had this huge project that took weeks to complete. He would come over a few nights a week, and we would work on the project and hang out. He was so thin and gangly. I don't think he realized, but I would see him sneaking extra food into his backpack in the cafeteria. He was poor and I think his father may have been abusive. My dad mentioned he had a drinking problem.

"So whenever he came over, I would always pretend I was hungry after school and make pizza, and give him tons of snacks. Then I would ask him to take the leftovers home, saying I didn't want them so he and his twin sister could have more to eat."

The revelation causes a sinking feeling in my chest. She always made me feel so comfortable that it never occurred to me, she was making food just to feed Jude and me. *Feelings. I hate when she makes me feel.*

"That was kind of you. You mentioned he vanished?"

"Well, the last time I saw him, he gave me what I think were lab notes. But I lost them like an idiot. I think they fell out of my pocket on the way home. Anyway, the next day was the day my mother died unexpectedly. Well, we knew she was sick, but I didn't get to say goodbye or anything. Actually I remember it vividly, because you don't forget those moments. I was walking down the hall, and I saw him in the distance. I was going to let him know that I lost the notes and apologize, but the principal called me into her office and my dad...he was in there with this look on his face...and I knew..." Her voice drifts as she relives that moment.

I remember her hidden fear, how she giggled with her friends, but when she and I were alone, there was an aura of sadness about her. She would try to have fun, dance, act silly because she didn't like to linger on the gloom. But she saw my sadness, and she felt safe sharing hers with me, even if it was only for brief moments.

"It was hard, my dad took me right out of school. Well, snuck me out so people wouldn't see me crying."

Oh fuck.

"So you never found those notes or whatever it was?"

"Nope and I felt so bad because he probably needed them back for the presentation. I didn't return for a week, leaving him to present the project alone. When I came back and tried to find him to apologize for leaving him stranded without the materials he needed, he was gone. My dad said his dad picked up and moved the family. That was that. I was kind of upset that he didn't say goodbye, but I felt silly, we only really knew each other for a few weeks. We hadn't so much as uttered a word to each other before becoming lab partners."

No. No. No.

"That's...a shame."

"Ya know, I wondered about him for a while. He was so different from everyone else. In our town there was a certain way you had to be, and if you fell out of that narrow box, then it was tough. Especially in high school. I guess I was lucky enough not to stand out, but I like interesting people from all walks of life. If you had looked at him, he might have been somewhat intimidating: gaunt, tall, long black hair, he wore a lot of black and chains. Sometimes he wore these terrifying contacts." She laughs to herself. "But as soon as I got to know him, he was a softie. I liked spending time with him. He exposed me to new things, and I liked that he didn't conform even though he was bullied. He was really smart too. He was a year below me, but was the same science class as me, which would have been two levels above his grade. So despite his circumstances at home, I am sure he's living a good life. Actually, that Radiohead cd I have up there, he gave it to me. He introduced me to a lot of music I would not have known of otherwise. I guess I learned from him how people can be so different from what they might appear to be on the outside. I didn't get a lot of exposure to diversity growing up."

I remain still, observing her voice for a hint of deceit, a hole in her story. There's nothing but innocent cluelessness.

It's hard not to lash out, not at her, but with a general sense of rage. I want to smash that fucking cd player, throw lamps, punch a wall. But I can't, I have to stay cool. She shouldn't have to see that, she's seen enough of my putrid hate.

This is a fuckup that cannot be made right. Even if I tell her everything now, how can I look her in the eye and tell her all this time, I have been blackmailing her for nothing? That I was so blinded by fury that I didn't consider the fact that her name was dragged into something she might never have been a part of? It was never virtuous of me to do what I did, but it was just. I thought eventually if she found out who we were she would understand. She might be angry, but she'd understand why Jude and I were so fucked up. I could try and rationalize with her. She'd understand why we felt she had to pay. Now there is no understanding. If I could bring Tripp back to life and kill him again right this second, I would. I bet that fucker is laughing in hell right now.

I am a killer. I planned to slit her throat with a serrated hunting knife. I dreamt about the look of terror in her eyes in her last few seconds of life as warm blood spurted from her neck. But like that stupid kid I once was, I got caught up in an illusion: that I am normal, that I can be with someone like Mia. In a way, Jude was right, I was allowing myself to get caught up in some sort of fantasy. Jude understands who I really am.

I am good for two things: scheming and fucking.

I was an idiot to think Mia would ever want anything more once she learns the truth. She'll hate my fucking guts. Even the "truth" I planned to tell her would have to be a lie. I was never going to tell her about my plan to kill her, swapping out her birth control, and the one thing above all that she could never look past. If I told her that, she would want me dead.

There is no debt to be paid. She's safe now. Trying to get her pregnant...what was I thinking? I'm not a father. I don't create. I destroy. That kid would end up just as fucked up as Jude and me. I thought creating a child was what I needed to do to save her and make things up to Jude, but there's nothing to save her from. Mia's innocent. All debts have been paid.

In fact, now I owe her.

She deserves better than me. She deserves better than a psychopath as a boyfriend and father to her child. She deserves better than for her womb to be used to satisfy the maternal urges of a damaged, vengeful woman. She needs the life she had before I came into the picture and fucked it all up.

This changes everything.

We are back to square one. There is no reason for me to be in her life any longer.

I need to set her free.

I am a destroyer. I am the desecrator of hopes and dreams. It's time to go back to what I do best and end this little paradise Mia thinks we have created. For her sake. Maybe I can do this one good thing. I can save Mia the way I couldn't save Jude.

All this time, I wielded my sword of vengeance with a shield of self-righteousness. Even collateral damage, I told myself, was still justified, because it wasn't my fault, but the fault of their loved one who had betrayed me.

But the truth is, I just like to hurt people. I am a predator. I hunt for sex, money, and pleasure. I only do things that make me feel good. This vendetta stopped being about justice a long time ago. I am no longer human. I don't have a soul.

I have been collecting on a debt from Mia that she never owed.

CHAPTER THIRTY-ONE

Mia

<u>Fiona Apple – Get Gone</u>

Is it possible Tax could be everything I need in a man? He has the fire that burns me and awakens me. That was the thing I had been looking for, and it is so uniquely hard to find. We are all told to snuff that side of us. It's immoral, it's vile, it's sick. But something about Tax is feral. He has all the trappings of a civilized man: wealth, material possessions, good taste. But the hidden part of him, it's untamed, untouched by convention, much like a boy raised by wolves. He turns me into that savage animal too, and I fucking love it.

But I need more than that. I need to know that he sees me. Despite all the urges we may act out, he doesn't really want to hurt me. It's a mating dance, full of teeth gnashing, and growling, and biting. But, when it's all over, I need a person there who will protect me, and care for my well-being just as I would do for him.

I felt it was always there. That hint of something other than just animalistic sexual rage. He cared, but he didn't want to. Now, though, he's becoming less greedy with it, putting his neck out to another beast who could rip out his jugular. I don't hold any power over him like he has over me, but if he does care, I could break him in other ways.

I don't want to break him though, I want to build him. I have found a connection that is nearly impossible to find and I want to make it better. I don't care how we got here any longer, I just like where we are going. And it means I am willing to let go of those circumstances if things go the way I hope. He is a bad man, and I think he can become a version of a good man. But if I want a bad man, I understand I will need to accept some bad things.

That's why lying here on my rug in the middle of my living room floor, after Tax's sudden and brutal attack, feels right. He's following the hard with the soft. He fills up the emptiness left behind when he pillages me.

I soak in his scent. It's like a drug, a hint of his masculinity lined with the warmth of musk, pine, and vanilla. He's asking me about myself, he's talking to me. He's seeing *me*.

And then something changes. Our subdued conversation, under the glow of a single lamp, halts. Tax tenses underneath me.

Is it because I touched his scars?

"Is everything okay?" I ask.

"I need to get up."

"Okay..."

Tax grabs his pants and shirt and disappears into the bathroom. He emerges minutes later, fully dressed, his face grim.

"Are you leaving?" I ask.

No answer.

I sit up, looking for something to cover myself with. His frost chills my exposed skin. "What's wrong? This is where you tell me what you are thinking, Tax. Remember what we talked about? No just up and leaving."

Tax grabs his phone off a side table and slides it in his pocket, his terse movement is a clear signal that he does not want to engage in discussion.

"Something is obviously wrong," I say, stunned by the sharp change in his mood.

"Enough, Mia," Tax says coldly. "Stop with the interrogation."

My stomach churns with anxiety. How could things have turned so quickly?

I watch in silence as he cracks his neck and adjusts his cuffs. I hope he'll start laughing and tell me this is one of his deadpan jokes, though I know it's not. Instead, he clears his throat and looks down at me.

"Mia, I am officially releasing you from the arrangement. You don't owe me anything any longer. Your reputation is safe with me. I will have all of the videos destroyed. You're free."

This is a good thing. This is what I wanted. So then, why does my chest feel like Tax just kicked it in?

"I don't understand...so does this mean we'll just keep seeing each other like normal people would? No more Tuesdays?"

"That's not how this works."

"What do you mean?"

"There is no arrangement. We don't see each other any longer. At all."

Now those words feel like a battering ram to the chest.

"There's something else going on here..." I don't want to sound desperate, but it's hard to contain the fluttering that travels from my heart to my stomach. "You said...you said you wouldn't go anywhere. Remember? On the boat? We were supposed to be here for each other? The video was a last resort. We agreed the blackmail didn't even really matter anymore because we both weren't going anywhere."

"You're free now. You don't need me. I was staying to protect you. You won't need that any longer."

"I don't believe you. How could anything have changed since you've gotten here? Did you get some sort of psychic message? You were just laying here with me, minutes ago, everything was fine. "

"Nothing was ever fine, Mia!"

Tears stream down my cheeks as the fear of total abandonment surges through me. "You care about me. I know you do. Why are you doing this? Why are you leaving? You came here tonight to be with me. What changed since you arrived? I don't understand! Was it something I said?" I try to think back to our topics of discussion, but the conversation moves too quickly for me focus.

"Mia, I came here to fuck you one last time. I already knew I would release you, but I wanted to use you anyway. I used you. I wanted to invade your home and come in you one last time because that shit turns me on. I promised you I would hurt you. I fucking promised, Mia. You didn't listen. I warned you."

The booming newfound optimism I felt for our relationship deflates when he utters those words. Had I been that big of a sucker all along? Would I continue to believe that he was doing all this for some greater good? Why should I believe that he is anything other than a soulless sadist?

It doesn't even matter if he cares about me or not. Because it's clear that he hurts the people he cares about and he hurts the people he hates. For Tax, it all ends the same way. Tax is poisonous, and if you are unfortunate enough to touch him in any way, his poison seeps into your life.

Tax told me he would hurt me one way or the other. I didn't listen. I could have tuned out, let him use my body, and then he would have vanished and our interactions would have become a distant memory, but instead I became a willing participant. I invested myself into Mia and Tax, and like a con artist, he's running off with everything I put in.

I hate him. I hate him so much for doing this to me. For making me become a lone beast. How could I go on without him? How could I have sex with another man? Go on some lame dinner with yet another online date? How could I pretend to be like everyone else after being with Tax? It's like never being able to taste again, smell again. When Tax left, he would be taking those things with him. My world would become dull again.

But I am tired of begging, trying to make him want all of me. As soon as I release that need, the part of me that withered, rises from the ashes like a phoenix, giving me the strength to do what I don't want to.

If Tax really doesn't want me, then he can go to hell.

"Why, Tax? Why did you come to me in the first place? You said I owed you. For what?"

"It's no longer relevant."

"The hell it isn't!"

He looks down, and one who didn't know any better might think it's with shame, but I don't think he has any. When he looks back up it's as if he's put on a mask, with black eyes and a cruel grin to match.

"Mia, there never was a debt. I saw you, I wanted you, and I had you. I thought it would be fun to fuck with you in the meantime."

"I don't believe you. You think I don't know you, Tax, but I do. I see right through your bullshit."

"Mia, you can tell yourself that if it makes you feel any better. Choosing you was random. There was no reason, or rhyme, other than I like the way you looked and I wanted to shove my cock inside of you. This was all because I felt like it. And now, I am done here."

"Well go then. I hope you enjoyed yourself, you son of a bitch," I yell at the specimen of physical male beauty encasing a rotten core. I stagger to my feet, trying to gain some semblance of control. "But do us both a favor and don't pretend you ever protected me. You only give a shit about yourself. You're not capable of caring for another human being. You are a parasite. You use and then when you are done, you'll likely find someone else to suck the life out of. That's the only way you can survive, isn't it? Sucking the life out of everyone around you. Because alone, you are hollow."

I think I see a flicker in his eye, the slightest twitch indicating my words might have had some effect. But I am sick of projecting my humanity onto him, and I won't do it this time.

He doesn't respond and simply turns away, walking to my front door. He stops and without turning says: "Mia, I am giving you your freedom back. You never had a choice, now you do."

"This isn't a choice," I hiss, my face contorting with disgust. I've never been one to enjoy hurting people, but right at this moment, my words are like venom and I want to spit them at Tax, like a cobra. To hurt him like he hurt me. And I want him to realize that I won't let him forget me. Sure, he can leave, but I will haunt his motherfucking ass until I have answers. "I've never had a choice with you, and I still don't. You are a coward, Tax. You might mistake my kindness for weakness, or my understanding for foolishness, but you have me all wrong. You are a bully. You might be tall, and strong, and have money, but inside you are frail. You don't have the balls to allow yourself to get hurt. I put it all out there. I tell you how I feel, even if it means I could get hurt. I am not weak Tax, but I refuse to hurt people to make myself feel strong. And I will never let anyone take my ability to care for people. That includes you, you asshole. I know you are lying. There is a reason you came for me, and if you won't tell me, I'll find out my damned self."

My words burn my chest and lips as I spew them like lava. Tax keeps reeling me in and throwing me back out into the loneliness of a dark ocean. This time he's going to let me drift with no hope of retrieval.

All my life I have been silently strong. Kind to people, but never afraid to tell them how I feel, if that meant giving a compliment or standing up for myself. All this time I was so afraid of Tax disappearing on me, afraid to lose this twisted thing we had, or afraid he might expose me, that I walked on eggshells. But now, he's leaving no matter what, and I want him to feel the pain of isolation that he causes me when he toys with my emotions like a frayed old rag doll. Let him feel some of the hurt this time, if he's even capable.

He stays with his back to me, facing the door, for a moment, as if he is absorbing the impact of my words.

In that stillness, I feel him just as I felt him the first time he showed me his scars. It's the humanity I always uncover in him no matter how much he tries to hide it under his black cloak of hate. "Mia, trust me. You don't wanna know."

He opens the door, steps out, and lets it close behind him. Just like that.

He's gone.

Tax

Nine Inch Nails — Only

What have I done?

Mia did nothing. Nothing. And I almost killed her. I can't even stand to look at her right now, knowing who I am, what I could have done. I stared at myself in the mirror of her bathroom for a while, resisting the urge to shatter my reflection. A dark, heavy feeling oozed over me like tar as I thought about the person she once knew and who he had become: shame.

I had never really felt that before. As a kid, I blurted out things that other people thought harsh or inappropriate. Despite getting picked on or beat up, I didn't try to be someone I wasn't. I never cared about what people thought. I did what I wanted to do and answered to no one. But I felt ashamed as I listened to Mia, as she faintly recollected her brief friendship with Sil and all those times she offered me food because she knew I was hungry and didn't want to embarrass me. That she saw past my exterior, designed to isolate and intimidate. That was the girl I fell in love with years ago, and she is the same person, not adulterated by one horrendous act as I had thought. She has always been the person I had hoped she was.

I tucked a knife behind my back, fucked her, blackmailed her, dreamed of carving her up, told her she meant nothing to me over and over. She has surpassed all of my expectations: it's me who is the disappointment. She says she imagines Sil is successful, living a happy life somewhere, having defeated all the odds. But I haven't. I am a killer, a sadist, and a con artist.

And so, I knew I had to hurt her one last time, so she would be free from me and the mess I have brought her into. I would tell Jude to let it go, and we would move forward. There is nothing left of that night except the ashes of devastation Jude and I left behind. Mia could go and live a normal life as if I never happened. As if that night never happened, because it didn't happen to her. She had nothing to do with it. She has no fucking clue.

Except there is one huge fucking problem: the possibility that I may have already gotten her pregnant. *Fuck. Father.* That word. That disgusting word. I don't even know if I have conceived a child with Mia and I have already fucked up as a father in countless ways.

The odds of her already being pregnant have got to be slim, but if she is I'll make sure Mia and our child are taken care of. But the only way I can let Mia be free of me and Jude is to go cold turkey from her. If Jude finds out she has a niece or nephew, she will absolutely find a way to be a part of that child's life. After all, that was the goal of getting Mia pregnant: to keep her alive and make her pay Jude back with a life. But now I know she owes Jude not a fucking thing. And if Mia is pregnant, Jude will latch onto that child like it is her own. If I am going to let Mia be free, I have to go all in, no matter the sacrifice.

The best thing for Mia, and our possible child, is for me to disappear from her life. She'll find someone else (whose face I would want to crush), someone who can be a normal father to our child, because she will always be at risk as long as I am around. I convinced myself the risk was something she had acquired through her cruel and senseless behavior years ago. Now I know better. It's time to man the fuck up.

The logical side of my brain prays she isn't pregnant so she can really start fresh. And yet, in some deep corner of my psyche, I still want her to be pregnant, so that I am always connected to her in some way. So that no matter if she ends up with some normal guy, I will always own a piece of her. And some part of me knows that the best parts of me and the best parts of Mia can make something — someone — amazing. Mia will always be the one, even if I can't have her.

I fucked up. I was an idiot to think I could have a woman like Mia. I would fuck her up like I do to everything. My touch is destructive, it ruins anything it lays itself upon.

If Mia were to know who I am, who I have become, what I did, it would destroy her. And she would hate me anyway. I'd rather her hate me now for leaving her than for knowing the truth about the monster that has been lurking in her bed.

I pull up to Jude's townhouse. It looks like it's time to break the silent battle we have fought these past few weeks.

A light drizzle begins to fall as I pound on her door.

Minutes later, she answers her door in a robe, her head wrapped in a towel.

"Jesus Tax! You scared the shit out of me."

I push my way past her. "We need to talk."

"What? Now you want to talk to me?"

"Jude, you walked out on me. You told me to go fuck myself, remember?"

She crosses her arms and sighs. "This better be you telling me your fucking master plan is finally coming to its grand finale."

I pace back and forth, running my fingers through my damp hair. "She didn't do it, Jude."

She takes a moment to digest my words and then laughs in disbelief. "Huh. What? You're fucking kidding me Tax. She's really gotten into your head hasn't she?"

"No...no. Jude will you just fucking listen? I know she didn't do it."

"Why, did she tell you that?" she asks, mockingly doe-eyed and innocent.

"Yes—no—yes. Not directly, but she told me about Sil. She never got the letter. It was all Tripp. It had to be."

"Oh come on, do you think she would tell you she set up a couple of kids to be nearly beaten to death?"

"No, but it was the way she told me...she didn't have to. I know she was telling the truth."

Jude circles away, and paces, a mirror image of me. It's freaky how sometimes we will have the same mannerisms and movements. Even I notice it.

"You're believing what you want to believe," she says, finally.

"No, Jude, you are."

Jude begins to shift from detached disbelief to desperate anger. I watch her small body tighten, her dark eyes narrow. She still feels that night as if it happened days ago.

"This is bullshit, Tax. After all we have been through, and now you wanna back out?" she shouts, holding back tears.

"It's not backing out! She isn't guilty of anything but being my friend. Do you know she fed us because she knew we were hungry? Her dad told her about pops, how things were bad at home."

"Oh so now we care what Sheriff Tibbett thinks?"

"For fuck's sake Jude, you can't even see the forest for the trees anymore. You just want to hurt people now. You don't even care what the reason is any longer."

"That's right, I forgot, I am taking to Gandhi over here. You enjoyed every moment of getting back at all those pieces of shit."

"Oh I did. I wish I could do it all over again. And if there was anyone left to pay, I would kill them with a smile on my face. But Mia is not one of those people."

"Just because you are choosing to believe her recollection of events doesn't mean I have to!" Jude shouts, stabbing a finger at me. All 100 pounds, five feet of her, never one to back down from an argument. "You know what Tripp said. She was part of it. How could he have even known about the fucking letter?"

"She said she lost it. Maybe he found it. I don't know!"

"And the letter she wrote back?"

"There was a group of people in on it, someone must have faked the letter to get us there."

"Oh come on! This sounds like bullshit. You sound like a conspiracy theorist. When you hear hoof prints—"

"I know, think horses, not zebras. That doesn't mean zebras don't exist."

"No...you aren't a reliable source anymore. She doesn't get to have everything and then get to walk away from this. For once, her looks and charm are not going to allow her to do whatever she wants! This isn't zebras. You know she betrayed you. This isn't some fucking series of freakish coincidences. You and I have spent years fabricating 'coincidences' to kill people. And you know 'freakish coincidences' only come from meticulous planning."

"I have seen crazier shit in my life and so have you."

Jude paces, shaking her head in disbelief. "Nope. Sorry, she was in on it. I hate to break it to you. You're falling for her bullshit again, just like you're in high school all over again. You got me into this mess Tax the first time because you were gaga over her, you promised you would make them all pay!"

"I would dammit, but not her. Not if she didn't do it. It's over Jude, let it go."

"Well, if you don't have the guts to do it, I'll do it myself."

I know Jude well enough to know she means it. And though I abandoned Mia, I did it to protect her, and that uncontrollable need to protect her again erupts out of me. No one is going to fucking touch Mia, not even my sister.

I lunge at Jude and she gasps as I grab her by the neck, driving her against the wall of her foyer. A lamp tumbles over on her entry table as she flails her arms.

"Jude, if you fucking touch her. I will kill you. Do you understand? I will kill you. This is enough. Everyone got what they deserved. We are done. DONE."

Jude and I look eye to eye, two halves, two allies, two fighters, always on the same team, and now we are torn, willing to alienate the only constant in our lives. She stares into my dark eyes with hers, and when she doesn't relent, I squeeze my hand, slowly tightening my grip. I have always seen Jude as an equal, but feeling her tiny neck in my hand reminds me that is an illusion. Jude needs to feel the grip of death. She needs to understand this is not an idle threat. If she hurts Mia, Jude won't be my sister any longer.

The lamp rolls to the edge of the table and shatters on the floor, breaking our standoff. We both look down and I let her go as she backs away several steps. Her robe is half off of her body, shamelessly exposing herself to me, the towel on her head lilts to the side.

Her red face, wet with tears looks at me with such anger and pity. How could this happen so fast? How could the only two women in my life who have ever mattered hate me? But Jude isn't even there anymore. She's like a cornered dog, and she snarls as the words collect in her mouth, almost as though she is tasting them before spitting out her poison.

"You love her? You love her! You fucking idiot Tax!" she screams. "She will never love you back! Even if she could accept the fact that you have killed Tripp and his dad, and Huck, and Tucker, and all of those assholes. She will never accept that you killed her father!"

Jude is not telling me anything I don't already know. But hearing the words I have been avoiding, shot at me like gunshot pellets, they sting. What Jude is saying is right and it's why I realized today that my whole plan was trying to fulfill Sil's dreams, not Tax's reality. If Mia ever found out I was the person who gave her father a heart attack with an injection of succinylcholine, she would spit on my grave, she would despise me. That's why I had to go. Mia and I and our child, it was all a silly fantasy. Maybe I could only tell Mia a half truth, but I would know. I would know I took away the one person she relied upon in this world, the man who was there for her when her mother died and protected her, even at the expense of me and my sister. I understand. If someone killed Jude or Rex, I would never forgive them. There are just some debts that cannot be forgiven.

"You don't care about anyone anymore, do you, Jude? It's all about you. I exist so you can pile on your guilt. I'll never do enough to make up for what happened. You don't want me to move on. You want it to just be me, you and Rex forever. You can have Rex, but I'm not allowed to have someone, am I? The world has to revolve around you. You'll keep finding ways to keep me to yourself." I shake my head in disgust, at Jude and at myself. "You don't have to worry though. I told her it was over. She doesn't deserve this shit. But don't for a second think I don't mean what I said. I won't just kill you, I will paint my face with your blood if you hurt her. I don't care who you are to me, because if you do it, then obviously neither do you."

Jude does what she always does, goes from lashing out to acting like a wounded animal who needs help, taking advantage of my need to protect my sister, the sister I couldn't protect when it mattered.

"*Taxtaxtax...*" she says in rapid succession, running to me and grabbing my arm. "I'm sorry. I didn't mean that. Come on, wombmate. We both say fucked up shit to each other. I won't do it. Okay? I won't hurt her. We can forget it. We can pack up and move to Tahiti or Malta. Remember all these plans we had?"

I look at her small hands clenching my forearm. "Jude, you don't fucking get it. We need separate lives. Until we figure out who the fuck we are. We're fucked up. We need to form our own lives in the real world. You're not my fucking wife, Jude."

"No, I'm not your wife. You can divorce your wife, but you can't divorce your twin." Jude softens her voice to almost a whisper. "Tax, we'll never be normal," she says through sad eyes, like she is diagnosing me with a terminal illness.

"Maybe not, but we can be better than this," I say, pulling my arm away and heading back out to my car.

CHAPTER THIRTY-TWO

Mia

Gnarls Barkley – Crazy

"I'll kill him!" Tiff says after I tell her Tax walked out on me. I kept it vague, but I said he was an asshole, that he said mean things to me. I let her think I was mourning our relationship, but it was so much more than that. I was mourning Tax as if he had died. I was mourning my former self, the person I was before I walked into the conference room in Alea and recognized the snakes slithering up a mysterious man's neck. I was mourning my new sentence to a life of ordinary love, not the explosively violent passion that Tax and I shared.

It's been almost a week since Tax walked out that door without even saying goodbye, and I have never hurt so much in my life. But I have put on my Mia Tibbett game face. No one knows about my silent and lonely agony. But with Tiff here, I can't hold in the emotion any longer.

I love Tiff, and she could tell me anything without my judgment and I have always felt the same way about her. But what I have become a part of is so warped, I am afraid of her judging me this time, and I am ashamed to admit this, but of her judging Tax. He is my secret, he belongs to me. She doesn't know him. Only I could judge him in my silent misery.

"I don't understand, at the bar, he only had eyes for you..." she says. "The way he looked at you, was like you were the only fucking chick in the building."

"Well, he was drunk and horny, I guess," I say. But I know it's not just that. He looked at me with fierce eyes full need and protection. I had never felt more needed.

"Shit. Why do men have to be such assholes! I am telling Rex about his fucking brother," she says.

"No!" *Shit, Rex.*

"Please, that'll only make me look pathetic. I can handle this on my own."

"Okay..." she relents hesitantly.

"I mean it, Tiff. If you bitch to Rex, I will be so pissed. Nothing leaves this room. I just need you to listen to me bitch, I can handle the rest."

"I just hate that someone would do that to you. You are the most generous, nonjudgmental, kind person I know. And you are successful, beautiful. What the hell is he thinking?" Her words, thrown out so casually, bring my tears to the surface again. Why wasn't all that good enough for Tax? Why did he discard me?

"Nonono...don't cry. I'm sorry!" she says.

"It's not you..." I say. "I'm just bummed. I'll be fine." I wipe a few rogue tears with my sleeves.

"I hate seeing you like this. I have never seen you like this over a guy, ever. What was so special about him? I know he's gorgeous and rich, but he's just a guy, right? There are others out there like him." She's trying to reason and help me see this is not the end of the world, but all her statement does is amplify the difference between Tax and every other man I have ever been with.

There's no one like Tax. No one.

"What about Blake? He wasn't just another guy to you. Was he?"

"At the time, no. You know I thought I would never survive that breakup with that bastard, but the feelings do subside. He didn't want to be with me and I deserved better than that; so do you. You deserve the world, Mia! You are a great person. You deserve someone who appreciates you and loves you. Someone who wouldn't just walk out on you." She adds some wine to her glass. "Do you want more?" she asks.

"No—Yes," I say. It numbs the ache that pervades through my chest. It makes me forget his touch, his smell. Maybe I will stop seeing flashes of that smile he rarely shows. Maybe it'll help me forget about the way I feel like an explosion when he holds me in his strong arms. How my world implodes around him when he is inside of me. I just want to forget he ever existed.

Several bitchfests and wine glasses later, there is a pause in the conversation as I begin to doze off.

"Mia, can I ask you something?"

"Yeah..." Tiff rarely asks if she can ask me a question, it's not her style.

"Did you...you used the card I gave you. Didn't you?"

"I, uh...why do you ask?"

"I booked another one, and my card was charged only half price."

"Well didn't you refer others?"

"I thought about doing it, but this stuff is too sensitive. I only gave you the card. Either it was a mistake on their end or it was you."

My drowsiness evaporates from the heat of nervous energy.

"You did, huh? You don't have to be embarrassed. I just wanted you to experience it. And, I wanted to talk to someone about it too. Not many people are like us, Mia. Not many people like it rough or painful. Or if they do, they never discuss it. We're lucky to have each other to share this with."

"I'm not embarrassed." I say, knowing that lying to Tiff about booking with Happy Kitty will fail.

"You did! I knew it!" she says. "But when? It had to have been a while ago."

I think about lying, telling her that the guy who came to me in the driveway fulfilled his duties. But, something breaks in me. The crying I had done earlier was subdued, it was a restrained version of the sadness I felt. Telling Tiff the modified story of Tax and me helped me almost believe it for a while: that we met for our first conference that Tuesday morning months ago, and we went out for breakfast and hit it off, and so began our whirlwind romance.

But this wedge of truth she has stuck into that tiny space between my fake version of Tax and the reality of the situation bursts me open. I begin to sob uncontrollably. It's deep, from a place I haven't cried since I lost my mother. A place of fear, confusion, heartache, and irreconcilable loneliness.

Tiffany's eyes go wide with concern. In all the years I have known her, I have hardly ever cried, never over a guy, and never like this.

"Oh my god, Mia. What's wrong? Did someone hurt you?" she asks, wrapping herself over my huddled body. "Did the escort hurt you?"

"No..." I choke out between shallow breaths. "Tiff, I fucked up. I don't know what to do..."

"Hey...take some breaths. It's gonna be okay."

"I can't...tell you." My diaphragm rages out of control, making it hard to breathe.

"Mia, you really have me worried here."

"I don't want to get...you...mixed up in things. And I know you. You'll...want to get involved, but you can't."

"You're freaking me out."

"No escort hurt me. If I tell you, you have to...promise, no one can know. You can't...do...anything about it. I am trusting you with...this information." My choppy speaking frustrates me, so I take a few slower breaths in an attempt to stifle the emotion.

"Sweetie, of course. I would never betray your trust. Tell me, you have nothing to be ashamed of."

I take a few slow breaths, but my chest rebels with staccato sobs.

"I promise. I won't tell anyone. This is between us."

"It was Tax."

"Tax was your attacker?"

"Wait..." I say, taking another deep breath so I can control my voice and tell the story clearly. "I went to the site. I paid for the service, but as soon as I did it, I thought it was a mistake. I was going to call it off as soon as the guy got to me. But then, on the first night, someone came, and I changed my mind. We had sex. I told myself I would say no, but when it happened, I wanted it. And it was unlike anything...and it scared me. How much I liked it. But then, days later, someone else came, and I panicked. I only paid for one service. I used the safeword. And he left. He told me it was impossible someone else could have arrived before him. I realized the first person I was with..."

"Oh my god." Tiff is a wild child. She has seen a lot in her thirty years, but the look of shock and horror on her face is one I have never seen since meeting her nearly a decade ago.

"I freaked. I thought someone random came into my house and I let him, no, I encouraged him to be with me. He had on a mask, but there were things I remembered about him, he had a neck tattoo..."

"Oh fuck." It's something everyone remembers about Tax and Tiff instantly understands the connection.

"Alea got bought out around the same time, I got promoted, and then I had my first meeting with the new owner...early when no one else would be in the office..."

"Are you fucking shitting me!" she says. Her voice has a tone of disbelief, anger, with a hint of laughter. *I get it, this whole thing is ridiculous.*

"It was an ambush. He told me he recorded it, that if I didn't do what he said, he would destroy me."

"Wait, do what?"

I look down in shame.

"That sick son of a bitch. Mia, I think I'm going to kill him!" she says, rising to her feet.

"No. You promised you would keep this to yourself. And I mean not a soul!"

"Yes. I know. I'm just fucking emoting Mia. But you can't let him get away with this. This is crazy. This whole thing is crazy. How did he find you? Why? Is he part of Happy Kitty?"

"No...he's been watching me, I guess. For all I know he can hear us now, but I don't fucking care. He knew everything about me. He said I owed him."

"Owed him? Why?"

"He refused to tell me."

"He was probably bullshitting you to fuck with your head."

"No, I think there was something."

"So you just went along repaying him for something you didn't know you owed?"

I can't help but feel judged by that question.

"What choice did I have? The debt didn't even matter. The reason didn't matter. He had my computer activity and video of me fucking him while he wore a mask and held a knife to my throat. He was going to post it everywhere, telling people I hired men to rape me. He told me he would send it to every possible employer, put it on the internet. Send it to friends and whatever distant family I have. He was going to ruin my life. He wasn't asking to collect, he was telling me he would."

And I know how fucked up I am when despite the sick story I am reciting, I worry I am painting Tax in a bad light.

"What could have possibly lead to this? For someone to come after you?"

"I don't know! You know me, I mind my own business. I am almost bordering on boring. My dad was a cop, but we grew up in a boring town. No big drug busts or anything."

"I'm still not buying this. I think he lied about your owing him something, like some psychological thing. So the grand reopening, were you under duress? Oh, god. How could I have not noticed?"

"No, I wasn't." I say, looking up at her with remorseful eyes, apologizing for my own depravity.

"I'm confused."

"I wanted him there."

"You mean, you wanted to be with him? The relationship was real?"

I fight so hard to keep from losing it again. "Tiff, I feel like such an idiot, but..."

"You're really in love with him?"

Again I buckle over. I am so good at controlling my emotions. When my mother was dying, I walked around with a smile, trying to make sure everyone else felt okay around me. But Tax rips me right open.

Tiff sits down next to me, stroking my back. "It's okay, Mia. You know, this happens...when people are forced..."

"I don't have fucking Stockholm syndrome. I made a choice." I confess to Tiff the words I hadn't even yet confessed to myself. "I allowed myself to fall in love with a bad person. I think he's dangerous. I don't mean he's going to hurt me. But, I think he's wrapped up in bad things. That's why it's important you stay out of this. And he started saying things about protecting me. And there's a part of me that keeps hoping he left because he thought he was doing the right thing. And then there's another part of me that is screaming at myself, telling me I am an idiot for thinking he even cares if I am alive."

"All this time you've been dealing with this alone?" Tiff asks.

"I was ashamed. I know what I have been doing is reckless, but being with Tax, when it's good, it's like nothing else. Hell, even when it's bad, it's good. He knows how to be that guy I need in a good way, and a bad way."

"Rex..." Tiff whispers aloud.

"He said Rex cares about you. He considers you a real friend."

"But?"

"He was planted in our lives to watch me."

Tiff riffles her fingers through her green streaks. "This is fucking nuts! So why did he leave you, really?"

"I still don't know. But he did. And I am going to find out why he really came after me."

CHAPTER THIRTY-THREE

14 Years Earlier

Me and Jude are splitting a couple of cans of pork and beans for dinner. Soon, I'll be heading out to meet Mia. I usually scarf down whatever is available for dinner, be it plenty or next to nothing, but tonight I can barely sit still in my seat as I push the beans around my plate.

"What's crawled up your butt?" Jude asks. She's already finished her food. For a tiny thing she can eat. She barely breaks 85 pounds, that girl.

"Nothing," I say. I usually tell Jude everything, but she knows I like Mia, and she already teases me about her incessantly.

"Liar! I can read your mind, Sil! We're twins!" she says, scooping up a spoon of my beans.

"Hey!" I say, striking her spoon with mine. The beans survive and make it to her mouth.

"Tell me!" she whines in an annoying voice that she knows I'll do anything to shut up. The truth is, I kind of do want to tell my sister. She's my only friend. She tells me about her crushes, which tend to change weekly, but I think she's due to be on the listening end. Poor thing, always stuck in the friend zone because she's so underdeveloped. We both are. I don't have any facial hair yet, my limbs are just bone and skin. Pops says we are late bloomers, that he didn't fill out until he was nineteen or twenty, then he got muscular, his beard came in, his jawline changed. It's a James trait: we develop late, but when we do, we blow up. At least that's what I am hoping.

"Come on Sil!"

"Fine," I say, sliding Mia's note over to her. "I gave Mia a note, and she put this in my locker."

I watch Jude's dark eyes intently scan the note, widening with each line they read.

She looks up, her mouth forming a big "O." "Sil! Oh my god. She likes yooooou!" Jude starts jumping up and down in her chair.

"Okay, relax. You're making me nervous," I say, but a smile has already made a home on my face.

"When are you leaving?"

"In a couple minutes."

"Dad's not home for you to use the truck."

"That's why I'm leaving now, so I have extra time to bike."

Just then the sound of dad's pickup truck rolling along the dried leaves and twigs alerts us to his arrival. *Shit.* Usually when he's late from work, he'll stay out all night drinking, come home when we're in bed, and pass out. If he gets in earlier than that, and he's hammered, it means he is going to make our lives a living hell.

The bright light of his pickup floods our double wide and then shuts off. Both Jude and I have learned to listen to the cadence of his steps and his breathing, sometimes accompanied by incoherent mumbling, so we can gauge if it's sober dad (rare), tipsy dad (less rare), or hammered dad (very common). The sound of his dragging feet, repetitive clearing of his throat, and his murmurs to himself as he trips over his feet let me know this will not be a rare night.

DEBT

Jude and I roll our eyes at each other. My stomach goes queasy. When you have a violent drunk for a parent, you pray that they'll just pass out, or maybe one day they won't come home plastered, but you always get that sinking feeling. You know you will be a human punching bag. Sometimes it's fists, sometimes it's words, but you feel like someone waiting in a pit for a lion to be unleashed.

I throw some beans on Jude's plate. The key is to keep your eyes down, let him scream, let him bash you. Fighting back only gives him what he wants, then the fists fly. You just have to take it. With food on our plates, it gives us something to look at.

We both slowly pick at our beans.

"Where the fuck—beans? That's what you fuckin' made?" he asks in a slur.

"That's all there was, dad." He loves to complain about the meager fixings at meal time, though he hardly gets groceries and doesn't give us any money.

"Are you being a smartass?" he asks, threateningly glaring at me. His feet are wide beneath him with his hips jutted forward so he won't topple over.

"I can serve you, dad," Jude says, to get the attention off of me.

"No...I got it. No one here has to lift a finger for me! I just do everything. I pay the bills, I work. But you both look at me like I'm a nobody...you ungrateful little shits."

He grabs the pan and Jude's spoon off of her plate and starts scooping up beans. About 80 percent successfully reach their target.

He opens the fridge. "Where's the fuckin' beer?"

"You drank it all." I say, as nonconfrontationally as possible.

"No there was beer here!" He whips around. "You drink it Sil?"

"No, pops."

"Don't lie to me!"

I know it's hard for him to believe, since though the fridge doesn't have much food, it always has beer. But he drank it all yesterday.

"Fuck it," he says, slamming the fridge door closed with his foot.

As inconspicuously as possible, I take the plates to the sink.

Dad gets close to me, so close he could sniff me. "Why do you gotta go all dressin' like a fucking freak?"

I look straight ahead. It's best not to challenge. He whacks me upside the head. "Answer me, you stubborn prick."

"I don't know," I say.

One day, I'll be big and muscular like him, and I will whoop his ass. I'll shove a can of cold pork and beans in his mouth and watch him gag.

I turn around and slide past Jude, noticing too late that the fucking note is on the table. I go for it, trying to slide it in my pocket before he spots it.

"What's that you tryin' to hide?' He asks, in a slurred voice.

"Nothing."

"You keep lying, boy. I'm getting sick of it. Hand it over."

"No."

He marches over, snatching it out of my hands. "Give that shit to me!"

He looks it over slowly, trying to comprehend the words in his drunken haze. "So you think you're going out tonight? On a school night?"

Not once has this man ever cared about my education.

"Just for a little while."

He looks me up and down with so much disdain. People say my mother was a good woman, but I have a hard time believing a good woman would have had children with such a piece of shit.

"You gotta clean the shed tonight. I've been telling you to do that all week."

"You've never mentioned it before."

"Don't fucking call me a liar."

"It's okay," Jude says, standing. She's been a spectator up until this point. Usually I get the brunt of the bullying, because I am the boy and I guess he likes to challenge me more. "I can clean the shed. Just let him go."

"So what? Now you think you call the shots under my roof?"

"She didn't mean it that way."

The clock winds down. It's already 7:55, I needed fifteen minutes to bike there.

"Now you both clean the shed. I want to be able to eat off the floor of that fuggin' thing."

It's at that moment I realize how cruel and hateful a man he is. It's one thing to dislike your kids enough to not want to provide or nurture, but to see one has a chance at happiness elsewhere and ruin it just for the sake of it, that's pure hatred for your own flesh and blood.

"No," I say. It's a word that does not get thrown at dad without something getting thrown back.

He throws the empty pot into the sink. The spoon rattles as it swirls, metal grating against metal, then quiet.

"Fuck you say?" he asks, coming closer to me.

"I'm going out tonight. I'll be back home at a reasonable time."

"You are going to clean the shed tonight." He takes the crumpled note from Mia, opens it up, and rips it in half, letting it fall to the floor.

There is tense silence as fear and anger wrestle inside of me, each trying to win access to my next words.

"Sil...maybe we could clean it fast..." Jude's tiny soft voice reasons with me from somewhere I can't see. She doesn't want to see me get hurt. Whenever dad beats one of us, it's like he's doing it to both of us.

Pops steps closer, and in his snarl, there are pieces of bean stuck to his teeth and sauce sloppily encircling his mouth. It's then I realize that for all the loudness, anger, and power he exerts over us, he is a joke. He is a bitter, pathetic joke of a man. A man who feels helpless in life, angry over things he couldn't control, probably gets shit on at work, and he exerts his dominance over the only two people in his life who have no choice but to take it: his own children.

"No." I say, my voice a little firmer this time.

His eyes flinch in disbelief, maybe panic. Things are different today: he might be losing control, even over us.

"Get your ass in the shed!" he says, grabbing the back of my neck and thrusting me towards the door.

"No. I'm going out. I'll clean the shed this weekend." No one is stopping me from seeing Mia today.

I can't see Jude, but I can feel her fear. It travels like an aroma, wafting in the air.

And then he slaps me. Hard. So hard it nearly knocks me off my feet. But I right myself and stare at him. He can't hurt me anymore. I might not be as big, or strong, but I'm not a child anymore.

"No."

He does it again, even harder this time.

"Stop!" Jude cries. I can hear her crying to herself, mumbling incoherent sounds.

Next is a punch, and it sends me to the ground. I open my eyes just in time to helplessly watch dad rear his leg for a kick.

"No!" Jude's little body sails over to him, her tiny frame throwing off a man who outweighs her by 150 pounds. My dad takes a few steps back, but regains his balance, and throws Jude like she weighs nothing. Her tiny body slams against the edge of the table and she cries out as she falls, clutching her side.

Jude's moment of bravery gives me time to get to my feet, and just as my defiance boosted her bravery, hers does the same for me. If my 80-something pound sister can confront dad, then so can I.

Coming to my feet, in a crouching stance, I tackle my father to the floor. "Leave her alone!" I say. "Leave us alone! You asshole!"

His drunkenness allows for a moment of reprieve, but he's a large man, with the muscles of someone who has labored his entire life. He lifts me off of him and rolls over me. He punches me once, then wraps his hands around my throat, cutting my air supply. I clench his wrists and scratch, but his eyes are vacant. It's drunken rage: all animal, no humanity.

And then, relief. I look up and see small arms wrapping around dad's head.

"Dammit Jude, you little bitch!" He stands up with her on his back and slams against the wall, but she holds on. My little doll of a sister has become a fierce bobcat. But he'll break her. He could kill her so easily in a momentary lapse of judgment. He slams again and she lets go, sliding down to the floor, gasping for wind.

He turns to her, and I know he has to be stopped. Now. Jude and I have arrived at a point of no return. If we don't stop him, he'll kill one of us tonight.

I grab the closest thing, the pot I made the beans in tonight, and I swing. He stops, standing erect. I swing again, harder. He looks at me in complete shock, a slit opens up on his cheek bone and then it starts pouring dark blood. He falls to his knees.

"Sil!" Jude says, encouraging me to hit him again. I do one more time, and he falls to the floor.

"Shit. I think I killed him," I say under my breath.

Jude stumbles to her knees and hesitantly leans in close. "He's breathing. I just think you knocked him out. You know he's going to kill us. We have to run away."

I grab his pickup keys. "Get your book bag and pack your stuff."

The clock reads 8:09.

I run to my room and grab my essentials. Then I go into my dad's room and look for his money stash. I find it in a coffee can, tucked into a drawer, and pull out a wad of twenties. I take one last look at my dad, his chest rises and falls. *Good, I'm not a murderer.*

Within minutes we are running out to the pickup. We throw our bags in the bed and hop in.

"What are we going to do?" Jude asks.

"I don't know," I say, bumping along the dark isolated dirt road that leads away from our home.

"You're still gonna meet Mia, right? That's why we did this. So you wouldn't miss it. You can't miss it."

"Yeah, I'm seeing her tonight. He's not winning. What time is it?"

"8:17..."

DEBT

"Shit!" I say, jamming the gas harder, making the old truck jitter along the rocks and uneven terrain. "We should be there in five minutes."

"She'll be there," Jude assures me.

"You okay?" I ask, giving Jude a succession of quick glances while trying to keep my eyes on the dark road.

"Yeah," she pulls up her shirt and winces at a welt on her ribcage where she hit the table. "It's fine, just a bruise. What about you? He hit you so hard."

I touch my face. That's when I realize I look like I'd just been through a battle. It'll freak Mia out. "Shit," I say, looking at the blood I've wiped off my face.

"I got it," Jude says, pulling out stuff from her bag. "I thought ahead." She grabs a rag from the back of the cab and pours the rubbing alcohol she took from the house. "It's gonna hurt."

"Just do it," I say.

She cleans my face as I hiss at the fire in each cut.

"So much better. Swollen cheek, but not as bad as I thought."

We pull into the clearing that leads to the abandoned lake house, a popular spot for high school parties and gatherings. It's quiet, being a school night. I pull up to the only other car. Both Mia and I usually walk to school, so I don't recall what her car looks like, but this has to be it.

"Just stay here, okay?"

"Good luck," Jude says with a smile. I kiss her on her forehead and she smiles. "Love you, wombmate."

"Love you too," I say.

I close the door to the truck and look around for a sign from Mia in the quiet night. The lake flickers with the reflection of the moon, crickets chirp, the occasional owl calls, but there's no sign of her. *Did she leave? Am I too late?*

I hear a rustling in the bushes close by. "Hello?" I call out.

"Psssst."

"Mia?"

I follow the sounds, past trees and fallen branches, to another clearing. Beer cans and bottles litter the floor, dozens of them. The scent of it in the air is fresh.

Something isn't right. The instinct to leave strikes, and I take a step back to head to the truck. Maybe I can find Mia tomorrow and explain everything.

Just then, I hear an eruption of collective laughing from a bunch of guys. And Tripp walks around from behind a tree.

"What's up, Sil?"

CHAPTER THIRTY-FOUR

Mia

<u>Hozier – Take Me to Church</u>

I peer through the glass of my windshield at the front of Tax's building. This is how I am starting my Saturday morning, at square one. My internet searches still aren't yielding much, so I figured the next best thing would be to try to follow him. I know, I have lost my fucking mind. But I will find out who he is and why he came into my life. Tax loved to mention that I owed him, well — now he owes me an explanation.

And I won't stop until I find out why he burst into my life.

Almost an hour passes with nothing, but I have prepared to be here all day, packing a lunch and prepping a playlist loaded with plenty of music. This is what Tax has turned me into: a crazed woman who follows a man around. But I have been left with no choice. If I just let him go, the question of why Tax came and went will linger in my mind for as long as I live.

Oh my god, I'm like that astronaut who wore a diaper to drive across the country to find her lover.

It felt great to tell Tiff everything. After the shock wore off, she promised to support me in any way she could, though she admitted she wants Tax's head on a skewer. I stressed to her that I didn't want anyone coming to my rescue and it was important to me that I solve this on my own.

My impatience begins to set in just as the front door opens and out comes Tax, in a pair of jogging pants and a sleeveless workout T. He's already covered in sweat, probably having just lifted, and he puts on his earphones and takes off for a run.

My heart sinks. This week has been hard, and lonely, but at least I didn't have to see Tax. I could bury myself in other things and ignore the pervasive ache. Now, watching him run: his body covered in sweat, his muscles gleaming in the light rain, his wet, messy hair, makes my body surge with desire. It's small things like watching him run that make me realize there's still so much I don't know about him. I run too. We could have run together. I mourn the things we will never do.

To my disappointment, Tax looks fine, and it hurts to think he's probably already moved on. But that hurt fuels me to push through the pain and get my answers.

I pull out of my spot, careful to stay a few cars behind where he is on the sidewalk. If I get too close, he'll spot me. He heads south, and I wonder if he'll go east, to the park, effectively ruining my tail. To my surprise however, he stays on the sidewalk and runs towards a more industrial part of downtown. At some parts I think I almost lose him, having to stay at such a distance, but somehow I manage to keep track of him. Eventually, we arrive in Walkers Point, a part of Milwaukee filled with warehouses, antique shops and gay bars, not the typical area one would go for a jog. It makes me wonder if he's headed somewhere specific. Why else would someone run all the way out here, when they were just minutes away from a beautiful lake and park system?

Eventually Tax runs down a quiet street loaded with warehouses that leads to an eventual dead end. I pull over a couple of blocks behind the dead end to keep my view on him without being too conspicuous. Tax turns abruptly into what appears to be an old collection of abandoned warehouses, maybe an old tannery. After waiting about twenty seconds, I pull out of my spot, and follow his tracks.

Could he be meeting someone?

I pull into the gravel lot in the middle of three warehouse buildings, all perpendicular to each other so that I am almost surrounded by abandoned buildings. Tax is gone. *Shit.* I think I really lost him this time. Or maybe he isn't gone, and he went into one of these buildings. I just spent 45 minutes following him to get clues and I might finally have one, there's no way I am quitting. I pull my car into a dead-end space between two buildings, doing my best to shield it from view in case he comes back out to the gravel lot.

I cautiously slide out of the car, looking for signs of life. The grinding of gravel underfoot is the only sound in the dead space. Then nearby I hear the sound of metal squeaking, just behind a door not fifteen feet away. I look side to side as paranoia kicks in. I am still alone. I tip toe towards the door, which is shrouded in graffiti, hoping to peer through one of the windows flanking it. Another squeak echoes from that direction. I hush my breathing though my heart speeds in anticipation of what I might see. *Crunch. Crunch.* Of all materials for a lot, this one *had* to be gravel. I near a shattered window, ducking underneath it, readying myself for what I might encounter.

A pigeon coos and flutters over me, escaping the broken window, and causing me to take a few flustered steps back. The shock is enough for me to lose my nerve.

This is crazy. I should just go back to his building at start over. It's clear I've lost him for now and I must be patient.

I pull my phone out of my pocket to check the time, when I hear gravel crunching behind me. Before I can turn, a huge warm body presses against mine, pushing me onto the cold hood of my car. My sensory memory explodes, and I don't even have to hear his voice to know that Tax has already busted me.

"You're following me now?" he growls into my ear.

My body heats up against his. The feeling of his pelvis pressing against my ass brings a mixture of rage and desire.

"I'm going to find out who you are, Tax. You can't do what you did to me."

"Mia, just let it go."

Just let it go. Like it was all nothing. Just let go months of insanity.

"No."

"You think you want this, but you don't."

"Don't tell me what I want!" I wrestle him again, and he only presses harder against me.

"You really want this, Mia? You really fucking want me? You want to know who I am?" he asks, his voice bursting with frustration. Suddenly, a serrated blade is pressing against my neck. "This is who I am Mia. That first night. That psycho, that's me."

"You are so full of shit," I sob out. He doesn't really want to hurt me. There is little I am sure of, but that, I know.

"This isn't a fucking game, Mia. I'm not some boy you can feed and make better. You can't fix me. I am not a project. I am not some charity case you can use to feel better about yourself. I'm not some guy you can fuck to take you out of the monotony of your boring life."

"Oh fuck you!"

"You want me to make you feel dirty? You like dirty? Huh? I am destructive. My danger is real, Mia. You should leave and never look back. Forget you ever knew me. Because I will only bring you pain. This is who I am."

Tax leans his upper body onto mine and his hips jut forward, rubbing his thickness against my lower back. The teeth of the knife dig painfully into my neck, always on the verge of breaking the skin, but his precise grip keeps me from shedding blood. "This is who I am. I am a fucking savage."

He pulls up my floral dress and rips down my panties, rubbing my pussy from behind. "Fuck, you're always so wet for me. Goddammit Mia. I gave you a fucking chance to be normal."

"I don't want to be normal."

"Shut up," he says, pressing the blade against my neck and I let out a frightened yelp as it bites into my skin. "Don't fucking say a word. Why are you out here? You want me to fuck you? Hurt you?"

His contradictions enrage me, but I want him like this. I want this beast to savage me, to hurt me while taking me to the apex of pleasure.

He pulls down his sweatpants. His essence reaches my nose, and like a powerful aphrodisiac, it stupefies me. "You want my fucking cock? You want it this bad?" He rubs the head along my slit, between my cheeks and back down.

The drizzle turns into a light rain, and it falls on us, mixing sweat with water, filth with cleanliness. My wet hair clings to my face and shoulders, droplets collect on my eyelashes and slide down my cheeks, onto my lips.

Whatever desires stir in me, I won't give him the satisfaction of knowing it.

"I want the truth, you fucking asshole."

He presses the knife against my neck again.

"Watch your fucking mouth or I'll watch it for you."

He runs his hand up my ass, my waist, reaching around and squeezing a breast. "These fucking tits," he mutters.

He slides his hand down my stomach and massages my clit through my lips, sending waves of pleasure to my belly.

"You get so fucking wet for me. My little slut," he says, almost affectionately. He bites my shoulder and sparks dance out from the spot. "You keep asking for trouble Mia, you're gonna get it."

I crave him in my bones. It's been barely a week, but it might as well have been a month. I hate him. I want him. And I want the truth, but right now, I just want him inside of me. I miss our bodies melding together in a mixture of fear, anger, passion, and affection. I am strong, dammit. But Tax, he makes me fucking weak. I'll get my truth, but his wet, hard body pressed against mine reminds me he is the only man who can give me the things I want.

Fuck, I want him so bad, but I won't give in to him until he gives me more. My sex is the only power I have because while he will never admit it, I think he's weak for me too.

My pussy is so ready, his head slides into me, almost effortlessly, and my walls clench, anticipating his cock filling its vacancy. Though the knife still digs into my neck, the pain dulls to a steady awareness of danger, but it's just part of the dance. He won't hurt me. I know it.

I curl my spine towards him, encouraging him to enter me, to make me forget who I am right now. If he thrusts inside of me, with a knife to my neck, I can blame him for making me do this, instead of myself for allowing this to happen. But despite the frustrated firmness of his cock, he resists, teasing me with his head.

"Beg."

My fists ball up in consternation. He always does this, makes me grovel, making it clear to both of us, that no matter how great his show of force, I want it just as badly as he does. But, I can't. I won't beg for someone who doesn't want all of me. Who abandons me like I mean nothing. I won't let him have all the power again. I won't fucking beg. Not until I know who this man really is and that he really gives a shit.

"No."

The knife digs deeper. *This is who I really am, Mia.* He's telling me, but I don't believe that's all of him. I have seen his other sides, he's already shown me too much for me to believe he is only some brute.

"I said fucking beg." He slides his head out and back in, it electrifies my labia with arousal. I bite my lip and scrunch my face to bear the agony of resisting him. I hate saying no to Tax.

"You followed me. I'm here Mia. I'll give you what you fucking want. But you better fucking beg for it."

"Fuck you," I wince. "Go to hell."

He yanks my ponytail ferociously, the knife pressed so tightly against me, that if I jerk, it will cut my skin. "No, fuck you," he thrusts into me once, punctuating his statement. We both let out gasps of intense relief and pleasure. We both melt in that moment of singular surrender.

But Tax doesn't surrender. He gives a little and he always takes more. Just as quickly as he is in me, he pulls out. The sting of the knife against my throat quickly fades, and his warmth leaves my body, leaving me wet and cold. His feet crunch the gravel as he tucks himself back into his sweatpants and tucks his knife back into his ankle holster.

I turn to face him, frigid from the rain and abandon, my panties still resting at the top of my rain boots, feeling naked though my soaked dress still clings to my body.

I glare at him, the rain on my face disguising the tears that mingle with it. But my lips tremble with disdain. He's leaving me. Again. Everything is always on his terms. I might see him again, I might not. I have tried to stay cool, to not meet his aggression with my aggression. I didn't mince my words the day he walked out of my house, but that was still restrained. I lashed out at him, but I didn't want to tell him how much he hurt me. In that moment, I just wanted to hurt him back.

But he needs to know. If he does want to protect me, if he thinks that what he did was good for me, he needs to know the truth. He has hurt me to the core. He has made me feel a type of emotional pain that no physical pain can match. He doesn't get to walk away thinking he's doing what's best.

If he really doesn't give a shit, then he'll walk away without a care. But if he does care, I want him to feel the pain he is putting me through. He will fucking feel it. He will know what a piece of shit he is.

Tax looks at me, his brown eyes determined, but the snakes along his neck swerve. His tat is a tell. He can't hide the tension in his neck and how uneasy he feels walking away from me.

He doesn't say a fucking word, looking at me with dead eyes, before turning to walk away.

I watch him, his body a monument to destruction as it walks away, leaving me in shambles again.

And this time, I fucking lose it.

I yank up my underwear so quickly it tangles in my dress and run towards him along the wet and muddy gravel.

"What the fuck is wrong with you!" I scream, tripping over my rainboots and landing on my knees. The tiny rocks pierce into my skin, but the pain is negligible compared to the fire breathing out of my lungs. I pick up a handful of gravel and throw it at him. "You ruined me! You son of a bitch!" I collapse down, on all fours, heaving tears. I grab another handful and throw it at him. Most of the gravel and mud, heavy with rain, barely makes it to him.

He keeps walking, but his body gets heavier with each step. "How can you be such a heartless bastard," I scream through tears. "You ruined me! You said you wouldn't leave and then you threw me away like garbage! You said you wouldn't leave and then you walked away like you hated me!"

I rise back to my knees, the pebbles digging deeper into my skin, like some sort of self-imposed punishment for allowing myself to get this low.

"What did I ever do to you, Tax? Why do you hate me so much? What did I ever do to deserve the way you treat me! You hurt me so much. You made me care about you and then you abandoned me. You fucking bastard! You don't even have the fucking balls to tell me, you asshole! Man up! Man the fuck up! Face the mess you made!"

Tax finally stops, like each word was another weight added and finally they were just too heavy to bear. In the moment of quiet, I have a moment of clarity as Tax's back faces me. He looks heavy, his rain-soaked body looks like it holds decades of pain. My words, they hurt him. My words matter.

And instead of screaming this time, I plead, with a week's worth of hidden tears in my voice: "Tax, what did I ever do to you?"

The rain begins to downpour, and I sink back on all fours, letting the drops wash over me. I look down at the gray rocks and dirt, unwilling to watch Tax walk away again.

His footsteps scrape along the gravel. But this time the sound comes closer.

I look up to see Tax standing over me, water cascading off of his head and shoulders.

His eyes are heavy. "Nothing," he says quietly.

It's not the answer I want to hear. I have to know why. I have to know this wasn't random, that there is meaning behind it all. He offers me his hand.

"Tell me, Tax," I say, refusing the gesture.

"Nothing." He sticks his hand out again.

"Liar!" I shout, slapping his hand away.

And now, Tax doesn't ask to help me up, he grabs my wrists and I wrestle him as he pops me up to my feet. I wrangle with him and he lets me go, allowing me to push him, shove him, and beat my wrists against his chest.

"You are a fucking liar!" I scream.

"I'm not, Mia," he says calmly. His calmness frustrates me. It makes me feel hysterical as Tax stands firm, taking the beating like someone who knows he deserves it.

"There's more. I know. And you need to fucking tell me. You owe me that. You owe me."

Finally, he grows frustrated and grabs my forearms, pulling me close to him. Our wet bodies cling to each other, and I stop wrangling with him.

Tax's lips brush against my ear. "You only get once chance to get away from me Mia. I'm giving it to you. I can't resist you. I was doing this for you," he breathes into my neck.

"No, you are doing this for you," I say. "You don't get to walk away from me. You don't get to set me on fire and leave me like a pile of ashes."

"I never left you, Mia. But, it's me who will hurt you. I am protecting you from me."

"Are you protecting me? Or yourself?"

The fire between our bodies makes the coldness of the rain evaporate from my skin. It's just me in Tax's arms. The elements bend to us. Time freezes. Sounds go quiet.

"Fuck," Tax says as he digs a hand into my wet hair and pulls me into a kiss so passionate it hurts. Not just my lips, but my heart twists and contorts in agony. We both know we are fucked. We keep fighting whatever this is, and we keep losing the battle.

I become pliant, molding my body to his. His apology is in the way his tongue slides against mine, the way his arm wraps around my waist, the way his hand knots the soaking fabric of my dress. "I owe you," he says, as his lips graze my neck. "There's no one like you, Mia."

While my mind wants answers now, my body cries out much louder, screaming for the relief of Tax's touch. He slides his hands down to my ass, and boosts me up as I wrap my legs around him. He carries me back over to my car and presses me up against the driver's side door, pulling out his cock. He guides it as I slide down onto him. The sensation of him filling me is agonizingly pleasurable. I moan out a half laugh, deliriously overwhelmed by the explosion of ecstasy.

His powerful hips thrust me up and down over his weighty, curved cock as I cry out curses and warped versions of his name. His strong fingers dig into the mounds of my ass, bouncing my pussy against his cock. Wet flesh slaps against wet flesh. The straps of my dress collapse, my dripping breasts bouncing against Tax's lips. He grips the flesh between his teeth, sparking an electric path from my breasts to the walls of my pussy.

"I miss fucking your tight pussy. Tasting your cream. You were made for me," he huffs out as he handles me like a beast ravaging his prey.

I wrap my arms around Tax's strong neck, smothering his face in my breasts as I attempt to muffle my cries into his hair. He grips the meat of my ass firmly, boosting me up and down his shaft, stabbing me deep inside. I throw my head back in euphoric agony every time his head plunges deep inside of me.

My body locks up, as I clench his, tense from pumping into me, as a burst of energy shoots through me. "Fuck, Tax!" I cry out as the pressure of my weight on his cock makes the intensity of the orgasm inescapable. I grab frantically at his hair and crash my lips onto his plump pout as I grunt and moan into his mouth. He rubs his pelvis against mine as his cock draws out every last wave of pleasure from my body. His dick swells as my orgasm tapers and he releases himself inside of me, pressing me against the car for leverage as he pushes himself as deep as he can inside of me, filling me with his warm cum.

I slide my legs down to the ground, but I won't release Tax from my arms. I don't want him to freak out and leave. He needs to face me. He needs to tell me everything.

But this time, he collapses onto me, panting, the cords of his muscles softened with relief. We both really needed to get that out of our systems.

"You drive me fucking crazy, Mia." It's like a poem coming from Tax's lips.

"Then I guess we're even." I let out my first genuine smile in a week. I cup his face in my hands. "Tax, it's time for us to talk."

"I know," he says, his eyes full of dread. He motions to say something, but then he hesitates.

"What is it?" I ask.

"Not now."

"Now. I need you to give me something. Anything."

He sighs, looking down at the soaked gravel below us. His body winds up in my arms, the relaxation from our sex already becoming consumed by his secrets. Whatever he has to tell me, he must think it will change everything. I tense up in response to his touch, bracing myself for whatever words come out of his mouth.

Finally, he looks into my eyes. They are clouded with remorse. "Mia, I am—was—Sil."

Tax

I knew Mia was waiting outside of my building before I ever stepped out. I had a feeling she might show up eventually after her little vow to find out why I blackmailed her. I told the doorman and security if a car with her plate numbers parked in or around the building, to call me. Mia's no fool. She's kind, but she's tenacious. I believed her when she said she would find out who I am and why I came into her life.

I have to admit, this whole following me thing is kind of badass of her.

And then there is the other possibility, the one I pray doesn't come to fruition: that she might show up at my door telling me she's pregnant. It's not that I don't want her to have my child, it's that I want for her to be free of all of my baggage. So, I bury that thought, tell myself it's not going to happen. I left her before I could do more damage than I already have. And if it does happen, I will have to battle with every fiber of my being to stay away, because that's what would be best for Mia and our child. She would probably hate me for abandoning them, but she never know how much it would torture me to stay away. And I would deserve for her to think that of me, even if it's a lie.

I thought following Mia this week would make things easier. Selfishly, I could watch her from a distance, get a dose of her while she would be protected from any further drama I could bring, but it only made me crave her with an intensity that was torture: sleepless nights full of internal deliberation, an unrelenting ache in my gut, a cock that wouldn't calm the fuck down.

I tried to make her think I didn't give a shit. That would be better than the truth, but she sees right through my bullshit, and she isn't afraid to call me out on it. Usually, I can shut people out, it's a shield I have used all my life, but Mia doesn't even notice the shield. She cuts through that shit like a welder. Her words were like bullets, each one piercing through the once impenetrable armor.

When she called me a coward, she was right. Mia exposes herself to me with such fearlessness. I respond by leaving. Yes,

DEBT

I am doing this to protect her, but I also don't want Mia to hate me. I like that she wants me. I could leave while I was ahead, or I could stay and earn her eventual hate.

And if Mia discovers the whole truth, she will hate me. There is no other way. I will be the one who is left alone in a pile of ashes.

But seeing her on the ground, broken and abandoned, knowing that it was me who did that to her, for no good reason, I couldn't convince myself any longer that what I was doing was good for her. I couldn't let her think I didn't care. She deserved to know that she is so much more to me than I ever let on. And if she is carrying our child, I can't let her do this alone, I'll have to find a way to control Jude.

I saw her puffy eyes as she went to work every day last week, tucking away the memories of what had happened between us so she could continue to run Alea. All week I had been fighting the urge to end up on her doorstep and make the tears stop. But I kept telling myself I needed to do right by her and that her temporary pain would be worth avoiding the greater pain of knowing. But then she got on her knees. She begged.

And I can't say no to her when she fucking begs.

If anyone had a debt to pay, it's me. She deserves to know who I am, what happened to me and Jude, why we turned out the way we did.

I'm in now. Mia and I don't have a choice, we can try to run, but we each keep getting pulled back in, like our connection is a strong current, pulling us on its course no matter how hard we swim.

I will tell her as much as I can, it'll be ugly, but it can be enough. Though there are some things, she can never know. She doesn't deserve that kind of pain.

"Sil? What? Sil as in Silvio? That's not possible. You don't even look like him..." she says in response to my confession, her face masked in confusion.

"Mia, that was 14 years, 80 pounds, and a delayed puberty ago. No one would recognize me. Do you really even remember what Sil looks like? Aside from the most obvious superficial characteristics? Long hair, tall, black clothes. You haven't seen his—my—image in fourteen years. No one remembers Sil, no one cared about Sil. Sil vanished one day and no one even noticed."

"I did," she says.

I watch Mia observe my face, searching her memories. Her mouth is parted open in shock. "It doesn't make sense. The things you said about yourself...that wasn't Sil's—your—life."

"Well, some things were true to Sil, some were true to Tax."

"I can't believe it..." her voice vanishes in disbelief. "Your eyes...I thought there was something familiar. I think it's why I always felt safe with you. No matter how hard you tried to be, there was something familiar inside of them."

I look to the side, now feeling that my eyes are some sort of vulnerability. I don't like vulnerability.

"But you never had a brother..."

"I met Rex right after I left Clint."

"What about your sister? Jude...Of course...Judith...I never knew her by anything other than Jude. You said she was your younger sister, not a twin."

"Technically, she is younger by a few minutes. Semantics."

"You said you weren't close to her. I remember you being so close."

"That was a lie, I'll admit. I didn't want you sniffing around with more questions about her."

"I can't even wrap my mind..." She slumps back, shivering as a breeze sweeps in.

"Come to my place, we can talk, but let's get you into some warm clothes," I say, feeling protective.

"I don't understand..." she mouths to herself as I guide her into the passenger seat of her car. "But, why? I never did anything to you...I thought we were friends."

"Let's just get back home," I say, pulling out of the abandoned lot.

CHAPTER THIRTY-FIVE

14 Years Earlier

This is bad, really bad. I'm not sure what's going on, but every base instinct is telling me to get the hell out of here. I don't want to run and look scared, so I slowly back up.

"Nothing man. I didn't know you were hanging here tonight," I say, as if Tripp being at the meetup point instead of Mia is some huge coincidence.

I scan my perimeter and see that Tucker, Tripp's older brother and lifetime delinquent, is standing nearby in the shadows. Unlike Tripp, who is seen as a golden boy and a future D1 college star football player, Tucker has always been a blatant troublemaker. Instead of going to college, my dad bitched that Tucker got a cushy office in the factory doing nothing. He doesn't even show up half of the time. He's been known to love late nights at the bar and for slapping around a few girlfriends. Tripp and Tucker together, drunk, is bad fucking news.

I glance to each side looking for an escape route. Flanking me are Huck and Curtis. My stomach twists and bile climbs up my throat.

"Just wondering why you wanna fuck my girl," he says, with a smartass smirk, his posture lilting from his drunkenness.

"I don't know what you're talking about."

Tripp laughs, looking around to the others for assurance, and they join his chorus of mockery. "Awwww, he thinks Mia would want some poor, part backwoods trailer trash, part immigrant, skinny fuck like him." Tripp pulls out a note from his pocket, waving it in the air.

He clears his throat and squints to read the letter in the darkness of the dimly lit forest.

"Mia, I think you are an amazing person, and you deserve the best. I know you think of me as a friend, but I see you as more. Awwwww!" He reads the words in a high-pitched voice, mocking the sweetness of my words.

My cheeks burn as he reads the private words, now made public for teasing and humiliation.

"Oh, this part is my favorite: I think you deserve someone who will treat you like a queen. It might not be my business, but you deserve better than Tripp." He looks up and sneers at me. "So, you trying to get my girl to break up with me?"

"How did you get that?" I ask. My insides quiver with mortification. How could I ever show my face in school again?

"Dude, she laughed her ass off when she read your letter and then she gave it to me. Mia was just trying to get her project done. She's nice to everyone. She doesn't like you. You've been creeping the shit out of her. She wants you to leave her alone and asked me to make sure you get the message."

"Fine. I got it. There's no need for four people to deliver the message," I say.

"I think there is. You seem to have forgotten your fucking place, you fucking weirdo." Tripp bumps his chest against mine, and the smell of hot beer assaults my nose. It reminds me of the man whose head I just bashed with a pot.

"I don't want any problems," I say.

"Well then maybe you shouldn't go around causing them."

DEBT

I take a few steps back and hit a wall. I turn and see it's Tucker. Tripp and his friends are all seniors. They all play football and Tucker used to play when he was in high school. While we are all around the same height, each guy outweighs me by at least forty pounds.

"Come on guys, point taken," I say.

Tucker pushes me forward into Tripp's arms and he pushes me back. "Oh, you wanna start something? The freak over here thinks he's a tough guy!" Then he peers at my face, tilting his head. "Looks like you got your ass beat once tonight already. I guess nobody likes you, huh? What happened? Daddy beat your ass again? Everyone in this fucking town knows what a drunk loser your dad is."

"Shut up," I say, seething under my breath.

"It's no wonder your mom offed herself. Who would want to live with a husband like that and a fucking freak for a son?"

"My mother died giving birth. You don't even know what you're talking about."

Tucker laughs behind me. "My dad said your mama killed herself after you and your sister were born."

Shock flashes through my body like a stun grenade. This can't be true. Jude and I had always been told she died giving birth to us. That's why pops hated us. But why would Tucker say these things out of the blue?

"Sil?" The small voice calls out from the trees, searching for me. *Shit, Jude.*

"Just go back to the car!" I yell, but it's too late, she reaches the clearing and sees the commotion.

"What's going on?" she asks, her eyes darting to the guys encircling me.

"I was just telling your brother how your whore of a mother killed herself," he said. I don't even think. Tripp's words, designed for cruelty, set me off. Maybe if it was just me, I could have resisted. But Jude, my best friend, the little spitfire who tackled my dad to defend me, shouldn't have to hear this bullshit.

I swing and land a punch right on Tripp's cheek. My hand shoots with a sharp pain as it connects and he stumbles back a few steps. The satisfaction only lasts a second as I feel Tucker's arms lock onto mine, exposing my torso.

Tripp rubs his lips and looks down at his bloody fingertips. "So you wanna roll with the big boys? Maybe you forgot who I am. I fucking own this town!" he yells.

"Hit him," Tucker says, tightening his arms around mine.

Tripp stomps forward and punches me in the gut. The punch feels like a missile directly shot into my stomach, triggering a tsunami of nausea. Before I can gasp for air, he does it again and again.

"Stop it!" Jude screams, trying to push Tripp away. But this is not two of us on one man so drunk he could barely stand. This is four strapping older athletic teenagers. We are no match. Tripp pushes her to the ground. "Huck don't let her go. She'll tell," he says.

"Run, Jude!" I scream through raspy gasps.

Jude tries to get to her feet, and Huck, all six feet of him, grabs her. She kicks and screams as he pulls her away.

"Jude's gonna watch," Tucker says into my ear, his stale beer breath adding to the sick feeling in my stomach.

Then punches rain down on me, my body, my face, my neck. The warm moisture of blood and snot coats my chin. My ribs ache so deeply, that if it wasn't for Tucker holding me up, I would wilt to the floor.

Finally he does, and the cool damp earth catches my body. *Relief. This is finally over.*

But soon I realize it's not.

"I want in this shit!" Tucker says, like it's his turn in a game of miniature golf. A huge thudding sound booms in my chest as a foot makes contact with my upper back. Pain shoots up and down my spine as stars explode in my vision.

"Wait...wait..." Tripp says, with a hint of laughter in his voice. "Let's show him who his real daddy is." I look up through swollen eyes as they whip off their belts.

"Please..." I moan, weakly raising a hand to shield myself.

That's when I tune in on the sound of Jude screaming. I had shut it out earlier. Her guttural pleas for them to leave me alone were too difficult to bear.

"Shut her up!" Tripp screams.

I want to tell her to stop, but every time I speak, I choke on blood and saliva.

"You're going to kill him!" Jude cries.

"Maybe we should stop," Huck says. "Guys this is getting out of hand."

"Huck, shut up the fuck up!" Tripp screams. "Don't be a pussy. Cover her mouth."

Then the belt buckles rain down. It seems each brother is competing with the other to see who can slam down the hardest. Tripp eggs Curtis to join in and he adds his belt to the violent flogging. Somehow, my shirt comes up, and they directly attack my flesh, tearing it open with each lash. Each time a cold buckle lands on my skin, it immediately bursts into flames of pain. Viscous warmth leaks from each new wound.

"Shit my belt broke," Tripp complains.

"Woooh!" Curtis shouts with a rush of adrenaline.

"Gimme that!" Tripp yanks Curtis's belt.

"Shit man, he looks bad," Curtis says. "Fuck dude, we are going to be in so much trouble."

"Shut up!" Tripp shouts, wailing down on me with Curtis's belt over and over.

Finally, it stops. The world begins to slowly darken, but I fight to stay awake. I can't leave Jude alone. I have to get to my feet and get her out of here.

"Naw, man," I hear Huck say, as he and Tucker discuss something in a low murmur. I roll over to my side and arch my neck to look up and see Tripp feeling up Jude. She bucks and writhes underneath his hands.

Without even looking back at me, Tripp speaks. "How about I let you fuck Mia, if you let me fuck your sister? I bet her pussy is tight. She's so fuckin' little."

This cannot be happening. This must be a nightmare. This doesn't happen in real life. Only in the movies. Tripp and Tucker are bad, but no one is this bad.

"Don't," I say, trying to get to my feet. Every time I get one body part off the floor, I collapse. My ribcage feels like ten knives plunge into it with each breath. Blood and spit dangle off my chin, swinging like a pendulum with every movement.

"Huck, don't be such a pussy," Tucker says. "Hold her."

"No!" I call out, but my voice is hardly a whisper.

Huck's face is full of dread as he clamps down harder on Jude and Tripp pulls up her shirt. He laughs. "She's got no titties!"

Tucker squeezes one of her nipples. "I bet she doesn't even have a bush yet," he says, tugging on her waistband.

Her tiny body kicks and wrestles underneath Huck's grip, but he'd rather hold down a defenseless girl instead of standing up to his friends. Curtis stands to the side, shifting his weight around uncomfortably, but laughs with the Pettits when they make their disgusting comments.

DEBT

I take a deep, painful inhale. It feels like nails are dancing in my lungs, stabbing them remorselessly. I finally come to my feet, dragging myself over to Tripp. They are so engaged in tormenting my sister that they hardly notice me.

I muster up every ounce of strength I have left to attack them all, but with one heave, I simply collapse on top of Tripp.

"What the fuck?" he says, pushing me to the ground and kicking me in the stomach.

He picks up a bottle from the ground and swings it in my direction. Then everything goes black.

Wet warmth awakens me. At first, it's almost comforting, like I am swimming in a warm ocean, but then the smell hits my nose, the acrid taste of ammonia cloys on my lips. I can barely focus my eyes, as my entire body pulsates in one unanimous throb of pain. Then my hearing hones in on the noise of a single stream of fluid coming from above. Someone is pissing on me. I barely have the energy to care. At least it's warm, and it's gotten so cold this late into the night, that this seems to be the only physical relief available to me. I'm probably going to die tonight. I don't see how I can make it out of this.

Then I remember Jude. My eyes shoot from one dark shadow to the other, and I finally spot one moving.

"Do it, Huck. You're not in it with us unless you fucking do it," Tripp's voice is more slurred. He's even drunker than he was earlier. The shadow is a hump and it thrusts back and forth, jaggedly, stopping for seconds at a time, over a limp figure. I moan, trying to do anything I can to make them leave her alone. The thrusts stop.

"I can't!" Huck's sobbing. "I put it in, okay? I pumped. That's enough. I did it."

"Then fucking use this!" Tripp picks something up from the floor and hands it to the figure. I squint my eyes to focus on the shape and I see it's a glass bottle.

I open my mouth to scream, but only raspy weak noises come out of my throat. I rise up to my forearms and drag my useless body across the spongy forest floor. I'll use the last bit of life I have to stop them from hurting Jude any more. Something grips the collar of my shirt and pulls me up.

"You just don't fucking quit. It's too late. We all had turns popping her cherry." He lets go of my collar as tears stream down my cheeks and I fall back to the ground. An explosion of pain shoots out in every direction from my torso and I curl into a ball as I groan in agony.

I have nothing left.

I never thought life was fair. I learned that from an early age. But today, I learned that life is cruel. It isn't random. It targets some people. People like Tripp and Tucker live with impunity. They get money, and girls, and parents who care. People like Jude and me are forgotten. No, we are worse than forgotten. We are the playthings of fate. Fate is a cruel bitch, and when she sets her eyes on you, you cannot escape her plans.

And so I appeal to the only thing left. I never really believed in praying. I used to do it when I was little. I used to ask god to make my daddy nice. I stopped asking at about eight years old. It was clear my prayers didn't matter. But now, I am willing to put my pride aside for my sister. I brought her into this mess. She should never have been here. She should have been home getting ready for school tomorrow. All this came from my obsession with a girl who laughed at my heartfelt letter, and passed it along to her boyfriend so he could use it as a torture device. Mia knows who Tripp is. She knew this would end badly for me. Maybe not death, but pain and humiliation would be guaranteed. She's not who I thought she was. I was an idiot to think a girl like her would love me back.

Please, If there is a god, if you let me and Jude survive this, I will make this right. I will be strong. I'll make it up to her.

Boots crunch along dry leaves and twigs, arriving in front of my torso. Tucker kneels, grabs me by the collar and rears his fist.

Darkness covers me again.

CHAPTER THIRTY-SIX

Tax

Mia sits across from me, her hair still wet from the rain, covered in a blanket as tears streak her face. It's the first time I have ever told anyone about that night. The events have replayed in my head more times than I can remember, but never have I recalled them out loud. Even Jude and I speak about it using vague references: *what they did to us; that night; what happened*. We never allow ourselves to relive it openly.

For me, it's to avoid self-hatred that brews because I allowed my sister to be gang raped and beaten. For Jude, it's the shame of knowing her brother witnessed much of it.

I've never even spoken to Rex about it other than in a passing reference. He knows the gist of it from Jude. In a way, it's our fourth sibling. That night has a life of its own. It lives with us, it fuels us, it gives us purpose and strengthens our bond. Rex loves Jude and me enough to know that the scars on my body and the scars in Jude's womb were from the same attack. That's all he's ever needed to know.

Uttering the words to Mia, I was surprised at how numb I had become. It was like I was recounting a horror story, not something I had lived. But for Mia, I could sense her feel every hit, every violation, every harsh word. I watched her feel the pain for me that I could no longer summon.

"I am so sorry this happened to you. Poor Jude..." Mia says, choking back more tears. "I don't understand how they could have gotten away with this," she says, shaking her head in disbelief.

"I was in the hospital for days under sedation, as was Jude. By the time we woke up, Pettit had paid off anyone who mattered, including my own piece of shit father."

"I can't believe I ever dated Tripp, that disgusting piece of shit. I broke up with him as soon as I came back to school after my mother died. He was a narcissistic nightmare. And I am sure he cried to his father telling him he made a mistake, begging for his help. That's all he ever did, was do whatever he wanted and then cry to his parents to make it right."

"Well, whatever he did, it worked. Because everyone was silenced."

"So, you thought...I set you up? You thought I could do that?" her eyes refill with unshed tears. "Tax, tell me you didn't think I could do something like that?"

"Tripp had the letter. He said you gave it to him. It made sense to me. I didn't think I was worthy of you at the time. It made sense to me that you might react like that. Actually, it seemed more likely than you liking me back."

"Tax...I would never. How could you think that? I was good to you." Her lips purse with indignation.

"Mia, you don't know what it's like. You were loved from the day you were born. Jude and I, no one ever cared about us but each other. It was really easy for us to think yet another person didn't."

The tense line of Mia's lips soften. She sighs, closing her eyes for a couple of seconds. The tautness of her muscles dissolves as she digests my perspective. She opens her eyes, nods, and reaches her hand out to my thigh. I tense. But this time, I allow myself to receive her touch. She's not the one who caused the scars, or the brutality. I have to train myself to remember that.

"Never, Tax. I would have never, ever let that happen if I had known," she says remorsefully.

"I know that now. But, Mia what happened to us, it changes you. I don't just mean it traumatizes you. I mean it infects you with rage. It fucks you up in a way that can't be fixed. The world kept taking and taking and never gave back. You can only give so much without getting back. Love, understanding, empathy. Jude and I only gave those things, they rarely came our way. And that night took the last of what we had left. We lost something. I don't feel remorse. I hate the world. My life became a mission to spread the pain tenfold. Pain. The world gave us that in droves. I had plenty of that to give back."

"You have more to give than pain, Tax. You are not those assholes. You are not," she says firmly. Her eyes widen. "My father?"

I don't have the heart to tell her the truth. It would break her. And if she knows her father was involved, it might lead down a line of questions I don't want her to follow. "He didn't know."

"Why didn't you tell him? He would've made it right."
He's not the man to me that he was to you, Mia.

"I was too scared of my own father. He threatened to hurt Jude if I didn't lie to the police."

"Dammit. I wish I had known. I would have helped. I promise you I had no idea. And if I had known, I would've gotten my dad to help you."

"I know."

"So you found me because you thought I did this to you?"

I nod. *Shame.* She's the only person who can make me feel it with the slightest gesture or look. It's not because she intends to, but because for the first time, I really care what someone thinks of me.

"And because you thought I was responsible for Jude's rape...you wanted to do the same to me?"

Fuck. I don't want to admit I am a rapist. I am many things, but not that. I never intended to fuck her. I intended to kill her. But I know only in my warped mind does that sound better. I try to find some way to explain it all.

"I wanted to scare you. When I saw you booked that service, the timing was perfect. The rest just happened. When I came to your house that night, I wasn't going to rape you, I promise. But then when I touched you, and you responded, I couldn't help myself."

"It was like a perfect storm..." she thinks aloud.

"Yes. And then, once we were together, I wanted you more. I know you did too. And the way we wanted things wasn't typical. But I was still angry. I convinced myself that I could do both: have you and make you pay. Of course, I was fooling myself. I knew as soon as we started the arrangement that something was wrong. I couldn't reconcile that you were the person who set up Jude and me. And I started wanting to see more and more of you, and I hated myself for betraying my promise to make things right. You have to understand, up until last week, I thought you had set Jude and me up."

"So despite thinking I had done all that, you came to see me in Miami?"

I realize how confusing this must be for her to understand, but it was just as confusing for me at the time. "Yeah. I just couldn't stop myself."

"Knowing me now, as an adult, how could you have thought that?"

"I bet you didn't think I would be who Sil would have become. It was my truth, Mia. What I did to you was wrong. It's the only thing I regret."

"It is. But I am part of that too. I let you do what you wanted. And I don't have an excuse."

"It's not that simple, Mia. Don't you dare blame yourself for anything. This is on me. And you don't need an excuse to be who you are. You are perfect the way you are."

She looks down, and her soft smile lights up the sadness in her face.

"If what happened between us wasn't supposed to happen, then what was your original goal? What did you plan on doing to me?"

I don't want to keep lying to Mia. But I must. She can never know I intended to slit her throat that first night. Some things can never be forgotten or forgiven.

"My original goal was to scare you that night in your house, then to purchase Alea and stun you when you realized I was the same person who broke into your house. Then I was going to tell you in the boardroom during that first meeting that I was going to close down Alea. You would be without a job and so would all of your friends."

She gasps. Up until now, she didn't understand the depths of my vengeance. And she still doesn't, but this small truth is a taste.

"You would do all that? What about the money? The company was worth tens of millions."

"It was the price I was willing to pay. I knew how important Alea was to you."

"I would have been devastated."

"That was the goal."

She bows her head in her hands, letting her damp brown hair cascade over her shoulders. I don't insist on forgiveness. There is no excuse. It's the truth. It's what I wanted at the time. She takes a deep sigh.

"But you didn't do it."

"I didn't."

"Because?"

"Because I met you."

"So you went after me. Did you go after the others?"

"Mia, you don't want to know the things I did. And I can't tell you. I don't snitch and others are involved. I promised I would tell you who you were to me. Why I came for you. And that's what I have done. I can only say, I have done some ugly things, but I never asked for the life I was given. Everyone who got theirs deserved to get got."

She can't know that the tattoo she subtly admires whenever we are together is a tribute to all the people I have killed. Each serpent, another person I have gleefully ended. It's something I take pride in. And there was one spot left for her. Because of Mia, this tattoo will never be completed. Its incompletion is a dedication to my commitment to protect her.

Mia stands up and comes to me, settling on the oversized ottoman and resting her head on my shoulder. "I know some ill fate fell upon a few of those guys. You don't have to tell me if you did it. But whatever you did to them, after what they did to you and Jude, I am sure they deserved it. I knew you, and you were kind, and generous, and you had—have—a good heart."

"Sil is dead. He doesn't exist. I'm not Sil, Mia. I want to make that clear to you."

"I understand."

She slides her fingers through mine. "Jude, is she around?"

"She and I aren't speaking right now."

"I thought you were close."

"We are. Very. We just have a hot and cold relationship. Right now, it's leaning on cold."

"Maybe I could talk to her. I could explain to her I didn't know."

"She knows. I told her. And she's not Jude anymore either. She kept the name, but she's nothing like that girl you remember."

"Does she hate me too?"

"I don't hate you Mia. But, Jude's having trouble shifting her perception of the situation. She needs a lot of time. I don't want you meeting her. You know that Shakespeare quote: And though she be little, she is fierce? Maybe I don't have it exactly."

"I know it."

"Well, that's Jude. Let me handle her."

"She is your twin. Fierceness is in the genes. But if I can help, let me know."

Mia tracks a finger over the top of my hand, and onto my forearm. The softness of her touch sends warmth through my veins. I don't want to hurt her. But it's what I do. I inflict pain and suffering. How can I become the man that this strong, beautiful, kind-hearted woman deserves? All I can do is warn her, like I always have, but she is persistent. She has a way of getting what she wants, even with someone like me.

It's a hopeless fucking endeavor. I keep pushing her away, trying to get her to safety and she keeps running back into the burning house to grab me. That's who Mia is, that's who she has always been. Ever since I have known her in a previous life, she has been trying to save me. Whether it be pretending to be hungry so that I would eat, befriending me, or allowing me the joy of falling in love during a time in my life when I felt so alone. Sil got to know what it was like to fall in love because of her. Tax knew what it was like to loathe because of her.

And now, maybe she is finally getting her way. Maybe despite the burns, and the cuts, and the smoke that have hindered her, despite my persistence that she run and save herself, she is becoming my savior.

"I'm a harsh person. I say mean things even when I don't mean to. If another guy lays a hand on you, I'll break it. I don't make love, or have sex, I fuck. Sometimes hard. Sometimes brutally. I don't get upset, I fuck shit up. I don't play well with others."

"Tell me something I don't know," Mia says with a snarky smirk on her face. It's that sass that makes me want to bend her over and smack that tight ass of hers.

I want to tell her I am a liar. That I have betrayed her in the worst possible way: I killed someone she loved. Or that I was set on taking her own life in the most brutal way possible. That I even take something that should be a joyous gift, the gift of life, and pervert it with my warped mind. I thought that, somehow, getting her pregnant might make up for everything I did to her by saving her life and giving her the family she had lost. But to normal people, lives are not interchangeable fucking Lego pieces. You can't trade one for the other. I can't make up for the person I eliminated by gifting her a new one.

And yet, I still pump my cum inside of her, because despite what my rational mind knows is right, some part of me still wants to connect with her at that level.

Mia sees my good intentions and she thinks that's all that matters, but intentions are fucking worthless when you are like me. Because by the time intentions travel through my fucked up psyche and burst onto the world as action, they have been shredded and warped until they are mangled with sharp edges that cut to the bone.

I thought I could save Mia from death by giving her life, but it's all the same shit with me. Even when I create, I destroy.

But I won't tell her those words, because I want her to stay. I gave her a chance to leave, and she came back. And I don't have the willpower to push Mia away again.

"I'll never be a normal person. And I can't be controlled. I shouldn't be with anyone. That's what I need to protect you from. I don't operate like most people. You are a good person, you should find a good person."

The words are pointless, because I know she doesn't give a shit. She's made up her mind.

"I already have,' she says, her soft lips kissing the snakes on my neck.

Mia

I finally understand. And maybe I should be angry, but I'm not. Tax doesn't want my pity, but what happened to him and Jude, it's horrendous. How could they be anything other than full of rage and vengeance?

I'll admit, it hurt to hear Tax say what his original intentions were with me. It hurt to think he even thought I was capable of those things. But, all he ever knew was hate. No one, besides his sister, had ever been good to him. Why would he think that would have changed in the few weeks he and I had been friends? It wouldn't take much for a young man who had been let down over and over to believe another person had followed suit.

And maybe I should be upset that he took the law into his own hands, but sometimes circumstances call for other forms of justice. Who knows how much harm they were allowed to do to others because they were never held accountable for what they did to Sil and Jude? How many other victims were paid hush money? I just can't find pity for the men who raped and wounded tiny Jude. There are so many other people deserving of my empathy, and even I have my limits of who I can extend it to.

As I watch Tax irrigating the wounds on my knee, I try to physically see Sil. He's transformed so much over the years, that I can hardly see it, even now that I know who he is. But I see Sil in ways that aren't physical. Tax says Sil's dead, that there's nothing left of the sarcastic yet sweet boy I knew fourteen years ago, but that's not true. I see it in small moments like this. When he doesn't feel the need to protect himself with aggression. Tax may be hard, but he is not heartless.

"So after it all happened, you ran away?"

"Yes. We didn't feel safe. As soon as we both could walk, we ran away while my dad was at work."

"How did you survive?"

"You do what you have to do," he says. "I hustled. We all did. Jude did things I didn't want her to do. But like I said, some things change you." I don't ask for any details. I can only imagine what had to be done.

"How did you get from that to all this?" I ask. I have to admit, as someone who is ambitious, his tenacity impresses me.

He looks up at me from the corner of his eye. "Someone owed me," he says knowingly. "There are many ways to pay a debt. That's all I can say, babe."

Babe. I love how his throaty, husky voice wraps itself around that perky word and manhandles the shit out of it.

"So, your last name? Draconi?"

"It's my mother's."

"Did you ever find out the truth? About how she passed?"

"My father wouldn't tell me. After Jude and I recovered, we ran away from home, lived on the street for years. I didn't have the resources to investigate. But eventually I did. She did kill herself. I don't know why my father lied. Maybe it was the one nice thing he did. Or maybe he was trying to be even more cruel. I think he was embarrassed. You know our town. Suicide has such a stigma. We were infants anyway. In either version of the story, she dies because of us."

"Tax, postpartum depression is no one's fault. It's a chemical imbalance."

"But if we weren't born..."

"No Tax. You are here because you are meant to be. If she never had you, I would never have met the love of my life." *Oh, shit.* Sometimes, I am a little too open. Tax has already shared so much, and this word, this little word can be like a bomb, even with an ordinary guy. I didn't want to drop it like this. Not so soon after all we had just gone through.

The Band-Aid Tax is applying jolts almost imperceptibly, like the word is an invisible gust of wind. He quietly smooths it onto my knee.

I am paralyzed with uncertainty at my choice of words. They were honest, but raw. I should've allowed more time for those words to cure before saying them to him.

My heart races, and now it's me who is stiff and uneasy. He turns to me, his freshly dried, soft, dark hair lays flat so that he looks almost boyish, and kisses me on top of my head. "You're pretty fucking special too."

CHAPTER THIRTY-SEVEN

14 Years Earlier

After being informed by the walking piece of excrement that is my father that I would have to tell Sheriff Tibbett a boldfaced lie, I am filled with rebellion. I don't care if pops chokes me to death, I won't let those bastards get away with what they did to me, much less what they did to Jude.

A doctor comes in and does a round of tests on me. He proceeds to tell me how "lucky" I am to get out of the attack with no permanent injuries, just broken bones, deep contusions, and a severe concussion. He laments to me that the lacerations were the toughest part, and when he lifts my blanket and unwraps my torso, I understand why. I look like fucking Frankenstein. There are stitches everywhere. Just the wounds on my torso required hundreds of stitches. The doc also tells me I'll need to stay a few more days for observation, and then they'll discharge me.

Afterward, I'm left for a few minutes alone, sobbing, Sheriff Tibbett struts into the room in his tan police outfit. He's got that stereotypical cop stride, with his hips shifted forward and his small belly pushed out. He pulls off his aviators from his nose.

"How ya feelin' boy?" It's like he's asking someone who has a cold, not someone who had been beaten with fists, bottles, boots, belt buckles and then was pissed on.

I wipe my eyes with my less fucked up arm. "Not good. I want to see my sister."

He sighs and pulls a chair up beside my bed, grabbing a box of tissues and putting in next to me. I don't touch them.

"She's resting. They have her sedated to deal with the pain."

My hands shake with boiling hate for what those animals did to her. Even Huck, that coward who fucked her while he cried. *He cried.* Like he was the victim. Like he didn't hold down a defenseless four foot nine girl instead of letting her run to safety when she had the chance.

"Well then when can I see her?"

"After we talk, I'll get the doctors in here to see what they say."

"Okay, I'll tell you everything I remember. And I know more now. Pettit is paying my dad to keep me quiet. The Pettit boys and Huck McKinley and Curtis Collins, they attacked me and Jude—"

"Woah, woah, woah, now slow down and take a breath here, Silvio."

I pause, understanding he needs a chronological account of things. This includes my embarrassing letter to his daughter. But before I can even debate that internally, he goes on.

"Now, from my understanding, you and Jude assaulted your father after he told you you could not go out on a school night. Then you stole his truck and money and fled the scene. You stopped at the lake to have some beer with your sister and some passersby coming through on an early morning run came upon you two. They heard some rustling in the bushes, like some folks ran away. The runners must have spooked them. You and your sister are lucky." *I wish people would stop using that word to describe us.* "We have reports of an unknown vehicle and group of men driving through town just hours before. We think that's who attacked you."

"No. I'm telling you I know who did it...and I didn't steal my dad's truck. He attacked me, we fought back. And me and Jude don't drink."

"I've seen your dad's face. That looks like assault kiddo."

"Anyway, I know who attacked us...it wasn't some bandits. It was the Pettits—"

"The Pettits?" He leans back in his seat and sighs. "That's not possible, kid. They were with their family that night. Huck and Curtis spent the night at the Pettit's house. We've got several witnesses to vouch for that, including their parents. Now, you were hit pretty hard..."

"Are you kidding me? They're lying! Can't you test my sister? She was raped."

"I can't talk about those details with you, son."

"But—"

Tibbett leans in, and almost whispers. "Listen, I don't want to have to press charges on you and your sister. Assault and battery, grand theft auto, petty theft..."

And that's when I realize the Pettits didn't just stop at my dad, Tibbett has been paid off too. No one is that stupid, he's looking exactly where he wants to look. He's feeding me my story. Everyone who matters is in on this. Jude and I are alone. We are surrounded by people who have been paid to allow our suffering to linger.

"Fuck it," I say.

"Excuse me?"

Using the bed remote, I lower myself, keeping my eyes trained ahead. The blank ceiling of my hospital room looks just like how I feel inside. "Yeah, it was dark. I don't know who it was. I just remember walking into the forest and that's it. They must have hit me right away."

"Okay." I notice he doesn't write anything down, because what I have to say is irrelevant. "We've got a APB out for a truck that meets the description of the one seen in the area. We'll be in touch with you and your dad with any new developments."

I don't look at him. I just focus on the ceiling, trying not to blink. But every time I cave in, tears roll down my temples. I wonder if god is punishing me for not praying and using him only when I needed him at the last minute. I promised if we lived, I would make this right, but he's going to make doing that as difficult as possible. No one, not a single damn person is going to help us. Not even the law.

Sheriff Tibbett, pushes himself up off the chair and calmly walks towards the door. Before opening it, he turns around.

"Silvio?"

I don't respond.

"I know you've been working with Mia for a project. And I know that's done now. I want you to leave her alone. Tripp told me you've been giving her trouble, getting the wrong idea of your friendship. She's a good girl. She's going to college soon. She's all I've got. I don't want her getting caught up with troublemakers. So, your visits to my home are no longer welcome."

Look ahead. Don't cry. Don't let them see the pain they've caused.

The door closes behind Tibbett, and then I am all alone again.

My chest spasms as I let the tears flow.

CHAPTER THIRTY-EIGHT

Tax

I'm waiting for Mia to wake. She made me promise I would go for a run with her this morning. I usually get up around seven, and on the days I'm not strength training, throw on some running gear and head out. But this morning, I am up earlier than usual, and Mia looks so peaceful, I don't have the heart to even touch her.

So I lie beside her, watching her stillness. She sleeps so peacefully. I remember when I used to sleep like that. Ever since Mia came along, I toss and turn a lot. Never have I had so much to lose, and so many reasons to lose it.

I don't feel bad about killing Tibbett. He was in poor health, he traded justice for money. Aside from my own father, no one else owed me more than Tibbett. It was his fucking job to help the defenseless. But he traded in his ethics for cash. As an adult, I understand better. He had just lost his wife, he was faced with raising his daughter alone. Money does a lot to help with burdens like that. But he wasn't just anyone, he had an obligation to help Jude and me, and he chose to side with the corrupt. I only feel bad that what I did hurt Mia. I hate that I have to keep this truth from her. But that's my problem, not hers.

I love looking at Mia up close: her smooth skin, the softness of her curves, the way her dark hair drapes over her bare shoulders. Flashes of that body twisted around mine as I fucked her last night play in my head. Her lips: soft, plump, flush with color. They wrapped around my cock as her tongue swirled around it, making it burst. Her fat tits, with her perfect soft nipples, I love the feel of them in my mouth. Her smell, light and floral, lingers on everything so that when she's not with me, I find myself thinking about her at unexpected moments. Everything about her turns me on, as if she was created to my specifications.

But it's not just about sex. Because I don't want anyone else. I never have ached before when someone walked out the door. I never felt the need to protect. I never wanted to just sit around and do nothing with someone else since the first time I met Mia as a teenager. That is, until I met Mia again.

My phone buzzes with a call from the front desk downstairs. I quietly slip out of bed. It's way too fucking early for unexpected visitors.

"Hello?"

"Good morning Mr. Draconi. Your sister is here to visit you."

I can hear her bitching in the background. She's always had a free pass to come up, but now that Mia's been spending some nights at my place, I revoked that privilege. Jude's just too much of a hothead to randomly discover Mia at my place.

"Tell her I'll be down, but don't let her up."

"Yes, sir."

I look through the heap of clothes on the living room floor that Mia and I left behind last night and throw on a t-shirt and sweatpants. I slip out the condo and head downstairs.

As soon as I spot her, Jude looks pissed. I understand, she's feeling shut out. That wasn't the goal, it just had to be done.

"What's up?" I ask. I haven't seen her since I threw her up against her wall and threatened to kill her.

"So what's this now? I can't even get buzzed upstairs? It's like that?"

I rub my temples. "No. I just want privacy."

She sulks a bit. "Why are you doing this?" she asks, tears forming in her eyes. I look around to see if anyone notices our interaction and then pull her by the arm into a lounge area.

"Why are you here?"

"I thought about what you said, and you're right. We need to look forward. And I was being a bitch. I'm going to give you your space, but I didn't want to just stop talking. So, I wanted to see how you were doing. Maybe we could go to breakfast?"

"I'm glad you are starting to see my side of things. I would love to go, but I have company."

"Since when have you ever cared about kicking out one of your hoes?"

"This is the shit I am talking about."

"Okay, okay. Sorry!" she says. "You're just acting weird. We haven't spoken in weeks and you won't even let me upstairs. Having a girl upstairs has never stopped you from letting me in before."

"Maybe I am trying to have a healthy normal relationship."

Jude laughs mockingly. "Okay, I can appreciate this whole new leaf you're turning, but you're not going to ever be Ned Flanders."

"Oh fuck you," I say, shoving her half playfully. "That's not what I meant."

"So, who is she?"

"Huh?" Just then, my phone buzzes with a text. I glance at it:

If you went running without me, you're dead.

I slide my phone back in my pocket as inconspicuously as possible, trying like hell to hide a smile.

"I gotta go," I stand up.

"It's her. Isn't it?"

Fuck. It's that twinstinct shit.

"Jude, now is not the time to talk about this."

She paces away from me, then sharply turns, jabbing her finger at me.

"You said you ended things with her. That was the compromise. She would be gone. You made her miserable. You made her love you and then you left. That's the only way I can live with the compromise."

"Not now," I say firmly under my breath as I glare at her.

Jude snickers. "She must be something else for you to risk our relationship over her."

"She didn't do anything. And I'm not risking anything, Jude. It's you who is."

"I don't believe it."

"You gotta go Jude."

"So just like that, I don't mean anything anymore. After everything we have been through together. We used to hang out every day. You don't need me in your life anymore now that you're the new Tax."

"You'll always be my sister and you'll always be important to me. Stop being so dramatic."

"I hate when you call me dramatic."

"Then don't be so fucking dramatic."

"You're still a fool for her, all these years later," she says, shaking her head.

"Go fuck yourself."

"Right back at you."

"Well, on that note, I'm glad we're talking again and you are willing to change course. Everything is fine. And when I am not busy, we'll have a long talk about it."

She crosses her arms and glares at me with disapproval.

"I'll call you and we can hang out just you and me sometime this week. I'll explain everything, but I need to go."

"I can't believe you," she says, genuinely hurt. "It's like you hate me now. You want nothing to do with me ever since she came into the picture."

"That's not true. Our issues have nothing to do with her."

"They have everything to do with her!" she hisses loudly.

"I don't have time for this shit. We'll do dinner. We'll talk. I'm not shutting you out. I promise. I'll call you and take you anywhere you want for dinner. Maybe we go to Door Country for the weekend or something. Okay? Now I gotta go," I say, backing out of the lounge.

Jude sulks, arms crossed. "Maybe I won't be around when you finally have time for me."

"I'll see you this week..." I say, running back to the elevator.

The aroma of coffee hits me as soon as I open the door to my place. Mia's standing in the kitchen completely naked, waiting on the brewer.

"Well damn," I say.

"Where did you go?" she asks, leaning over the counter. Her eyes are still puffy from sleep and her hair is a rough mess from all the yanking it endured at my hands.

"The doorman had a delivery issue. I didn't go running without you. I always keep my promises," I say, my cock rising as I take in the view of her naked body glowing in the morning sun.

I walk up to her and press against her. The softness of her pillowy breasts rubbing against my stomach makes my cock ache with need.

"We need to run," she says, pushing away from me.

I grab her ass so hard she flinches. "You know what you're doing. There is no version of a story where you walk around this condo with your tits and pussy out that doesn't end in me fucking you."

I spin her around and bend her over the kitchen island and she gasps as I rub my hand over her wet pussy. "Goddamn Mia, I knew you fucking wanted it."

I slide a couple of fingers inside of her, and her creamy warmth engulfs them. My dick pulsates in anticipation of being wrapped by her pussy. But I love to tease her. Even if it's a quickie, there are ways to make her cunt gush for me.

I curl my fingers on her g-spot and she purrs like a fucking lioness. "Stop, Tax. We never get anything done," she moans, thrusting her hips against my finger. Her protest conveniently simulates her fucking my hand.

I glide my fingers out, they glimmer with her pussy juices and I pull her up by the back of her neck, using the slickness of my fingers to rub the tip of her fucking gorgeous tits. She curls her body against mine, groaning from the back of her throat. I grab a nipple and stretch it out as she lets out this sexy fucking whimper that makes my cock flinch.

I grab her tit hard and press it up. "Lick," I say. She bites her bottom lip, looking up at me hesitantly, teasing with her brown eyes. "Fucking lick," I say, squeezing it harder. She tucks in her chin and rolls out her tongue along her light brown nipple. Watching her lick her nipple like that makes my cock scream to be touched, so I stroke it to alleviate the throbbing.

I turn her just enough towards me so that I can lick the rest of her juices off her breast and that's about all I can fucking take before I burst.

"Shit, Mia. I'm gonna fuck you so hard, this whole building is gonna hear," I say, facing her away from me again and gripping her neck for leverage.

"Fuck me," she begs, reaching her hand underneath to rub her pussy. *Fuuuuuck.*

"Say please," I groan in her ear. "You like to beg, don't you?"

"Please Tax, stick your huge fucking cock inside of me." *Holy shit, she is so fucking hot.*

I push myself into her tight pussy, growling from the tight warm grip that takes a hold of my cock. She lets out a moan that sounds like a cry. The way she moans could make my dick explode right on the spot if I let it.

I plunge into her, then keep my cock inside, massing her g spot with its head. I spread her tight ass cheeks apart and tease the tight button of her asshole.

And then the knob on the front door starts jiggling.

"Oh shit," I moan, on the verge of coming. I whip myself out of her. The door hinges open.

"Who is that?" she asks covering up her chest.

"Duck," I say, just as Rex walks in from behind the door. She drops to her knees. "Oh for fuck's sake!" I scream. "Can I get some fucking privacy!"

Then I feel Mia's lips wrap around my cock. *Oh this kinky little minx.*

Rex isn't looking at me when he starts saying: "Since when the hell has privacy ever—what the fuck?"

Just at that moment, Mia starts doing some voodoo shit on my cock with both of her hands and her mouth: sucking, twisting, licking.

"Oooh fuck..." I say, gripping the table.

"Are you naked?" Rex asks.

"Go away, come back in like an...hour." Just as I say that, she takes me balls deep. Her cock sucking skills are about as magical as a fucking unicorn.

"Aw come on man, what the hell am I going to do for an hour?"

Rex can be so fucking daft for a genius.

"Rex, I am literally having my cock sucked underneath this counter as we speak. Do I need to fucking build a sign? Go somewhere else!"

"Oh shit, man. Okay." He backs out. I let out of sigh of relief. Then the door pops open again.

"Holy shit man, is Mia here?"

"Are you fucking kidding me!" Mia's laughter hums against my cock. I should have totally put him on that list with Jude. I haven't gotten around to telling him about my reunion with Mia, thinking it would get back to Jude before I could tell her myself.

"Alright!" Rex says, backing out and slamming the door behind him.

"Uhhhh..." I dip my head back and relish in the feeling of Mia's gorgeous hot mouth on my dick. "Come here," I say, pulling her up. "That was really fucking bad, what you just did."

"You're a bad influence," she says with a smirk.

"Now I'm gonna fuck the smartass out of you."

CHAPTER THIRTY-NINE

Mia

I feel like shit today. I woke up nauseous and under the weather. To top it off, my period is starting. This whole thing with Tax has made me less productive these past couple of weeks because I want to spend all of my time with him or thinking about him. I know? How pathetic, right? I've turned into a lovesick teenager.

Anyway, because I do have a company to run, I have insisted, against Tax's wishes, that I spend most weeknights at my place away from him. That way I can get a good night's sleep and also take some work home with me. Work, I might add, that I have been behind on ever since that week he left me. I kept a happy face for everyone at Alea during that time, but my output still suffered. I like to remind him this is *his* investment I am taking care of after all, although I now know he originally had no intentions for it to flourish.

Now as I walk into Alea at noon this Tuesday, I feel like I'll never catch up. Thankfully, whatever the hell I had seemed to work itself out, though my period decided to pop her head in for a monthly check-in. *Bitch.*

"Good morning—oops—afternoon Mia!" Laney says as I make a beeline towards my office. "Are you feeling better?"

"Good afternoon! Yes, I think I ate something funky or whatever. Anyways, I feel like a million bucks now! Anything I should know?"

"Yes. Adam and Eve called, I pushed them through to your voicemail. Oh and Pete was looking for you. Aaaaand Mr. Draconi is in your office," she says pressing her lips into a tight line as her eyes go wide.

"Wait what?"

She keeps her lips pursed and mumbles, pointing her head towards the direction of my office. "Miiisstterr Draacooniiii is iiin theeee offiiiccce."

"Yes, that I got."

"Sorry, normally I wouldn't let anyone in, but he insisted and he does sort of own the entire company."

"No, it's fine," I say, dropping a folder and then spilling my coffee on the floor as I bend to retrieve it. "Shit!" I haven't seen Tax in these offices since our last kinky Tuesday morning meeting weeks ago, and having him here so unexpectedly takes me back to that feeling of delightful anxiety.

"Go ahead. I've got it," Laney says, taking my folders from my arms and nearly shoving me in the direction of my office.

"Hold my calls!" I call out as I head towards my door.

I straighten out my flowing dress, smooth my hair, and open the door.

Tax is sitting in MY chair, grinning just like I knew he would be. He loves to see me on edge. He's wearing a black suit, with a white shirt and a mustard tie that brings out the olive undertones in his skin. My dear ovaries, does he look hot in a suit with that tat peeking out just above the collar. I close the door behind me. "What are you doing here!" I whisper.

"I expected a much better reaction than that," Tax says, leaning back in my chair.

"Well, it's been a while since I've seen you here. And, I didn't expect you."

"Are you feeling better?"

"Yes I am. Thank you for asking."

"Good, because I came here for something," he says, licking his lips.

"You wanted to play checkers?" I ask.

"Hey, it's you who insists on going home alone, Ms. Independent."

"Well, you know, I am running your company, and ironically you are a huge distraction to that task. And that's my chair you're sitting in, Mister."

"Don't forget who's boss here," he says, standing up. I immediately revert back to the woman who was at this dark man's mercy. When he's not in Alea, I run the show, but as soon as Tax stands in front of me, his hair slicked back, his body finely wrapped in an Armani suit, I become his secret whore. And yes, it turns me on.

"You know I'm leaving for a few days this afternoon. I thought stopping by yesterday would hold me over, but I decided I need your pussy one last time before I go."

"Or you can just stay in town. You're probably going down there to sunbathe anyway."

"Why does everyone think I don't work?" Tax asks, exasperated. I know Rex loves to give him crap about it, so I join in on the jabs occasionally. "If I was going to sunbathe, you'd be coming with. It's boring real estate development shit, as you know."

"Maybe it's because you make everything look so easy."

"That's a good point. Some of us don't struggle as much to keep it together," he says playfully.

"You're just jealous because I work at a dildo factory as you like to call it. So much more fun than the lame stuff you do," I say.

Tax walks up to me slowly, a hungry look in his eyes as he presses against me. I step back into the door, and his firm chest traps me against it. His lips approach a near invisible distance from mine and then he reaches past me.

Click.

That sound brings back a flood of memories. So much has changed since that first day. It happened tear by tear, thrust by thrust, kiss by kiss, but over time Tax and me have evolved into something beautifully ugly. The painful journey is just as important as this moment here because without it, what we have now would not have the same meaning.

Tax is still a savage beast, but now, he is *my* savage beast.

He slides his fingers around my neck and pulls me towards him, pressing his lips against mine. He mutters into my mouth, his warm breath mingling with mine. "I came here for my pussy. Now give it to me."

He takes my mouth, sliding his tongue against mine, drawing on my upper lip with his teeth. Heat spreads from between my legs, my panties dampen, like a conditioned response to his sexual aggression in this building.

His kisses wander down to my neck followed by angry bites. I offer my nape up to him, like someone inviting a vampire to plunder. Tax grabs my ass, dragging me over to my desk. He sits me on its edge, pausing to unbutton his jacket. As he tears it off, I grab at his shirt buttons, undoing them as he grips behind my knees and yanks me towards him. My pen cup falls over and pens roll off the cliff of my desk one by one.

"Wait...wait..." I say, pressing a hand against his bare chest.

"No," he growls, pushing my dress up.

"I have my period," I say remorsefully, as if it's my fault.

He pauses, tilting his nose into my neck, as if caught off guard. A faint sigh blows along the fine hairs on my neck.

For a moment, it seems as if the mood might change.

But then Tax laughs into my neck, his breath tickling the crook behind my ear. He straightens up, looking at me through his chocolate-colored eyes. "Mia, do you think a little blood scares me?"

"Well, I didn't think—"

"I don't give a shit about your period." He pulls my panties to the side and gently tugs on the string of my tampon so that it taunts my pussy with promises of pleasure. "Do you want to do the honors, or should I?"

Jesus-h, why do I find this so hot?

"Which do you want?"

"Smart woman." He looks at me through eyes heavy with arousal. "Why don't you pull it out for me? Slowly." His voice is raspy and low, emerging from a deep place of yearning.

Tax steps back for a better view. I come to my feet and let my panties fall to the floor, then slide back on the desk and bite my lip as I slink my dress up again. Tax watches with a devious smile as he unbuttons his pants and reaches in to pull out his dick. His thick fingers grasp the shaft, and twist up and down as he draws out a lingering breath. He watches me through hooded dark eyes as I stroke my fingers down my inner thighs, to my knees, and push my legs open.

"Your cunt is fucking gorgeous, babe," he tells me.

I lick my lips as I trail my fingertips back up my inner thighs, reaching for the white cotton string.

"Pull it out. Slow. Let it tickle your pussy lips as it comes out."

Holy hell he is so kinky.

I tug on the string firmly this time, jarring it loose. I just started my period, so the dryness causes some discomfort, but once it's free, I slink it out gradually, letting the fibers tickle against the flesh of my opening.

Goosebumps raise on my arms and thighs as Tax watches me do the filthy act while massaging his cock. I hover the string over the trashcan and it makes a small thud as it falls to the bottom.

Tax stands up, still holding his girthy, curved cock in his hand. He comes over to me, and glides it up and down my opening. "My perfect little slut," he says to me. It's a term of endearment. I'm a slut for him and no one else.

"Are you going to be able to stay quiet?" Tax asks. He makes me scream.

"Do I have a choice?"

"Here's an insurance policy," he says, grabbing his tie and rolling it into a ball. I open my mouth without being prompted. "Now I am going to fuck you hard. I'm gonna hurt you, just the way you like it." He props a breast on the neckline of my dress and rolls his thumb on my nipple. "And you are going to keep quiet."

I jut my hips back and forth, signaling that I will comply. He spits in his hand and strokes his thick cock, glaring at me like a predator honing in on his prey. And then his eyes narrow as he thrusts deep into me. I moan loudly and it's only muffled by the tie in my mouth.

"Mia, you didn't last one fucking pump," he groans. "You need to do better."

I nod intently. Again, he plunges in and out of me. I collapse my face into his warm chest as I wrap my arms around him to muffle my sweet agony. He propels himself deep inside, pulling on the flesh of the back of my thighs so that we crash into each other with every pump. "Mia, your pussy is always mine, I don't give a fuck what time of the month it is," he groans out between one of his powerful thrusts.

The skin of my thighs burn from the friction of his grip, but it only helps accelerate the blazing need erupting from my core. He lifts me off the desk and crashes back onto a chair.

"Fuck me Mia. Use my cock to make yourself come." His fingers drag down the sleeves of my dress so that my breasts fall out.

I plant my feet on the ground and bounce up and down on his rigid firmness. Instantly the buildup begins.

"Make your fucking tits bounce," he says, squeezing them both together in his hands as he runs his wet lips against my nipples then tugs one with his teeth. "Make that dirty pussy come on my cock, Mia. Come all over it."

His hips join up to meet mine each time I land down on his dick, and the depth he reaches sends ripples of energy from deep inside. I clamp my mouth down on the tie and bury my face into his neck tat, letting it muffle the sounds of my orgasmic cries.

Tax lets out a sigh from deep within his chest as he uses his own strength to pace me and I let out another groan as his fat cock expands, shooting his cum far inside me.

I lay on his heaving chest for a few minutes, my eyes navigating the collage of scars on his chest. Once they were like his tattoo, just a physical manifestation of his mysteriousness.

But now, when I look at them, my heart hurts for him. And then I get angry. I try not to show it, because he doesn't need any more anger in his life, but the scars remind me what an unjust place the world can be. And yet, despite the injustice, beauty emerges. His scars shield a beautiful physique, ruggedness and beauty combined, they are uniquely Tax. I never looked at them as a flaw, but as a signature. When I used to trail my fingers along his chest, he would lock up, but now, it's different. There's no secret. And he knows I am not the one who ripped his flesh open.

I glide my index finger along the mound of his pecs, occasionally encountering the raised flesh. I feel him watch me in silence. There's something in the air between us, like he wants to say something, but holds back. It's okay. I know he'll tell me when he's ready.

Tax

It used to fill me with feelings of rage when she touched my scars. How dare she take the liberty of touching the brutality I endured at her behest? How dare she fucking pretend like her touch could heal me? It would take everything inside of me not to lash out, but even then I was battling something.

Even when I thought she was the one who set me up, her bold touch made me feel things I had never allowed myself to feel. And now, as she runs her delicate fingers along the permanent reminders of the suffering Jude and I endured, I no longer feel conflicted. I can just allow whatever it is that happens when she touches me.

When I was a kid, I used to have a compulsion to destroy soft, pretty things. If I walked by a patch of beautiful flowers, I would stomp on them. If I saw a bush blooming, I would grab a branch and beat it until the ground was littered with scattered petals. Things that were born beautiful, that were watered and tended to, agitated me. Nothing should be that easy. Softness should be defiled, and true beauty should be earned.

Mia lets me still fulfill that compulsion. But with her, I can do it without destroying her beauty. She is strong and compassionate, and unlike those flowers that withered and died when I ravaged them, she blossoms. There's no one like Mia. She is delicate and fierce. She comes alive when she faces my ugliness.

I think she understands that, but I've never really said it. I can't push the words out from my thoughts. I did it once, fourteen years ago, and when I did, everything fell apart. I don't want this to fall apart. I don't want this to end. Maybe if I don't say it, it can't go away. She can be vulnerable for the both of us, but I won't ever open up. Whenever I do, the cruelty of the world finds a way to seep through those fissures.

So instead of words, I give her sex and touch and hope she understands that's all I can give. I've already warned her that's all I have at my disposal.

When Mia told me she had her period, my first gut feeling was disappointment. It was pure instinct. Somewhere in my bones I yearned for something to express the closeness I feel to her. I fucking suck at showing it, or saying it. And there is no greater connection than a child. But moments after, relief washed over me. We can really move forward, free from the consequences of the lies I believed about her.

And so there's one other thing I will do for her. Something she will never know. I'm not replacing the next set of birth control pills with placebos. Because Mia deserves a choice. And it's no longer the strategy to keep Jude happy while having Mia in my life. If Mia and I ever have a child, it will be because we both want to, not as an offering to Jude. Jude will have to learn to accept things just as I have. What I have with Mia belongs to us and only us. No one else can have a piece of it.

I grab her hand, so small curled up in mine, and nibble the fingertip that grazed my chest.

"I've got a flight to catch, babe," I tell her.

"I know. This meeting is also beginning to run suspiciously long. Laney probably has her ear up against the door," she sighs.

My phone rings and I glance over. It's Jude. I haven't spoken to her since she came over to my building that morning. I have been meaning to stop by, but most of my free time has been with Mia and now I had this last minute trip come up. I ignore the call. I'll get in touch with her as soon as I get back from the trip. There's no point in trying to catch up with her over the phone. She'll just bitch and moan like she always seems to do these days. I shoot her a quick text telling her I am going out of town and I'll talk to her when I get back. Then I toss the phone to the side and get back to talking to Mia.

"Sorry about that. Jude. Anyway, I'll be back on Thursday. Then I am having you all weekend. And then I am locking you in the condo, selling your house, and moving all your shit in."

"Is that the Tax Draconi way of asking me to move in with you?" she asks. I feel her cheek press up against my chest as she smiles.

"Actually, I think I am."

She pauses for a moment and nuzzles into my chest.

"Well, since you asked so nicely...but only if there's room for my pink and silver CD player."

"Oh fuck. My property value is going to plummet, but I think I have a spot for it. Hidden. In a box. Deep inside of a cabinet. Where no one can ever see it," I say, enjoying the music of her laughter.

CHAPTER FORTY

14 Years Earlier

It's been three days since I woke up and I still haven't seen Jude. I keep asking to see her and everyone avoids the subject, saying she's sedated, or she's recovering. Today's the first day I am allowed to roam the hospital in crutches. Up until now, the pain in my ribs was too severe to bear my own weight.

Of course, my first stop is Jude's room. The hospital is small and it only takes minutes to find her, even at my slow pace. There are two beds in the room, but the one closest to the door is empty. The curtain is drawn between them, blocking Jude from view. On the television is a rerun of Saved by the Bell, her favorite show.

I trudge into the room, peek past the curtain and a strong current of nausea rocks me in the gut. She looks so tiny in the bed, her body covered in purple and green bruises. Her face is scratched up. She's sleeping, and I choke back the tears and snot that erupt out of me as I take in what they did to her while I lay unconscious just feet away.

I tuck my face into my forearm, stifling the heaving sobs that erupt. My muffled sobs stir Jude and she turns her face and opens her eyes.

"What are you doing here?" she asks groggily.

I suck back tears. "I wanted to see you."

"I don't want you to see me like this," she says.

All along, it was Jude who asked not to see me these past few days.

"Why?"

Her lips quiver uncontrollably, her eyes go red and glossy with tears. "I—I—I'm—embarrassed."

Then a flood of tears stream down her face and my choked sobs break free. For minutes, she and I just cry. Not just about this, but everything. We had never allowed ourselves the privilege of self-pity.

But if there is any time to wallow in our sorrows, it's now.

I sit next to her.

"I should be embarrassed, not you. I was the idiot who believed Mia would ever want to see me. They used my stupidity to set me up. They hurt you Jude. You didn't do anything wrong. They should be embarrassed."

"They made you watch—" she starts crying again. I understand the shame. Though it's not her fault, the idea of her brother witnessing her lose her virginity in such a disgusting way still stings with humiliation. I'm embarrassed I had to see it too.

"I didn't see much. I'm sorry I couldn't stop them. They knocked me out over and over. I tried so hard to stop them."

"I wish we were stronger. That we could have killed them. Another thing we can thank dad for, being late bloomers." She says it like a joke, but I know she means every word.

We sit in devastated silence for a while, until Jude summons up the strength to speak again.

"Sil...they told me—that I'm—I had bleeding and they had to do surgery. That I won't be able to—have—babies."

I wince in devastation, tears that may as well have been fire rain down my face. Ever since we were little, she cherished every doll like it was a real child. We didn't get toys a lot, so when we did it was a big deal. She told me she wanted to have kids who would have a nice mother and father like we never had. She wanted to rewrite our lives through her own children. And now, even that inherent gift she was given, the ability to make her own life, was gone.

"When did the doctors say you would be able to walk?" I ask.

"I can stand to go pee now. But I think it's another week before I can really move. Why?"

"We're not safe here. Did dad tell you?"

"I know. He said that he would hurt you if I told."

"It's not just him, Sheriff Tibbett, the Pettits, they all know and they are covering it up. We can't live here. I won't let you go to school and have to face those assholes."

"I wish I could kill them all, make them suffer forever."

I nod, wishing there was a way I could blow this whole fucking town into smithereens.

"What are we gonna do?" she asks.

"As soon as we are both discharged, when pops is at work, we're running away. And then, I promise you, one day, we will make every piece of shit in this town pay."

We sob in silence until there are no more tears.

It will be the last time I ever cry.

CHAPTER FORTY-ONE

Mia

He can't wait to see you.

That's the text I get from Tax on Thursday morning, accompanied by a pic of his gorgeous cock.

What about the other head attached to your body?

You know the answer to that. I meant what I said before I left, about you staying. That's not just Hercules talking.

Hercules? Please tell me you just made that up.

I did? ;)

I can forgive anything but naming your cock Hercules.

I was jk (not really). But serious about the other part.

I know. And I meant what I said as my answer.

Good. Now you can stop pretending that you do anything other than think about me all day.

Likewise, Tax.

Boarding. I'll see you in a few hours.

I spend the next few hours working at my desk, trying to keep my mind off my reunion with Tax. At about 11:30 Laney rings me.

"Hey."

"Hey. I have a call on the line from someone with Draconi?"

"Draconi? Really?"

I've never spoken with anyone other than Tax regarding Draconi. And I find it unusual that he wouldn't give me any advance warning that someone else might be calling.

"Did the person give a name?"

"Yes, she said it was important. Name is...Judith James."

Jude? "Yes. Yes, put her through."

Laney patches the call to me.

"Hello? Jude?" I ask.

"Yes, hi Mia."

"Oh my god it's been so long. Is everything okay?" For a moment I panic, remembering Tax is a on a flight and she is his closest relative.

"Yes. Sorry, I didn't mean to worry you. I was hoping I could speak to you in private as soon as possible. Maybe meet around lunch?"

DEBT

"Ummm...yeah...yeah. Sure. What's this about?" Tax said she had a hard time coming to terms with what happened. Maybe she's ready to hear my side of things.

"It's about Tax. I'm worried. I need to ask you a favor. Please don't tell him I am reaching out to you. At least not until after we speak."

"Okay..." I respond hesitantly. "Could we do this outside of the office?"

"I would prefer that as these are personal matters."

"Okay. Does noon work for you? There is a park across the street from Alea. Do you know where that is?"

"Yes. I'll see you then."

My knees bounce up and down as I wait nervously on a park bench for Jude. I almost feel the need to apologize to her. Even though I didn't do anything, all these years she thinks I did. All these years, in her mind, I set up her brother and her eventual torture.

And I want to say sorry for what happened to her. I know it's not my fault, but it's just like saying sorry to someone when they lose a loved one. You aren't accepting blame, rather expressing your regret for the tragedy itself.

In retrospect, I feel like I was part of the problem. I befriended Sil, but that wasn't enough. I didn't invite him to sit with me at lunch, I didn't introduce him to my friends. As a kid, the impact of those small acts didn't even occur to me. It was easier to just keep Sil to myself. In a way, I liked our secret friendship and I didn't want to share him.

And Jude, she came to my house a few times and kept herself occupied while Sil and I worked on our project. She was always nice, a little more rambunctious than Sil. I liked her. But I never really reached out to her. I could have invited her to hang out with me and my girlfriends, but I just let the status quo be.

I should have done more. Being a nice person on the sidelines isn't good enough. I know that now, but I didn't when I was 16.

At about five after, I spot a petite woman walking through the park entrance. She is still a tiny thing. Of course she's a woman now, so a few inches taller and a maybe a hundred pounds. It's almost comical how tiny she is compared to Tax. Her raven hair is cut into a sharp bob, and she is sharply dressed in all black: pants tucked into high-heeled boots, a buttoned up black blazer, and black cat-eye sunglasses. I remember in high school, she used to wear so much color, while Sil dressed like he was in a perpetual state of mourning. Right now, she looks as though her next stop could possibly be a funeral.

I stand up and wave in her direction, she nods and walks towards me.

"Jude, it's so good to see you. Really," I say, extending my arms out for a hug.

She accepts, but the hug is tentative.

Jude pulls off her sunglasses, revealing her big dark eyes, framed by long thick lashes, just like Tax. She has grown into a very attractive woman. "I appreciate you taking out the time to meet me. I imagine Tax might have given you a certain impression of me. So, thank you for giving me the chance to explain my side of things," she says as we both sit on the bench.

"Of course. And well, Tax just said you were having a hard time accepting that things weren't what you originally thought. And I just want you to know that I never, ever knew. I thought I lost the letter. I didn't even know it was a letter to be honest. If I had known, I would have told my father and made sure he brought everyone to justice."

Her dark eyes grow, and she leans back a bit, seemingly taken aback by my statement. She adjusts her position on the bench to face me. "I understand that. But Mia, I'm here to tell you, there are some things you should know about Tax. Things he clearly hasn't told you."

CHAPTER FORTY-TWO

Tax

"I'm sorry Mr. Draconi, Ms. Tibbett stepped out to lunch and then she called saying she wasn't feeling well and was going home. She's been fighting a bug all week. I cancelled her appointments, but I didn't see anything with you today," says Mia's assistant, who stares at me a little too obviously every time I come into the office.

"No, that's fine. I was just in the area and thought I would stop in for a quick chat." I hoped to surprise Mia for lunch. I dropped a text on the way from the airport, but she didn't respond. She must be resting at her house.

On the way to her place, I stop by the Milwaukee Public Market and get her soup from her favorite spot. That's what good boyfriends do, right? I'm learning as I go here.

When I get to Mia's, I use the keys she gave me to enter just in case she's napping. I have my own pair, from my vendetta days, but I like using the ones she gave me instead. I enter the foyer and turn into the living room, where a single lamp is lit. And that's when I see her, sitting on the couch, bent forward, her chest trembling. She's crying. Something is wrong. She must be feeling really sick. Or someone hurt her. I'll fucking kill whoever it was.

"Mia? What's wrong, babe?" I ask, placing the soup on the nearest table.

She looks up at me, her eyes puffy and raw. I've made her shed tears before, but this time she looks torn up. This is different.

"Jude told me everything," she says.

I'm going to kill that little bitch.

"Woah, woah. What are you talking about?"

"You know damn well what I'm talking about!" She pauses, like she's afraid to ask. "Did you...kill my father?"

Shame. There it goes, wrapping around my chest and squeezing tight. Fear. Pounding on my heart like a tribal drum. I'm going to lose Mia today. I'm going to lose the best thing that ever happened to me.

"Calm down. Let me explain."

"I won't calm down! Explain? It was a yes or no question. You were going to kill me that night. The night you came into my house. You didn't come just to intimidate me. You were going to slit my throat you sick fuck!"

Though I stand tall above her, my insides wither to their smallest point. Now I feel sick.

I tried to explain to her who I really am, but she didn't fucking get it. I didn't want to see her like this, I was trying to protect her from the ugly truth.

"Mia, I would never hurt you."

"All you've done is hurt me. Over and over. And it's my fault for being an idiot and thinking I could save you. It's my stupid savior complex bullshit."

DEBT

"You did save me," I say, desperate to hold onto any shred of respect or love Mia might have for me.

But those words don't touch her heart, which is shielded by anger and betrayal.

She scowls at me. "If I had evidence, if my father wasn't cremated, I wouldn't hesitate to call the police on you. You're lucky your sister made it clear that there's no trace of anything you did."

"Jude is trying to sabotage us."

Mia laughs incredulously. "She told me the real reason you didn't want us to meet. Because she wanted to tell me everything. You made her sound like some sort of unhinged psycho. She was perfectly calm and fine when I met her."

My desperation converts into manic rage as I ball my fists up at my temples and shout. "Mia, she's nuts. Can't you see what she's doing? She wanted you dead. I have been trying to keep her from hurting you!"

"Well, I was right in front of her today and she didn't do anything."

"Are you sure about that?"

Sometime during the shouting, Mia had stood to her feet. I was too overwhelmed to notice, but I do notice when she breaks down again, sitting back on the couch.

"Why, Tax? My dad was a good man. I get the others, but you took the only person I ever could trust. You took him from me and left me alone in this world. My mom was taken away and then my dad...You sick son of a bitch."

"You have to understand...I didn't tell you things because I didn't want to hurt you."

"Stop! Just stop saying that!"

"Mia, he might have been a good dad to you. But he was a different man to me and Jude. I didn't want to tell you this...but he was part of the cover up. He took money and even when I tried to tell him what happened, he told me he would arrest Jude and me for stealing my dad's car and attacking him. He told me to never see you again."

She rises up to her feet. "Shut up! You don't get to talk about him! He was a good man!"

"I understand why he did it. He had to raise a daughter all by himself. How do you think he sent you to Marquette on his salary? Helped you buy your house? Mia, it was blood money! My blood, my sister's blood!"

"You're a fucking liar! My mother had life insurance."

"Her life insurance policy was shit."

"How would you know? Oh yeah, you've been spying on me for years. You're crazy and I'm fucking crazier for ever trusting you."

I can't get through to her. Panic sets in as I stand there, watching Mia slip away from me. I have to get through, through the anger, pain, and fear. I can't lose her again.

"Mia, my little eighty-pound sister was gang-raped by a bunch of drunk teenagers who each outweighed her by at least one hundred and ten pounds. They beat me within an inch of my life. Then they fucked her with broken bottles, tree branches, they beat her, they kicked her in the stomach. I saw her lie there lifeless while they fucked her limp body. Your ex-boyfriend and his disgusting brother forced his friends to do it, so that none of them would tell. They were so brutal, they took away her ability to have children. And your fucking father turned a blind eye. Two teenagers who he knew came from a house full of abuse, who never even knew their mother, who had no other person to turn to but him, who he had a responsibility to protect, he turned his back on them! Who knows what else he turned a blind eye to? Whatever good you think he did, that single act defined him."

"What defines you?"

"I don't hurt people unless they hurt me first."

She snickers. "Really?" What a hypocritical thing to say to her.

"Your dad thought I was trash and he made that clear to me the day he came into my hospital room. He told me to never come to your house again. I was lying there, covered in stitches, bones broken, spirit crushed, and he told me I wasn't welcome. He wasn't all good Mia. He might have been your daddy, but he was another person in a long line of people who hurt me."

"Shut up!" Mia howls. "Get out! I hate you! I don't ever want to see you again. Ever!"

I take a breath and soften my tone. "Fuck. Mia, you don't want to do this."

"Get out! I don't care if you fucking put a billboard of us fucking on Times Square. Fire me from Alea. You can't ruin my life any more than you already have. You're a fucking psychopath. Leave! Don't call me. Don't try to come back. If I see you anywhere around me, I will call the police and I will get a restraining order," she cries.

"Mia, I'm not gonna give up on you so easily."

The woman who has grown to look at me with happiness in her eyes now looks at me with devastation instead. "It doesn't matter, Tax. Because I have given up on you. Now leave, or I am calling the police."

Mia

Fiona Apple – Love Ridden

"I'm sorry, Mia."

Those are the last words the love of my life will ever say to me. I expelled him from my life. I had to do it. There are some things that cannot be tolerated. I'm doing the right thing, but the ache in my chest is so deep, I don't think I can breathe. I don't think I can survive this pain.

I hate myself for wanting to chase after him and try to make this better. But it can't be made better. He killed my father. What kind of person would I be if I stayed with the man who admitted to murdering my dad?

I hate Tax for telling me what my father did. I had wondered in passing how my dad could afford some of the niceties he had access to during the years after my mother died. My mother had life insurance, but we were saddled with a deep hole of medical bills. I just enjoyed the benefits and never put any deep thought into how he could have come upon it. My dad probably got the biggest payoff. As the local arm of the law, he had the ability to divert the investigation. The buck stopped with him. My college alone was tens of thousands a year. I did a semester abroad. He put fifty thousand down on my house. How could I have been so naive not to ask how a man making barely fifty thousand a year could afford to send me to a private college free and clear, no loans and no questions asked?

Jude only said Tax killed dad because he blamed him for not digging into the truth. If she knew more and didn't tell me, it's possible she was trying to sabotage us. Jude and Tax are both liars, people who never had a chance to develop and blossom like I did. The sun shined on me. I was loved, my mother nurtured me, my father protected me. I was born into a world of safety and security. Jude and Tax were born into the shadows, right in the path of a predator. Every time they reached towards the sun, the beast snapped at them. And so they have grown into warped and misshapen souls.

When torn between two liars, who am I to believe?

If what Tax said is true, then I am a hypocrite. How can I take Tax's side, turn a blind eye to the other people who he ruined, and then hate him for what he did to my father?

How can I say he was justified in going after everyone else associated with the cover-up, but somehow exclude my dad? When Tax told me what my father did, it was like he was killing him all over again. I couldn't take it. I couldn't accept the fact that my father might not be the man I thought he was. Now I realize he might have been just like everyone else in Clint: if you weren't one of "them," then you didn't matter.

Memories of my dad talking about how the James family were trash come to mind. I recall the cutting tone with which he would say it. He would mention how Mr. James was always getting thrown in the drunk tank or starting fights. How Sil had been caught shoplifting a few times. How they lived in the woods in a ratty double-wide. How Clint would be so much better off without trash like that. Maybe my father treated me like a princess, but that meant that he saw people like Sil as peasants.

But he was still my father. The man who held me up when I collapsed at the news that my mother had died. The man who taught me how to ride a bike. The man who coached my middle school soccer games. How can I stay with — much less love — the man who ended his life?

Tax can blame Jude all he wants. Maybe her motives weren't pure, and maybe she omitted certain facts, but Tax killed my father. That's the undeniable truth.

I wish I could say I hate Tax, but I can't stop the tears from falling. There is already an empty space inside of me. I just can't turn off my feelings for him. Even if I never see him again, I will always long for the man who killed my father, and had plans to brutally kill me.

I sit on the couch for a while, rubbing my temples to subdue the throbbing. Finally, I rise to my feet to do the thing I have been avoiding all afternoon. I walk over to the Walgreens bag on my kitchen counter and pull out the pregnancy test. My hands tremble uncontrollably.

This can't be happening. My life can't be crumbling around me like this. I am responsible. I run a successful company. I have never missed a day of the pill. Hell, I have a daily alarm for it. I am fucking responsible. Yet somehow, I have fallen in love with my blackmailer, the man who killed my father, and I may be pregnant with his child.

That morning I first got sick, I thought I had gotten my period. But it turned out to be nothing more than about two days of spotting. The period never came. I had the symptoms of a period: breast swelling, lethargy, moodiness. A few mornings I was sick to my stomach. I thought maybe I had a bug on top of the period. Only after being a full week late did I think that those could all be symptoms of something else.

I take a deep breath, and walk to the bathroom, just minutes away from news that may change the entire course of my life.

I stare at the blue plus sign for an indefinite amount of time. Despite all the signs, I had convinced myself this would be a false alarm. Never did I think I would have an unplanned pregnancy. That only happened to irresponsible idiots. Conflicting feelings of warmth and anguish overtake me. Tax and I have created a life. From the barren rubble of everything that has happened, grows a small sprout. *Our baby.*

I think back to our last moment of happiness together in my office, as I straddled Tax and rested on his chest. He asked me to move in with him. We were genuinely happy. When it's just us, things are better than a dream. But it's not just us, there is a sick world out there, and it has festered everything good. Tax is broken beyond repair. Is it even right to expose a child to a man like him? But I know Tax, his intentions come from a good place. They just become so twisted that the goodness in them becomes unrecognizable. He would never hurt our baby.

Abortion is off the table for me. Not because I am against it, but because I already feel attached to the one piece of Tax I have left growing inside of me. Out of all the pain and death, a life has been created. Something good and innocent to outshine the horror.

I want nothing more than for Tax to be here right now. For him to hold me and tell me that he'll be here for me and our child.

Then a flood of grief storms in. He killed the grandfather of our child. I cannot reconcile this. How can I ever forgive myself if I forgive Tax?

I wrestle with these emotions as I sit on the lid of my toilet, staring at the plus sign. I already miss Tax like a part of my own soul has departed, and the knowledge that a part of him is inside of me only makes the longing deeper. If it was just me, I could do it. I could muster up the strength to move on. It would hurt every day, take every inch of fortitude I possessed to keep the pain hidden, and I would mourn him for the rest of my life. Even if I learned to love someone else for who they were, they would never be Tax. Even if I married someone else, I would feel like a widow, my life always overshadowed by the ghost of Tax's memory.

But if I have to look into eyes of a little girl who has his long lashes, hear his subdued laughter, or one day watch my son crack his neck when he gets out of bed, I couldn't bear the daily agony of those tiny reminders. Echoes of Tax in our child would be like a razor cutting the same wound open every day. I would never get the distance I needed to live again, because I would be living with a piece of Tax. I would live with a physical manifestation of our unique bond and love him or her more than life itself. Loving someone who is half Tax would always keep my love for him raw, leaving no room for anyone else.

Tax has only seen pain and betrayal. He deserves to know that he is capable of doing something purely good.

My father is gone. He did something reprehensible. We all do bad things, even good people do. But just like Tax said, sometimes one thing is so horrendous, it defines you. The man who covered up the brutalization of two innocent teenagers was my father. He was other things, but he was that man too. Maybe even that man first of all. What happened to my father would never have happened if he had done the right thing.

And our child should not have to pay for the sins of his or her father. Both Tax and I know what it's like to lose a parent. We both know what it's like to pay for their sins: he for his mother's suicide and me for my father's greed.

Our baby will not pay.

So, I make my decision. I don't know how I can move forward from this, but I need to tell Tax that I love him. Not in passing, not a slip of the tongue. But to tell him that I love him, and it's not a mistake. And I don't know if I can be with him after what he's done, but he needs to know I didn't mean those things I said. About giving up on him, or about him only hurting me. Because he has done so much more than hurt me. He has brought me to life. He has made me feel emotions higher and deeper than I ever thought possible. And I will never give up on him, especially when it comes to being the father of our child.

I lay the tester on the bathroom vanity and exit the bathroom to find my phone. As I reach the end of the hallway, I see a shadow in the living room.

"Hello? Tax?"

He came back.

I walk into the living room and find Jude standing alone.

"What are you doing here? How did you get in?"

"The door was unlocked when you kicked my brother out."

"What? How did you know? You were outside?"

"I needed to show Tax you never really loved him. The real him. I won't let you take him away from the people who really love him. It'll be easier for him to move on this way."

"Jude, what's this about?"

"I know you gave Tripp that letter. You two walked home together that afternoon. I saw it. I am sure you didn't think it would go so far. But it did. Nothing personal, right? Huck, Tripp, Tucker...none of that would have happened if you hadn't manipulated the boys around you. And now you're doing it to Tax again. You always get your way."

"Jude, I thought you understood. I never even saw the letter. I swear it. I would never have done something so malicious. I'm sorry, but you need to leave." I should have listened to Tax. Something is off about Jude. The kindness she displayed in the park has been shed like a snakeskin. Her dark eyes curve in frigid satisfaction as she faces off with me in my living room.

"It should never have been him to come after you. It should have been me. Woman to woman. It's time for you to pay, Mia."

CHAPTER FORTY-THREE

Tax

"Hi, you've reached the voicemail of Jude James. Leave a message."

"Answer your fucking phone Jude! Answer your motherfucking phone!" I scream, slamming my cell down to the passenger seat. I whizz in and out of traffic as I race to her house.

I don't know what I'm going to do to her when I find her, and it doesn't matter. I am just blind fury. She took away the only person who ever truly made me feel less than dead inside. Jude doesn't want the vendetta to end. She wants Rex, her, and me to be one twisted little family forever. Sure, Jude and I fantasized about a "normal" life, but now that we're close, I think Jude's scared. She doesn't know normal. Fuck, she might not even like normal. I don't. The difference between us is I want more and she just wants the same.

Jude always loved the fact that I was detached from the women I fucked. That I only loved her. I devoted myself to her. But I always saw an endgame in our mission, and now I see Jude doesn't want this to end. She has the men she wants, she doesn't need to look elsewhere. She was always the center of Rex and my world. My moving on with Mia was a threat to that. And she had to ruin it for me.

Ever since that night, everything I did was about making it up to Jude. But nothing I ever do will make up for the pain and loss. She's just angry, and she wants everyone else to roll in the filth of rage with her. She wants to believe Mia did those things. Because otherwise it was all random. There's no one to blame. And it wouldn't even be my fault. Because I wasn't manipulated by Mia, she did like me as a person. It was just fate. That bitch. Somehow Tripp got the letter, and fate found the perfect way to manifest her cruelty.

She hates Mia because Mia is everything she never had a chance to be. She hates Mia because I love her. She hates Mia because she sees Mia as those flowers I liked to trample: Mia had it too easy.

Jude would be damned if Mia would get me too.

Mia was pretty, and smart, and popular. And her dad loved her. Sure she lost her mother, a pain most kids should never endure. But Jude would kill to have the sixteen years on earth with our mom like Mia had. Life was too fair to Mia, and Jude was going to stomp on her petals.

I slam the door to my car and run up to Jude's townhouse, pounding the door with angry fists. I am about ten seconds from kicking it down when Rex answers, shirtless, in just his boxers, sleep still in his eyes at two-thirty in the afternoon.

"Tax, what the fuck is going on?"

I push past him.

"Where the fuck is Jude?"

"Huh?"

"Where is she!" I ask, slamming him up against the wall.

"Tax calm down. I don't know. She went out yesterday and hasn't come back. I thought she was out seeing one of her guys."

Her guys. It's what Rex calls the other men she fucks while she keeps him close.

I step back and let go of him. "She told Mia everything. That fucking bitch. Mia just lost her shit on me."

"Fuck."

"You told me you would make sure she didn't do anything stupid!"

"Dude. I fucking swear, she told me she believed you. She was acting normal and shit. She was better than I have seen a long time."

It's because she knew she was about to get what she wanted.

I circle away, running my hand through my hair. "What the fuck is she doing?" I think aloud. What's her goal? She knows I would be enraged. If she did this to keep me to herself, why would she do this and disappear? Maybe she's waiting for me to cool down, I don't know.

"We need to find her. Now," I say, jutting a finger in Rex's direction.

"Okay man...okay...lemme think," Rex says. "Come on," he says running up to the main level. "Let me look in her office to see if I find anything," he says.

I pace the living room, taking turns calling Mia and Jude. I don't care if Mia calls the cops on me. I need her to know I will go to the ends of the fucking earth for her. She needs to know I won't give up on her.

I feel like I will fucking burst with each missed call to the only two women I have ever cared about.

The sounds of Rex fumbling around in Jude's office are broken up by him saying "shitshitshit..."

"What is it?" I ask, from the threshold.

"Oh man...I don't know...this isn't good."

"Fucking tell me!" I yell.

"Her safe. It's like something she keeps for emergencies. You know, our getaway plan."

"Spit it the fuck out."

"I have the combination too. I just looked in, it's empty."

"You think she's leaving town?"

"Tax, there was at least two mil in cash and—"

"And what?"

"A gun."

"A gun?"

For all of Jude's desire to kill, it was always me or Rex who did the dirty work. I wanted to keep her from having to do that. Jude is not the type to walk around with a gun.

Rex and I both look at each other and instantly realize the implication of that missing gun. "Mia," we say in unison. In a fraction of a second we are sprinting out of the house. Rex throws on pants as he runs, grabbing a jacket to throw over his shirtless body.

I toss the keys to him so he can drive while I call Mia. Rex and I don't even speak. We operate without words on pure adrenaline.

"Babe, please answer your fucking phone! Lock your doors, or go to Alea and call me from there. If you see Jude, run. Don't speak to her, just run!"

I end the call and follow up with a text.

DEBT

If Jude comes to your house, do not let her in. Stay put. Lock your doors. Pick up your phone pls!!!

"Come on...come oooon..." Rex says to himself as he speeds on the freeway.

We come to Mia's block and Rex jumps the curb right by her driveway. The car isn't even at a full stop when I open the door and jump out, tripping over her lawn as I reach the porch steps. I dash up the stairs of her porch and barrel through her unlocked front door.

"Mia! Babe! Mia!" I call out. There's no response. Underneath my own panting, I hear a groan coming from the hallway that leads to the bedrooms. I look down and see a foot peeking past the corner.

"Mia?"

I race over and turn into the hallway to find her lying on the floor in a pool of blood.

———✦———

"Nonononono," I say, scooping Mia's limp body in my arms, slapping her cheek to keep her conscious. I lift up her shirt to find the wound. There's so much blood. So much fucking blood. My hand slips and slides along the slick warmth until I find a wound in her lower abdomen. "Babe, you're gonna be fine okay?" I press down on the bullet hole and she moans.

"Tax..." she raises a hand to my face. "Our baby..."

"Baby? What?" My mind is running a thousand miles per hour, trying to make sense of it all. "You're pregnant?"

She nods.

"Oh god. Oh god," I groan, rocking her back and forth in my arms.

"Oh shit man..." Rex says as he comes upon the scene.

"Where's the fucking ambulance!" I yell.

"They're not coming. That gun had a silencer attachment. Let's just get her in the car, it'll be faster. She's gonna make it, okay? But we gotta go!"

"Babe, I know it hurts, but press down," I say, ripping a throw from her couch, pressing it on the wound, and placing her hand over it.

I pick Mia up off the floor, almost slipping on the viscous pool of blood.

"Come on!" Rex yells. Usually, I am the one with the cool head, but right now, I can't think straight and it's Rex who has to keep it together for the both of us.

I run towards the car and thrust into the back seat with her. Mia's droopy eyes are locked on me, as she rests on my lap. "Go! Go!" I yell to Rex. The car bounces as it jumps off the curb, and the engine groans as he slams on the gas.

I press my hand over hers, doing everything I can do make the bleeding stop. She says something but it's inaudible in the chaos, so I lean in. "Talk to me baby, stay with me," I mutter. "We're getting you to the hospital."

"Jude," she whispers.

"I know. I am so sorry. I fucked everything up. I should have never left," It's at that moment I realize I am crying. Not just crying, I am sobbing in a state of hysterical helplessness. I haven't shed a tear since the day I first visited my sister after the attack. 14 fucking years without allowing myself to feel anything other than numb rage. I promised I wouldn't let myself feel that kind of pain again, and I keep my promises. But ever since I met Mia, all I have done is break them. I'd fucking gladly break any promise for her. My chest heaves jaggedly, pushing out an endless stream of tears.

I press my face to hers, kissing her clammy forehead. Her body temperature is dropping. I rip off my jacket and cover her.

"You're gonna be fine. Our baby is gonna be fine," I tell her. It's a lie. Mia is slipping away, and there's no way a pregnancy this early on could survive a shot to the lower abdomen.

I should have never left Mia alone. But never did I think Jude would do something like this. She had only killed one person, and that was with me by her side. Above all, I never thought Jude would hurt me like this. For all of Jude's barking, it was me who did the biting.

I don't even think Jude cared if Mia lived or died, she just wanted to make sure Mia suffered the same curse as she did.

"I'm sorry. I didn't mean what I said," she says to me in a throaty voice. "I didn't give up on you."

"I know, babe. Don't worry about that. I am so fucking sorry for everything. But you can't leave me." I mush my face harder against hers and plead into her ear. "You can't leave me. I can't live without you. You're the best fucking thing, babe. There's nobody like you," I whisper, tasting a mixture of her blood and salty tears on my lips.

"No one like you," she says, pushing out a thin smile through the pain.

I look up to see where we are. "How long?" I shout. "Hurry the fuck up!"

"I'm going as fast as I can! Another minute," Rex, says frantically. "Hold on Mia, we're almost there," he chokes out from the driver's seat. His eyes are red, his face is wet with tears. Rex had watched Mia for years and I don't think she realized that he had grown somewhat attached to her too, especially when he found out she was innocent.

Her face, usually illuminated by a peachy glow, grows grey. And I cry the words to her I have been too much of a fucking asshole to even think to myself. "I love you. I love you, Mia. Please don't die on me. Oh god, please."

Tears flow from her eyes. "I love you," she mouths. "It's okay..."

Flashes of the helplessness I felt when I watched Jude get ravaged overtake me. So I do what I did that night. I don't know if it'll work, but I'll try anything. I don't care if I am punished again for only praying when I need something. Or not even believing in the deity I pray to. Let me take the fall, let me suffer, just please let Mia live.

The score will never be even. There is always collateral damage. It's like a rogue form of interest. When I killed the people who hurt me and Jude, innocent people were hurt too. Children lost their parents, an entire town lost its livelihood, sisters lost their brothers. It never ends. All Jude and I have done is spread our pain like a virus. Now the score is racked up against me. And now I have a debt to pay. And I'll spend the rest of my life paying if it means that Mia doesn't have to. I deserve the punishment, but she never deserved any of this. She never deserved the bearer of destruction that is me. I'll live in misery everyday if it means she can live a good life.

The day I found out she was innocent and I walked out of her house, I should have left town. I should have changed my name. I should have never let her find me again. Because I knew better than to think I could stay away. I can't say no to Mia.

Still whispering into her ear I mutter, "If you exist, please, let her live. I'll go away. I'll let her have a normal life. I'll let her have the life she deserves. I'll let her be happy. I'll make this right. Please, don't let her die."

The car comes to a screeching halt. Rex pops out and opens the door. I look down and her lids are barely parted. "*Nonono*," I murmur to myself as I run out of the car towards the sliding doors of the hospital.

"Somebody help!" I scream running through the emergency room. Patients gasp and cover their children's eyes as nurses swarm us. "She's been shot!"

"Sir, you need to hand her to us." Like a colony of ants, they sweep her away and I stand there in shock, my white dress shirt soaked in the blood of my girl and the child we will never meet. "Sir? Sir? What happened sir?"

"Someone shot her. I walked in and she was on the floor. I don't know how long she was lying there."

Her pulse is tachy!

We need a surgeon stat!

BP is plummeting!

Get a blood-type and match!

We need a crash cart!

"Sir? Sir! Do you know if she has any allergies to medication?" A nurse asks loudly, as I desperately watch Mia disappear behind some double doors.

I collapse against the nearest wall in sheer devastation. "She's pregnant," is all I can muster. There's nothing I can do to save her. Fate, that cruel, heartless bitch came back for more.

"Are you her husband?"

"No—but I'm the father—I don't know anything about her fucking medical issues. Stop talking to me and go save her!" I shout at the nurse.

"Bro..." I feel Rex's hands rest on my shoulders and my knees buckle for a moment. "I got you man," Rex says, sympathetically. "She's gonna be okay."

I turn to face him. He looks like a fucking mess. His hair is every which way, he has no shirt on underneath his jacket, his eyes are red. That's when I notice he's not even wearing shoes. He understands how bad this whole thing is. Rex knows me well enough to understand my typical reaction to death. He knows this is different for me.

"I heard her coding." I can't bring myself to say she's dead.

"The cops are gonna be here soon," Rex whispers.

Ever since the attack, I have had an inherent distrust of the law and it's ability to bring justice to those who deserve it.

Jude. I need to find Jude.

The cops should be here any minute since it's a gunshot wound. If I don't leave now, Jude will be long gone. I made a promise I would make this right. And when it comes to anyone but Mia, I keep my motherfucking promises.

CHAPTER FORTY-FOUR

Tax

"Fuck! Fuck! Fuck!" I scream. My hands leave imprints of Mia's blood all over the dashboard as I beat it. "I need to find Jude right away. She had to have left some hint of where she is going on her computer or something. You know how to look that shit up, right?"

Rex scratches his head uncomfortably. "...What are you gonna do to her, man?"

There's an uncertainty in his eyes that I don't like. His loyalties are divided. Of course. He's in love with Jude. "Pull over," I say through my teeth.

"What?"

"I said pull over!" I grab the steering wheel and jerk it towards the side of the road. A driver blares his horn at us and narrowly misses the car's bumper.

"Tax, what the hell?"

I grab him by the collar. "Where is she?"

"I don't know!"

I twist the fabric of his shirt in my hands. "Where the fuck is she! You know something dammit. She tells you everything."

His eyes turn down. "I didn't know about any of this Tax. What the fuck? You know I would have never let her do what she did if I had known. I like Mia, bro." He sighs, shaking his head. "I'm the one who convinced you to give her a chance, remember?"

I ease up on my grip, realizing I am spiraling out of control and need to keep my head on if I have any chance of making this right.

Rex sighs, the words come out of his lips bitterly. "Jude sent me a text while we were driving to the hospital. I didn't see it until you went in."

"And you were gonna hide it from me?"

"I don't want you to kill her!" he shouts. "She's your fucking sister!"

"She *is* MY sister. And I need to see to her. Rex, you don't get to sit this fucking battle out. You don't get to just step out of the way. You are in it, right in the middle. If you don't tell me what you know, you are fucking dead to me." I tighten my grip around his collar.

"Tax, I think we all need to lay low. Just cool our heads."

I pull him up and slam him back down against his seat. "You get one more fucking chance to tell me. Do the right thing. Don't fucking choose Jude over me. I swear to god you will regret that for the rest of your life. You know no matter what you feel about her, what she did—she fucking shot Mia!" I scream in frustration.

Tears stream down Rex's eyes. "I can't choose, man..."

"You don't have a choice," I say, easing up on his collar. "This shit ends."

Each word comes out of his mouth like a heavy weight. For once, he has to choose between the two most important people in his life. Rex isn't like me or Jude. He does fucked up things, but it's out of fierce loyalty to us, never out of malice. But he knows deep down inside that whatever attachment he has to Jude, she is dead fucking wrong on this.

"Her message came from a different cell number. She wanted to know what was going on. She wasn't sure what we knew. She only knew you were pissed at her for telling Mia everything. I don't think she knows we found Mia or that we even know what happened to her yet."

"And?"

"I ignored the question. I asked where she was. She hasn't answered. I just wanted to stay out of it."

"Sorry brother. Not this time."

I piece together the timeline of events. The last time I called Jude, I was on the way to her house, angry about the argument. If she's hiding somewhere, she doesn't know I know she took her gun and money. She doesn't know I found Mia dying in a pool of her own blood. I can use this to my advantage.

The best way to find Jude is to give her what she wants: to be needed. To be the shoulder I lean on.

I release Rex's collar and grab my cell phone.

"What are you doing?" he asks.

"Give me the new number. I'm sending her a message."

Where are you? I need to talk to you. I'm sorry I overreacted. You were right about Mia. She kicked me out of her house. Now she's in the hospital and no one will give me details. I think she might have hurt herself. Or...was it

you? If you did, I understand now. I never should have gone off course. I fell for her shit again. I should have finished things the way we planned.

It's a longshot, but no one knows Jude like I do. She's never been alone. It's her greatest fear. And now, I am allowing her to believe that the scheme is finally working. That she has a chance to ride off into the sunset like our original plan. Jude can be cold and calculating, sometimes seemingly impenetrable. But I know the parts of her that are easy to manipulate, parts of her that are almost childlike.

We start to drive back towards the house when I get a message from the new number.

I did this all for you. I love you. I couldn't stand to see you falling for her like that. I knew she was going to hurt you again. She doesn't love you, she only loved a version of yourself that you put forth. I had to show you that to spare you the pain. She's not like us. Now we can all move forward.

Where are you, Jude? If you did this, things are gonna get hot for you if she makes it. I need to make sure we get you out of the country safely.

She knows she needs my help. She already fucked up by messaging me and Rex on our main cell phones. Jude is all emotion, and emotion clouds your judgment.

You promise you won't hurt me?

Never. I am pissed. Not at you, but at Mia, and myself. I'm sorry I didn't listen. I'll move on like I always do. It's what we do.

Please remember I did this because I love you. I miss you. I've gone home.

Of course. She's going home. Clint, Iowa, the place where we lost our innocence, a ghost town, the perfect place to lay low.

"Get me to the garage," I say to Rex without hesitation.

The warehouse. No matter how much money we have, we will always be outlaws. We are always ready to drop our lives in a moment's notice. The plan was always to run together if the need arose, which is why Jude might be struggling a little. She doesn't have Rex to help cover her tracks. She doesn't have me leading the group. She's put herself on an island now.

The warehouse, the one where I led Mia on my run, is a property I own. In it, I have a several vehicles stored. Each with new passports, cash, and burner phones. The vehicles have fake registrations. It's exactly the kind of shit one needs to vanish.

"You gonna go like that?" he asks softly, motioning to me with his eyes.

I pull down the visor mirror and peek at my reflection. Things have moved so fast, I haven't really had time to absorb the sheer brutality of it all. Only small hints of my white shirt peek through deep red. My face, hands, and neck are all streaked with crimson. My hair is crusted with dry blood.

Mia. Mia's dead.

There's no way she could have survived. And if by some miracle she did, I'll never see her again. My vision starts to tunnel, but I take a few deep breaths to shut down the flood of emotions. I have to keep my mind focused on finding Jude. It's the only thing I can control right now. It's the only thing I can do for Mia. But I don't want to take off the shirt. It's all I have left of her.

"Yes. Let's go," I say.

"She took one of the cars," Rex says, as we open up the garage door.

"No shit," I say, tossing my phone to him so my whereabouts won't be traceable. "You know the burner number. Now go find out about Mia, and tell me what you know. Sweep Jude's place just in case. We don't want this shit falling back to other things we've done. Get in touch with our lawyers, you know what to tell them. We need to buy me some time before we talk to the cops." I am in mission mode. I can't think about Mia. If I do, I'll fucking lose it.

"I got you, bro." Rex looks at me with mournful eyes. "Please..." he says.

Three hours and forty-five minutes. That's how long the drive from Milwaukee, to Clint, Iowa is. I blare the music in the car as loud as I can, trying to distract myself from the intense agony. I keep hoping Mia is alive, but I know she won't make it. I'm going to live with this burden. Or maybe I won't. If Mia's gone, I have no reason to live. If Mia's gone, I will make Jude pay. Not by killing her, but making her watch me kill myself.

There is no bigger price for Jude to pay, than to lose me after trying so desperately to keep me in her grasp.

DEBT

I drive as fast as I can without drawing attention, dusk shields me from the prying eyes of other drivers or police on the road.

Fierce determination to get to Jude numbs the devastation.

Rex messages:

> **Trying to get word. Can't go to the hospital. Tiff cursed me out when I called. She's hysterical.**

I just need to make it these next few hours. *Don't think about Mia. Don't fall apart. Find Jude. You made a promise you would make this right.*

No matter how many times I chant that to myself, despair rips out of my chest at random moments. I'll bark out a cry, or scream, or punch the steering wheel. It only lasts a moment, then I stuff it back in, like a beast that momentarily escaped a cage.

The sky turns from swirls of orange, red, and blue into indigo as I exit for Clint. I haven't been here in eight years. I never thought I would find myself here again. I wiped this shit hole off the map so no one, including myself, would ever have a reason to come here.

Moments later, I am driving along main street. Boarded up windows, shattered glass, half-fallen signs, and trash is what's mostly left. It's hard to believe this town once thrived, that families walked their kids to the ice cream shop, parades marched down this street. Now it's a corpse.

I turn down several streets and towards the road that leads to the forest where I once called home.

Home.

That word gives most people a sense of comfort, belonging. For me, it has always been foreboding. A place of fear, isolation and anger. A place I longed to forget. And yet, I find myself back here again. It pulls me in. No matter how far away I go, it never fucking releases me. Or maybe it's the other way around.

I pull into the path leading to our old house. It's overgrown from years of never being accessed, but still manageable.

My thoughts go back to the night Jude and I raced down in our dad's pickup, desperately trying to make the meet up with Mia, completely unaware that we were about to face our destruction.

I pull up to the dilapidated double wide, covered in rust, siding dangling. My stomach churns. All these years, and this place still makes me uneasy. There is a glow coming from the inside, radiating brightly in the darkness of the surrounding wilderness.

I check my phone. Nothing from Rex yet. This should make me hopeful. No news should mean she's alive, but I won't allow myself to feel hope. I am damned.

The door creaks loudly as I pull it open. The stench of cigarettes fills the small space.

My eyes go to the single light in the home.

Jude is sitting at the table, a small handheld lamp resting on it just beside her, a trail of cigarette smoke slithering above her head.

CHAPTER FORTY-FIVE

Tax

I resist the urge to smash her face into the table. I'm here to end my life, and let her walk this earth in a state of limbo.

"I found this old pack of cigarettes in a tin. Stale as shit, but I figured today is a better day than any to start smoking again," she says, without looking back. I think she's in shock.

I don't say a word.

"I know this is hard Tax. But I can tell you are already understanding," she turns to face me, but I remain tucked away in the shadows.

"I am," I say through a clenched jaw.

"Remember the last time we were here?" she asks.

"I do," I say, taking a few steps forward, but stopping just short of the glow of the small lamp.

"Eight years ago. We came back for dad." She laughs wistfully. "You worked out so hard to be big and strong so you could take him on. And when we got here, what we found was a weak, broken drunk who could barely lift his head off of the couch."

I spot the gun she used on Mia resting on the table. My veins surge with rage so strong, I begin to tremble. *Breathe. Keep cool.*

"You held him down, and we force fed him can after can of beans. He would puke and we'd make him keep going. That's who we are. That's why I did all this. It was only a matter of time before Mia turned on you again. Her life has been too easy, she could never understand the things people like you and me have to do. I knew that she would turn on you without hesitation. We had to make the first move. You were slipping away," she says, coming to her feet to face me. She gasps when she gets a good look at me. Her lips quiver. She's never pulled the trigger herself, and clearly when she did with Mia, she left before she could even see the damage.

"That's Mia," I say. "She's all over me."

"But I thought you hadn't seen her."

"I found her, Jude."

Jude takes a half step back.

"I'm not here to hurt you. I lied because I wanted to see you, that's all. If I told you I knew right away, I thought you might not give me the chance."

"Do you know if she…"

"Not yet."

She nods. "It's for the better. I didn't mean to kill her. I just wanted to be even. I wanted her to know what it's like to have the ability to conceive stripped from you."

"What happened to you?" I ask.

"What?"

"What happened to the girl who I used to sit with at this table who would steal my food? Laugh about life no matter how bad things were? All this time, I kept thinking if I made everyone who ever hurt us disappear, I would get her back.

How could I not have seen that girl died that night at the lake?"

"It's the same thing that happened to you, Tax. We never had a chance. I thought you said you understood."

"I do, Jude. I understand now more than I ever did."

My phone buzzes with an alert.

I pull the phone out of my pocket.

She's gonna make it! That's all I know.

Those words, they rip me open. And everything I tried to shut out erupts. Tears trickle down my blood-stained face, puffs of air release from my chest as I mask the smiles of relief.

"What is it?" Jude asks.

I look down for a moment. *Pivot.*

"She's dead," I sob.

"It's gonna be okay."

"I know," I say through a mixture of joy and heartache.

"I'll lay low, go somewhere far and establish a new identity. You and Rex can meet me soon after. Right? You guys can cover this up, can't you?"

"Yes we can," I say.

"Then we can travel the world, just like we planned we would. Finally, we get to move on."

"I know," I say, my chest heaving with the knowledge of what I have to do. Mia's not dead. But as long as Jude is alive, she will never be safe.

"I know things feel like shit now, but they are all going to go back to normal. I promise," Jude says, cradling my face in her hand.

"Can you grab the gun? We have to get rid of it," I say. "It's a murder weapon."

"Of course, it's why I didn't leave it at the scene," she says proudly, reaching over for it. She grabs it, and as soon as she turns to face me, I bear hug her tiny frame.

She stiffens at first from the pressure of the hug, but then she relaxes.

"I love you," I whisper in her ear.

"I love you too Tax. I'd do anything for you."

"I'm sorry, Jude."

I slide my hand down to the one with the gun and grab it. "Ouch, Tax...what are you doing?" she asks. She tries to fight back, but her resistance barely registers. "Tax, what are you doing?" Her big brown eyes grow with fear.

I lean in and whisper in her ear. "She was pregnant. You killed my baby, but you didn't kill Mia. I promised if you touched her, I would kill you," I say. "I fucking warned you."

"Tax!" she yells, as I push her against the table, holding her down with my bodyweight. I turn the gun up under her chin. "Tax!" she yells, her eyes watering. "Oh god. A baby? I didn't know...If I had known, I would never!"

"I know. Because it's all about what works for your needs."

Her eyes fill with tears. "Please, I love you, Sil. Don't let her do this...I didn't know. I would have loved that child..."

"I would never have let you touch my child."

And then I pull the trigger. A guttural cry escapes my body as my sister's skull explodes onto the ceiling and wall behind her. I let her lifeless body fall back and I collapse onto the floor, soaked in the blood of the only two women I ever loved.

Jude killed my child. She almost killed the only other woman I ever cared for. Jude stopped caring about right and wrong a long time ago. As long as Jude existed, she would keep pulling me back to that night over and over. Jude was home.

I sit there in stunned silence, overwhelmed by the sheer volume of loss. When I regain some presence of mind, I clench Jude's small limp hand and wail. I hold it until it goes cold.

My wombmate, my tiny little sister, is now just another corpse in my wake.

But Jude's been dead for years now, and she'd never be whole again. I had no choice. Even if I would never know my child, I had to avenge its death.

Now I am untethered. Mia is alive. But I made a promise that if she lived, I wouldn't selfishly come back.

I have destroyed Mia.

I killed her father. I tormented her. I put her in Jude's path. Without her consent, I gave her a child she will have to mourn for the rest of her days.

We will always be a reminder of the other's pain. Looking at Mia will always remind me of the fact that I killed my sister. But Mia never had a say in that. All of the pain I caused Mia was willful.

I've never cared about doing the right thing, I just wanted the just thing. An eye for a motherfucking eye.

I knew I would hurt her, and I kept going back to her, because I am self-serving. Just once, I want to do right by Mia.

She will never have the life she deserves with me. She'll always have to mask the agony I put her through. People don't forget pain.

I of all people should know that.

Mia

The first thing I notice is how hard it is to swallow. When I open my mouth to speak, nothing comes out. My blurred vision focuses on the collection of tubes hovering around me. I become acutely aware of the beeping sound just beside me. *My baby.* I want to ask about my baby, but I am trapped. I feel for the tubes, grasping for them, trying to pull them off of me.

"Mia, calm down honey, you're in the hospital. Don't pull on anything." Tiff says, grabbing my hand. I try to take a breath, but the tubes make me feel like I don't have control of my own body. My eyes dart around the room for Tax. The memories crash upon me like violent waves, each one threatening to pull me under again: How Jude told me what Tax did. The argument. The pregnancy test. How Jude showed up to my place and after saying only a few words, quickly pointed a gun at my abdomen and fired, leaving me to slowly die as I begged for help.

I thought about all the things I would never get to tell Tax. I thought I would die having only said that I had given up on him, that all he ever did was hurt me. I felt myself getting weaker, drifting away to a quiet place. And then he was there. My dark knight.

And I knew that if I died, at least I could tell him about the child we conceived, and that I was sorry. But what I got was so much more. He told me the things I was never sure he felt. He poured his words and emotions on me. It hurt to see his pain, but I also felt comforted in those words. That if I died, at least I had been able to find what I was looking for and at least Tax knew what it was like to find that too. At least I had achieved that.

Doctors and nurses come into the room. Reading vitals, shining lights into my eyes. I keep trying to ask questions, but my voice is obstructed.

"Mia, don't try to speak. You are intubated. We are going to pull the tube out. It's going to feel uncomfortable."

They pull the long tube out of my mouth, a strong choking sensation makes me gag. And then I am free. I cough, touching my throat, signaling for water.

A nurse hands me some. My throat almost feels foreign, as I try to activate my voice. "Baby..." is all I can say.

The nurse and the doctor look at each other uncomfortably.

"Ma'am, I need to speak to her privately," he says to Tiff, who appears to be in a new state of shock.

"No," I say.

"Okay," the doctor sighs. "Ms. Tibbett, you were shot twice in the pelvic region. Your uterine artery was grazed, the force of one of the bullets fractured your ilium, a bone of your pelvic region. The other directly hit an ovary. We were able to remove the bullet and stop the bleeding. You lost a lot of blood Mia, we had to transfuse five pints. We believe your ilium will heal well, due to your fitness and age. Now regarding the artery, there was no way a fetus could withstand that type of trauma. We had to go in fast to save your life. And I am so sorry to say, it is highly unlikely with the trauma to your uterus and with the complete loss of an ovary, you will be able to conceive. I won't say impossible, but it will be difficult. We can set you up with a reproductive specialist. They can give you a better idea of your chances. There may be alternative options."

I glance over at Tiff, who squeezes my hand as her eyes fill to the brim with tears. I doubt she even knew I was pregnant.

I fight to keep it all together, but seeing Tiff's green eyes is like looking into a reflective pool of my own sadness. Tears fall down the side of my face. I don't try to wipe them, I let them stew, wetting the pillow just to the side of my ears.

"Where's Tax?" I ask Tiff.

"I don't know," she says. An angry frown emerges. I know she blames him for everything. "Rex called a few times to check on you, but he won't answer any of my questions. I don't know where they are."

"They saved me." I tell her.

She bites her lips together, for once keeping her mouth shut when I know all she wants to do is scream. She looks up, one tear, then two roll down her cheek as she shakes her head. She tries to move her lips to say something, but they tremble and she stops.

"Is my phone here? I'll call him."

"I think the police have it. They were in your house."

"Call Rex. I want to speak to Tax."

"You just woke up, honey."

"Just do it please."

She hesitantly grabs her phone, calls and puts the phone to her ear. "She's awake. She wants to speak to Tax...No, you fucking tell her...I won't do it."

She jolts the phone in my direction. I hold it against my ear. "Hello?"

"Hey Mia. How are you feeling?"

"Where's Tax?" I ask.

"Can I visit you?"

My chest begins to rumble as I fight tears. I need Tax. But I know what Rex can't bring himself to tell me. "I have some things for you. Have you spoken to the police yet?"

"No."

"There's nothing they can do. Tax made it right. I need to bring you something, but until you clear my name I shouldn't see you. Both Tax and I are people of interest."

"Made it right?"

"There's nothing left to do, Mia," Rex says. His voice is rough with emotion. "Just tell them Jude did it. Everything else is handled."

"I want to see Tax."

"We'll talk about it when I see you. I'm sorry for all of this. You never deserved it." Then silence.

I clutch the phone to my chest and sob.

CHAPTER FORTY-SIX

Mia

"Ms. Tibbett. I'm Detective Schuler and this is Detective Bishop. I know this is a very difficult time for you, but we have some questions about what happened to you."

I know Tax, they are already too late. He only trusts himself to take care of things. I don't know what that means in Jude's case, but I'll let Tax execute his own brand of justice. The truth is, I am too heartbroken to speak. I just want to lie here alone in silence. Just be as still as possible. Maybe if I do that, the pain will disappear.

"Ask," I say, choking back tears.

"Can you tell us what happened the afternoon of the assault?"

"I came out of my bathroom, and I saw my boyfriend's sister waiting for me. She said she came in through an unlocked door. She didn't like my relationship with her brother."

"Your boyfriend?"

"Yes, Tax Draconi."

"And his friend's name?"

"Rex. I don't remember his last name. He always just went by Rex."

"Could you identify these men?" He puts a still shot of Tax and Rex from hospital surveillance in front of me.

"That's Tax and Rex."

"And you and Tax. Were things good?"

"Yes. He saved my life. His sister had issues with our relationship. Tax and I were fine."

"Could you elaborate?"

"They were twins, she thought I was getting in the way, I guess."

"Have you spoken to your boyfriend? Since the incident."

"I'm tired," I say. "You know who did it. I don't want to talk anymore."

The detectives look at each other skeptically and sigh. "It's important you tell us everything you know. We're looking for Judith. Did she indicate to you where she might be headed? Even a small hint?"

"No. She only told me she wanted me gone. She didn't say much before she shot me. She only said she didn't think I deserved him, and then she shot me so quickly. I barely had time to scream."

"And your boyfriend? Do you think he might know?"

"He wouldn't protect her for doing this. I was pregnant with his child, as I am sure you know. We were happy. Why don't you ask him? Now, please, I want to be alone."

"Ma'am it's important—"

"I want to be alone," I say firmly.

"We're confident Judith will be found. Your boyfriend is a very powerful man," Bishop says, on his way towards the door.

DEBT

"He's got great lawyers. He's adamant about helping us find her."

They can sense I am hiding something. They have no fucking idea the extent of it.

A few minutes after they leave, Tiff returns. I use her phone to call Rex.

"I told them Jude did it, and you and Tax saved me. I won't speak to them again. You're off the hook. There's no way they can come after you guys when I am swearing your innocence. Now tell me what you have to tell me."

"I'll be there soon."

Soon is five days from my phone call. After my first day of physical therapy, I sit in my wheelchair, looking out a window, wondering when I will see Tax. I made Tiff go home and shower. She's been here around the clock, and she needs some rest.

"Mia," Rex says softly.

I turn around to face Rex. Normally carefree and bubbly, he looks pained. He's experienced tremendous loss too.

Seeing him makes the emotions I had been suppressing all week roar back to the surface. I hadn't cried since the day I awoke. I dissolved into a state of numbness. The pain was too much. Missing Tax, losing the baby, sometimes I thought I would stop breathing under the clutch of sadness. If I turned it all off, then maybe I could survive.

But Rex is my only connection to Tax, and seeing him reminds me how much I miss him. How much I need him.

"He's not with you?" I ask.

Rex looks down, his hands tucked into his pockets. "No."

"Where is he?"

"I don't know. He wanted me to give this to you."

He pulls out a thick manila envelope tucked under his arm. I slide out the contents. On top is a handwritten letter from Tax.

Years ago, I wrote you a letter that never found you. And for so long, I thought you had read it, and turned it against me. But now I realize, you never even knew the words that had changed the course of our lives. I think I owe it to you. I still remember most of it, and it all still rings true.

Mia,

I have to admit, writing this is one of the scariest things I have ever done, but I think telling you how amazing I think you are is worth it.

I've sat in the back of class all year wondering if a guy like me might ever have a chance with a girl like you. I still don't know if I do. But I want to tell you that being your friend has been one of the best things that ever happened to me. You make me feel like I'm not a freak. You make me feel like I belong.

I think you are an amazing person, and you deserve the best. I know you think of me as a friend, but I see you as more. Maybe it won't be me, but I think you deserve someone who will treat you like a queen. It might not be my business, but you deserve better than Tripp. You deserve the world. And if I was ever lucky enough to be that guy, I would make you the happiest. But if not, I hope that you find that with someone one day.

Sincerely,

Sil

DEBT

I fucked up Mia. I fucked everything up. I still think you deserve the world. I wish I was that guy. I wish I didn't destroy the things I love. But I love you too much to keep hurting you. And I have already done too much wrong to make things right.

I bet sitting here, you think you've seen the filthy pit of my soul, but there are still things you don't know. Your pregnancy was my doing. I snuck into your house and replaced your birth control pills. I did it because I thought having my child would end Jude's anger and keep you safe, but it doesn't matter why I did it. Even when I try to be good, I am bad. Even when I try to do right by you, I only hurt you. I wanted it all, and now you will live with the pain of losing a child and almost dying because I break things. I break people. Even when I try to create, I destroy.

You were right about me. I can't be saved. I am broken. And it's not fair to ask you to look past all the things I did. Mia, you are the closest thing to an angel, but I can't ask you to forgive me. I'm not worthy.

You will find someone who is good. I'll still want to break his face, but he'll never hurt you like I have.

I will never find anyone as good as you.

I will never love someone like I love you. Never. There's no one like you, Mia. No one.

But I'm not sure what we have is meant to last forever. It's too intense. That's why people write about it, to capture something so wild and fleeting. What we have makes us crazy. It makes us do things we would never do otherwise. I can live with being a monster, but I don't want to make you one.

I'll never be able to make up for the pain I have caused you. And I will mourn our child until the day I die. That was it for me. Only you would be the mother of my child. You would have been such an amazing mother to our baby. You would be the mother I used to wish for as I hid under the table from my drunk father.

I have taken so much away from you.

But I am giving you what I can: a new life and your other baby.

You are the best fucking thing, babe.

Tax

I flip through the stacks of papers behind the letter, using my forearms to wipe rogue tears from my eyes. It's hard to see the text as I gasp for air. He can't leave me. He's all I have. He keeps saying I'll find someone else, but there is no one else. It's him.

I scan the documents: My house has been fully paid off, the deed to his condo signed to me, a document declaring me the new owner of Alea for the sum of $1, a new bank account in my name. I crumble the stack and throw it onto the floor, sobbing his name. Tax thinks somehow his value in my life can be replaced with dollars. But he doesn't understand I forgave him the second that bullet pierced my womb. Holding onto hate is what has gotten us into this mess. We were just starting to get it right. He can't give up on us now.

"Where is he!" I scream at Rex who watches me from the corner of the room. "Tell him I love him. Tell him I don't care. He's not making it better. We can start over," I cry.

Rex can't even look at me. "I'm sorry, Mia," he says, battling to keep his composure. "I'm sorry."

"What about you? Am I never going to see you again?"

Rex smiles a bit. "You know Tax will always have eyes on you. I'm his eyes."

"I don't think I can do this..." I say, hugging the letter, the last piece of Tax I have left. "I know you know where he is. Just tell me..." I plead.

"Mia, I don't. He's gone. I communicate with him through attorneys," his cheeks flush red as he holds in tears. "I'm gonna miss him too..."

Rex walks over and sits on the bed beside me. "He's never going to forgive himself for what happened to you. I've never seen him the way he was when we drove you to the hospital. He's doing this for you."

"He's doing this for him," I sob. "I forgive him. That's all that should matter."

"Mia, he's made his decision."

"What about me?" I feel like I'll die. I can't take anymore devastation. "I can't do this. I'm all alone."

"Me too," he says.

"What happened to Jude?" I ask.

"I can't—" Rex's lips flutter as he pushes out the words. "Thank you for talking to the police. They saw the messages on your phone from Tax, trying to get a hold of you. Combined with your statement, it looks like for now anyway, they believe what happened. For a while they were pushing for some sort of connection. Like we put her up to it or some shit."

"I just told them the truth. Thank you for saving my life."

"I wish I had seen it coming."

I shrug. I have learned by now, that wishing for things to have turned out differently is the greatest form of torture.

"So it's you and me? The Draconis just march in and out of our lives. We're just left in shambles."

Rex nods, looking down to the floor.

"I'll never accept this. I won't live in this purgatory."

"I know," Rex says. "I've gotta go. But if you need anything, you call me. I promised Tax I would take care of you."

I barely nod. All this time, I wanted to open up Tax, make him the man I knew he could become. He has grown into everything I ever knew he could be.

And now the cruel irony is I can't be with him.

EPILOGUE

Mia

Everything seems normal on the outside. It's how I have always operated with loss. Don't let people see the pain. Don't inconvenience others with your sorrow.

When my mother died, I came back to school a week later, all smiles. No one saw how I cried myself to sleep for three months.

When my father passed, the service was on a weekend, and I was back at work that Monday, burying myself in work and the company of others so I wouldn't have to think of the loss.

And this year, as soon as I could get back on my feet, and against my doctor's wishes, I went back to Alea. My other baby. I worked days so long that people swore I never left the office. I couldn't stop. If I did, I thought I would cave from the emptiness.

I haven't spoken to Rex since he delivered the package in the hospital. I am sure he monitors me, but I don't look around for him. He's too much a reminder of Tax, and I can't bear it. Remembering hurts.

If it wasn't for Tiff, I don't know how I could have made it. She doesn't know Tax killed my father, or that he had plans to kill me. I don't want to tell her that and then make her keep that secret. That's too much of a burden to ask of someone who has already done so much for me.

I am pretty much healed physically. I can run again. And I am seeing a specialist to see if there is any hope for me to have children. But it doesn't matter, because Tax isn't here. It was supposed to be us.

I've tried. God, I have tried so hard. I've gone on a couple of dates, only to cut them short, go back to Tax's condo, and sob.

Every morning, I look at the surgical scar on my pelvis, and I remember the void. The desolation.

After Tax left me, I went through all the stages of grief. I was angry for a while. Sometimes I was so angry, I would stop by his place and punch his pillows, or throw his books across the room. Those shallow tokens were all I had left of him. I didn't have the privilege of a face to face confrontation.

Sometimes after I lost it, after books and pillows and sofa cushions were splayed everywhere, I would collapse and grab the nearest thing and hug it. I would clench it tight, and close my eyes, and pretend that somehow this extension of him meant he was still close. The tears would meander from my pursed eyelids, and I would let them fall onto whatever I was holding. A part of me joining a part of him just one more time. I was surrounded by vestiges of Tax: his furniture, his books, his bed sheets, his artwork, and yet I couldn't grasp him. Without Tax, the penthouse he left me was hollow. He left me. He fucking left me.

But what he did is why I will always love him. It's the reason why I can truly forgive him.

Shortly after Rex dropped off Tax's letter, the cops found Jude. She had gone back to Clint and committed suicide. I know she didn't. I could tell from the pain in Rex's eyes when he visited me in the hospital, that he knew she was already dead. I know what Tax did for me. And I know that's another reason why he won't see me. He loved his sister. Seeing me will always be a reminder of what he had to do. Jude's story is a tragedy too. I remember the tiny, dark haired girl who followed her brother around, looked at him with admiration in her eyes. So much was taken from her, including her soul. I wish Tax hadn't killed her. I would never have asked him to do something so painful for me or our baby. That's Tax though. He's a good man, but he's still bad.

He's light and dark, forgiveness and vengeance, beauty and ugliness. He's all those things. My beautiful savage. And even savages protect their young.

Today, I decided to call Rex and ask him for one favor. Just one. Because I can't keep living this lie. Going to work, having all this money, the homes, when I all I do is die inside a little more every day.

There's no one like Tax. And I can go on dates every day, scour the world for someone else. But they won't be even close to him. I tried to honor his wishes and move on. But, he's wrong. He's so fucking wrong.

We defied fate, who stepped in long ago and did everything in her power to keep us apart. Like two comets headed for a collision, our trajectory could not be stopped. We kept finding a way back.

Every choice, every kiss, every subtle nudge was destined for our inevitable impact. Fate thought she was pulling us apart, when all along, she was setting the path for spectacular crash. An eruption, a nova, a big bang, a constellation—That's what we are. We are the thing of beauty created from catastrophe. We are the light burning bright, forged from an impossible collection of coincidences.

I won't let all this death and destruction be for nothing. I won't just let us be a pointless catastrophe. We will be the swirl of stars that is born from the disaster.

My doorbell rings.

"So good to see you," Rex says, giving me a big hug. His hair isn't black anymore, but his natural strawberry blond with a light beard to match.

"I'm sure you've seen me more than I've seen you," I say with a smile.

Rex winks.

"You look real good Mia."

"Thanks, so do you. I love the hair." Just as I say that, it dawns on me that he had been coloring his hair to be more like the Draconis. Rex has become his own person.

"Thanks," he smiles. "So what's up?" he asks.

"I need you to do something for me."

"Anything."

"Give this to Tax," I say, handing him an envelope.

He looks down and it and sighs. "Mia..."

"Just do this for me. Please. Take the heat. I'm not asking to see him. Just give him this."

"Okay," he nods. He heads for the door and then turns around.

"Mia, he's never forgotten you. I know it seems like maybe he moved on. But, you are all he cares about."

"I know."

Tax

Ray LaMontagne – Empty

Rex visits me here in Miami once a month. We try to go about things like nothing has changed, but nothing is the same. He and I are all we have left and yet we are barely holding on. I try to live like I did before Mia came along, in that state of comfortable numbness, but Mia tore me wide open. I can't turn it off.

Rex and I don't talk about what happened to Jude. He knows it had to be done. And I can't even bring myself to utter the words about that night.

All I ask is that once a month he tells me in person, that Mia is okay. Just one or two sentences about how she's doing. It's all I can handle hearing about her.

Anything more, and my willpower will break.

So this morning, when he shows up to my house with a letter from her in his hand, I'm not happy.

"What is this?"

"Bro, she wouldn't take no for an answer."

I almost laugh to myself, feeling nostalgic. I know exactly what he means. Mia's so fucking persistent. Just as quickly, I stop myself from remembering her: forget her dissatisfied pout when I say no, her laugh, the taste of her tears on my lips, the feel of her skin on my fingertips.

That's how I survive.

I survive by trying to forget: The quiver of regret in my sister's voice as she realized she had killed her niece or nephew. The blood. Mia's blood swirling down the drain. No matter how many times I scrubbed, I would find it hiding somewhere. The Draconi curse: both Jude and I will never have children. Because Mia was the only one I could ever imagine that with.

But I can't forget.

My dreams are out of my control. And Mia visits me in them. I smell her subtle flowery scent, feel the curves of her body against mine, the wisps of her breath from her moans into my ear.

So many times I have picked up the phone and stared at it, just one button away from calling her. I can't tell you how many phones I have shattered, throwing them across the room to stop myself.

I wish I didn't love her. Because it would be so easy to go back to her. But I can't face her knowing what I have done to her. Seeing her will always remind me of what I did to her. She's moving on. Rex tells me she goes to Alea every day, that the company is growing at lightning speed. She's not with anyone, but I know she's at least tried. And I know I am still a selfish asshole because the thought of her even going out to dinner with someone else makes me want to break shit. Namely, the guy's fucking mandible.

Anyway, she's finally flourishing without me. She's getting over me like I knew she would. I was a dark cloud, and I blinded her from seeing any other possibility for herself. Getting the fuck away gave her the space to see beyond me and into a future where she doesn't have to hurt. Because parts of me have changed, but other parts never will.

I will always be the man who makes her beg, who inflicts pain in order to give pleasure. I'm broken and dirty. I don't think Mia can receive that anymore, knowing that the first time we ever fucked, it wasn't the acting out of a fantasy. It was real for me. I was going to kill her.

But then there's this letter. It's staring at me. I could toss it. But a piece of Mia is in there. The right thing to do is shred it. Don't let her get into my head. That's why I had to leave like I did. If I saw her, she would have pulled me right back in. The only way to quit Mia is cold turkey.

But opening this letter could be like having a piece of her, even if it's just in writing. Maybe it's her saying goodbye, or that she's moved on, or telling me to go to hell. Then I can have that peace of mind.

I grunt as I grab the letter opener, tearing through the cream-colored envelope and heading to the balcony to read it.

Dear Tax,

I don't know why I chose today to write this letter. It's been 330 days since I last saw you. I could have at least given it the full year. But, I've already waited too long.

I've lived a charmed life with some pretty shitty days peppered throughout: The day my mother died, the day I was shot. Hell, the day I first faced you in the conference room. Then there was the day I found out our baby was gone.

But without a doubt, the worst day of my life was the day I read the letter telling me you wouldn't be coming back for me. Because that was when I lost all hope. All this pain and tragedy had to be for something. But then it was all gone. It's like a tornado came through my life, ripping it to shreds, and then I was left sitting alone in the silent aftermath. Every morning, I wake up and try to pick up pieces of my shattered self. You were supposed to sweep me away with you, but you left me behind.

I bet Rex reports to you about me, and tells you everything looks good. I'm sure it does. I've mastered hiding in plain sight.

But Rex doesn't know about the nights where I hold your sweatshirt in your bed and cry myself to sleep. He doesn't know about how I run my finger over the scar left behind from the shooting and wish you were here to help the indescribable pain go away. He doesn't know how I dream about you coming into bed and wrapping your arms around me, turning around to see your tattoo, and knowing I'm safe in your arms. Only when I reach out for you, you vanish.

Sometimes I go home and leave the lights off, hoping you'll come out of the shadows like you used to. My dark knight. My angel of darkness.

It hasn't gotten easier Tax. It never will. You said you wouldn't leave me. But here I am, all alone.

I never had the chance to tell you that after you left when I said all those things to you, I took the pregnancy test and learned I had a piece of you inside of me. I was going to call you and tell you I wanted to make it work. That I could forgive you, because my father made a terrible, evil choice. But I never got to really say those things. Sure, we said our goodbyes in the car on the way to the hospital, but I wanted you back before I ever thought my life might come to an end.

So every day I wonder if my words made you leave and never come back. That even though I said I didn't mean them, you thought those were just the last words of a dying woman.

Well, I'm still here, and I meant every word that I said.

I heard the promise you made. About leaving if I survived, about letting me have a normal life. I know you think this is some sort of penance, that you are punishing yourself for the wrong you have done. I know you are making yourself pay. But why do I have to pay? Living without our child is enough, why do I have to also live with the pain of being abandoned by the man I love?

DEBT

My life is a flat line, I go through the checkpoints everyday: wake up, run, eat breakfast, go to work until I can't keep my eyes open, go home. Rinse. Repeat.

There is no color, no scent, no taste.

I miss your savagery and your tenderness. You understood what I needed, and I hope I did the same for you.

Sometimes the ache is so strong, I can't breathe. Even at Alea, sometimes, I have to lock myself in a bathroom stall just to pull myself back together.

I don't just mourn our baby every day, I mourn you too. I lost you both so quickly. I never even got to say the things I wanted to say. It's like you died with our child.

None of the past matters anymore, because I love you and I will never stop loving you.

You left me with money and things, as if they could ever replace you. You cannot be replaced, ever.

I'm begging you, please come back, please hold me, please fuck me, please love me again.

I can forgive you for everything, but I can't forgive you for never coming back.

There's no one like you. No one.

Mia

Some of the ink on the page is blotted with her tears. I should never have opened this fucking letter. I'm doing the right thing, but then why does it feel so fucking shitty? A year has almost passed and there is still a sick feeling in my stomach about leaving Mia.

I pace around the balcony and punch the stucco wall so hard, my knuckles trickle with blood.

She had to fucking beg.

Mia

<u>Alicia Keys – Try Sleeping with a Broken Heart</u>

Another week done at Alea. The job that used to bring me so much joy is now another reminder of the void. Memories of Tax are everywhere. I can't escape him. He's imprinted on every part of my life. I know it's weird I still live in the house where I was shot, but there are so many good memories here too. I am afraid if I move on, I'll lose some of them.

I enter my house, kicking off my shoes, but I leave the light off like an unspoken wish.

Today has been really hard. It's the one year anniversary of the day I was shot, the day I learned I was pregnant and lost our baby, and the day I last saw Tax.

I used every last bit of strength I had to keep it together at work, but in the safety of the walls of my house, I give myself permission to fall apart.

I go into my bedroom with my clothes still on, lie in bed, and weep. The heartache is as fresh as the first day. Somewhere in the darkness and tears, I drift to sleep.

In the tranquil haze of sleep is where I am most alive. It's where I get to see Tax, and sometimes even, our baby.

DEBT

Tax wraps his arms around me. His warmth, the firmness of his muscles, and his smell cloak me. My sadness lifts away as he fills the void he created when he left. He brushes my hair away from my face, and then wipes my tears.

"I'm sorry babe," he says, the gentle breeze of his whisper caressing the shell of my ear. "I'm so sorry."

This is the first time he has spoken in a dream since he left. I had almost forgotten what his voice sounds like: rich and haunted.

"I miss you so much," I say to him.

"I'm here, Mia."

He plays with the purple streak in my hair. I've kept it in, hoping one day he'd come back and twirl it in his fingers again.

"I thought I was doing the right thing for you. But I can't say no to you. I just don't know how to do the right thing by you. I don't want to keep hurting you."

"Just be here. It's all you have to do," I say.

"You always end up getting your way, don't you?" I feel his smile against my shoulder, then a kiss.

"Please don't leave me again. I can't take it anymore. I can't keep doing this without you," I say.

"I won't," he says, his baritone voice humming against my temple. "And I never did."

This is the part where the dream ends.

I always pray it won't, that when I turn around and reach for his face to kiss him, I won't wake up in an empty bed with only sobs to fill the silence. Maybe one day, the dream will become my life so I can stop living in this nightmare.

I turn to face Tax, the faint glow of the moonlight and a street lamp allow me to see the brightly colored tangle of snakes on his neck. Before reaching out, I look up towards the stubble on his square jawline, his plump lips, his warm brown eyes, and thick hair rustled against my pillow. I inhale his scent, arousing and comforting all at once.

I stare into his cocoa eyes, trying to take him in one last time, before I wake up alone, before I go back to my waking nightmare.

I reach for his face.

His stubble prickles my hand. His pillowy lips press against my tear-stained ones. His tongue flicks gently against mine, stoking flames that had dampened since the day he left. The taste of his kiss skates across my tastebuds. His strong hand slides up my shirt and grips my hip, as his thumb softly passes up and down against my scar.

I open my eyes.

He's still here.

ABOUT THE AUTHOR

Nina G. Jones is the author of the Strapped series and Gorgeous Rotten Scoundrel.

She resides in Milwaukee, WI with her husband and two fur brats.

You can connect with Nina on Facebook or on her website at www.NinaGJones.com

MORE ABOUT NINA

Have you read the Strapped Series by Nina G. Jones?

"I fell in love with these characters immediately. And I fell in love with Jones' writing immediately. She is able to ensnare every single sense and light them on fire with even the simplest of scenes and that ability combined with the incredible depth built into these characters and their story makes for a series that stands alone amongst its contemporaries." - Lightning Room Literary Reviews

"Bottom line, if you have yet to read the series DO IT NOW !! If it was too crazy for you and you gave up COME BACK AND TRY AGAIN YOU WILL NOT BE SORRY!" -Amazon Reviewer

"Wow what a storm of events. I feel like I ran a marathon." -Amazon Reviewer

By all appearances, Shyla Ball has an enviable life: a loyal boyfriend, a great job, and family that loves her. She doesn't realize how deeply unsatisfied she is until she has an embarrassing encounter with a handsome stranger at a coffee shop. Taylor Holden, a successful businessman, takes a sudden special interest in her and offers her a job she cannot refuse. Soon after, she learns there is much more to this intensely private man than meets the eye. He is hiding many painful secrets, including why it is that he has seemingly plucked her out of obscurity for such a lucrative position. Her "perfect" world is turned upside down by her infatuation towards Taylor and in just a couple of months, her life looks nothing like it did before. While she is frightened by the changes she sees in herself, she cannot resist the lure of Taylor Holden. As Shyla slowly gains Taylor's trust, she learns of his complex history and how it has molded him into the person he has become. When elements of Taylor's secret past resurface and threaten to destroy them, Shyla finds out there may be more to Taylor's story than even he is aware of. Strapped is a story of passion, manipulation, obsession, and family secrets.

In the mood for some hot, snarky humor?

Check out Gorgeous Rotten Scoundrel, a standalone novel by Nina G. Jones

"Gorgeous Rotten Scoundrel is officially on my top romance list for this year." - Danielle of This Redhead LOVES Books

"I loved this book. Easily a 5 star for me. I love a book where it is written so perfectly that you feel every emotion." - Give Me Books

"Gorgeous, Sassy, Witty, Flirty, Ballsy and Smoking hot.....grab me a washcloth I am ready to give a bed bath!" - All Booked Out

He was a pig, a jerk, selfish, callous, crude, tactless, prone to outbursts and gorgeous. The kind of gorgeous where you didn't even attempt to hide the fact that you were staring. I knew the type: His entire life he has coasted on his good looks, artificial charm, and sex appeal. Everyone wanted to be him or be ON him. I had been hurt by jerks like him before. He was like those guys but far worse.

I was the unfortunate sucker to be offered a gig I desperately needed as his live-in chef for a Summer in the Hamptons. But I wasn't like the other girls--the models and socialites who came through the revolving door of his bedroom. I would bite the bullet, take the job, deal with his sexist comments, his expectation that I would fawn over him, and have no problem letting the door hit my ass on the way out when I was done with the gig.

Then something unexpected happened that changed everything and I realized that there may be more to him than the labels I had affixed to his character. Maybe.

But if he really wanted me, it wasn't going to be easy, not like everything else in his life. He was going to have to work, I was going to make him miserable. He was going to hate wanting me just as much as I hated myself for wanting him back.

Heath Hillabrand: International Supermodel.
Womanizer. Gorgeous, Rotten, Scoundrel.

Printed in Great Britain
by Amazon